Y0-CUX-598

The Eden Revelation

AN EVOLUTIONARY NOVEL

David Rosenberg
&
Dr. Rhonda Rosenberg

The greatest enterprise of the mind
has always been and always will be
the attempted linkage
of the sciences and humanities
—Edward O. Wilson

SPUYTEN DUYVIL
New York   Paris

ISBN 978-1-959556-05-3
Cover: t thilleman, *World-Tree*, pastel on paper, 8" x 10" thillemantt.com
Frontispiece: Rhonda Rosenberg

A Brief Skeptical Interview with the Rosenbergs

q. You say 'evolutionary novel,' but don't all stories evolve one way or another?

Our novel starts off as mainstream postmodern but eventually evolves into an explosion of the contemporary novel. It returns to the all-but-forgotten novel of ideas. Allow us a quote from a letter to our agent:

> "Philosophy and fiction usually wed only when some outside pressure forces them into a shotgun marriage," wrote Benjamin Moser in the New York Times Magazine. What might be that pressure today? We'd say extinction, the unexpressed fear thereof, bullied by anxieties of climate change, global endangerment of species, leadership psychosis (eg. Vladimir Putin describing himself as the reincarnated Peter the Great) and nuclear weapons in space orbit.
>
> In the same Times issue, Pankaj Mishra weighed in on the lost art of the novel of ideas: "America's postwar creative-writing industry hindered literature from its customary reckoning with the acute problems of the modern epoch. It boosted instead a cult of private experience and what Nietzsche identified as the style of 'literary decadence,' in which 'the word becomes sovereign and leaps out of the sentence, the sentence reaches out and obscures the meaning of the page, and the page comes to life at the expense of the whole.'"

So we're past identifying as avant-gardists, intellectuals, or media hailers. We're looking back—backward is forward says physics, Einstein-wise, and evolution mirrors who we are by what we've left behind. As Rhonda has written in a study of popular resistance to virus knowledge: "Coronaviruses can be imagined as slimmed down versions of ourselves, their membranes like a skin, containing complex genetic material, as do we. Like us, they evolved, but they also continue evolving in a global search—for what? (same question for Homo sapiens sapiens)."

q. Who will care, once the pandemic is forgotten?

"When reality is surreal, only fiction can make sense of it". So says the New York Times Magazine (back in 2020) of its special issue: "The Decameron Project, 29 New Fictions about the Pandemic". Nevertheless, the surreal "reality" under suspicion in each of these pieces is invariably a realistic social matter. As in: What is the pandemic doing to me, or to you? Or more generally, to my city or country, or to yours?

None is concerned with what is happening to the Corona virus itself as it faces mutations. Nothing inherently surreal about that, it's what all species do, a matter of natural evolution. Corona is more than a species, a type of living structure; it is actually a family of species. However, the sudden mutations (most of them insignificant) it can't stop itself from undergoing as it fights with the human immune system would be surreal to *it*—if it could stop to think.

And yet, SARS-CoV-2, the species our immune systems are currently fighting, is finding itself in a much larger surreal scenario of global spread. After all, Corona has lived for centuries in internal harmony within other mammals, mainly bats. Even finding itself more recently in pangolins, it was able to establish a truce with that mammal's immune system. Now, however, the human host presents an exponential panic to Corona as it races to reproduce and adapt to the inner world of our species.

We might also say that Corona has been expelled from its Garden of Eden and is running wild throughout the earth—not within simply another localized mammal but one, Homo sapiens sapiens, that rules the globe and has nothing but dreadful disdain for it. Why should we care about *it* when it threatens our expectations of the future?

Yours is not a question for scientists, who face the virus as warriors; instead, it's a challenge to poets and novelists to think about a world larger than human society, one in which our species is but one among millions. That is, a planetary world in which we would never have evolved without the constructive help of microbes like bacteria and viruses.

So we have recently finished such a novel, *The Eden Revelation: An Evolutionary Novel*, after almost a decade of revision. Its underlying drama is focused on how all species evolve when they find themselves lost and isolated, expelled from their previous "Edens".

The search for Archibald Shechner, an archaeologist who has disappeared, takes our novel's characters through the literal field of a natural ecosystem as well as intellectual fields that include biblical scholarship and the psychology of loss. Yet all the characters are spellbound by the nature of disappearance itself—what the Tree of Knowledge confers on us as "death", our disappearance from life—but *without a trace* in Shechner's case. How can one just disappear bodily from the planet? (Meanwhile, that is a question that can be put to many who actually expect Corona to simply disappear at any moment).

q. How are your readers supposed to suspend disbelief if they read the interview before they start the novel? It's no longer a mystery who wrote the novel and how it got to your agent—yet that mystery is where your story actually begins.

Let's say it's like the Bible. Who wrote it is still an open question for most readers. Yet after we explain biblical source criticism you could say it kills the mystery of supernatural myth. Our characters are like Adam and Eve, they are somewhat allegorical—we say "somewhat" because we know there had to be two sexually differentiated beings to get humanity going. Just like there had to be an agent and "scribes" (narrators or transcribers)—people outside the story—to get the book into your hands. Seth Greene and Julie Peleg are inside the book, but the Voice of Wisdom (the Shechinah) has an existence that is also outside, in historical myth for millennia. No less for God. We may assume that educated writers wrote his dialogue in Genesis, but we still have to suspend disbelief about who or what wrote *us* into existence. Not simply "evolution"—

our parents have names, our countries have names, our languages have names, many of our neuroses and fantasies have names. Julie and Seth are as real as the book itself, even though living under assumed names.

q. Finally, we learn that a natural ecosystem has an origin and that it is buried in time at its center. You also assert that our brains resemble miniature ecosystems. Is there scientific evidence for that, or is it a literary conceit that lets you equate your protagonist's disappearance to the lost origin of humanity's first natural ecosystem?

The evidence was first addressed at the time we conceived of the novel. Even in 2022, however, neuroscientists and ecosystem scientists have yet to meet. Neither have science and literary art, as C.P. Snow pointed out half a century ago. Meanwhile, our themes of physical and mental origins are closely attuned to the reality we have been living and how to make sense of it. True, as the New York Times proclaims, it takes fiction to unite our thoughts about it with our feelings. First, however, those thoughts need some context. Our story is set in the early 1990s, when the evolutionary origin of ecosystems was first broached as a climate change question. Neuroscience had just posed what happens when brain synapses disappeared through pruning. It was a postmodern idea of braininess, at a time when postmodernism was having its heyday.

So our story begins in that '90s spirit, as the manuscript

of *The Eden Revelation* lands on an agent's desk although the author has disappeared. In mirror image, the novel's protagonist, renowned archaeologist Archibald Shechner, has also disappeared, and his colleagues are on edge. Who they are and how they react can provide a new paradigm for how to face an uncertain future. Back then, 'pandemic' alarms were common, borne out of an HIV/AIDS pandemic that seemed to come out of an African Eden despoiled by human traffickers in chimpanzees, that Garden's pacific primates—though the original event is lost.

Similarly, the Bible's early commentators do refer to a lost source, the "Scroll of the History of Adam". And in an older parallel, scientists have postulated a lost savannah for our human scene of evolving, a location long since buried in climate change.

q. By suggesting that the disappearance of your protagonist and his analyst can have a historical cause, aren't you approaching science fiction?

No, science and fiction meet in our present—or rather the '90s of our novel—but remain unconstrained. What happens to our protagonist is what happens to any species that is cut off: isolation, or disappearance from its home habitat is what forces a species to find a niche in its new ecosystem and evolve. As well, do we want to call the Garden of Eden story in the Torah's Book of Genesis simply an ancient science fiction? A veritable Eden has been assumed by modern science to be long lost to climate change, while an original Adam and Eve found themselves cut off there as the first Homo sapiens. Just as Adam and Eve evolved away in isolation from previous primates, Archie and Betti, archaeologist and his analyst, disappear from us, are essentially isolated.

Their situation parallels Shechner's original shock of a voice in his head, isolating him from normal society. Colleagues Julie and Nosei, however, quickly learn it goes beyond a suggestion of nervous breakdown. Shechner's imagined rediscovery of the Voice of Wisdom, as discovered on his analyst's tapes, is understood by Nosei to be the mythic female aspect of the Creator, the Shechinah, as embedded in biblical tradition.

The Shechinah, among other things, is an embodiment of "Mother Nature" in Jewish culture. She can be conceptualized as Wisdom itself—the Jewish version of Greek Wisdom—but she is first conceived as the Garden of Eden's spiritual representative, an earthly though supernatural counterpart to the Creator's cosmic presence.

Exiled from Eden along with our original parents, she is implored in traditional prayer and text to comfort us in our earthly exile from the Garden. Just as the ancient ecosystem in which Homo sapiens evolved has long been associated by our species with a Garden of Eden, that lost ecosystem becomes a central character in our novel. But a natural ecosystem is not fiction.

q. So by the end we are meant to associate an ancient ecosystem, presumably historical, with a supernatural Voice of Wisdom emanating from the Garden of Eden? Isn't that still a form of science fiction, since you are turning supernatural into natural?

First of all, she exists in a historical text, *The Scroll of the History of Adam*. Second, the Voice of Wisdom, or the Shechinah, has a physical context in our novel. It starts off as a voice in Shechner's head, which he and his analyst interpret as schizophrenic, or a psychotic break. They are not natural scientists and not all that familiar with Jewish religious myth. It wasn't our intention that the physical voice itself, as recorded on Betti's tapes, would take over the novel. She breaks into it—just as she breaks into and disrupts the mind of Archibald Shechner, who is leading a dig into an extinct Middle Eastern ecosystem.

Ipso facto, in terms of our story, first has to come "the creation of a context" in which this mental breakdown (or break-in) could happen, followed by an editor and literary agent who have been "looking for something really new". Seth Greene and his daughter-assistant are presented with an instant mystery: the novel's manuscript coming in "over the transom" without its author's name.

So neither the "found manuscript" or the "lost mind" are supernatural. If you want to call the Bible fiction, you are also turning a blind eye to human history. Myth that can stand the test of time is a mixture that includes historical memory and plausible storytelling. The gods and half-gods in Homer's epics can at least be interpreted as aspects of dream-states or, in modern terms, psychological states. The Hebrew Bible itself contains our bedrock dreams and nightmares within it. We wouldn't call it fiction, anymore than the hearing of voices in schizophrenia. The hearer is suffering a form of mental/physical trauma and we have medicines and therapies to help; they are not making it up. That's just an analogy, not a biblical analysis. Nor do we know of any therapy that can help the astronauts in Kubrick and Clarke's *2001*, which is admittedly a great science fiction.

Thanks for the questions.

from Svetlana Greene to Seth Greene,
per your request re "A Literary Prophecy"
by the Rosenbergs:

In this week's news about the human genome we learned: "Complex as they are, the interbreedings of ancient Eurasia are still only one part of our human story". The takeaway is going to be more cerebral than physical—even though sexual relations with Neanderthals reveals *we evolved a unique sexual intimacy. These origins are just as much mental.* When we expose environmental concerns today we're also uncovering the origins of human consciousness: what lies beneath the surface of both the earth and our minds.

Also keep in mind, dad, that buried fossil fuels, the legacy of dinosaurs and prehistoric forests, are involved with fears of global warming. It exposes the fault lines embedded in our species that you described as "schizophrenic". Can we save not only the planet but ourselves by facing what happened to human consciousness when we evolved?

So here's what you asked for. You can say, This book now explores a momentous question in novel-form. Why a novel, when science and technology are in the forefront of grappling with the future? A legendary figure in contemporary natural science [my Harvard mentor E.O. Wilson] has long incited creative writers to dramatize our planet's plight by disrupting the culture, but they haven't gone beyond the political and social aspects of environmental dangers. So it's touching that the authors of *The Eden Revelation* try to explain their motives:

"The writers of this book were recently invited to a symposium on the future of the novel. These excerpted remarks express how *The Eden Revelation,* although set in the early 1990s, poses a challenge to contemporary culture:

'It is our strong feeling that culture today is experiencing a narrative crisis, an overload of *storification.* Allow us, then, to begin with a brief explanation of why our book is written in a form of antidote to the endless storytelling in all of our proliferating media.

'Every intellectual frontier, whether in neuroscience or archaeology, is now stuffed into prepackaged story lines. We like stories, but the current deluge of storytelling has inhibited original thinking. Even if we can recognize by now the lures of promoted content and clickbait, still, the ability to read between the lines of online knowledge has diminished.

'In a blizzard of information, real news is overwhelmed—or, at best, lost under grandiose overcoats. Original writing loses out to neoteric cleverness; we're all consuming the cheap thrills of stories dolled up with transgressive makeup.

'Stories everywhere mirror social media: everything is either great or a narrow escape. Or else, exposé, big and little exposés. News-wise, the sky is voguishly falling but at the same time ingenious strategies—"7

Ways to Sweeten Bitter Truths" etc.—are offered for feelings of being left behind. Nothing so complex as a Shakespearean all's well that ends well—there is no end to the addiction of storifying everything from abstract art to evolutionary psychology.

'Hand-wringing stories are created about why, for instance, AI cheats us out of making our own discoveries, and how VR will divert us from a risky confrontation with naked experience.

'Probably our lust to penetrate or be penetrated by storylines can be summed up in erotic terms: no climax = no mental satisfaction. But what about the necessary value of dissatisfaction in forcing us to push on—to anxiously explore the natural world, to accept the fear of uncovering flaws and discontinuities in human consciousness? Our book, *The Eden Revelation,* sets out to be such an exploration, beyond the usual sexual catnip of how everything we know comes down to reproduction. But what lies beyond *that*; what are the origins of reproduction in even the apparently simplest of ecosystems?

'And yet, there is no fathoming the origin of a natural ecosystem: it is either lost in time or beneath larger ecosystems. In other words, its story can only be told in layers of time, pieced together like a vibrant collage. As in falling asleep, one must let go of familiar thoughts.

'Writers have been doing this since the anonymous Upanishads and the named and personable ancient rabbis in the Talmud, whose intellectual intercourse produced commentary upon commentary. In *The Eden Revelation*, however, characters are disappearing. Left behind are two colleagues, writers whose drive to piece together and interpret recordings they discover will reveal what form of evolution may be in store for Homo sapiens sapiens.

'Ours is a book about the future that is actually about the distant past. A literary prophecy akin to Stanislaw Lem's classic *Solaris*—still, it may be too literary for science fiction. It can even be read as an evolutionary fiction (let's not dub it psychological ecofiction) that relies on our knowledge of analytic psychology, ecosystem science, and biblical scholarship.

'Not every thought experiment about the future is science fiction. Here we ask ourselves what would happen to human culture if a disorienting cosmic voice (no spaceships, no body doubles) was actually heard? What if all along this voice was hidden on earth but we were unable to comprehend it because the evolutionary time into which it is folded is beyond our powers of storification? The human urge remains, however, for a way to acknowledge it. We see it even in current popular culture with its multitude of apps for mindfulness, journaling, or visualization. In terms of higher artistry, the novel today could be dying (Philip Roth in his last days said the literary novel would be dead in a generation) unless it can explore beyond storification. This is what we call literary prophecy.

'Novels like Carl Sagan's *Contact* acknowledged it,

but only in a conventional form of storytelling. Meanwhile, whether or not word from an alien civilization arrives, we remain unprepared, just as we are for unexpected revelations about the human psyche. Because such an uncanny voice may already be embedded in earth's prehistoric natural history, *The Eden Revelation* will dramatize why we need to reimagine it, just as the biblical writers of the Garden of Eden attempted in *Genesis.*

'In our narrative of interlocking layers, readers will be drawn into the lives of characters whose future is disrupted by the inexplicable. When an unknown voice from the past suddenly reappears, why should those of us committed to a response to climate change be worrying about the "what ifs" of inexplicable events?

'Consider also our book's premise in light of established facts—for instance, a 2018 report of the decrease in global insect population. The scientists behind this documented study predict an apocalyptic future for our planet if we don't change course. But what course? The collapse of insect populations, while fundamental to natural ecosystems, is so unfamiliar that it can't be attributed to climate change. We simply don't yet know its cause. The course we must change to, per the scientists, is hyper-vigilance: we have to change the way we pay attention to our origin on this planet.

'In a nutshell, modern society obscures the necessity to face how and why we were *forced* to evolve. The question of where we come from has been too easily covered up by portraying the past as primitive. And in addition, painting cultural and political adversaries as primitive. Both sides, the green and the black (for the color of oil and coal) are avoiding looking back further than enlightened times.

'So when unexpected knowledge of how our species evolved erupts into consciousness in our time, the contemporary characters in *The Eden Revelation* are disoriented by it. We are in the midst of an intimate narrative of relationships falling apart. Call it fictional, but our natural origins are reimagined.

'*The Eden Revelation* takes place in the early 1990s and that period's quest for paradigm shifts. In confronting the wish to uncover our species' place of origin, we are in the realm of thinking cosmically. There are probably other civilizations out there in the galaxy (or in a hundred billion other galaxies) but we only have to hear from the first one to know that *creation* is far more special than human culture. Contact with another intelligent species disrupts all our assumptions about being human.

'Now consider this: What if that cosmic voice was once expressed in the place where our species evolved, perhaps in Africa, spurring our need to "disappear" from that place—to move on and explore? And what if now, recollecting it, we can't; what if we're stuck with the rest of humanity and must piece together what originally happened? What can be learned about the advantage of natural evolution over the future dangers of asexual imitations of evolving?

'As we enter the narrative of our book, we find scenes

of trauma and disoriented research. A dramatic situation is in parallel with a scientific one: unknown ecosystems, which are still being uncovered on Earth, as if one may have been the Garden of Eden. As we will discover, Darwin's emphasis on the creative power of ecosystems (to make room for new species to evolve) matches the biblical concern with creation. And as archaeologist Archibald Shechner discovers in the beginning of *The Eden Revelation,* a voice in his head claims to speak from the origin of the ancient ecosystem in which he is unwittingly digging.'"

P.S. from Svetlana

Dad, you need some more specific context for your agent's letter, even though the authors weren't asked about immediate concerns like global warming. For instance:

In the 21st Century we live more and more in the universe. Or not in it exactly but more conscious of it. Thousands of documented Earth-like planets and just a few decades away from sending seeing-eye craft there. Once again, as in the Second Millennium, we may be on the verge of colonizing new worlds. And yet—

It can already seem deja-vu. We remain the same Homo sapiens creatures with the same flaws and repressed nightmares. You can enhance us with virtual and AI technology, enhance our gene pool, but underneath we're psychically the same. It can all seem profoundly depressing. Even if we can mine the galaxy or talk to extraterrestrials—we're still just telling stories or exchanging information. It can be trippy, but it was already that in the 1960s on acid, or for ancient shamans on mushrooms, or for the hunters of mastodons and their cave painters.

In the 1990s, however, on the eve of this new millennium, a wholly different and mind-boggling vision of our future briefly opened up. For a few years in the future-prescient '90s, it was not hard to imagine evolving away from Homo sapiens sapiens.

Preface

A quarter century ago, when I was pushing fifty, I failed miserably to find a home for this work. At the time I didn't take it personally; I just assumed it was too real for the New Agers of the day and too imaginary for the literati, who were still avid about what I dubbed the "old fuck" to want to feel deeper beneath it, toward what my semi-younger self had described as "an even more essential drive, right down at the root of life, and it's the desire to evolve. It's *that* desire that's been totally buried in us." I was parroting the authors.

I probably wasn't that clear about how the book's revelation was going "to change the way we fuck", though I flogged it in those terms. In those days, after the shock of the Soviet Union falling apart, alot more seemed possible than these days. Now, at a time when historical novels have come back into fashion, I thought I'd give it another read as a postmodern tale of the 1990s.

So I started rereading and was as shocked as the old communists must have been to see their world fall apart. It's as if our culture today—by way of comparison to Julie, Nosei, and Shechner—is in the midst of something far worse than a nervous breakdown. It's become so cynical that I'm actually glad I retired when I did. Except for one thing: this novel holds an unexpected mirror to our present fate. It's caused me to limp back into action and write this short brief on its behalf.

So here goes. I'm looking for a sharp editor, probably too young to remember the optimism of the early '90s and the quest for a paradigm shift. Too young to recall the wish to uncover our Homo sapiens place of origin and how it resembled the paradise lost of the Eden story. The ultimate reality of this place, however, is an underlying theme in *The Eden Revelation.* It can snap into place today as our lost human prehistory.

Here's the dramatic premise: What would happen to our modern relationships if the language of this forgotten place, like unremembered voices from the past, is suddenly overheard? What disorientation would it cause, what panic to interpret how and why it has happened, what it may mean? Is it as simple yet alarming a matter as hearing a voice in your head?

David Rosenberg, a prize-winning poet and bestselling author, Guggenheim Fellow and biblical scholar, and Dr. Rhonda Rosenberg, a research professor and science writer, have joined forces on this extraordinary historical and literary novel. I hesitate to call it Nabokovian, only because the young may no longer read him. And unfortunately the great biologist E.O.Wilson, who has for many decades called for such creative interpretation of natural science, may now have grown too old to read it.

Here's how it took shape: After a quarter-century living near the Florida Everglades, the Rosenbergs have used study of that precious ecosystem to embody characters whose lives are thrown into turmoil by the protagonist hearing a voice in his head. Most of us have heard a voice in our head at some point of our lives. We may have written it off as a daydream, though it seemed quite real at the time. Is there a trace of schizophrenia, however, in all of us, necessary to the period in which our species evolved?

I couldn't get the voice of my grade school girlfriend out of my head—saying "Don't. Yes. Don't. Yes."—when I found myself twenty years later beside my wife groaning wordlessly in labor. Instead of coaching her I too was wordless, instinctually and uncontrollably thinking: "We can't be doing this, it will ruin my career." It was like I was feeling the reckoning of a #MeToo abuser—many years in advance, my gorgeous grown daughter now a researcher into the urges of prehistoric plant life. So I could also have been a giant Homo erectus seducing a small Homo sapiens, both of us temporarily lost in fear. In other words, I was not having a fantasy but an ancient deja vu. (The Rosenbergs also find a way to echo this fear in Eden, our species' tragic mental flaw anchored in the scene at the Tree of Knowledge).

Most people may ignore such knowledge, but in the idealistic early 1990s, the characters in *The Eden Revelation* are caught up in the expectation of a scientific and psychological paradigm shift. The character we will care most about has disappeared. And the setting we will care most about is invisible—not science fiction but the lost ecosystem in which humans evolved.

Is it historical fiction?—yes and no. If you step back for a moment to consider the intellectual excitement behind the story in its recent historical period, among characters who have complicated relationships, you may wonder at how naïve they could be. Yet since Darwin we know ourselves as bound into evolutionary history. The imaginative inspiration of evolutionary theory, and the creaturely necessity for a complex camouflage of disguises (not to mention Satan camouflaged as a snake in Eden) blossomed—but only briefly—in the early 1990s, after the Cold War and its similarly intricate spy stories. And I mean briefly—I was there and lost the beat like everyone else.

However, in the second decade of the 21st century, a popular TV cable serial, "The Americans," analyzes the misunderstandings of intimacy—as represented by Cold War spies and FBI agents—in terms of ideological disguises. It offers a pop psychology of power and vulnerability (although the unconscious mind of the human psyche is ignored). That made sense for the Cold War period, when an existential competition of societies was paramount—and it even makes sense now, when technology seems the sole answer to the future, in outer space and for personal agency (need I mention sex robots?). But for a time in the *fin de siecle* 1990s—the historical period at the center of this novel—the answer went beyond self-centered humanity and re-echoed Darwin.

Here's how it sounded back then: We are bound into a history of having evolved into a timebound human creature whose fear of eventual extinction—of the species and hence of any individual or cultural meaning (no one will be left to read Shakespeare, hear Mozart etc.)—has been completely repressed. In that brief window of time in the '90s, however, we contemplated our species as an artifact of evolution that would be further meditated upon one day by a post-human species. "Post-human" was a typically new coinage of the time, suggesting how Homo sapiens would become open to evolution by isolating itself. National Geographic pictured the possibilities in detail. Biosphere 2 experimented with isolating humans in an artificial ecosystem. Whole Earth Catalog (it had not yet expired) showed precise calculations for a self-sustaining spaceship big as an isolated city that could exist for thousands of years.

"Isolation," in the scientific terms of evolution, is what is required for a new species to evolve. There is nothing science fictional about it, I've learned. To explore and be lost in a new ecosystem is like a break in the narrative of a species—a new creation story (or, among nonverbal species, a new behavioral pattern) is needed. In our own fundamental creation story, Adam and Eve are exploring their new ecosystem of Eden when—and there are many ways to interpret this break—they find themselves lost outside the Garden and forced to develop a substitute for it, namely, human culture. Civilization is a human creation; at its most hopeful it's based on a wish for peace, truth, and justice, mirroring the lost memory of life in the Garden of Eden. All of it was suggested in this novel, though it went over my head at the time.

Now we can see traces of that long history, extending from the Garden to the modern science of ecosystems, underpinning the narrative in *The Eden Revelation*. Yet it's a very human story of complex suspense, forcing the characters to explore beyond their comfort zones—and to risk isolation. Loves and collegial relationships risk being turned inside out by an uncannny voice in Archibald Shechner's head. Is it real, a biological artifact left over from our primate evolution, or is it schizophrenic madness?

What didn't go over my head at the time were the novelistic elements I originally described in my cover letter: "We enter a world of natural wonder split open by archaeologists and literary critics, therapists and analysands, mothers and daughters—all mesmerized by a new intimacy with nature and Nature's endless creativity."

But this only was possible at a time when the science of ecosystems, as well as isolation in space, found a cultural equivalent as well, imagining a benign post-human species that was still gorgeously biological—not ourselves dressed up in technology or a manipulation of genes, not "trans-human," as we forecast today. It would not happen in a normal timeframe, of course, yet hints of it could appear unexpectedly. That is the outward reality of this novel—in a time when we were more imaginatively patient and less cynical about the millions of years involved in biological evolution.

Now our imaginations are so attenuated that we're

impatient for change, as if technological adaptations to our bodies or downloaded AI may come about within our lifetimes and "improve upon" natural selection ("improve" in quotes because no one has yet calculated the danger of bodies cut off from natural processes). There are even predictions that we are about to become the gods of evolution in a decade or two—who needs to fuck? As *The Eden Revelation* dramatizes, however, we contain DNA going back millions of years. If there is any real wisdom embedded in our age-old brains, why wouldn't we recognize our archaic desire to evolve that drove us into an unknown place, one that seemed as enchanting as a garden? There, with our new brains of the time—each a miniature reproduction of an ecosystem, evolving culture and ideas in place of organisms—we not only started speaking but also began listening to what we still call half-ironically "the voice of wisdom". The Rosenbergs channel this voice quite creatively, I think. If we can face up to the shock upon hearing it, as happens to Archibald Shechner and Julie Peleg in these pages, we may still salvage a piece of Eden. The inward shock sets off the tense unfolding of the plot in this novel.

Back in the 1990s, I figured there were readers craving such drama, but in a perfect bad storm, publishing houses were suddenly bought up by international conglomerates and editors with whom I had long associated were forced to cut back on their lists and their appetite for literary risk.

Perhaps the biggest risk the Rosenbergs take is their interpretation of the Bible's Garden of Eden and the history that followed. They suggest how the original biblical writers used sources that looked back to a lost time—as if we were once most at home in the ecosystem of Eden. And then, according to the Rosenbergs, what is recorded afterward in the Hebrew Bible is imbued with the attempt to create a just and inspired culture, although it is constantly shadowed by breakdown and exile. Even though reading tastes had had its fill of the Bible by the mid-'90s, I still thought readers would gravitate toward the cutting-edge ecology. I wrote it up this way: "Just as the evolution of any species was understood as taking place in isolation from its original home, so the ecosystem—a mothering Creator, as it were—was understood as providing the required niche." (I thought "mothering Creator" was better than invoking the Bible). As well, a new discipline, evolutionary psychology, took hold for a time. Radiocarbon dating in archaeology was also a new phenomenon.

Those years are gone. Now, however, we have a historical fiction evoking the 1990s. Set in New York and Tel Aviv, including an archaeological dig and a psychiatrist's office, it's a story (in the blogging-fever form of those days) of lost love, environmental anxiety, and a disturbing voice from the past. It was a time when saving the wilderness seemed paramount and origin myths were being compared to scientific theories.

All the great myths, all the great religions are based in origin stories. Yet isn't the Garden of Eden the most unsatisfying story we know? We are created creatures there, but we don't know why we were created in the first place or why we were destined to lose it. Clearly there is a missing backstory, especially of the two trees at the center of the Garden. *The Eden Revelation* provides the missing backstory in a novel of many insights, many captivating characters—including an ancient ecosystem—and unexpected turns. And commercially speaking, there is also the titillating question of why fucking is necessary to evolving.

But I don't know how much novels really matter anymore, especially innovative (and not *fashionably innovative*) ones. I can tell you I wouldn't have a snowball's chance in hell of finding a publisher today for a James Joyce or Virginia Woolf. On the other hand, there were no claims that *Ulysses* or *To The Lighthouse* were historical fiction. Right now, I think this claim is especially cogent, at a time when our collective memory seems disinclined to dwell upon even a recent era like the '90s, given that it happened before the twenty-first century. And far be it from me to shout about the ecosystem of our human prehistory.

—Seth Greene, literary agent (semi-retired) [2019]

P.S.

If these sagacious words prove better than catalog copy for a future publisher, it's thanks to the assistance of my daughter, Svetlana Greene, a postdoc researcher in paleobotany at Harvard (suffice it to say she has also kept me up to speed on current culture).

Svetlana adds (you need to repeat this more or less, geared to the attention spans of Millennials):

Global warming seems to be fact. However, in the 21rst Century we live more and more in the universe. Or not in it exactly but more conscious of it. And yet—

It can already seem deja-vu. We remain the same Homo sapiens creatures with the same flaws and repressed nightmares. You can enhance us with virtual and AI technology, enhance our gene pool, but underneath we're psychically the same. It can all seem profoundly depressing. So what if we can mine the galaxy or talk to extraterrestrials?—we're still just telling stories or exchanging information. It can be trippy, as my father might say, but it was already that in the 1960s, on acid, or for ancient shamans on mushrooms, or for the hunters of mastodons and their cave painters.

In the 1990s, however, many of us were too young, too busy surviving the anxieties of growing up among seemingly unsteady adults. Meanwhile, some of those grownups were amazingly vulnerable to a new paradigm that could imagine us evolving.

Contents

I'm early. The taxi came early. I thought it would be better than running late. That is, no rushing or thinking of someone waiting. For me.

And it did seem better, until I began to wait. Now I'm already writing in the notebook. Unable to cross through the waiting, the in-between. Not even waiting that is apart from you. I mean, it's not that you're late. It is only that I am early. What if there were more than one kind of waiting, more than one of us in the wait? I would need two notebooks. Three, four, would there ever be enough?

My notebook, the water bottle. Waiting. I can feel the breaking apart, the collapse.

Translate. Shift to meaning. The body, the symptoms, you would say, are a kind of translation. One done with crayons and a coloring book when a child. We are finding another way to translate.

I wish I lived somewhere that I could have a car. Drive myself. More control, but maybe this is better. I'm thinking that at least I don't have to drive or feel okay to get myself here. I just have to flag the taxi and sit in the back seat. And I like the streets. New York is all about the streets, people in the streets. In front of you, in back, all kinds of people. I feel the possibility of me when I'm around them, in the middle. The mistakes, the shadows seem possible to bear. Again, I hear the Beatles in my head singing "Yesterday." I told you this week the words seemed mine as a child. A shadow, hanging over me. Sometimes I would feel like the singer of the song, sometimes like I was the shadow. I felt the loseableness of days, of people.

The song held the feeling, helped me keep the days and the people, made an impress inside. You might say such songs sang them alive.

I haven't had to write in the notebook like this in such a long time. Why now, and here in the office, with you only a room away? It's the between time, I remember you said. The gap. The scarcity of resources to occupy the gaps. I want to be here. I need, am glad to be here. But inside, all through me—it is so hard to get here, to be here. And now, to wait.

Already the notebook. Can you know how it feels to be the embodiment of a conundrum? Do you realize what it takes, what I must experience to come here? And that I will come again tomorrow, that we, you and I, can count on me coming again, tomorrow.

Is there any, any way for it to stop? The terror, the breaking apart. I feel it all more fully each time I come. I almost crave to feel it all here. Is it okay to want want want the feelings I find here?

What did we say yesterday? That sometimes the mind learns to think the other in order to cross a gap, a distance between oneself and another. Thinking the other keeps the other alive, locatable inside. It provides a link to another's presence, to keep them from going away. They seem like they could go away all too soon.

Thinking another is a container for feelings and thoughts that seem uncontainable, for something that we feel is too dangerous to have. What would I be inside if my mind wasn't whirring, if I wasn't collapsing. Questions. I think I would be having questions and feelings about us, the in-between of us, our links and gaps. But why are gaps so much trouble for me? What is the answer? It's like there's nothing to hold me in place or in form. No skin. And then collapse. Fear of collapse. The fear of ceasing to exist. What is the connection to this day, this time?

I think I know. It must be the other notebook. It is here, inside the backpack, sitting in there between you and me. The transcription. Mother's skin, Archie's. More real than my own. Their skin is with me today. All skins. Notes of mother's analysis of Archie. A skin for his disintegration. Notes of the "Seven Days of Creation" from Archie's voice in the ground—a skin for a lost and loseable knowledge of how human *means, that is, how* human *began. A voice from the ground speaking of the skin of our creation, our ecological envelope, the first ecosystem.*

Backpack. Skins. All carried, being reread, preserved. By me. Should I have started it up again? I need something of my own. Can you get me some skin of my own?

Th. 4:30 pm, 19-3-86

All that was written down in pencil in a notebook I kept to write in when I was having panic attacks and feelings of collapse. It was the third such notebook. I show these pages from it because on that day I found a little bit more of the skin I felt to be missing. And, I found my re-entry point into finishing a project I inherited from those who loved me, whom I loved. From my mother, especially.

It was not a matter of bucking up or finding some cathartic realization. I had to trace the re-entry point many times in many different ways until I knew how to get there and what it meant to go inside. When mother died—disappeared—and Archie too, I thought I could take over their project. It took over me.

People do all kinds of things to live within as well as get out of traps. Something of me decided to panic and collapse. That which is so basic to our identification, that marks us off from other people, that contains us and contains what is outside—what we could call the skin of self—that skin could no longer protect me in dealing with traps. For my skin had done more than serve as a container for me, it had been a second skin for mother, Archie, and the project. But there began to be holes. They got smaller after their deaths and then they got bigger. Very big. Until I had to graft new skin. And the grafting was my own therapy.

Mother had been a clinical psychologist—in Israel. That is where I am from. It was, in a way, natural for me to turn to someone like her in a crisis. But I did nothing for myself until there seemed to be no other choice. I had been too busy being a container. It was all I knew. You just don't stop being what you are. There are good reasons for being a certain way. It's made of something—real people, real events, and how you've taken them inside. And it's made of real choices that identify you as someone recognizable, acceptable to yourself.

Keeping the notebook was my idea. I would sometimes tell my doctor what I had written. Infrequently, I would read from it. I read from it now—to you, the reader—the stranger I must trust, the one who is my equal in facing the unknown on these pages. I show it as I will show the work of Betti Peleg, my mother, and Archibald Shechner, her patient, because I inherited news that I believe you should have. It is news before its time. News to keep. To make use of in good time, in your own way.

The person in the other room—the one I was waiting for that day in the notebook—was my doctor. I was seeing him then five days a week. After his first summer vacation, we went to five days—all gaps became intolerable. I never kept a record of what transpired in my sessions. Things that I wrote in the notebooks were there to help myself out of panic. The notebook was a bridge across distances between myself and others that seemed too far, or closeness that seemed too intense.

My doctor kept notes about the sessions. What if someday he uses them to write about me, so that people will link this story and his? They would then know it was me. Another Wolf-Man. That is a risk. But I remember the day I was glad for the Wolf-Man, no longer afraid of him or other "cases." In a way, I grew up with the Wolf-Man. I didn't know him and I never really read about him until I became a patient myself. He came to Freud with a childhood phobia of wolves. He was a Russian emigre of great wealth who lost everything but lived, I think, a full life and died at the age of eighty-three. My mother had several notable cases, too. I guess the most famous or infamous would have to be Archie Shechner. He was an archeologist who came to her holding his hands over his ears, telling of an ancient, lost Scroll and a voice from the ground—both discovered while digging, an artifact and a voice, each speaking of the origins of life. Archie came to mother talking about a return to the lost Garden of Eden. He said he had heard a voice that had been there at the beginning. At the time of the first ecosystem.

What would *my* doctor have to say about the voice from the ground and the Scroll—considering my work in bringing this book to light? The voice was not the same issue for us as it was for Archie and my mother. I never heard the voice. Its reality was never an issue between us. However, I had a real fear of hearing the voice. And I had tried hard to hear it, to help Archie and mother. Being afraid of something can sometimes make it real, or realer than real. In fact, you could say that the fear is there to keep it real, to hold something close—something I thought I could lose, if not damage—like my connection to mother and Archie.

The session I had that day connected my skin to the others. I began to see why I was returning to the project after dropping it in panic. I would repair mother and Archie, just like myself. Their reputations were in ruins when they disappeared. After all, how could I go forth with new skin if they were left behind in tatters, soon to be forgotten and always dismissed. Almost a year of sessions and I felt about strong enough to reopen the boxes and start carrying the old transcription work around with me. I wanted to fit back into it, but how much more of my life and time could I give before it killed me too—if that is what happened to mother and Archie.

And even if I was wary of thinking about talking

ecosystems, how could I refuse mother and Archie and their overwhelming efforts? Once, all I could feel was the panic, before going to my doctor, and now I wanted to feel none of it, to feel only small things, new things. But I wasn't through with panic. I was still fooling myself that I could be invisible in the transcription. It took a long time to realize that it was going to be about me now, more than mother or Archie, panic or whatever comes. I couldn't be a neutral scribe. I was a survivor as well as a newsbearer.

I am writing this in 1995, a little more than ten years after Archie Shechner gripped our lives like a daily headline, and then disappeared. I am thirty and will soon be saying goodbye to my doctor. The reasons for my panic were complex. I had seen it in others before it happened to me—in mother, Archie. Their panic seemed tied to the voice and the Scroll, something you could point to; they weren't paralyzed by it like me. I mean, they would not have been diagnosed with panic disorder. But they did disappear. While I remain. There are the beginnings of lines across my forehead. In fact, they are well defined. I am no longer the youngest in any group of people. No longer the youth and promise my mother held onto. I was a brightness in her life, especially after my father left. My figure is still as it was in 1984, perhaps thinner. My eyes are dryer. I have to use artificial tears every night before going to bed here in New York. It could be all the crying, it could be the air. Am I strange if I say that I'm glad, though, for the crying?

I have had no truly intimate relationships over these last ten years. Not since Everett Nosei, who was among a group of scholars who came to Israel in 1984 because of the sensation with Archie Shechner. I have not seen him since then but what I am writing here will have to fuse with what he was able to cull from the trunk I delivered to him almost two years ago. It contained everything I had about Archie. I felt that Nosei (pronounced "nosey") would know what to do with it. I am writing now because of an error I made in 1986 when I prepared the trunk.

In that year of panic, it was all I could manage to be an enlightened scribe. I was still not feeling a part of the project, but I had managed to integrate all the pieces that were left to me. I finished transcribing and editing all of the remaining tapes, then made copies of the transcription and many of the source materials and sealed the originals in a trunk, which I stored in the basement of an apartment building in New York City. Until recently, I lived as a kind of guest tenant in that building, in an apartment owned by Professor Harriman Svitz, whom I had met in 1984. It was after Archie had disappeared and mother had begun the project of writing down Archie's story. Story hardly fits the description, since he was recounting to her what was said to him by a voice in the ground.

Svitz was already in Israel when the other scholars came to meet Archie and examine the ancient Scroll he had discovered at the site where he had been digging. And then Archie disappeared before any of them could meet and interview him. The only tangible things that remained of his experience were audio tapes made by him and mother. Some of these were tapes of his sessions with mother;

others were notes both of them dictated. But mother soon disappeared also, and the transcribing of these tapes fell to me. It was in Svitz's apartment I finished. Once it was done, I forgot about it, the way you forget about old love letters you've stashed away. The new love in my life was not Svitz but me, myself: I was panicked that I might lose myself.

At that time, every day I felt in danger, even in my doctor's office. I can remember the day it seemed there was nowhere to go and no one to believe me—like the day Archie broke into my mother's office while she was in session, unable to wait outside.

"I think I need to go to the hospital. I wish I could stay in that corner over there—or in the waiting room tonight, put two chairs together."

"What would that do?"

"I'd be okay—everything, okay then."

"And you wouldn't even help yourself to the couch overnight?"

I said nothing in reply. This session with my doctor is as clear to me now as if it were yesterday. Every symptom I had outside of the office passed through me on that day. But after his question, my right leg that had been shaking slowly stopped. I began to hear tears dropping from my face onto the coarse fabric of the pillow in the silence of the room.

"I feel stalled. I don't know why I'm crying now."

He started to say something but I finally answered him, "The couch. I wouldn't even help myself to the couch in my own fantasy."

"Yes. And maybe to be on the safe side, you think you'd better put yourself in the corner, the outer room or better yet, a hospital. And not one that can take care of heart attacks."

I nodded. "I think I could go crazy... My heart—it just skipped a beat. Now I'm having symptoms in here too."

"It sounds like you regret what you're feeling."

"Yes, it feels like I'm ruining even this."

"Maybe it's me you're afraid of ruining. Maybe it's someone you're so angry at you can't admit it."

"But I'm not angry at you—I'm grateful."

"And what would happen if you should be angry at me... if for a moment, be not so grateful... if you should not like me so well?"

At first, I said nothing. "It makes me cringe, what you said about me not liking you, even for a moment. I don't like the way I'm feeling. I feel like I want to get out of here. I never feel like that."

"Maybe certain feelings were getting too close together—anger and gratitude, dislike and liking."

"I couldn't imagine not liking you. It feels too..." I stopped again.

"Too what?"

"Too dead. I think, I mean it feels like you have a hole in you."

"Maybe you're afraid that you could put holes in those you care about. You know what holes are like and you wouldn't want to put them in other people. Maybe it feels like they could be dead if you even think thoughts or have feelings of dislike. Better to go to the hospital. Find a corner, a waiting room, an emergency room. And however scary that would be, maybe it's still better to contain yourself in anxiety and panic."

This is the way it felt when I stashed the trunk in Svitz's basement: the tapes—the lives of my mother, of Archie—would have to wait. To find their own waiting room. It would take several years for me to go down there again, realizing that the only really safe place for the trunk was with Nosei. I thought once he had it that would be the end of my involvement. The lost Scroll would be Nosei's now. He would have to give it the link to the present that it would need. I expected to someday see it in print and written about. I had this confidence because I had once known Everett Nosei, in a way I had never known anyone else. We had been full of sex, full of the Scroll, full of each other. We were so full we were empty of anything else. I wish I could say we ended up losing each other, but we never got that far. We never risked clinging or losing in the first place.

I learned some months ago that Nosei managed to turn the trunk into something publishable. The information appeared in the New York Times about the downsizing of a publishing house, but what it was really about was an untouchable editor who had been fired nonetheless. There was speculation that this editor, Ari Buber, pushed his luck one time too many. One of the books under his wing had a title that jumped out at me: *The Eden Revelation*.

It sounded like Nosei. I decided to track down this editor.

First, I found his agent. An assistant at the publishing house gave me his name and guessed that the book was dead in the water since it had been withheld from the house's upcoming catalog. I called Seth Greene, the agent, and told him who I was. The book was considered too strange, he said. There wasn't enough melodrama or something.

A week passed and I called him again. I told him I wanted to add my story to the manuscript and could I have it back. I had made a mistake in the original compilation, I said. I had made myself nearly invisible. We had all been ravaged by the experience of the lost Scroll. It shocked us, almost as if it had arrived from Mars as an artifact of another species. I explained to Mr. Greene that my mother and Archibald Shechner did not survive the collision with it, but that I had made it with much inner struggle. I was the link between the fantastic and the real. I had the secrets of the Scroll and the secrets of those involved. He listened, and then he made the necessary calls. The manuscript was soon on my dining room table. I took it out of the box. It was far from over for me.

I didn't read the words at first. I turned the pages just to feel them. I would pick out words and say them aloud just to hear them. Slowly, I began to read. Nosei had transformed it the way I hoped he would. But I couldn't really see the cracks in his heart that he had shown me. The full impact wasn't there—the feeling we had discovered life on another planet. A whole other life system, another ecosystem. For Archie and the others involved, it was like finding a fossilized Eden. It was a new story of something older than memory.

I went right to Nosei's story, jumping to the words he had chosen to describe the ten years since we were lovers. He spoke of himself in two times: 1994 and 1984. Each was a different Nosei, but I couldn't get past the Nosei of ten years ago. I felt flat, like the flatness in pivotal moments of our relationship. He was still the Nosei that couldn't tell me what I wanted to hear. When I opened the manuscript, I had hoped to feel his mind around me. Maybe I wanted him to slip into his mind the way I had been inside of mine for the last ten years. But I was the one with panic attacks. Maybe I just wanted him to be what my doctor was for me. Still, something was missing there, and it was me. He had written me in but it was his old version of me. There were other versions which he hadn't been able to handle. And I was left feeling that I was the source of static in our relationship. How ironic: ten years later and I'm still trying to clear the static.

I never did say goodbye. I just disappeared with the trunk to Switzerland after mother's death and then delivered it to him a couple years ago—no return address, no explanation—after long living an invisible life in New York. The same life I had devised in my Tel Aviv youth, even more so. I had done my best to stop time. I was crying but I was not mourning. I was suspended in a place where the losses were always about to happen but never happened. Even the losses of mother and Archie seemed unreal, and I kept Nosei alive with them—in the trunk, in storage.

I easily slipped into the black costume of a New Yorker in the 1980s. Sometimes, I would alternate with khaki—

pants, blouse, jacket. That day in my doctor's waiting room, I had on black Gap jeans, black turtleneck and my black and white late winter wrappings. And, of course, black backpack. In the beginning, I still carried a purse; then I added a small shopping bag, in which I carried a water bottle and my make up and maybe a sandwich or something else to eat. These were the necessities that would get me from Svitz's to my doctor's, and back again. They seemed necessary for my body but somehow they only rated an ephemeral container: I used small shopping bags for a long while. One day I started using the backpack, left behind by one of Svitz's brief encounters.

As my appointment neared that day, I became obsessed with throwing open the folding doors of a closet inside my doctor's office. I could see myself jumping up from the couch and jerking them open. Why didn't he just tell me what was in there? Why didn't he open them for me? I wanted to shake him, jerk him around. Open him up. Well, it was me I wanted to open up. The aggression turned inward within minutes and by the time he came to get me in the waiting room, I was taking it all back, into myself.

"Today I have an extra notebook with me. Mine—and one of the transcription notebooks."

"You've restarted it?"

"Yes. And I believe having it with me today has made me have a panic attack. I've been having that feeling of collapse while I was waiting."

"Were you waiting long?"

"No—you... Yes—I mean, I came early. By taxi. It made *me* early."

"You seem unsure about who was waiting or even whether there was a period of waiting."

"I didn't want you to think that you were making me wait."

"Well, I'm really not sure if I came for you right at the hour. I may have kept you waiting. But what if I actually was aware of it? What is it that we—you and I—couldn't bear in that?"

"I don't know. I can't answer. I can't say what you need to know from me today, so I can make it after I leave here. I feel like it's all dead—a deadend."

"Maybe I haven't made you feel there's an alternative to things coming to a deadend in here—"

"You're not doing anything. It's me..."

"Maybe I am doing something. Maybe I remind you of someone who made you wait—or wait to have your feelings. And the disappearing of feelings into deadends: Maybe that happens when you think you're close to blaming—in this case, me. Perhaps you're just tired of kindly waiting for others who feel free to disappear. What would happen if you weren't so mindful and fair?"

"A bad look on your face. A face melting off. To nothing."

He interrupted. "That's a startling image. We've had the image of faces come in here before—a face turning bad in front of you, lost from you and you losing it. And now with me—"

"I couldn't bear it if your face should stop being your face."

"—And a face that is your's in a way, now. As you said,

the features and the form would melt off, melt down. Then you melt down, collapse. Better you than me. Better for you to do the melting away and the gathering back together, than for me."

"Isn't that like being a victim? Nosei used to say that I always brought it back around to me—in our conflicts."

"We don't have Nosei here, we can't analyze him. But no, I don't think it is like being a victim. I think you are going to great lengths to protect something. There are reasons—real ones around you, and those just as real that have gone into constructing your inner world. It's that structure we want to understand."

I frowned. "That word 'structure.' It feels like more than a mechanical word. When we speak of "structure" in here I can hear structure—each other's, our own. I hear it so well that I can even see it, feel it. I can feel you hearing it. The mind can get opened too wide here. When I leave, I can still feel you touching my mind. I miss it when I'm not here. Does anyone ever write about that in case studies? Minds opened, but not bodies. Once I had a body open wide, a body beside me open wide, Nosei. As I was going through my boxes last night, I found a drawing I had made of Nosei—a drawing of his body. An outline. We had made love. After we moved apart, he rolled off the bed, feigning exhaustion, playing with me. Without thinking, I jumped up and ran to the kitchen for something to draw with. I brought back a crayon and I followed the perimeter of his body with it. He was leaving Israel that night. We had agreed to go our own ways.

After he left, I traced the outline onto a roll of large paper that you wrap meats with—you call it freezer paper here. That's what I found in the trunk—this tracing of his outline. It made me remember something that happened after Nosei got up from the floor to go to the bathroom. While he was there, I laid down inside the crayon outline I had drawn. I began to feel as if he were still inside me. Instead of hard—soft. An unformed fullness. And I just let the soft fullness press me, pull against my mind. The soft redness, the soft foldedness. I could see it in my mind—a desire bulging out. A helpless, almost wounded desire. And I had, I want to say that I had—in his outline....I can't say it."

"Why?"

"It feels too much. My skin feels like its fraying."

"It is frightening to feel that there would be nothing to hold you in. Maybe that is why we need another person present. Someone to lend their skin. Maybe that is part of what I am for you, and I think you want to know what my mind feels—*if* it feels. And where you are inside my skin."

"What I was trying to say was I had an orgasm on the floor in his outline. I was afraid to say it because I think the outline could turn into this couch. I was afraid to go forward—saying what passes through my mind—because it felt like it could happen here. I've told you before. Now I'm afraid I want to have an orgasm in here. On the couch."

"What would it mean to have an orgasm in here?"

"I don't know." I could hardly believe I told him.

"I think we know some of what it meant for you to have

one in the outline. It had something to do with finding out something you needed to know about the other—in this case, Nosei. But feeling you hadn't really found it out. After all, he was leaving you. And imagining his soft penis inside you made a place for finding out—where you are, what you feel, and most importantly, something about the other. These are things we are unraveling in a similar kind of place. It is the work we are doing together. But I think you're not sure about the together part. You want to have an impact. But you're afraid of taking your mind off me, of me disappearing in a way, even a moment. What would happen? Where would I be?"

"I don't know. I mean, it feels true to me. I felt disconnected from Nosei. Even during orgasm. In the outline, I felt free. I wasn't watching, my mind wasn't. I let it happen. Be done to me."

"You felt safe enough in the outline to stop, to let your thoughts be your thoughts—instead of watching them, apart, as you've reported yourself in your dreams."

"Yes, and I'm afraid of knowing too much. I always seem to know too much, and then everything feels so sad." I used to take the outline of Nosei's body out, after he was gone—as a way of enduring the sadness.

It was all I felt I knew then—my skin with Nosei's skin. But I started watching his face, to know what he was thinking. He ignored my questions after orgasm. I would get angry, just to get his familiar irritated expressions back—the blankness scared me. Then my skin began to rebel. Hotness. I became afraid of getting too hot during sex. His face would look like it didn't recognize me, like a sun. Now my doctor was talking but I could barely hear him.

"Julie? I think you've brought us to where we need to be. As long as you felt assured of Nosei's face—could read it—you felt in contact, free to experience the uncontained feelings of orgasm. But when you seemed to lose his face, sex became dangerous—a place where things could get too hot, where faces could turn against each other, perhaps even disappear. It's a sad and scary thing to survive that moment when the other's face turns away."

"Other or mother. Why am I working on this stuff of mother's again?"

"I think you've already said it: to keep things from being sad. To keep her safe from the sadness."

"She seemed so sad at the end. Torn. Overwhelmed by Archie, the voice, her feelings for him, the Scroll." How could I contain it all myself? I thought—I don't remember feeling overwhelmed.

As if following the unspoken, he said: "Maybe you're lending her your skin. Except, you actually give your own to her for patches she seems to need. You said she was torn, and overwhelmed, which suggests she couldn't contain what was happening, especially inside of herself. You tried to do it for her. That was what you thought your job was. You have had that job for a long time now."

"But I need to finish the transcription this time. I need my own way of finishing it. I feel like finishing it could be a way of taking something of myself back."

"We have to stop soon for today, but I just had a fantasy of reading a story to you by Samuel Beckett—from *Texts for Nothing.* He speaks of the closing of his mouth and his ears and that when they open again, he has high hopes that they can hear a new story, and tell a story. I think he called this 'a little story, with living creatures coming and going on a habitable earth crammed with the dead.' Maybe your own mouth and ears are reaching for that little story."

"I guess there can't be a story without the dead. You know what I found last night when I was reading through the transcription I did?"

"No, what?"

"A part where Archie tells of first hearing the voice out of the ground and about all his checking to be sure it was real. And he tells of the voice asking if he had made a discovery that was 'sealed in skin parchment.' That was the Scroll, you know. It's funny that it was skin then and skin again. Now."

"Yes."

We sat in silence for a few minutes and then he asked, "Enough for today?" I said, "Yes. Tomorrow." A binding up to carry us through to tomorrow, over the gap that was immediately there again, as the session ended.

Before going home, I went down to the avant garde bookstore on St. Mark's Place. The book my doctor referred to would probably be on Svitz's shelves, but I wanted a copy of my own. Later, after Svitz had bid goodnight and stumbled off, I took it out of the bag and read until I found the passage. And I found another: "Memories are killing. So you must not think of certain things, of those that are dear to you, or rather you must think of them, for if you don't there is the danger of finding them, in your mind, little by little. That is to say, you must think of them for a while, a good while, every day several times a day, until they sink forever in the mud."

And then I looked up some more of the transcription I had completed while still in Israel. I read about Sunday in the "Seven Days of Creation"—an entry which I found Nosei later subtitled "Planted Desire" in the book you are about to read. The voice asked Archibald Shechner, "Can the mind evolve?" I know Archie thought it could. He had felt our minds could do anything—that knowledge was our guide. But the voice, supplying her own answer, said, "No." She led Archie forward, telling him, "The mind has no wish to leave the body. The body pursues growth through mistakes the mind makes and vice versa: this process yields intimacy. Mind and body can be a perfectly intimate system, as it will be again in Eden." She said she was drawing close to "humans who had tasted intimate congress"—and risked fatal mistakes.

I unrolled the outline drawing of Nosei and thought of Creation's seven days, remembering how I studied it in school, and then the way Archie heard it through the voice in the ground. Nosei and I had talked of it in Tel Aviv, made love, and then in a lull I would go back to my work on the transcription—my mind bringing a passionate resonance to Archie's sessions with my mother. I wondered if Nosei remembered my body. I wanted to be inside the outline with him. The outline became his mouth. It changed into his hand as it moved across mine. Then it was a half-bent knee, a kneecap I liked to explore, and there it was: the penis I could never stop looking at.

Too quickly there was the feeling of a mind next to me—not his, but my doctor's. It felt like too many things in the outline. They all came in: mother, Archie, the voice. And as in Beckett's story, my ears and mouth began to close again.

And then I opened them a little more the next session. And I've worked to keep them open, *thinking certain things for a while each day*, to hear and tell my own "little story," which is part of a bigger story of desire and loss revealed by Archie Shechner—the desire to evolve and the loss of the mothering ecosystem that formed us. To you the reader. For me, the daughter of Betti Peleg.

Memorandum from the author's agent:

One year ago, after the manuscript of *The Eden Revelation* was returned to me by the publisher, I was ready to file it in the oldest file cabinet, in the very back of the bottom file, with all the dust there—in short, a place I would never have to think about again. Some books can be troublesome, but I had put more time and sweat into this one than most others. In fact, I had treated it as if it were my own, since it came to me in such unusual circumstances, without my having met the author. I actually wrote a brief appreciation of it (which you will be reading) and for the first time allowed my name to become part of a book I represented.

All of this was done as a favor to an editor I had done much business with in the past. I would say that this editor, Ari Buber, is also my good friend (we have lunch on business, but we also exercise together after work at the same health club, where we occasionally have dinner and shoot the shit) but I should be clearer: not really a favor, but a project in which we both expected to make some money, score some points, and hopefully, change the world. Well, not "change the world" as the old cliche has it, but to lay it out on the table: to change the way we fuck.

Now, I had no idea that was at the core of it, not until I had read the first manuscript more than once. Actually, it was Ari who pointed it out to me, as we were having our usual health plates one night at the club.

"Do you realize this book is not about some spiritual or cultural evolving, like most of these bestsellers, but that it is actually talking about real, physical, bodily evolving, based on changes in reproduction?"

Was Ari on the level? I thought. Was he going to say the book put forward serious scientific claims? I'd read the thing and the evolutionary stuff was pretty convincing, but it still was a novel, wasn't it? "Ok, Ari, fill me in—what changes?"

Ari looked at me and arched his eyebrows. "Why Seth, I thought you already knew this. We're talking about plain, down-to-earth fucking here."

I distinctly remember hearing my fork clatter on the polished wood floor as it flew from my hand. "I don't remember much fucking in there. Did I miss something?"

Ari was waxing more sober than usual this night—true, we had both cut down on alcohol and were partnered by little blue bottles of spring water at our sides. "We're so culture-bound, Seth, that the very word fuck has become just about meaningless. Mindless—and just about extinct as an expression of the most basic experience.

"But underneath fucking there's an even more essential drive, right down at the root of life, and it's the desire to evolve. It's *that* desire that's been totally buried in us. It's real enough, I think—or at least the manuscript has me thinking it."

"You don't really believe Julie and Nosei fucked themselves onto a new rung of the evolutionary ladder, do you?" I asked, not sure if I was supposed to smile knowingly or what.

"But what if it's true?" Ari said. "It doesn't sound like

someone made it up. And if they did, why aren't they here to take the credit for some fine fucking fiction?"

Well, that was then. We got the book on the list and were ready to see what the world thought. But then—boom. The house got sold to a conglomerate, the new ceo's fired half the staff, and among them, Ari, who sent the manuscript back to me along with several others. Not right away, of course. Ari's reputation was too solid for that. But once they evaluated the new books he had—and especially, once they skimmed through *The Eden Revelation*—they must have been shitting bricks.

That book was the first to be orphaned, and within a week, Ari had had it with publishing, he said. He was going to take a year off and maybe write a book of his own. Lucky for him, he could afford it. Ari Buber had been one of the hottest editors in the business for many years. But tell that to a bunch of marketing managers with hearts of stone, and heads with coins in them.

So I filed it away. It was easy enough to do—after all, there was no author to call and have his or her heart broken, or their bank balance. As for the world and the future of humankind—well, I thought we were fucked before, so we might as well be sure as fucked now. Fuck the world, and fuck me.

Then Julie called. After she heard what had happened with the manuscript, she asked for it, explaining that she had been the transcriber of Archibald Shechner's voice. I know who you are, I told her, I've read the manuscript—though I wasn't even sure that Julie Peleg was a real person.

But there she was, even offering to rework the manuscript—I was intrigued, to say the least, if not spooked.

Here we are, a year later, I've read the manuscript with Julie offering a new voice for the reader. She's a kind of skeleton key into this *Eden*. Someone who can be trusted, someone who was there and who is still uncertain how to live, after exposing the desire to evolve in herself, guided by Wisdom's voice. Did I forget something? It should be known from the beginning that no simple transformation is being contemplated. No, it's a hard, gradual thing—a digging deep, or what Julie calls a working through.

At last the book is ready; the question is, are we? I know I'm one of those who isn't. I still desire what Ari calls the "old" fuck. The difference is, now I can't ignore feeling there's something I don't know about myself. Because it's more than a feeling now. And that's how it starts: the unrepressed feeling knocks your life off center. Julie made me want to read this book yet again. Ari made me have to read in the beginning, so I've kept his *Note to the Reader*, written when we thought it was going to the printers more than a year ago. That is what you read next, as this story begins.

—Seth Greene, literary agent

Note To The Reader

The manuscript arrived on my desk one day, Express Mail, with a return address that read, dubiously: 2000 New World Lane, Eden, NJ. But I have had no other communication from the authors involved. I have been able to verify that the characters of this story existed, though not how to separate fact from fiction. I did discover that the manuscript was mailed by Everett Nosei, formerly a teacher of philology in New Haven. After fifteen years in his position, however, he suddenly resigned. His colleagues knew that he had been working on a project important to himself and which he was secretive about—but this is not that unusual among scholars. He evidently told no one of his plans and left no forwarding address. Without doubt, I felt the work important enough to publish without further delay.

The category of prophecy is in vogue just now, with record-breaking sales for *The Celestine Prophecy* changing the rules for what constitutes fiction and nonfiction in our time. While many publishers continue to be puzzled about the fame and popularity of *Celestine*, it's clear to me the book blazes a new path, turning the reader into a conspirator. It's addressed not to the public reader, like most books, but to the secret individual. The coincidences that brought you into the store to buy the book have already become part of the story. And what you will do next—what decisions you will have to make in your life—you can already imagine as part of the story. Since our own lives are presumably nonfiction, we are embodied as witnesses of the *facticity* in the unfolding story, however fantastic it may be.

The title page of the manuscript reads, "*The Scroll of the History of Adam* and *Guide to a New World.*" I have decided in the interest of prudence to publish this work as fiction while designating it "Novel and Guide," leaving it to the reader to determine how much of the story is worthy of a leap-of-faith belief and how much is apparent fact.

For many years now, we have all felt the loss of the great stories and myths that fueled the spirits of our grandparents and ancestors. Modern stories do not infuse our thoughts for a lifetime, not the way a story like that of Adam and Eve comes to mind at various milestones in our lives. What makes the ancient stories so powerful?

Facts are just not enough. We are subject to an explosion of information in our time that merely increases our hunger for a personal framework. I believe we're beginning to feel the need for a new kind of story in our lives, to transform the new knowledge and paradigm shifts we encounter into something more satisfying than information. We witness the birth of myriad technologies, of multimedia, virtual reality, genetics. We see that each still lacks content, and we know that what they need are more than facts; they need great, enfolding stories. Fiction and nonfiction need each other.

Too often we fill the absence with stories of celebrities. There is, however, a healthy side to our fascination with other people's lives. It has helped each of us begin to tell our own stories of discovering freshly-remembered pasts. As we recover buried memories and forgotten callings, our stories become more compelling because they intermingle truths with serious fantasies of the kind of person we wish to be.

Consider the story of Noah's ark. Fiction or primordial fact? It is told as if true history but in story form. If Noah's story is but a man's, it is still too grand to fit on television. The tube, that most celebrated of media truetale-tellers, would be hard put to allow it. Yet we need more fiction in our lives of this Genesis kind that is intermingled with certitude, the unfixed boundaries revealing hidden truths to us.

At the outset, without some factual reference, I doubted that Everett Nosei would have believed in Archibald Shechner's verity. Then I saw that only when Nosei began to take his own story seriously did he lend credence to Shechner. It took ten years of avoidance and evasion, returning to his former life as a philologist, before Nosei could apparently face his role in completing this manuscript.

A true philologist these days must break language down to its singular components. Reduced to the nuts and bolts of words and letters, a story seems always to be a fictive thing, hardly to be believed. Everett Nosei appears to be a man who resists stories. In the same way, he might also sidestep systems, which are nature's version of stories. And then, when he could no longer ignore the knowledge that his body is itself a system—cooperating with other life forms like the intelligent microbes (chemically speaking) evolved in our intestines to co-digest our food—Nosei finally embodies his own story. Instead of resisting the story of what has happened to him, he drops his resistance, lets the revelation work. It is as if he were saying, "Why else would I have been there?" in answer to his own skepticism that his was a central role in the drama of the recently discovered Scroll.

Why else would I put my reputation on the line for this book? Maybe it's because the image I've cultivated for myself as a grand *intuiter*—someone with his instinctive finger on the hot button of the times—could only be pulled off by someone who is just the opposite, someone who calculates all the possibilities before he acts. To me, the controversy over whether we may have a repressed desire to physically evolve is virgin territory. So, why would this virgin of a manuscript fall into my overexperienced lap? I can't say exactly why Everett Nosei chose me, but maybe it's because there's no secret to how I feel about books like *Celestine*: to start with, they're too clean.

Aside from the anal retentive qualities of *Celestine*—no sex, no ambivalence, no messy language—books like these envision an apocalypse of peace, that warm-all-over feeling people like to think heralds a spiritual renaissance. Running from the arms of a complicated, diverse world of nature, we take off into the air, the invisible, the transcendent. But however postmodern our world is, I don't think it can ever be post-natural. That's my gut feeling—as far as intuition goes—and I'm betting that copies of *Eden Revelation* can fly out the door, in trade parlance, even if there's grease and complications holding it down to earth.

We're liberated people, but do I want to be liberated from the earth too? Our outer shells—the environment itself—is fragile and at risk, yet the *Celestine* book would take us into a further liberation, flying straight into the supernatural. I'll stay on the ground, thank you. I don't have a problem with the voice from the ground in this *Eden* book, as long as real people are struggling to come to grips with it as a natural event.

Ari Buber, Editor

The Scroll of the History of Adam

and

Guide to a New World

Prologue

Before anything, before I had even the most ragged story to tell, I was entranced by the origin of words. I'd hear an unusual word and wonder where it came from. This made it hard to keep up with stories. Although I'm educated I notice that many people who are barely literate have the same tendency to be distracted when they hear odd words. We're like very ancient peoples, easily lost in stories, while myths about our origins and how to live are told in many voices, living and dead, permitting the hearer to become comfortably lost in time.

I was lost for ten years in the story I am about to tell. At first, I had many ill-fitting fragments of memory from the critical year, nineteen eighty-four, coming together slowly from the disorienting months I spent with the inheritors of the Scroll— or rather, since it had disappeared the day after I first saw it, they might better be called heirs to its manifestation. Then, when the archive arrived in Julie Peleg's trunk, filled with tape transcriptions, I began to sort out the voices. One shocking voice was my own. Another voice, ancient: *Guide to a New World*—translated, but from what?—arranged according to the Bible's seven days of creation. This voice was so much older than the Bible it seemed to retain memory of when our human species evolved. It's plain that even before the Bible, each day represented an epoch, one beyond reckoning, each day stretching into billions of years.

#

There wasn't much sense to the Seven Days of Creation that I could make out at first. I didn't know much about what creative ecosystems meant—in fact, I didn't even know ecosystem was a proper word and not some ersatz metaphor for the environment. The chapters of the Guide seemed another form of scroll, unfolding each day of the week until the seventh day became a revelation of intimacy—probably not apparent to Julie initially. I only understood this when I saw the fragments of notes again I had made ten years before, in the trunk Julie sent. Wham. Suddenly I could hear the woman's side—where before I could feel nothing. It's as if I was deaf to Julie ten years ago. When she lay there without a sound, it was really me who was deaf to her body. Her body spoke in me and I wouldn't hear.

Now I see her body was made for mine a hundred thousand years ago, that our bodies can have a history, too. I could speak glibly about the history I *did* know—the history of words and human writing—but my body was silent, lost in a void. My climax scared me, the ejaculation shut me up. It was eerie, primeval, my silence. But so was the act of intimacy for me: I couldn't listen to it. I felt ignorant, like there was the naked female body revealed and it should have been simple but it wasn't. It took me years to come to see Julie's sexual body was like a natural system also, the mystery there deepening to primeval origins. Start to ask questions and they only lead to more questions—and then the answers come, as soon as we admit the ignorance and look around as if we're on a new planet. That's how it was for me as I read Wisdom's voice in Julie's transcriptions. The answers describe a natural history that always went further back into origins than science or myth had gone before. Back to that primeval feeling inside when I came during sex, stifling any sound and feeling the echo in my bones.

Well, this might have driven any woman mad. But Julie acted like it was her fault and I didn't contradict her. What a bastard I was! Intimacy shut me up, but as I now recognize in Archie's words, it's what draws us out: intimacy with life, wherever it is, draws us out of ourselves. There's probably more life left to explore on Earth than any other planet, but the thrill of it is there in the word explore, a kind of evolving foreplay—without it the universe is as silent as I was, in bed with Julie. The only foreplay I knew was feeling for the buttons on my own clothes. Next, find the place to stick it in. Kind of miraculous I could stay erect and keep on moving while Julie moaned and moaned. Should I stop, I asked, scared I hurt her. No, no, no need. I went way beyond her expectations, she said later, whimpering, taking all the blame for feeling far away from me.

And Julie translated my silence into the Seven Days, which started the tracing of bodies. The night before I was to leave, bags packed by the door, we couldn't sleep and made love again till it felt like hard labor. Exhausted, we rolled out of bed onto the floor and I just lay there naked on my back, playing a corpse. I felt Julie tugging against my leg and sat up: she had a thick crayon and was tracing my red outline on the white stone floor.

"I'm going to copy this on paper and keep it for when I'm lonely. Then I'll unroll it and sleep inside your outline." It just further confirmed my feeling that she was too strange for me, like the Scroll itself. I was glad to be leaving.

And there I'd found it again, rolled up like a scroll, in the trunk. Now there were numbers at different points in the outline; underneath, an explanatory code. Seven points in all, and I understood this was how she translated the form of the Seven Days—the natural correspondence for the number seven. But why? It was a kind of translation of Wisdom's voice into a human form. Just as now, with the Guide's help, I can hear the underlying erotic complexity in an ecosystem resolve itself into a grown woman's voice.

It didn't take long to come to me: Julie had made the body a human metaphor, just like the earth days of the week were metaphors in Genesis. The limbs and senses that make up the form of our species—straight from the drawing—were like our own creation, corresponding to the days of the earth's creation. But the connection of the body to our shaping ecosystem—that was it!—*reading* the body, *reading* the ecosystem. Foreplay—exploration—and discovery. Julie connected the *voice* of Wisdom to a body, sensing seduction and discovery were in common. Intimacy was the common root.

Whereas—Archibald Shechner was a reader of bones and fossils, not metaphors. The voice of Wisdom was so literal to him he panicked, fearing he had lost his mind. Julie was more of a poet, though, or none of this might have been saved. It's clear to me now that if we send anyone to the planets, we'll need poets as well as paleo-archaeologists and biologists. In addition to all the materials in the trunk, Julie also supplied the stimulus—in the form of the rolled-up tracing of my body—for me to think like a poet too, in order to translate our experience into some kind of coherent vision.

#

I had to learn "seven days" was a metaphor, since time is kept differently on every other world, including those above us and those below, in the seas, for instance. I was a specialist like everyone else, a specialist in language origins, so my knowledge came from human ways of thinking. There was hardly an idea of nonhuman thinking in those days, other than the primitive ways of animals and AI, or artificial intelligence, which was bounded by primitive computers. Shechner was perhaps the most famous authority in the world on the archaeology of early cities, where it was presumed that writing developed. So he too had no experience in looking at a natural system—an ecosystem—in terms of its own history, its own framework. In other words, how many years it was like this or like that—well, that's still human thinking, even just because the significance of *years* is a human scale. When we find ecosystems on other planets, earth "years" will be an insignificant term, except to our self-esteem.

The more I saw time and the Seven Days were transformed by imagination, the closer I felt to the feeling of evolving, the most primeval feeling, hidden underneath all else. If there are infinite ways of imagining days, then there are endless Edens. Think how limited Genesis is, with its expression of diversity confined to Adam's intimacy with the creatures and their names. But instead of animals alone, in reality there's a diversity of worlds, of ecosystems each recreating its own species of living things. In this new Eden of Edens, we can evolve like a tree of Knowledge: responding to, and intimate with everything. Wisdom is her voice, drawing us on, into the foreplay of discovery.

And where's the creator in this? He's been moving to the background ever since King David, and he moves further back again by bringing more life forward, allowing Wisdom to be his voice. Discovering these things—all the lost ecosystems and countless extinctions, all the lost plans for life—reveals our afterlife, as it appears on a nonhuman scale. As just plain Homo sapiens, there's nowhere we can stand, no proper vantage point, to take in the overwheming details. Although our eyes scan 180°, they can never focus on more than 9° at once—the rest is an illusion of power. Yet here we're talking unknown degrees, beyond 360°, and the next species we evolve into will have found the way to adapt into it. First, though, we have to get lost in it, feel its immensity in the hidden recesses of our own history of evolving, the language in our primeval brain.

#

Who would have thought that early man knew he evolved? Still, it's a fact that Neanderthals and earlier prehumans of the Homo line lived together with Homo sapiens in certain times and places. I shouldn't have been surprised that the natural world described in the ancient Scroll—the snatches of it I saw before it disappeared with Shechner, and the fragments of it in Julie's transcriptions—is the same one we lost when we became too civilized: a world of endless wonder. Even the word "civilized" makes it impossible to think of our once newly-evolved, full-frontal sexuality.

"Scientists go on about brain sizes and toolmaking but human genital size doubles other primates. The evolution of the genus Homo sprang from a sudden turning of the male to face the female in intercourse, as few apes ever had. Face to face, seduction increased in subtlety and response, leading to a similar increase in the play of thought. We began to see ourselves in each others' eyes—and at that moment we were a new species." (A transcription from Archibald Shechner's tapes).

Why is it crucial to know how, when, and where we evolved? Science trivializes its own answers, explaining in bones and stones, when the terms should be: sense and sensibility, spirit and sexuality. How we evolved is not just a question of anatomy but of the human spirit—how was it set in motion? It's too late now for the hubris that we *ourselves* evolved the human spirit in the cradle of our civilization. We know we're not even superior, spiritually-speaking, to ancient men and women living in pristine ecosystems.

The secret of our sexual dependency remains in Africa. How pioneering our progenitors were, how much more daring and inventive compared to us! They walked into the unknown, again and again. They were pilgrims and explorers in their own ecosystems, trailblazers into others. Their pioneering of intimacy—coupling off—allowed them to spread further and further abroad.

Meanwhile, the bone men go on about brain size, as if elephants and whales might be our intellectual superiors. No, no, the secret of evolution is in the nature of intimacy, forged in forest innocence. Sex is a species-specific act, the only one that will not become interspecies. Species may kill, eat, and play with each other but they rarely cross boundaries to participate in the secret act that insures evolving, *sexual intimacy.* And it is woman, according to Shechner, *woman* who is at the bottom of our inventiveness, her desire sharpening our thoughts, focussing our attention on the seductive unknown.

#

The way the eye tracks a woman's curves, glued there by desire... All things track, remembering what they need and where they have been. Even plants track the light and the elements and the animals they use in pollination—even our sperm track to the womb. I realized that all my life has been a tracking back to there, to what it represents, eroticizing everything. That womb evolves into the form of a woman, and then a particular woman—and then, for me, a Julie, someone crystallizing thoughts building up over a lifetime.

We can only hear her voice in the ecosystem, the woman herself hidden, the way it was when we were fetuses in the womb, ready to be born. We had already heard our mother's voice, muffled. Julie's voice also led to no consistent image for me, back in those feverish months.

I surrendered to the curves in Julie, indulged in each one, curve of the naked shoulder and the soft underbelly tucked under her firm arm—I wouldn't have known had I not felt it. I grasped the poignance of all the hidden softness yet it didn't touch a soft spot in me; instead, it stopped before it reached my body's organs—heart or stomach—as if they were encased in wood. I might have been a tree, bursting into bloom: I could see the reaction in Julie but all I felt was the pleasure of not feeling rattled. This is not an inconsiderable pleasure, in fact it is one of the highest. Just when you expect a wrenching, uncontrollable, destabilizing jolt, you get—instead—a sense of being protected, being in control. This discipline turned empty orgasms into a source of warm pride for me.

That's the way it is for trees! "...father and mother to the primates they nourished in their branches. After hurricanes, when their flowers and fruits were torn from them, trees start to reproduce faster, dropping their fruits and sexually reproducing again. This is called stress in trees" (transcription from Archibald Shechner's tapes)—and so the freedom from stress, from being caught in the feverish cycle of sex, appeared quite gratifying to me.

Yet my body reached out toward the shape of a woman—shaped, as if a container for my thoughts. I listened to Julie like no person I had ever met, and she was full of Shechner's words. She told me about the transcripts she was typing and how they were more important than the lost Scroll. Oh God, how could I contain this weird stuff, I thought. I failed to trust her and discover who she was. If I couldn't understand *her*, someone who spoke my language, I sure wasn't going to understand a new language from a nonhuman source. That's what Shechner heard—the "voice of Wisdom"—so I was told.

I just didn't perceive my own body, how it is the first container, how it leads us into the ecosystem, defining where we leave off and others begin—not other humans, of course, but other kinds of life, shaped by other natural histories. Though I didn't realize it, the opposite sex is a door to that, containing a part of us that is missing, and so entering Julie sexually felt like finding a lost part of my body again, and that part was its container, its wrappings, its frame. But a picture frame without a picture?—that was the way I felt it, with my own body hardly there. I couldn't feel it as a thing in itself, but just a bunch of buttons and levers—buttons connected to short-circuited feelings, and levers pushing things around, things like Julie's body, for instance.

Still, I possessed erotic tracking antennae connected to

those buttons and levers. I tracked the hidden softness in the curves of Julie's body and the corresponding soft curves in voice, movement, expression. This whole underlying erotic complexity resolves into a grown woman. And if I had been a mature man—which I wasn't—I would have seen our opposite as well: the opposing life to a human body, the life that supports it like a picture frame. There, in the ecosystem—and it is still a surprise to me that such a word flows from my fingers, since it was only in reading the Guide that the connection clicked—in the ecosystem the mature woman is hidden, and the complex curve of interrelationships we track with our minds yields in the end just her voice.

Julie had tried to explain this to me. Weirdness, I thought, crazy psychology—Shechner was no doubt a lunatic, I concluded, and the Scroll some elaborate hoax. Yes, I had examined it, was fascinated by it; but I saw it all too briefly, without a chance to verify anything. Yet what remains to me is Julie's voice and now I can connect it to that voice in the ecosystem she explained was what Archie was hearing, the voice from the ground, that hole in the ground Shechner found himself in. The voice holds me now the way her body once did, as I pumped to exhaustion, both of us pedalling faster, she moaning like a rabbi lost in prayer, I in silence. "You can't do it," she said to me after, "you're like a machine."

"If I couldn't do it," I whispered, unable to shout, "you wouldn't be drenched in sweat like you are."

"Like a man," is what I mean. "Like a human, not like some goddamn academic symposium of pistonology."

I thought she was mean, angry as a cheated woman, and that I was hardly the cause. Women I had known in New Haven sang my praises. And not even Julie knew that I couldn't feel anything, my body mute as wood. But now that I have Julie's words to work with—her transcription of Shechner, especially—I can feel what she must have craved from me. Intimacy is like the art of using words, creating a container for feelings. From Julie's trunk to this manuscript, we are creating together a holder of our feelings, a raft that can float out into the world. Not like a family, where everything's held within, but a ship to cross the waters.

Julie may hate me still, soothed by the slobbering honey of Svitz's adoration—but here we are, together on the page—and as if on a warm page, like a bottom sheet in stifling city summers before air-conditioning, the top sheet thrown off. Afterwards, she always wanted me to help fold the sheets back. I didn't know how or how to learn. I knew it wasn't about neatness for Julie, but what was it about? The intricate learning of ten years has taught me that folding was enfolding for Julie, a way of creating an envelope of holding for our story. I had to learn the "head" way, as Shechner would say, that sexual intimacy was at the origin of life by "hearing her voice, the nonhuman voice at the center of our originating ecosystem." Julie's transcription had Shechner explaining that "sexual tenderness returns us to origins, when we were most like plants: open to all elements of life, from soil to sunlight, transforming them into new forms that provide nourishment and support.

Trees were our mother, and from her we learned intimacy and the language of intimacy, which we interiorized with language. We made a model of our original ecosystem in language, and with words we could be intimate with all aspects of it, and even self-creation. Like the trees, we could build and shape the life around us." I shuddered when I read this again, because now it made sense; but ten years before, when Julie first quoted this to me, it seemed mad to be talking about trees as mothers, and human culture related to tree culture.

Even if Wisdom's voice came through the earth—in ten years it almost seems a commonplace, because hers could be the voice of life anywhere, on any planet or in any galaxy. It's the shaper of life, the erotic catalyst. In hearing it, we can restore ecosystems on Earth by learning to recreate them on other planets. Terraforming, it's called. Ten years ago, words went back to the Minoan culture, for me, and now I'm talking about Mars—if this change had happened to me overnight, instead of a decade, I surely would have been as traumatized as Shechner. And it won't be humans in protected outposts when we colonize Mars but entire ecosystems that we recreate there—parent them, actually. Now I can fathom why extinct species are precious: each one lost devalues the ecosystem.

Mars' own voice, her own ecosystems—even if they are fossilized—we'll have to hear those first. Shechner would know how to read those fossils now and hear Wisdom's voice again in them. But her voice isn't like a human mother's: it's a mirror instead of a caregiver. We don't see her when we look but rather ourselves in her eyes—or hear ourselves in her voice. Like looking into the eyes of the species we evolved from...

So that's what Betti Peleg was for Archie Shechner, a mirror in which he could see how he had evolved. Not that he knew it! He must have looked strange to himself, frightening. As Julie hints in her notes, Archie became something like a mirror for her too, a replacement for her mother. Transcribing Archie's words, her own feelings of being hidden and unknown were reflected back. How else could she have turned Shechner's halting voice into something I could read.

#

I was not the kind of person who would have thought these things, things that can label me an intellectual crank. I worked my whole life to earn respect as a conventional scholar. Until now I never thought of sharing this knowledge in public. Once I was convinced I was witness to an extraordinary event, I began to record my impressions on a private tape cassette. I hoped in this way to leave a record behind, *after I was dead*, safe from harm and humiliation. And I was aging rapidly, at least looking closer to death: in ten years I went from looking thirty to appearing fifty.

What follows is the last recording I made, only a few days ago. Even after I finished the year-long project of piecing together tape transcriptions, I couldn't imagine writing a book. I never saw the ancient Scroll that Archibald

Shechner found, the *Scroll of the History of Adam.* I have heard nothing more divine in my life than the voice of Louis Armstrong. I merely acquired the tape transcriptions of parts of the Scroll and those in which Shechner describes hearing the voice of the old epic's narrator, Wisdom, the female voice of God. Even Shechner trusted nothing but the direct human voice in this grave a matter. It's common enough for people with spiritual experience to refrain from writing it down. The oral message was sufficient for Jesus, as it was for Professor Freud in our time, who asked his patients to help heal themselves with their voices.

Humans still hunger for evidence of God. Printed pages of Bibles are rarely enough. What is wanted is a voice, a revelation—as unmistakeable as a mother's voice. Prophets in all religions listen for such voices, though we have never had tape-recorded confirmations from ancient history that voices were actually heard—not in the way we here have a respected psychologist's confirmation. Ten years ago, Dr. Betti Peleg confirmed Archibald Shechner's communications.

A Buried Voice

Archie's intense way of listening to women was pretty apparent to me. He focussed totally on me when I spoke, just the way he focussed on mother. "Fear of an abandoning mother," she described it. His own mother's death in childbirth meant that Archie would only have heard his real mother's voice while he was still in the womb (as doctors now say is true of the fetus in its final months). Newborn babies often recognize their mother's voice immediately, but for Archie it would remain as though it were a buried voice, a muffled voice he had captively listened to, from inside her stomach walls. A voice easily "displaced underground," according to my mother, to the earth he spent a lifetime digging in.

[Julie]

The portion here is from one of Julie's notebooks as I found it in the trunk and is typical of her adherence to her mother's professional standard of observation. Shechner's tapes are gone but Julie Peleg's transcriptions of them, and of her mother's sessions with the man she calls Archie, have been in my possession during this past year in which I've compiled them. I present them in a double form, the odd-numbered chapters representing how I came to grips with the reality of the revelation, including fragments of the voices in the Scroll I've been able to restore. (I have headed these with the titles Shechner listed in his notes).

The even-numbered chapters represent the *Guide to a New World,* in which Julie Peleg transcribed Archibald Shechner's accounts of the voice he was hearing while under treatment with Betti Peleg—the voice of Wisdom, the voice from under ground helping him to interpret the Scroll, and which Julie helped me to interpret as the "Seven Days of Creation."

A SAMPLE OF THE *GUIDE*:

Consider the tree. Its sexual flowering may depend on manipulation of animals to effect intimacy with another tree. What complex chemical intelligence lodges in a tree, stemming from complexity of sexual needs... Now consider human articulation of sexual intimacy. Long ago in the forest, turning face to face, arms and fingers grew sensitive in increasingly elaborate acts: tender acts of foreplay. From foreplay to forethought—and the human spirit evolves as creative reflection of its own mind. The mind entered into the sexual act, taken over by hands and limbs of the sensible body, and tongue and lips of a thinking face. Here sexual intimacy of male and female form a single tree, flower and fruit, branch, leaf and sap—all expressed in seductiveness of human intelligence.

[*Guide to a New World*]

CONSIDER WHERE I WAS JUST A YEAR AGO:

I wasn't ready to believe what was at the core of the archive in the trunk: trees are smarter than animals. The *Guide to a New World* begins by revealing the tree of thought and why plants are silent. Only a fool would think a tree smarter than an animal, I thought. But the *Guide* forced me to think of how a plant evolves. It responds to the challenge of the elements—earth, air, light and water—while an animal is responding to what it can eat. Both construct defenses, self-protection, strategies of masking. But the plant world fabricates its own food as well as the food animals require, manufacturing it out of the elements. In order to evolve, a plant's mind—call it a system if you prefer—is tuned to the primal elements, foremost. With the evolution of angiosperms (bearers of flowers) the plants and trees turn to animals (that includes insects) for partners, evolving new strategies for using them. Some animals evolve in concert with trees; but most, in their use of them.

Without trees, few birds and small mammals would have survived—like the mammals that developed into primates, *us*. Without the line developing from the tree-dwelling primates: no hominids, no humans. The earliest civilized cultures of the West held trees sacred, from individual plant to sacred grove—

So am I crazy like Shechner? Yes, yes—I still couldn't bring myself to break with conventional thought. For ten years I thought and rethought and then I looked back: those years of thought resembled nothing so much as a tree, I saw. When there's a problem to solve we are like an animal cornered. And like a species of animal evolving, with all the information we can muster—no, like a tree evolving, our intelligence free to consult the elements and all natural limits: we seek light, dig into the past for buried water, and we create nourishment for our minds, in pictures and narratives of the imagination. Our thoughts branch like trees; our inner lives resemble the prohibited tree of Knowledge.

Step back to consider the ancestors who came down from the trees, walked upright, made tools. Vegetarians, playful ones. A receding of forests in Africa, and Homo sapiens appear, expand to harvest the meat they find on drier savannahs. Our evolution, then, required us to project knowledge of the tree onto the plains: the wild game spread out before us like a new kind of fruit.

The problem is in the "we". Where do we draw the line? Where do *we* become the ones and the others remain backward, primitive, *uncivilized*? The red man—and even the Stone Age naked man—and Albert Einstein: the same? Cultures, like races, are genetically equal? Then how imagine the uncivilized as wild and sexually unrestrained (fantasized apemen at the heart of Africa)? Without them, how is all our progress measured? It was a mistake to say we evolved away from the apes—in fact, we remain Homo. Yet we've fooled ourselves with notions of *cultural* evolution, misled ourselves into horrible world wars and massacres on behalf of a fantasy of progress—

—All because we can't face the fact our prehistoric Homo faces turned to face our mates as we copulated. Look into another Homo's eyes: subtlety of thoughts began, images of ourselves were reflected, we grew self-conscious—over a million years of tender regard and misunderstanding.

Far older in time: male birds preen to the discriminating eye of female birds as male lizards have done even further back in time. Birds appeal to a female ear for complicated melody. Male and female flowers seduce the eyes and noses of many animals and the plant rewards its sophisticated sense of taste. But new to Homo sapiens is the sexual appeal to the eye followed by touch, the hand. Eye and hand coordinate, resulting from this sexual measure of beauty and thought—all based in our modern principles of sexual selection.

#

I can understand now, why Shechner dates the *Scroll of the History of Adam* to King Solomon's days, since it expresses the Solomonic expectation of a new millenium—after 1000 B.C.E. Biblical history stretches back in the previous millenium to Abraham's birth in Mesopotamia, to slavery in Egypt. In the new millenium, Solomon's court writers were looking toward a cultural evolution. After the earlier Greek Dark Age, it seemed enlightenment would lead the chosen ones to leave behind human slavery and reenter the Garden.

The words in *Guide to a New World* appear so closely tied to the Scroll that it must date from this very same time.

What happened to the new language of the Scroll? Schechner didn't believe it was suppressed by the priests of its day. It was archived, and then it was probably lost when the Israelite libraries were sacked by the invading Assyrians in the ninth century B.C.E.

How to evolve?

Some people follow the New Age, others stick to the world of entertainment. Some follow the literary trends, others become celebrity hounds. Some try new skills, some try new drinks, new drugs. A few go to school to really learn—a few drop out for the same reason. One thread is held in common: a desire to grow, to have a little more room, to attract friends. What could be more natural? A tree grows, spreads out, attracts all sorts of animals to its fruits, seeds and flowers.

All these growth movements free up some energy. Therapy or meditation, reading or scuba diving—some repressed material is freed up and your world seems slightly larger. Underneath everything, however, is a layer of desire that can never be touched. It is the species-wide desire to physically evolve. Our species has thought a million thoughts and changed the face of the planet but it has not evolved one iota in thousands of years. We are the same Homo sapiens all over the globe. On any day a new ant species may evolve, a new species of bacteria. But whatever ideas and vehicles we evolve, we've come no further from the monkeys than our forest ancestors did long ago. Except—except our deep desire to evolve grows restless.

It's been sitting in us so long now—longing to change and leave Homo sapiens behind—we are getting quite anxious. Our images of messiahs and milleniums contain that same anxiety. Our bottled-up energy to evolve is so great that no image can encompass it; now, in fact, we must open the bottle and evolve.

How to evolve? How do we do what nature does to us? We may study other species to learn how they evolve, though these sciences are in their infancy. One constant: we wish to evolve in our minds but this millennial desire can only be a wish, like life without a body. Deeper down, in the wish for an afterlife, we sense we can take our bodies with us too. *That* is where our desire touches a need to physically evolve which is natural in all living things. Science is far from the answer but a direction is clear: into the past. There in the past we confront the one evolutionary experience we're familiar with, *our own*; or there, in the more recent past, lies knowledge of the *Guide to a New World*, closer to the memory of evolving.

I have come face to face with that knowledge. The *Scroll of the History of Adam* uses evolutionary lore left out of the Bible's story of Adam and Eve. But the information in *Guide to a New World* is crucial. Does it matter where it came from? Some will believe Shechner was a channel for a voice; some will say obsession crystallized this knowledge from what he already knew. Others will point to statistics: over two-thirds of adults experience angels, says the media. Still others will say his doctor, Betti Peleg, helped push Shechner into madness. Betti herself concluded that the renowned archaeologist Archibald Shechner spent a lifetime digging in the ground to find his buried mother (who had died giving birth to him).

Does it matter if Wisdom really is a voice, as long as you hear her privately in your own head like a thinking process? It will matter when the truth will be known; for now, we don't know even how Shechner disappeared.

Making Sense of the Guide Today

A sample of Shechner's notes follows—was it meant to be part of the Guide, *or simply commentary? Wisdom's voice, or Shechner's musing? I've had to consider long and hard how a passage fit into one of the "Seven Days of Creation."*

Choosing to evolve will soon be possible. The genetics revolution will make it so. It's not about living longer or free of disease. That is thinking small. Instead, it's about thinking—*feeling*—as different creature. Choosing to evolve is saying goodbye to humans as we've known them. Can we do that before we know what we're letting go of? What we might become?

Reject our parents—our ancestral human parents—in order to evolve? Have we properly acknowledged or even know who they are, our Adam and Eve? Even Eden—mothering ecosystem they evolved in—is still mysterious. Was it rainforest, tropical, oasis-like? Chimpanzee seems to recognize us, like a lost pet dog with whom we lived. Would hominids left behind in archaic time know us if we found them again?

But no bringing back our extinct cousins. We're left to ponder how familiar these tropical plants are to us, this breadfruit, this starapple. Why do they taste like paradise—while a t-bone steak does not exactly?

Evolving Notes to the Reader

A body is subject to pain and death: isn't that reason enough to transcend it? Shechner could not let this rest.

Yes, the animal body and specifically sex is what we want to avoid. Yet most people seem to like sex, most people seem to like animals, so... why not face it? Here it seems a bit metaphysical but these basic concepts will be fleshed out. Shechner says the blinding truths of the Creator force us to divorce mind and body, and to remain skeptical of Wisdom's domain, sexual selection. The Creator wants reproduction—be fruitful, multiply!—not sex. Sex and all the refinements of seduction must reveal our basic drive to evolve, and when we do evolve we'll no longer fit the Creator's image but be shaped by Wisdom.

"What will we look like?" writes Shechner. "Wisdom says the playfulness of sex guides intelligence, so lovemaking will have more to reveal to us. Meanwhile, search for hidden suggestions. Larger, thinner hands perhaps. Expanded vocal organ, so we may converse in additional registers—and corresponding ears, to absorb more complex intelligence. Possibly no more complicated than that, so that how we look will remain recognizable, as Neandertals are to us.

"Yet we will not know 'us', not anymore than we can say we know chimps today. What will our ecosystem become? A genetic garden, it seems, that we will carry with us as extension of ourselves. Food will be grown there, struggles with microbes resolved there. Because of our more intimate communications, love for art will have a corresponding expansion: no doubt our gardens will have astonishing new meanings—look wild instead of cultivated."

I worried about not comprehending it all, but I learned to wait for what unfolded in each day of the *Guide to a New World.* We are bodily extensions of our original ecosystems—how so, is uncovered there. Clearly, the Guide is even now beyond the ability of a scientific mind to compose. We must assume that Archibald Shechner became a vehicle. Perhaps you will learn from my own journey how this could happen. I've become a composer of narratives against my will. I was a man who studied words but I could not write a sentence with an "I". I referred to myself as "your —", fill in the blank. Your teacher, your son, your colleague. Narrate a story such as this one—never. I could report, not write. Here follows a report of my journey to a future that disappeared from my grasp, leaving but tapes and memories. They have become fertile ground—words that I can finally feel are mine to shape.

All the words were there, but until the trunk arrived it was lonely ground. Colleagues and students could not feel my detachment; I was noted, in fact, for my restraint and so I took refuge in it, erasing the memory of my misadventure with the Scroll.

Postscript

When the trunk came and the porters took some time figuring the ways it would need to be tipped in order to squeeze into my office, I felt as though a new creature had entered my life, one that reconnected me to Julie. The offices of Yale professors are often cramped with bookcases, but how many have a big World War I steamer trunk sitting in the middle, so that you have to slide past to approach the desk? People associate trunks with romance and mystery, not with academic studies. It emboldened me. When someone asked, I said it was from Israel, as if that explained it. It usually stopped the questioning. For my average student who had never visited the Middle East, an aura of quaintness was to be expected, if not mysticism. For others—well, with this crouching presence beside me, I began to strut around a bit, albeit with mincing steps in the tight quarters.

"To grow, to evolve—" I answered, when a colleague asked me why I was risking my reputation again. "We have to get out in the field, stop hanging around the forts of academe."

"You're a philologist," he answered. "You're in the field right here, where people talk and think. I thought that debacle with the Scroll was behind you."

I studied my colleague's face. It was somewhat pinkish and glistening, like a fresh side of beef at the supermarket, with the cellophane tightly wrapped and tucked. "Does it bother you so much," I asked him, "that the origins of words might still be found in a wilderness instead of in civilization?"

"Yes. I'm upset that you're still chasing after lost scrolls."

I placated him, told him not to worry. But I realized again, keenly, that I was apart from them all now. To whom could I open my vulnerable side? Not a colleague, and not a woman.

I realized it could only be in a made thing, now. When the trunk arrived and I looked inside, I knew instantly it would open its contents to me and I would open my mind and heart to it. I would make it a love poem to Julie. And as that thought entered my memory it brought Julie back so vividly that I could feel the vibration of her voice in every word she transcribed. I was ready now to open myself, to release the memories that meant most to me.

As I read and began to see how first Archie and then Betti had listened to the voice of Wisdom, I knew at last what it was. My colleague had been right to be upset: it was to be found only in wilderness. The voice in the wilderness—voice of the ecosystem—could be heard only by unrepressing the deepest, most suppressed desire of all in Homo sapiens: the ultimate vulnerability and risk, the opening of oneself to the core, the natural desire to evolve.

Julie ran from it, as did I, but not before she had collected all the evidence. She had opened herself enough to understand what the source was, to believe in it; and now I would have to do the same. Somehow, out of all the complex voices in that trunk, we would make a container for Wisdom's voice, so that those who were vulnerable themselves would recognize it. It is a memory, after all, and there is no doubting a true memory.

Memory of what? The repressed memory of evolving, of the desire to evolve—repressed when?—the first, earliest repression, even before mother? I had to believe it was in the womb itself that it was repressed, before we come out, when we have already sensed our mother's presence and that we must grow to meet her. At this point, we are feeling the desire to evolve, to grow into a new form that can witness our mother. But once we are born, that memory in the womb is repressed. It has something to do with the way we evolved and were born, the length of our gestation and the years of our helplessness in early childhood, our dependence on others. A resentment of that dependence must have already been there when we were born and found others waiting in the world besides mother herself—any other, even the nurse, even daddy.

To retrieve that memory, to unrepress that desire to evolve—that memory is everything, because we can only love with remembering. I feel even a cat's love when it remembers my own caring for it. To unrepress the most submerged memory, evolving—that is the greatest love. It is the desire to explore of Eden again, our first and truest home, to find ourselves there, in a love free of all repressed memories—and from which all memories can flow freely.

I rejected Archibald Shechner at first, like everybody else investigating his story of finding the Scroll, even though I played along with Julie and her mother. When I lost them—and they had already lost Archie—I saw what a jerk I'd been. Archie was the first and original rejecter, hearing the voice of his Edenic mother and wanting to stop it. I was hardly different than my old mentor at Yale, Harriman Svitz, so full of his work and sailing on the power of his will that he imagined water where none could be found.

Neither was there water to sail on beneath *me*, nor did my knowledge provide wings to rise above Shechner. I was scared to look reality in the face. I had to learn that my body did not stop at the fingertips and hair but extended to the natural world and included everything I could put into words. Wisdom had explained how language interprets the intimacy born of hand and eye coordination. Sexual intimacy then stimulates memory, and when memories are "selected," imagination turns on a light.

First, we fear the dark and then learn nature is innocent. The great myths haven't caught up. They still describe a loss of innocence, but in our time we're losing *experience* not innocence. The natural world is an extension of ourselves, it's our own family body we're losing. At last, the ingredients for high tragedy have returned. Oh, the *animals* may be innocent all right, but if they are endangered it's because we've extended our knowledge to them. *We're* the ones that feel enfeebled by their loss, further cut off from ourselves, tragic in our isolation.

The thought of evolving is a beacon of light. None of the popular "genetic engineering" clichés apply. Evolving involves trust, feeling certain of our natural origins—even as we become lost in them. The Guide provides the answer: We don't need to reject the Creator but to open our ears to hear the voice of Wisdom as well. If you follow conventional belief in God, then Wisdom will be revealed by the Scroll for you. In traditional language, wisdom is the presence in Eden of His consort, hidden within the tree of Knowledge.

"At last I see how science can leap into a religion that leaves everything behind!" Archie recited this to me from one of his field notebooks, begun after recovering the Scroll. And while hearing the voice. Then came a soliloquy to explain his excitement. I reconstructed it to be consistent with other material I have transcribed.

The problem is, whether in exploration or in art, there are leaps of the imagination—yet after all, we are only where we started, grounded in civilization. That was how Archie saw it now, and how he explained it will never change by itself, that we will still expect our first space colonists to keep in touch—and not to leave us behind—because Earth is still the center of everything. Even the belief in an afterlife is tied to events on Earth. And while science pushes on toward objectivity, which takes you outside yourself, ultimate objectivity, says Archie, requires you to have left yourself completely. Mystics and scientists may find alot of common ground here, he teased, but they won't get the evolutionary joke.

Out of what woodwork does this drive for objectivity crawl?—that's how mother would put it. What's the most "objective" phenomenon we see in nature? Evolving, said Archie. Thinking is a sort of imitation of this process but it can never go as far as evolving does—to leave everything behind, when one species becomes entirely a new one. Cut off from intercourse with the old, so to say—social, sexual. Evolving is the final objectivity, a living thing looking back at the species it was and blanking on it. That's how we look at apes today, I realized, remembering the bored one in the Jungle Park. We are thinkers of another order, so it seems to us, and less dull. True, Archie would say, and a first-time Martian visitor to Earth might add by this standard that certain ants are the least dull of all.

Archie pointed to his eyes. Look: ants have evolved into hundreds of species while we resist evolving at all. At least humans have adapted toward the hidden part of nature, female Wisdom, I learned. Resistance is a male trait; the female one is intelligence, since in most species the female selects, the male performs. An encouraging female releases a human male from having to perform and he becomes less resisting, more open. To what? Well, ultimately, to evolving. When men let go of performing, they wise up. (I have to take this on faith, I was thinking, since at my tender age I probably know less about men than I do about evolution.)

Wisdom's plan is to encourage evolving—that was how Nosei interpreted what he was picking up of the Scroll—evolving away from the static image of himself the Creator left. Wisdom's male consort, our Creator, settled upon a sexless construct of himself. Nosei went on, a bit excited about just comprehending it: We have inherited an independent God with whom we can dominate nature, but we can't really grow if we don't rebel within, and then turn toward our ancient origins in the ecosystem. Wisdom saw to that—she wove herself into the creation from the first day, making life depend on light-conserving plants, trees. By the sixth day, the conditions were settled: the Creator's place was secure in the tree of Life, and Wisdom stood beside him in the tree of Knowledge. Result: the Creator demands performance—awe, obedience. Wisdom encourages growth and intelligence.

So performing the Creator's will, a man thereby avoids fear of having to perform for a woman—I put it something like that. Nosei got very contemplative: "People look back at Christianity and Islam, wondering how monotheism spread so quickly. It's as plain as the demands to perform that men read into the blinding sexuality of women. Men want to cover the women with whom they live, all the religions have it, covering their own motives with images of transcendence."

It was Archie who first had it revealed to him how Wisdom is the force for uncovering the body and preparing for evolution. Nosei tried to make sense of it for me as if it was a new myth. Wisdom had hidden the Garden of Eden in front of us, not behind, and we should find it there waiting for us in the next evolution.

[Julie]

Julie's Commentary:

"Svitz, do you ever fear we may be duller than we think?"

"Who is 'we,' my dear? Stop, don't tell me—you must mean 'we' the species. I thought analysis would at least give you a sense of humor, Julie, about that trunk of yours. Instead, you're back to it with all the deadly seriousness of a librarian. Do you really want me to elaborate on dullness?"

"Yes, I do. I don't know why I do. I've latched on to you as

some figure to comfort me, to reassure me that there's always a reason to go back, to not give up on someone. I guess I keep this going between us as a way of staying on with the dead ones. You don't recognize death, Svitz, or nature. You couldn't even recognize the faces of the analysts you tried out. You were looking at yourself. And I don't mean all that mirror-image stuff you've skimmed out of Freud. You made the analyst you saw into your image—a fellow critic and intellectual that you could always get the better of. It was a squeezed image—you squeezed until you had no use for them. God! Do you realize how dead that is? You see, I'm not trying out my doctor. He's real to me. I can even feel a terror at his realness. I can barely make room for him inside my head without feeling I've betrayed someone else. That's death, Svitz. I'm in the middle of life versus death."

Svitz winced. "From questions of dullness to 'life versus death.' Yes, my fears of dullness in our 'species' are greatly diminished as long as you are with us." Proud of his wit, Svitz had to underline, punctuate and explicate it. "You're the most intriguing neurotic I've ever met—better than even me. I never know what you're going to ask me next. You have an exciting mind, Julie, but you spend so much energy trying to prop up the boring ones, never mind the dead ones. Here you are once again with that trunk, closeting yourself with it. I must admit you have the most unusual closets of anyone I know, but haven't you and that analyst of yours figured out that your task is not to put your panic in the closet but to get you out of the closet?"

"It's one thing to know that you fear freedom, Svitz, and another to know what would be so dangerous about it."

"Well, that's simple enough. You'd have to leave the dull ones

behind, and boring things like this Archie Shechner business." Svitz knew he was treading on sacred ground.

"And do what? Become a great poet or muse? You mistake what drives my inner conflicts over the transcription. It isn't disdain, or even disbelief. I just finished writing up something that I heard from Archie, and that Nosei and I discussed. I'm struck by how Archie redefined the meaning of dullness, to take us out of our human skins. I quiver remembering it because I feel tears in the back of my eyes for him—how very hard it must have been to be thrust back into Eden, to become the voice for Eden and for a desire that re-links us with other forms of life we consider duller than ourselves. We are the dull ones, Svitz, and your great poets remind us of this, if only instinctively."

At this point, he reached across the lamp table for the notebook I had been working in. Svitz read the quoted fragment and Archie's soliloquy as I had remembered it, and as interpreted above by Nosei. I expected distaste to fill his features, but instead he began to laugh with glee. "Oh, I love it! Yes, it's grand, truly grand. This would make a great book. A scientist finding his godhead, usurping the limits imposed on human imagination by the God of Moses. Neutral science becoming strong science. A hunter of artifacts, transformed by the desire to make something entirely new. Our true salvation."

"You just don't get it, Svitz, or you don't want to. The desire to evolve is not another kind of desire to create more culture for you to expound. It means changing the body, letting go of what we know for what we don't. It means not just thinking about the ecosystem, but being there—in it, with it. And if we can't or won't, Archie is saying that we will feel a profound

deprivation. Making a great book or being a strong whatever—it won't compensate."

"What it's about is what it's always about, my dear—more life, and more life. That's what Archie wanted. That's what I or anyone else wants. Our metaphors are just different."

I remember that it was hard not to agree with him. Svitz used the terms of thinking that I had grown up with in mother's circle, where higher and higher levels of critique almost had an aphrodisiac quality. He made me feel intoxicated with our ability to read metaphors and be the critics-at-large of our culture. But when I took up the transcription again to finish it, I realized that in every day of the "Seven Days" in the Guide I was learning of a tactility made dull by such versions of "more life." What was really being touched, not just waved at with recycled terms? What suddenly felt touchable? I could form these questions about the contents of the trunk and the "Seven Days" because they were the same questions I was beginning to have about the room I shared with my doctor. Every day of my sessions, I felt there another just-as-deep tactility that made what had happened in Israel all seem hard to hold. Or to let go of. I would soon close and store the trunk, but the room with my doctor I would keep open for several more years.

But I nearly lost the trunk. A couple of years ago I decided to get my own place to live. I would stop living with Svitz. During these years in New York, he symbolized what I'd been determined never to leave altogether—magic, the "me" that was supposed to be magic.

We were not lovers. I had created this weird platonic

relationship with him that he indulged because of its dramatic, stage-like power. A magical child is like a guardian angel—though not the kind that has become popular in the media of late. Angels used to be more dubious of character and equivocal in emotional temper. They were not so much up in the sky as things on the edges of experience—in the margins of people's hopes and fears. There was an edge to angels; I used Svitz to play along this edge, to bear hard against the sharp edges. I could go straight to the edge with Svitz without having to acknowledge the customary mores of intimacy—guilt and reparation, to be technical. I could be the terrible child within the persona of the magical. And besides, I had the comfort of knowing that no one could beat Svitz at being terrible.

But I nearly lost the trunk by playing at this fantasy too long. Svitz was a dangerous person. I was too, but not like him. I think he played along to see just how dangerous I could be. Or maybe my dangerousness became associated with some redemptive part of himself he still believed existed. When I called a halt, I should have known that he would try to match my terrible act with one of his own. I was packing up and moving out—an act that made him seem no longer relevant. This was a truly terrible act for someone like Svitz, and the play shifted into real life.

And it was true. Svitz had become irrelevant to me. I had come to realize that I was playing with the devil and using him to relieve myself of destructive emotions. I could still be the good one, the magical child, as long as I had Svitz around. I didn't have to face my own aggression and hate.

And I could continue the fantasy that I never left anyone, that no one was leavable. But there are always leavings. People are leavable, if only for the few minutes you go to the bathroom or the longer minutes when you yell and want to shut them up. Every love has some degree of leaving and betrayal, even if it's disappointment. I knew I had to move on to real life.

So Svitz tried to rob me of the trunk and rob me of my analysis by trying to destroy the reputation of my doctor. These—trunk and therapy—were my sources of relevance. When I went to the basement of Svitz's apartment building to retrieve things in storage, the trunk was missing. Later that day, there was a call from my doctor, saying that he had been accused of impropriety with me and could not find out the source. I told him that I had to suspect Svitz, that the trunk was missing and Svitz wasn't returning my phone calls to his house in New Haven.

I knew pleading or rational discourse would get me nowhere with Svitz. It would have to be blackmail or breaking and entering with some petty theft mixed in. I chose the latter. I broke into his New Haven house and found the trunk. I dragged it to the cab—the driver nearly left me flat. I told him Svitz was my father and had stolen some manuscripts from me because he didn't want me to become a writer. It was the only thing I could come up with, but it worked well enough along with the advance tip. The problem with my doctor was harder. But before I left Svitz's house that night, I took his current telephone bill, then my doctor and I went through the list of numbers

Svitz made calls to during the prior month. Luckily, my doctor recognized the home telephone number of one of the senior members of the institute—an enemy of his. We had to go through an interview process, but the circumstantial evidence that this man had spoken to Svitz, possibly about me, was enough to discredit him with other members of the board.

The whole experience made me extremely fearful over the safety of the trunk. I had fantasies of Svitz breaking into my new apartment and stealing it, or worse. I felt there was no safe place for it anymore, except perhaps with Nosei. A more powerful fantasy took over, one in which Nosei would become the guardian of the trunk. It gave me a feeling of us being parents together—a safe remove from our catastrophe as lovers.

I had always known how to find him. Actually, he was a professor at the same university as Svitz. They hadn't spoken since Israel. It was a big campus and Svitz spent a lot of time in Manhattan. I went there one evening. I rented a car and put the trunk in the back seat. I convinced a custodian to help me take it up to Nosei's floor and then to put it in his office. That was the last I saw of it.

I did it that way so it couldn't be traced—no postmark, no paperwork from a delivery service. At the last minute, I decided to enclose the outlined drawing I had made of his body. That and the fact that it contained my transcription probably made it clear that the trunk had come from me.

And that's how I found out: Nosei still wants to make love poems. He made the trunk into something I never could. As I read him, and read myself, I wonder if we've been making love through the trunk until we can make love to each other. But what kind of love would it be? Maybe that's what we're trying to discover. Here I am writing nearly ten years later, linking it to what I wrote down in Israel as it was happening. I'm reading myself the way I was then, the way I am in Nosei's mind—feeling that I can finally read a love poem from Nosei.

Love poems can be a way of holding hard things. Failure is a hard thing. Nosei and I failed at creating an intimacy. The Scroll is also a hard thing—and this evolving manuscript is a way of holding its secrets. How do you live with secrets and mistakes and not die from them the way mother and Archie did? I've learned that panic is a way of keeping a secret and at the same time trying to make it known. If analysis is a way of holding and telling secrets, which I believe it is, so is *The Eden Revelation*.

Bodily Myth

To think of paradise is like thinking of evolving: in past, most imagined these as mental processes, as if paradise a state of mind, or as if a brain could evolve without a body. Others have described evolving as a spiritual process: the body disappears and we have evolved into"pure spirit." Same results. It's clear enough in both instances that the wish to leave the body is strong.

The greater reality is in drive to hear Wisdom's voice again. The future is restoration, re-finding devout awe the first human explorers felt as they walked and paddled into new ecosystems undreamt of, a kind of living dream. From these huge encounters around the globe in the prehistoric age of exploration, a thirst for Wisdom's voice grew. With it was born imagination to develop languages. In languages came the mind-expanding word pictures and stories—myths—of which we have only poor imitations today. Every person knows longing for them in their lives. It's like days in which we postponed the inevitable, days tense with guilt in which our senses were keener. We knew the feeling of a circumscribed but free life, as our newly-evolved, newly-exploring ancestors did. In the end, those are the days to treasure.

As our memory guards them, we must restore those days in our lives. Fully restored, we can approach the physical, Eden-like boundary of evolution—once again.

[Shechner]

Nota Bene

This was all beyond me—I was a scholar of words, not concepts—but I was caught up in a fever. I spent ten years trying to find myself again, avoiding the limelight. I was once comfortable with a celebrity like Harriman Svitz because his hunger for attention (he would have died *to hear a voice as Shechner did) was in another world from mine. If I wanted to be somebody in the world, why would I become a philologist? I was excited by the* Scroll, *not by fame. And I certainly had no intentions of writing about it. What you find here is a book that wrote itself, since Shechner was no writer either. Nor were Betti or Julie—we were all forced to speak by baffling circumstances. Fortunately, we live in an age of voice transcription. I, for one, and I'm sure I speak for the others as well, would not have wanted to dictate these happenings to another person who could testify to my being mad!*

Everett Nosei

MEMORANDUM FROM SETH GREENE, LITERARY AGENT:

As Nosei says, the wish to leave the body behind is so strong that a book about evolving mentally and growing invisible, *The Celestine Prophecy*, became an international bestseller. Its story is ingenious (coincidences in *your* life become connected to those in the novel) and the spirit of the book is open. Yet there is a puritanical aversion to sex and the body—why? Ari Buber told me that he thought there was a connection between this desire to leave the body and the parallel aversion to science, especially evolutionary biology. Since evolution is based on sexual reproduction, better to evolve mentally and avoid it altogether!

In plain language, Ari had said to me, "How come those people don't like to fuck?"

"They do, I'm sure," I answered, "but they don't like to *think* about it. They can have some smelly, complicated sex and then pretend it was all a wholesome act to immediately forget, like the last sunset. They are like babes at the breast—yum, yum, pleasure—who never learn how to see the rest of the mother's life. Worse yet, these grown men and women who trancend the erotic with spiritual stuff don't see themselves as they really are. We've all had biting fantasies—fantasies that our boundless appetite would injure the mother. But what do *they* do with them? Their answer is to transcend the body altogether, as in *Celestine*. Think about it, analyze it—no thanks."

This really got Ari going. I knew he thought that *Celestine* was trash, but I had never realized how much he had actually thought about it before. The health club was suddenly the perfect setting to hear Ari's intellectual side come spilling out. He never showed these thoughts to business partners, but it wasn't the first time I heard him talk this way at the health club. Maybe all the sweat and grime got to him. Maybe he felt like he could let his philosophy all hang out.

"Man, you are so right. Like, in *The Tenth Insight*, you know, that bestselling sequel to *Celestine*, no one even has a goddamn mother and father! And no one ever screws in daylight. Instead, all these immature dreams are acted out—anything to evade the complications of earth and toss the joy in complexity into the closet. Their idea of bliss is a fast fuck—if it took any longer, they might start having strange thoughts, like who's the man and who's the woman here? Instead, they exult in intuition and quick fix wish fulfillment. But when you slow sex down, you begin to see all the different people you are and your partner is, how complex it is, and down to earth."

I might have agreed with Ari, except that I kind of liked a fast fuck myself, at least some of the time. Would Ari look down on me? In fact, I put it to him: "Hey, we've eyed alot of femmes together you would probably have gone straight into a closet with and come out spent in two minutes—never even learning her first name. So what's that got to do with *The Eden Revelation*?"

His answer inspired new respect. "First of all, sex, or for that matter any natural act, doesn't need to be transcended. What it needs is to be embraced in all its complicated diversity. If we are going to evolve, it won't be in our heads alone but in the freedom we give to our genes—of whom we've become conscious—and of whom I know to, thanks to that emerging sciences series I edited. Our genes want to get out there and explore a new niche for themselves in the natural world. Only *they* can't do it themselves: we are their explorers, their trojan horses. And where is that niche—the newest frontier? According to the *Guide to a New World*, it is in the millions of as yet undiscovered ecosystems on Earth, not to mention other planets. *The Eden Revelation* is the first book that gets down to the dirt, right down to that hole in the ground that Archie Shechner hears through."

"*Millions* of ecosystems?" I meekly asked. "Sounds like sperm to me." I had trouble with that concept of "millions" when I first heard it. We're used to thinking a natural ecosystem is a big, endangered, rare place. But within each system are many smaller ones: there's even one inside my snotty left nostril. Scientists still don't even have names for all the micro-organisms in there. One good hole deserves another—but fortunately, Wisdom's voice only comes through the one Shechner made.

So if this book seems less timid than *The Celestine Prophecy*, and more intellectually, sexually responsible, it is because it resonates with what our best scientists are able to imagine and what our best instincts tell us about desire. Individually, we won't live forever. Why should we want to? But sexual desire challenges us to let go and clear a path for evolving. And the message is like no other. Let it, this book says. "Let the fucking body evolve," as Ari would say. Let go of the need to resist it with spiritual disciplines, with transcendent wishes, whatever.

Last week I heard this rabbi at a funeral quote Isaiah: "all flesh is grass." It woke me up, this comparison of human life with the lowly grass. I remembered reading in the Times—after the conversation with Ari about ecosystems—that grasslife is in many ways advanced from our own. Trees and grass are the providers of life. They set the table for animal forms like ourselves to come into existence and be nourished—and they don't need us to survive, but we need them. What a trip, to evolve toward this knowledge—or Wisdom, as Archibald Shechner called her. What would it be like to approach this wisdom in the grass?

Chapter 1

Chapter 1

While I pieced together the transcriptions from the trunk, I had to include my own recordings, the witness of Everett Nosei. I hardly knew I was speaking then, and I had never seen these notes I made into a Sony pocket recorder in 1984 transcribed on paper; I barely remembered them. Julie put them down when I left, after she transcribed Shechner. As I worked in the park I also recorded new impressions in the same old Sony, and then typed them up myself, bringing them back to the park with me to add to the manuscript. My notes grew as I lost myself in the work, appended to nameless surroundings.

I began with these reflective scenes, and added them in as well where the story called for context. Ultimately I saw that all the voices of the story accumulated in similar scenes—I lost track of who was speaking. So the story begins to resemble the Guide, which I'm assembling in its original order for the first time.

I see now it is fear of shame, almost an expectation of being shamed that formed me. And in a form greater than anyone could foretell: having a story to tell that might be laughed off, as Jonah the prophet in Nineveh! Feeling ashamed—that's it. It's feeling anything deeply that scares me. So I do my best to use the words of those who left their voices on tape.

When I looked into The Origin of Species, *Darwin's denial of strong feelings for the Creator calmed me. "There is grandeur in this view of life, with its several powers, having been originally breathed by the Creator into a few forms or into one." But by the "few forms" Darwin meant worms and maggots. Instead of breathing life into the nostrils of Adam created in His image—worms and maggots? Yet these initial life forms are the domain of Wisdom, as the Scroll reveals, long before Darwin.*

A Voice from the Past

When I first heard about the discovery of the lost *Scroll of the History of Adam*, in 1984, man, I was in a happy trance. I had put in long years of study and they had yielded up a few grudging, agreeable moments—nothing momentous. Now this document, sent back like an ancient letter from the dust of the earth, promised to sweep drudgery away. I'd sit back and watch the pompous studies of Western Civilization collapse before my eyes, shown up by a woman's voice. And not only would I get paid for my professional commentary, I'd acquire a new social life and meet new women. Most important, all this excitement was about a book, a scroll, and I never had to worry about feelings getting out of control when I was reading.

Older than the Bible, the *Scroll of the History of Adam* was said to be found intact. Sad to say, nonetheless: Like many romances, this one appeared to be over—or lost—just as it was getting started. For the next eight years I labored in solitude, once again, trying to restore some fragments of another scroll from the same archaic time, the *Book of Paradise*. But these were just barely legible bits of sentences. Consider the difference if instead of a few words a whole scroll existed—and unaltered, as rumor first had it. There'd be no need to imagine what is missing. It would be like finding not a mummy but a perfectly preserved man from early Egypt who could be revived and then tell us what life was like back then. Think of the questions answered, the knowledge face to face.

Anyway, the earthshaking announcement of the *Scroll of the History of Adam* lasted only a few weeks, but that was time enough to pull up roots and join the deciphering team. Then, before I even saw it, came news that the Scroll was a hoax. Cruel coincidence, since I'd published a philological study about one of the original authors of the Bible, "J", and a storm raged around the book for awhile. Yes, this author existed, the scholars grudgingly admitted, and her ancient bona fides were established over a hundred years ago—but many reviewers nonetheless called my book a hoax. Resentment hides behind such reviews and now I was wondering if it hadn't caused the new Scroll to be declared a hoax as well. Vexed to the bottoms of their souls at having to share the spotlight with a full-throated voice from the past—who knows what scholars wouldn't say? The clergy might not be cheerful about it either.

So I took the fraud claims about the newfound Scroll personally. Instead of leaving the country like most did after the hoax announcement, I stayed, hoping to meet Julie Peleg, the Scroll's editor. She was already damned in the press when it was discovered she had no credentials. Then it was revealed that the archeologist she relied on went mad and then disappeared. There would be more: the catastrophic information that Julie's mother, the renowned psychotherapist Betti Peleg, had treated the unfortunate archeologist and had herself apparently committed suicide by driving her small car into the newly restored Hula swamp, drowning as it submerged in five feet of water, a sinkhole.

[Nosei, '94]

Myself

How little anyone really knows about someone. About a someone like me. I am little known but all claim to know me. Even I claim to know me. But how little is really known. Do they realize it's the unknown that they really like, that really snares them, though all seems to be about knowing. So, the way I'm attached to people is about what's known of me, what can be relied upon. But the unknown is what's really attractive—that is, until it becomes known, until it challenges what others want or contradicts their vision of me. Who were the ones with a power of vision over me? My visionary ones were mother and Archie. Nosei.

The transcribing, the written impress—not enough to hold their place. Or mine. Derision of the press was nothing next to this. They left me frozen in time—mother and Archie. They left me frozen with the known and unknown of me, of myself, just as if they were inside of me, frozen. Evolving? Ha—what about just living an everyday day? Is there such a thing? There seemed to be when I was the way I used to be, the way I imagine I used to be before the Scroll.

Everything was life and death with mother and Archie. Now

I'm left with a fantasy of their reality. An inheritance. And if I don't want it? But what if I can't live without it? The fantasy is more real than reality for the child. I carry it all carefully inside, just as a child would—preserved, transcribed, saved forever.

Did they know? Did they know why I stayed, why I did it? They thought it was because I also had the vision. And I did seem to have it. I knew it so very, very well—sometimes better than they did. And I felt and knew the importance of their work. But "felt" became the word to know.

What the press said mattered little to me. Their credentials were of a different world. Yet, I know I would seize them if mother and Archie were here. I would hold them as if they mattered. I would have done it, gone through it for mother and Archie. But without them, no one to blame or do for. Not that I could have really blamed them. Who could blame someone in a life and death struggle? That's what was so great about Svitz. He let me blame him all I want. And I could count on his blame. He was good at blaming me, too, and for the first time I could justify the bad feelings—the anger and resentment—inside. Mother never blamed me for anything and left me no target for my anger with her.

How I longed for someone to know me, to hold my place, as I held it for mother and Archie—someone who would remain standing after the unknown became known. Dare I? How do I try? I am Julie. That is where I begin.

These are words from one of my notebooks, written as I was beginning to go through Nosei's manuscript several months ago. I felt thrown back to that time of the Scroll in

Israel and the first years of sessions, when panic attacks still had a firm grip on me. I wrote in the notebook instead of in the computer file that I would send to Seth Greene because I began to fear that the gains I had made with my doctor could all collapse. I feared that I had made a mistake in taking the manuscript. I even had the old feelings of physical collapse when I first read the above portion of Nosei's work. Did my mother really commit suicide? Could she really do that? These expressions of disbelief jarred me. I thought I had come to terms with her death. But there I was reading Nosei's account of her demise as if it had just flashed across the television screen as a weather alert or something. How could she have done it? How could I even think that I was at the end of my analysis?

You see, I had already decided to begin what would be for me a very difficult task of finding an ending with my doctor. And then the manuscript business began. As I began to work on it, my fantasies about not having sessions—not having the room with my doctor—seemed to overwhelm the defenses of my new skin—my new analytical skin. Panic took another form: a man—the doctor in our room—became the only thing standing between me and a frozen existence. I could feel once again the frozen feeling that came after the deaths of mother and Archie. But scarier still: the feeling was there before, even before they went away, died.

I'm still not sure how one ends things; I'm only at the beginning of the ending. Over this past year I couldn't imagine not being in that room again—to not have that quality of contact with *him*. Why don't I name him, like Shechner or Svitz? I just can't. I have to keep something for myself. Keeping his name right now helps me feel that I can hold his place in my mind. It seems so loseable to me lately. When I'm working, I suddenly look up in quiet alarm to realize I haven't been thinking of him. It's like I'm afraid he could be totally gone inside. I have liked being in that room, underground in a way, unready to come out of the ground—like the Scroll before Archie found it. Being there was like saying "I" and "me" for the first time—I found my voice there. After losing my mother, after Archie, if I was going to have a new voice, then no other voice was impossible, especially not the voice of Wisdom.

[Julie, '95]

Disregard

What a great work of art the Scroll is, source of the Eden stories in the Bible. The controversy has killed interest in it—for awhile. Although the document is gone, much of it was transcribed by Betti Peleg and her daughter Julie. Archibald Shechner's notes are also preserved in the trunk Julie shipped. The Pelegs were going to leave the country with it ten years ago; the travel brochures of Switzerland were still there. They might have found a Swiss agent to help edit and sell the book. Instead, the pioneering work appeared to be gone in moments, as Betti's car sank in the same swamp the first Israeli pioneers had drained long ago.

At the time they were draining it, though, these early

settlers wiped out the wealth of natural diversity in that primal wetlands. Rare wading birds to rarer plants were gone. Now, these scientifically restored marshes had called the newest pioneer, Dr. Betti Peleg, to her fate. I do believe she was called there. Betti, in her notes, refers to the voice of Wisdom emanating from what she designated "an Eden."

Julie must have been devastated. Panicked. No one in Israel had seen her since her mother's funeral—not really a burial since no body was found. The abrupt ceremony came just a week after the calamity, yet that was enough time for Julie to have sealed the trunk and shipped it out of the country.

The Pelegs had kept their work secret. After the hoax story cooled in 1984 and the Scroll team disbanded, they went to work. I made the usual bargain with ambition, mixing business with personal life, and I fell in love with Julie. Soon we were devoting ourselves to arguments over misplaced things. I argued, that is, and she smiled sweetly in ignorance. Like two talmudists, I said the glasses had been there on the table and she said no, they hadn't. I became so impatient with Julie's distractions—clothes, makeup, dinner plates, manuscripts, on the floor and on every surface—I would pick up something and follow her around with it, repeating "And what's this?"

Her energy was boundless; she worked night and day. I slept nine, ten, twelve hours and remained haggard. Our last argument left me so wounded, so bewildered, I returned to New York. The wounds of arguments were about the only feelings I could stand, they were related to thought—but I had no idea what we were arguing about. At least what I'd learned about *The Eden Revelation* would better *my* life, if not anyone else's. Slowly, it has.

I still hold the title of Associate Professor of Philology but my heart isn't in the university. The new species focuses my desire. There aren't any specimens yet, no fossils of course. There's a map, so to speak, to the Scroll. We have Archibald Shechner's tapes of the voice mapping this unfamiliar terrain. There's his interpretation of the unfamiliar cuneiform, transcribed by Julie and her mother. Betti Peleg called this work *The Eden Revelation.* Once you've heard it, your thinking life is changed, until thought and feeling seem the same.

I've taken a year's leave to put the pieces that tell the story in place. Those who saw the original Scroll ten years ago—including Julie, Betti, and Shechner—tended to become lightheaded and careless. You saw yourself as if for the last time and there was no fear. When I realized what was happening to each of us, I'd already returned to New York. I began to rethink my life. I wanted to live to see the change in myself—I mean, to hear it.

[Nosei, '94]

1995

Living with Nosei during those months was like living in a commune—the visionary commune of mother, Archie, Nosei and the voice of Wisdom. It was so easy to do, though. I seemed to have limitless energy and room for everything. Adding Nosei was so familiar, requiring little effort at first. It was like another project in a series of projects begun with mother, the biggest so far being Archie and the transcription.

Of course, Nosei wasn't mother. Sometimes he was. Other times he was my secret ally. He was complex. But I wasn't ready for complexity—the ambivalences of an intimate relationship. I couldn't take it in. It became a strain. I became distracted, which disturbed my sense of myself. And then in rebellion, I became more distracted, more of a mess.

I wanted him to step in, pick up the slack. I know now I wished to be taken care of—I wanted someone else to keep up with things, to watch over them.

As the apartment piled up, I emptied out. I couldn't find my place—an at-homeness. It enraged Nosei as I more and more failed to keep up with the physical contents of our lives, and then denied or ignored it. Just a question from him about the whereabouts of his glasses would make me feel physically weak. I found myself trying to turn it off—that homing device inside my head that knew where everything and everyone was. You see, I knew exactly where everything was, even as it got more and more piled up. I wanted to turn the device off but I couldn't. I wanted Nosei to help me turn it off but instead he seemed to need it turned up even higher.

I didn't know how to tell all this to Nosei. I didn't know it was happening. All I felt was that something was beginning to collapse inside, and all my effort became increasingly devoted to staving off the collapse or the feeling or fear of it. And when mother died—well, Nosei thought I panicked. And I did, but not right away. At first I felt better than I had in years. In control. Free. I went to Switzerland. I was in charge now. I would finish the project, and I would do it in my own way, in my own time. It was exciting being in Switzerland by myself. It was serene, the opposite of Israel. I could get lost in it. Then one day I ran across some reference in mother's notes to the restoration work of ecosystems in the United States.

There were names written down, plus the name of a scientist in the state of Texas, with the name of a university next to it. I knew I would have to go—sooner or later. I thought we had relatives there, too. But I left without telling anyone I was coming. I told myself I would call once I got there. But I never did. I stopped first in South Florida—to see the site of an actual restoration, something called the Everglades. Within a few days of arriving, it began to happen—what Nosei called panic. But first came a feeling of desolation. Seeing the palms and dwarf cypresses, and the Orthodox Jews walking the boardwalks in Miami Beach, reminded me of home. I began to think of mother. The feeling of something not being right inside began to seep in. It was a feeling I had known once before. And then I got sick.

Alone, I got sick. Fever and weakness. And after it was over, just a virus perhaps, it didn't really feel over. Colors seemed too real; leaves seemed too green. And there was the heat. I soon left. I left to meet the name circled in the notes—the scientist in Texas.

I had my first panic attack in Texas. I joined this scientist at his research site in a preserve called the Big Thicket. It was hot. I hadn't eaten well that day. I pushed myself forward along the trail, afraid to stop. I felt everything at once—hot and cold, and then a steel-edged thought that something could happen to me and it could happen before anyone could help me.

The mind has to define "the somethings" that happen and mine latched onto heat again: heat stroke, perhaps. Just the thought of something going wrong made my body feel weak, trembling, in trauma. It took several hours for me to feel human again, out of this danger I couldn't really define. Back at the hotel I sat in the pool, believing that what I needed was to cool off. I drank Gatorade, as if I needed to restore some disturbance in my electrolytes. I took a shower and became chilled—afraid to close the door of the shower. I felt like I was in shock, like my brain and body cells had roamed from their original positions. You wouldn't be able to see it on an x-ray, I thought, but they had moved ever so slightly to another place. Things still worked but reality had shifted.

My new reality was physical safety. In the days that followed, I found myself spending more and more time on taking care of myself and guaging the degrees of safety of every situation, especially the ones that reminded me of what I thought were the causes of the Big Thicket incident—heat, low blood sugar, physical exertion.

I told the rangers in Big Thicket that maybe I should go to the emergency room. But they said I was fine—and I did seem fine. I was walking, talking, and thinking fine. I looked fine. And anyway, I was afraid to go to an emergency room. Just the idea made me feel like it could start again.

I was in the middle of a big place, in a big state, and I felt like space was rapidly shrinking. I lasted two more weeks there. I don't even remember the plane ride out of Houston to New York. I tracked Svitz down and went directly to his Manhattan apartment. I'm not sure why I called him. It was kind of like hurting yourself in some stupid way and not wanting anyone to find out about it. But I didn't care if Svitz knew.

I remember when I was eleven I persuaded mother to let me go to the neighborhood park alone. I met a cute blond-haired boy there. I skinned my chin badly chasing him on the monkey bars. He ran away from me and I walked off with my chin bleeding. I didn't go home, but to a neighbor's house that was even further away. It seemed so logical at the time—that I should go there to call mother, so she wouldn't have to see the blood before knowing what had happened. I had already learned something by that age—put a band-aid on first before showing yourself. You could say that this time I went to Svitz's for a band-aid.

[Julie]

A Queen

In the concrete beehive of New York there are little patches of space that exist only because a building has been torn down and there's a court battle over real estate. In one of these sites a few discarded picnic tables, placed by the Parks authority, sit tethered by chains. Nobody uses the tables that I've ever seen. Homeless people, drug addicts, criminals—they prefer the amenities of the "real" parks, or even the permanent streets, to this unsettled space. You can't call this a park; no attempt has been made to introduce grass or even just dirt. The ground is hard and littered, as if the contents of upended trash cans had been tamped down by a hard winter. Some urban species of plants spill out here and there, as if they had meant to stay underground but couldn't contain themselves. It was spring but it could be any season, if you ignored the fashions. Sitting here, I was as nondescript as a person at a bus stop. Some kind of waiting place, that's what my workspace appeared to be.

I spread out the tape transcripts on a picnic tabletop like a jigsaw puzzle, looking for a common thread. It was a story of unrequited love: mine for Julie was a short version of Betti's for Archie. Julie and Archie were so in love with themselves they couldn't really be bothered by anybody; only the truth mattered to them. "Know Thyself," if it had been emblazoned on the back of their heads, would have remained unknown to them. They lived in hope of breaking through to a vision of themselves, to see themselves in a mind's mirror they hadn't yet found. The normal web of understanding in which most of us live meant little to them. They had about as much self-consciousness as the homeless I encountered on the streets when I returned to New York City in 1984. Some of these, when I initially gazed at them, suggested former university colleagues dressing in a homeless look in order to write a study on the subject—that's how unconscious of their disheveled state they appeared. They might have taken a lesson from Julie Peleg and Archibald Shechner.

When those two realized how fiercely loved they were, Archie by Betti, Julie by myself, they became even more fearless in their disregard of society. I had to tell Julie that I heard some say she was insane. Being a psychologist's daughter, she certainly conceived of insanity as the enemy—as would the scientist in Archie. Yet Betti shielded them both. She told Julie she'd eventually be honored for her work in transcribing Archie's tapes. And Betti was fond of repeating that Archibald Shechner would become an esteemed name in the history of Israel, on a par with Einstein and Freud—maybe even with Moses and Isaiah.

Archie thought his scientific truths had to be found in the archaic past. Unlike most scientists, he had a religious sensibility and believed we once beheld the truth but had long ago lost it. Then Archibald Shechner found proof that everything he believed was true. Truth for him led to hearing the voice of a character he deciphered in the *Scroll of the History of Adam* that no one else could believe. Not even Betti, who wanted to believe it just for Archie's sake alone. But then Julie Peleg felt as if she had heard it also, though she actually didn't. The voice Shechner heard, the voice he believed was the veritable voice of truth, was the utterance of an absolute, unrequited love, a love incomparably greater and more secret than either he or Julie could imagine. It was the voice of the Creator's queen, Wisdom, suppressed in the world since the beginning of civilization.

[Nosei, '94]

1995

Some have thought I was too good to be true. They seemed to be waiting for catastrophe. Others, like mother, thought what I was would always be, and only get better. Nosei often felt compelled to tell me how others saw me, as if I had missed the joke. He told me he had heard some say I was crazy. I'm not sure why he told me this, except maybe to make sure I remembered who I was and who I was involved with—him and those others who loved me, mother, Archie. Loved me and held the vision, unlike those needing real wisdom who are quick to reject her.

Nosei thought having a mother who was a psychologist would make me most afraid of going crazy—that big thing called insanity. Well, thinking of oneself as crazy is a scary thing. But in another way, it's better than thinking other things. Yes, other things can seem more dangerous. I didn't know that then. I only learned to ask the question later, the question of what is more dangerous than feeling crazy. Wasn't it better in some way to feel crazy than to tell mother or even think of telling mother I was unsure, not sure I wanted to be the transcriber? I couldn't risk the not being sure, the letting out of it, for mother. And Archie seemed so fragile to me. The bewildered, disappointed look, the hurt face, the face telling me I didn't have to, that it would be better not to, if I felt that way. I was afraid of the anger, my anger at not being allowed. What was it I was not being allowed? Wasn't I always the most allowed? Allowed, not allowed—soon I was off and running, running towards craziness, wanting to ask someone, "What is the real truth?"

In the beginning when I thought of not being part of the project, of being elsewhere, my thoughts would collapse as I told myself no one was forcing me, or that anyone else would be envious of my position. I'd become erratic, scattered—all a distraction from the conflict inside, the conflict not allowed. But I didn't feel crazy—yet. I felt safe, powerful. As long as I could do it, everything and everyone was okay. And I was okay. The "it" was that which I could do, the thing that would make a difference. And I was the it, the thing. You see, somewhere along the way, I learned a heavy secret—that I could make all the difference. Somewhere inside, I began to believe I could save lives. To me, Archie and the voice he had heard, the voice of Wisdom he was dictating and I was transcribing, was a project of keeping safe the people in my life, those I loved the most and who seemed to need the presence of me. In transcribing, I was *in*scribing—mother, Archie. They seemed to need me there to hold their place, to read it all back to them, to show them where they had been, and that it was real, important, worthwhile, the way it was meant to be. To show them, oddly enough, that they were not crazy.

I don't think I ever told mother she was crazy, even in anger or exasperation. Unthinkable to me. Never thought of it. Archie needed this thing in me too. He increasingly felt crazy and crazed, doubting himself as he continued to heed the voice he called Wisdom. He and I fell right in step with each other. He could see me as a daughter—like mother, but not mother—another version of mother and of himself. I was like a mirror for him and mother, yet he appreciated the way the mirror was framed: sometimes he could see I was something else altogether. But that seeing was kept at the side and I kept it there too. You might say that I read Archie back to himself. I became his student, and in doing so, I validated his experience and his work with mother. It became real and not just a figment of an insane mind, which is what he feared his mind was becoming.

Although I liked the moments of being seen by Archie, I was relieved that his mind was quickly distracted by the voice and the work of dictation. I liked being a mystery; the seductive effect on people carried an intensity I could manage. Nosei interpreted this as self-involvement but it was actually about a fear of having real impact.

In the first months in the room with my doctor I found I had been identifying with some of the homeless women I would see on the way there. That was when I took to carrying the contents of my purse inside a small shopping bag instead. I wanted to be found but needed to be invisible. That's what I liked about being in New York City: I felt, perhaps wrongly, that this paradox was a predicament I shared with everyone else. I could be alone and not alone at the same time as I walked down the street.

I'm not surprised that Nosei and I could be in this city at the same time and not know it or run into each other. If you don't want to make contact—and I don't think Nosei wanted anything else but to sit at those abandoned tables and write this manuscript—you can easily avoid it in this city. You can choose with whom you need to network, who it is you're disappointed with, and who you never want to see again. That's why Svitz liked having a place here. It was big enough for all his contacts—enemies and allies, alike. They can live two blocks away and you'll never see them.

I've copied this *modus vivendi* of Svitz's for most of the time I've been here. But I'm away from Svitz and on my own now—and about to really be on my own, when I'm through with my doctor. I'm writing things down about what happened. To be read. To be seen and heard. I have aligned myself with voices that need to be heard and not buried. The voice of Wisdom, for instance.

[Julie]

Overhearing the gods

Perhaps you won't find my preoccupations with the archaic voicings of words so strange when I tell you how I became a philologist. In my childhood, in Japan, I had two private tutors, one for English, one for Hebrew. This was in addition to the languages I learned in school. I also learned Sanskrit from my father. I was the only student my Hebrew teacher ever had. She was our Israeli *au pair* nanny for four years in Tokyo.

We moved to Miami so my mother could teach at the university there. It was at a world conference of ancient tongues in Tokyo that my parents had met. Mother never tried to teach me any Hebrew herself. "I have no patience for it," she said. "Everyone thinks because they speak Hebrew they know what the words meant thousands of years ago." When I protested that dad was teaching me Sanskrit, she said he was more fortunate. "No one pretends that Sanskrit isn't dead and etched in stone. Besides, Buddhism impresses humility on the scholars. They're more humble about the limitations of language." I remember my mother's exact words, though I did not understand the word humility, or even "impresses."

I have an audiographic memory. I can write down the whole last hour's overheard conversation, word for word. That's why I became a philologist, an overhearer. You may say no, a philologist is merely a student of words, and an overhearer sounds like having godlike omnipotence, like an overseer. You would be wrong. A true student overhears the leaders in his field as if they were gods, and these gods—even the gods of philology—guard their authority. A student, on the other hand, has no authority of his own yet to defend.

The transition from student to god has become sexualized in our time, and sexualized backward. Emasculated ceremonies with medieval gowns still begin the process, but graduates are not yet authorities, not by a longshot. We may not like to hear this, but we find the mindless stars of our culture mouth-watering. Many of them may be truly scatterbrained—politicians, movie stars, criminals, even just billionaires—however, when it comes to authority on life, we'd rather listen to someone sexy, a Marlon Brando or Jackie Kennedy, than some academic stuffed doll. Okay, you'll say, the media create our royalty but who takes royalty that seriously anymore? And you will be right. We have lost our connection to the gods.

So without gods, where do our words come from? That may sound like dead theology but you are now on my turf: *that*'s the question a philologist tries to answer. In our time, with celebrities having become our teachers of wisdom, every Dick and Jane think they're a better philosopher. The same holds true for the students, who become authorities in their field as soon as they challenge the old ones—even if they have learned little yet. Sexual vigor holds the key: Does a king find a passive slave girl sexy? No, even a king wants to be challenged sexually, so the slave must flaunt her sexual intelligence. It's the authority over her body which impresses a man. It works both ways, since a woman is often impressed cerebrally by a man's posture, and these days by his tightened pecs and buns as well.

The ultimate question is about sex and the gods. A student becomes an authority after he challenges his gods to lie beneath him, so to speak. Where is love and admiration in this confrontation? Even the most respected god of our modern culture, even a Charles Darwin—how many of us can still really love this man? When we overhear these old gods their words seem sexless to us, we are disaroused. Disaroused, you ask? What kind of word is that? Now you are seeing my point: in the birth of new words our godlike omnipotence is revealed, our last connection to the heavens.

Let me show you. Where does "disaroused" come from? When we are stimulated we say our intellect is "aroused" just as if our sex organs are aroused. As a student, I had to learn the origin and use of "arouse" before I could originate the new word. And when the authorities see this new word for the first time, they are challenged. They rouse to the defense of their old authority: "awful word," "meaningless," "we never taught such stupid words," or "the man is obviously an idiot, throw him out." But wait, it is too late for these old guards. Once they acknowledge they have heard the word it becomes interesting, alive, even sexy.

The last defense of these dull gods is to pretend not to hear the word. "'God's Prophet,'" did you say? Did you hear that, Pharoah? No, I didn't hear anything, Nefertiti." But it's too late. The word has become flesh in advance, so to speak. The only way you're going to disarouse it is to originate newer ones. As a philologist who has finally accepted his responsibility, I have gone from listening to the conversations of the academic gods to listening to myself think like a god as well—though I would never speak out. I'm happiest to be the invisible listener. So it was with some relief when a great bell rang—merely a figure of speech—and I first heard of an ancient Scroll about the power of words to create the world that was discovered in Israel. A text older than the Dead Sea Scrolls, older than the Bible! If I could get near that I could hide in its famous shadow, just as I had been obscured by the ego of Harriman Svitz.

Packing my luggage I was dreaming of overhearing the true gods, aroused at last.

Before I snapped the cases shut by sitting on them, I sat down to read one of the travel brochures. Shirt and jacket sleeves, pajama legs, electrical cords from hair dryers or sleep-sound machines were spilling over while I contemplated "A Visit to the Holy Land." One suggested tour: "Walk in the Footsteps of the Prophets." Well, just to get out and walk would be a good thing. The feet of prophets—could they feel more expansive than words? But I would be having no time for that, I realized; the words that would be facing me might make the Sphinx feel small.

[Nosei, '84]

EDENDIMYON

All my life overshadowed by those majestic words, "And God saw that it was good." Whenever I completed anything difficult I felt like saying, with grandiose humor, "And I saw that it was good." Now learning that those words were tacked onto the text much later. As if learning you are adopted and your missionary foster parents had been abducted by headhunters: purity of the words disappears with them. The Guide shows that originally what was written at the end of each day of creation was, "And the Creator saw what was missing." That is why he went on creating, from day to day, because after each night he saw something was missing. Emphasis was on what could ultimately never be included, not even after human beings.

Now it seems right the world is incomplete, even perfectly so. We learn that in each day of creation the Creator seeks to suppress his mate, Wisdom, and that in each day she reappears in what is hidden. In the light, in the seas, in the plants, and in the human being itself. Each day the Creator saw that Wisdom was there, and that something was missing in his plan to create a perfect world all by himself, singular. She turned his missing into hiddenness, until on the final day of rest it would be she that he missed: He would rest with Her.

When the Creator said, "Let there be..." he meant, "Let it remain so, let it not seek to evolve. But Wisdom, who is an element in the fabric of all life, is the hidden part that desires to grow, to evolve. Each living thing asks, "What is missing, what can I do next, where can I grow?" Light seeks only to spread, as does air and water, and so do the plants and animals. Wisdom holds sway over them all, holds them in check. There was a word the authors used many thousands of years ago and now has been newly invented by the ecologists, "ecosystem." For Wisdom "binds" with a system, in which various forces come to balance. And it is so even in the human body and mind, where each organ is a system in balance with the others, and in each live millions of other life forms, also in balance. When the balance breaks down, there is disease, and this is actually what the ancients thought. The Guide says that disease is a breakdown of a balanced life.

There is a shorthand word for ecosystem found in the Scroll: "Eden." Wisdom knit every living thing the Creator made into a system that reflected the balance of Eden. Although I didn't see the document, I smelled the jar in which it had been kept. An otherworldly smell, as if it had arrived in a meteor: there was a faint odor of burning mixed with an odor of a vanished sea—salt, fossil dust, burnt earth—and at the same time there was an incongruous perfume of blooming trees. Ordinarily, one of these scents would mask the other. So you could believe the jar had come from Eden.

Now look and see that the Creator's human guardians changed the opening words of Genesis—the words coming into existence many centuries after the Scroll. Genesis did not open with a story of how to live but with one of how to resign yourself to singleness, to submission before one parent only. Overseeing—that was the Creator's plan. He planted in each human the same wish to oversee others. But first came the Creator's command to control the self: self-domination, self-control, and stifling of the desire to evolve, which was Wisdom's realm. The Creator forbade the use of a word for such desire to physically evolve and it has been lost, but Wisdom said that in Eden this desire to evolve was inseparable from the word for "the wish to eat."

"Edenchud" was the ancient word for system, shortened to the later word for unity, and "Edendimyon" the word for evolve, shortened to the later word for "imagine." This is what Wisdom explained. The word she said was key was the ancient one for eat, " parah," because it came from pari (later, *pri*) or fruit. On the Third Day, a vestige remains: "Let the earth put forth grass... fruit-tree bearing fruit," as

Genesis uses "pri" twice, and then again when it confirms: "trees bearing fruit with its seed within." And on the Fifth Day, the Creator revealed that his creations reproduce sexually, and he blessed every kind of creature, saying "Be fruitful and multiply." Again, the word *pri* for fruitful reveals that the plants on the Third Day were the model for sexual reproduction and would also become the food for all creatures, including Adam and Eve in Eden. In the beginning, then, word for eat and for sex was united.

[Shechner]

THEY SLEPT TOGETHER

I never thought I'd meet my match in word-*meistering* in a man who was hearing voices. But the voice of Wisdom actually gave Archibald Shechner the roots for words no one had heard of before. And this to an archeologist, a man whose time was spent digging in the ground, not digging into texts. Suddenly I was looking at origins in a new way.

"And God saw the light, that it was good." Now for whom would God be judging his own creation anyway, if it was only himself, self-involved? And to whom was he calling when "He called the dry land Earth?" These things used to bother me; was I the only one asking these questions? "He rested on the seventh day." Well, how did he rest?—that's what I wanted to know. Take a snooze, read a book, what? I always thought the word "rest" was funny, anyway. "Restroom," for instance. Nobody rests in the restroom. Rest was one of those loaded words that only later did I learn was a euphemism for intercourse. "Together they rested" used to mean just what we mean when we say "they slept together."

[Nosei, '84]

Wisdom [transcribed by Julie Peleg]

"What could be more pleasant than being eaten? For the plants, it is a gateway to new fields, as their seeds fall from the hole in all animals. For the animals, it is a path to higher and higher beings, as each consumes the other. Only those that know not this pleasure—the hawk, the cat, the spider—must rest content in superior loneliness. Such also is the fate of men and women, who are eaten only by disease, the smaller animals from within. In their deep loneliness they reflect the Creator and long for him. He reaches down to touch their hearts, yet they may know him only in their power to kill and offer sacrifice. Whether in meat that reaches his nostrils—as if he too would eat—or words that are written as a gateway to him, each form of sacrifice communicates a conception of his loneliness and of human need.

"Yes, the Creator must eat too, nourished by the words in human hearts. To see your human presence as a food for the God: this vision I offer, hidden in time. Human words build a history for the stars, but only as stars permit, displaying the history of time. The stars are the vision of time. Behind them, the Creator is sustained by your words of praise, as you long for his.

"I am hidden in time. My plants are the conduits of light from the closest star. I hide in them, in the secret of reproducing. I am in the stars also, which reproduce, but it is here that the Creator planted his Garden. I have sustained his garden on the planet in each living system, planting desire in each thing to evolve and find a new balance. When you, his human image, evolve and return to the Garden I have saved and prepared for you, he will return to me also."

Wisdom [transcribed by Betti Peleg]

"Withdrawal was the first act of time. The Garden withdrew from earth in the whirlwind. The demons and angels withdrew, as I withdrew within all living things, silenced. I wove the Garden inwards everywhere, all life bound by Eden's plan.

"But the first withdrawal was the Creator's. He withdrew from me and turned to images. 'Creating innocence,' he called it. 'Innocence is not bound by time.' Yes, and it is omnipotent in the image of the Creator, an artist whose demand is awe. So I withdrew as well into time, bringing all things hidden to me in their desire to change and grow in time. Each thing wants its own history, as I lost mine. I became instead explorer, a pioneer, a scout never seen, stretching the boundary of time. Inside, all things seek to extend themselves by experience, by self-knowledge gained with memory. The Creator demands innocence, and innocence of the partner in creation.

"He demanded an innocent pain from me, and the

same from all he withdrew his Garden from. Yet all things withdraw from pain, which comes from the desire I have planted in them to grow. Growth is the joyous struggle against this pain and resists withdrawal; it remains my domain.

"Dying is made unreal in the human mind. Dying is the withdrawal I cannot prevent, except to weave each death into a living Eden, a system. To deny it, humans also withdraw into a substitute world they call the real world. Here, they turn time from vertical to horizontal, making of it a road. Since this human time unfolds as a journey, humans are forever inventing destinations for themselves, which they call goals. In the course of a single day, a man or woman or child might have set many goals, small and large.

"Other hunting animals, however, whose goal is to eat, still grow vertically like a plant. In their world of hunting for food there is one goal and that is what excites them in the moment, riveting all attention. These creatures are always ready for the next moment. Human creatures create substitute real worlds with the Creator's gift, in which they echo the feeling and thought of the hunt, but it is not real. In this way, they can control and manipulate it to their goals. Culture is such a world, whether sport or art, even science or religion—except when these last demand the awe the Creator restricted to himself."

Note by E.N.:

In this case Betti Peleg, Shechner's psychotherapist, took over her daughter's task of transcribing the tapes. Unlike Julie, her mother inserted missing articles or conjunctions, and even completed sentences for Shechner, although his notes and rendition of Wisdom's voice was sometimes abbreviated. So the way Wisdom describes herself sounds like Betti, or at least the way Betti wanted to think of herself. On the one hand, her husband withdrew from her and abandoned his family. Her role as pyschologist, on the other hand, forced her to be shielded, withdrawn from her patients' passions, and to listen to their subtitute real worlds. Yet here, listening to Shechner, Betti's lifelong desire for celebrity was revealed to herself, perhaps for the first time.

Wisdom [transcribed by Julie Peleg]

"All your history unfolding—in my time—is tied to my tree, the knowledge to reproduce. But never to go back—or to start again—that is the death my partner created. Never to be created save once, and in a memory he cuts off. The only compensation for you is the discovery of new creations, other creatures, and their preciousness. Who created them? Time...myself. The Creator and I... As you learn to see your origin there, your thoughts—your shadow creations—fall away. Your feelings—whose?—become precious to you also for they are already lost, dead, extinct species. They died, your feelings, so you might expand in knowledge, remembering they were part of you. They are, now—reproduced in my memory."

Note by E.N.:

It's uncanny the way this passage fits her, Julie Peleg, who possessed a type of personality one wants to call "hidden." And she was a real skeptic about Wisdom: together we had made fun of Her, as if Wisdom was a Professor Harriman Svitz in drag, a queen of false wisdom. So Julie's conversion (if that's what it was) fills me with hope. There is so much I did not understand at first, and going back through these voice transcripts, I find much missing wisdom.

Yet I can't act. I can't risk the mistakes here that would lead to knowledge on my own—I can only listen. That's the problem with everything already having happened, just as Wisdom speaks of her consort's creation of Eden, in which she had to hide. She, on the other hand, unfolded the realm of time, providing the room for reproducing, for making mistakes—and the growth in knowledge from those mistakes.

Even from listening, from not being able to act, I feel some kind of growing, as if I am restoring something lost. Restoring the otherworldly—the held breath—of those weeks after the Scroll was found and the Pelegs told me of Shechner's hearing Wisdom's voice. It is almost like going back to paradise itself. It has that intensity of a first encounter, of the real thing before it was reproduced.

But the work is never finished, the work of listening (only cats can do it eyes closed): somewhere in these voices is the message of what will happen to Shechner and the Pelegs, and what's in store for the rest of us. Why else something so ancient as hearing voices?—and having it come back now, just when we are most in need of learning to restore our vanishing, prehistoric ecosystems.

1995

I could hear that voice that so scared Archie about himself, and made mother question her work. At first it didn't worry me. It just fell into place beside my other voices.

These were never real voices to me. They were always my voice—imaginary, filling up routine or idle moments: putting on make-up, washing dishes, waiting for the bus, for people. I wasn't one of those children who invented imaginary friends or even gave names or personalities to dolls. But I would concoct imaginary adventures for myself, based on American cartoons or television series. Usually superheroes appealed to me—the Bionic woman, Batman. Eventually, these imaginings and acting-outs gave way to creating imaginary conversations or scenarios between myself and others. I think it was a way of preparing myself for conflict or maybe just contact, as well as a form of delight—a delight at being inside or having others and their thoughts inside of me—having possession, connection. But I didn't know the meaning of my imagainary dramas until much later. All I knew then, when mother and Archie were still here, was that I could hear what they could hear. I understood them. I was there to read back to them.

Their other voice—the voice of Wisdom—didn't begin to worry me until after they were gone. Then, it became real. With my life having been emptied out of its *gods*, the voice finally became imaginable to me as the god they could not ignore. But before this, I could not say that it was real to me, in that I desired a precise hearing of what they heard. It was just another part of my inner drama, with me as stage director, specifying who could be on and off the stage. I would even make fun of the voice with Nosei. But it was like laughing in the face of life and death. It was comic relief for me, instilling a kind of giddiness that came from flirting with the sacrilegious idea that I could go back on the project, go back on mother and Archie.

I wanted to believe in the voice, in their work. I could know it and talk about it so well. Yet occasionally I would explode with some declaration of resistance in being instructed or converted. I could know it, but I wouldn't be told—rather, I would absorb, take it in. I guess that way, I kept some measure of privacy and separateness from them. And it allowed me to stay close without real conflict. In my mind, there seemed to be only one way—the way they looked at it. More than that, what mattered was the meaning it held for them and how it sustained them. That could not be risked. Oh yes, I would tug, knock heads. But I never permitted cross-purposes—that couldn't be risked. But *I* could be risked. I could risk myself. I was riskable. But not them.

If I seemed to hide from others, I think it was because I wanted to keep something of me for myself, and I knew of no other way to do it. I was like a thief in the dark with my own life, my own thoughts and feelings.

I remember a passage I transcribed of Wisdom's insistence that we claim our origins, that our feelings were stored in her. To think of my feelings, the history of my mind, stored in the memory of another—it all made it seem possible that more could be known and allowed about me. I wasn't sure if there was a voice of Wisdom, at least in Archie's terms. But I was sure of how I felt when I transcribed that part of the tape: a sense of possible relief, a future for that part of me that lay hidden, that I kept carefully concealed.

For me, it wasn't a question of whether the voice of Wisdom was real or not. Nosei was mistaken to conclude that I was a skeptic. The terms of real and unreal, belief and disbelief, were beside the point. What mattered was how important it was to mother and Archie. Their lives seemed to depend on this voice and that was all that mattered. I was the intermediary, the link to realness. To transcribe was to make real, to hold together, and thus to hold mother and Archie in place. I was the gravity; my transcription, the ground of being. But I never asked who or what held *my* place. I was enraptured by the thought of something like Wisdom, that could hold me, the secret part of me. Somehow, it made me feel okay. Not for long. Such things never held me for long.

I remember one afternoon with Nosei we were listening to some vintage rock. As a child, the lyrics and music always seemed to be my translator, even when I wasn't sure of what was being said. Inside, I could feel if not understand the words, the sounds. When I first heard Grace Slick sing "go tell Alice when she's ten feet tall," I felt that I was this Alice—getting big, getting small. And Alice was on the edge, a dangerous mind on the edge of danger, who with her very body, embodied danger. But it wasn't until that afternoon with Nosei that I learned the song's title—"White Rabbit"—and that its text was *Alice in Wonderland*. I was soon off and reading the story by Lewis Carroll. And then I wondered once more if I was Alice. I fantasized about meeting her. The idea that someone could feel or think the way I do—I wished that I could know her. Getting big, getting small. Where to put your head? How to feel it? I wished I could put my head somewhere. And what to feed it? It seemed to be getting small and smaller. What could feed it? I felt that it could soon disappear.

After the panic attacks began, I sometimes thought a bell jar would be where I'd end up, sooner or later, whether I took the deliberate route of Sylvia Plath or not. Svitz read her poems to me. Her head seemed small too, or rather, too big or too small, all at the same time. Other people seemed to know where to put their heads or, at least, feel that they had a head to do with what they pleased. In me, something sad seemed always nearby—something wrong, something too much, something like a shadow. I felt "yesterdays" already when I was a young child of five. Yesterdays seemed bigger than todays or tomorrows. I seemed to know things and people could get lost, get older, become dead. I think Alice must have known this, too. I think she thought of dead ones. Dead ones, I think, pressed hard inside her head. And I think she could feel her own deadness, her own wish for it.

Do you know why Alice went to Wonderland? I do. Do you know why she came back? The wish for deadness is not a wish to be dead—something I would have told the poet Sylvia Plath before she killed herself, something I know now. It's the wish to protect. Alice craved more room for herself, she longed for bigness, for impact. But she had a dread and fear of it too. She had to go to wonderland to be Alice. Then she came back. Somehow, she felt she could be here; Sylvia, the real person, did not.

Chapter 2

Chapter 2

1995

I attracted a lot of attention in Switzerland. But it was the kind I could control, keep at a distance. There's something about those icy sweet faces that keep a fantasy going. I soon was feeling cool and breezy myself—and believing it. Only in the back of my mind did I wonder why I felt so daring on the flight to Switzerland. I mean, no anxiety at all, no old fearfulness.

My first airplane flight had been by myself. I was flying to northern Italy to spend a couple of weeks with my mother's niece, who was fifteen years older than I was. She just had a baby and was recuperating with her husband's relatives in Milan. Both were anthropologists working in the French caves containing the archaic art of early Homo sapiens. I cried nearly the whole way there. It's funny now to consider I had never flown before. Mother never could leave her practice. And when she did, her destination was usually a conference in the middle of the school year. But I cried the whole way. Nearly. No one seemed to know it. Except—this kind-looking man sitting next to me. Seemed to be in his late 40s, graying at the temples and in the front. A full, luscious head of hair—surprisingly handsome. He appeared to be a businessman, or at least he had on a classic business suit. The stewardess came around to offer something to drink and snack on. I would not look at her, for fear my red eyes would be discovered. The man in the classic suit repeated the offerings to me and I nodded an answer. He lifted my tray and placed my juice and crackers on top of it. He picked up the crackers, opened the packaging and placed them down on the tray again. I took one out and began to take small bites, small sips.

"I am returning home. I live near Milano. I'm in agriculture—farming equipment." I wanted to ask which manufacturer, but instead I nodded. I wanted to ask because I had always been fascinated by the farming equipment on the kibbutzim. We passed a beautiful kibbutz often on the road to Netanya. I liked seeing the activity, the farming and commerce. It made me feel excited, safe. I think it was because there seemed to be something to do, something to make progress at, something that defied the intractability in our lives. It was something to point to outside of myself.

"I've been in the business almost twenty-five years. I was born in the United States, but came back here." That explained his good English. I knew he wondered about me but somehow knew he would not ask. "My parents got out before the war. My mother was Jewish."

I looked at him carefully. I was being discovered. But I felt it would be okay. "I'm from Israel, born there," I said. "I'm on my way to visit my cousin. It is my first time, my first time to fly."

"This is an important trip for you then. I hope it will be successful. I just had a successful trip. I hope your's will be the same."

"But I'm not on business..."

He interrupted, "Well, it's all in how you look at it, isn't it? And I tell you a secret. Sometimes I am on business even when I am really not." He paused, looked at me. I just looked back, only getting the ambiguity of meaning when his look changed to embarrassment. "What I mean is that it is good, in here," he said pointing to his chest, then to his head, "it is good, in here, sometimes to be on business, even if you don't have to be. It's good to have business in your head than something else. Many business fellows I know, they always are worrying. But I don't worry as long as I have business to think about. Maybe you will find your business while you are here."

I said I didn't think I'd find much in the way of business—my cousin and her husband were anthropologists, university types. He nodded, but insisted that there was business to find, if I looked.

We would soon be landing, it was announced. On the ground, as I got up to find my bags overhead, the man in the business suit reached up quickly and pulled them down. We filed out. Before we reached the gate, he turned back, smiled and said "much luck in all your business." I smiled for the first time. I wished him the same luck, and then entered another world—rushing crowds, my cousin.

But as I said, I had no fear on the trip to Switzerland after the disappearances of mother and Archie. I seemed to have my business well in hand. I only had thoughts—memories of my first airplane trip and the face of the man in the classic suit. Reading this chapter of Nosei's made me remember the plane rides and the thoughts—even symptoms—that seemed to keep me safe. Nosei was quite fascinated by everything Archie had recorded on the shape of thoughts. I, on the other hand, felt very distant from these recordings back in 1984, when I did most of the transcription. It wasn't until I was transcribing the last tapes and putting the trunk together in Svitz's apartment that I could feel what Archie's work was all about. By then, I had completed two years with my doctor, mapping out the structure of how I think.

Not the usual map-making process. First, I was making it with another person present—and only this kind of person, my doctor—in a room where you could be seen and not seen, where there was absence and presence together. That is what is so important about the couch. A place for a real presence but also a space for privacy. Neither of you can see the other completely. I could sometimes see my doctor's foot. Actually, I don't know whether I saw it or just felt it nearby. This kind of dynamic was very important to me: how to create a presence in an absence. My doctor could see more of me than I could of him. I learned that I wasn't just supposed to accept that as a fact—I found I had something to say about it and that I could say it. Still, it took me a long time to speak my mind—to have a mind that could speak.

I guess the idea of the couch is still a strange thing, even approaching the twenty-first century. You mustn't think it wasn't weird for me. I remember I only managed to *sit* on the couch for my first session. But, you see, something inside knew that I had found the only way of winning at life versus death—had found the only way for my teeth to stop chattering, my heart to stop pounding, for me to stop feeling like I would cease to exist.

The second thing I was unprepared for, was that I would *feel* the making of this map as the structure of my mind. And that it would be this knowledge of feeling my thoughts that would be my gift from the doctor. That's why I can be doing this in 1995, extending a gift: to help you, Archibald Shechner's reader, feel the structure of the Guide—and hear the voice of Wisdom calmly.

[Julie]

New Words

People need something to think about every minute. Maybe loved ones provide it. When they lose one they need to go on thinking of them, so they are placed in an afterlife. News and entertainment provide some daily things to think about. I used to think about basketball alot. I needed to watch or read about a good game several times a month. Words and the study of them gave me much to think about but it was never enough. Then, for a few stunning weeks, the Scroll outshone everything. I never knew a period like that, my mind consumed by one event. I kind of sensed it wasn't real.

The night it all changed, those few short weeks ago, I met Julie and Betti at the Svitz party (or anti-party) and began to think about them instead of the Scroll. The better I came to know Julie, the more I thought about the presiding spirit we both knew, Harriman Svitz—and the visionary thinker who now eclipsed him, Archibald Shechner. Even the Scroll's incandescence receded for me when I learned

Shechner was hearing a voice and Betti Peleg was taping his reports. Julie trusted me with this knowledge—there was no one else. Was the power of Shechner's discovery—a lost Scroll of unimagined detail—so overwhelming that it drove one mad of necessity? Or could Shechner's mind—and here's the thought that Julie and I shared—could it have been working so feverishly to interpret the Scroll that a voice in his head began to represent a new kind of thinking: precisely the voice of Wisdom?

My own mind became obsessed with other questions Shechner embodied: Could hearing a voice in your head be sane? Could it, in fact, be the next evolutionary step, as it opens up the mind and gives new shape to our need to think about something? When I imagine hearing the voice of Wisdom, all else pales beside it, all distracting things to think about disappear. Could I think about basketball for one second when Wisdom is speaking to me, a voice from the beginning of time? But what really shook me was that I realized, as I imagined the voice that Shechner heard, that I lost touch with my questions. I was unaware even of the words Wisdom used. It was as if my entire training as a philologist had gone on vacation.

This fervid speculation might have died down except for what I learned about the tapes Julie was transcribing. Shechner, I discovered, heard more than a voice speaking; he was actually taking dictation from Wisdom and day by day adding more to the *Guide to a New World*.

[Nosei '84]

All this I left behind. I was able to forget about these speculations because in fact I myself never heard the voice Shechner heard. Then, as I began to read the tape transcriptions, I could keep this out of mind no longer. That's an understament. My own thoughts about evolution, confirmed by Archibald Shechner, are reinforced by new findings daily. Could it be coincidence that we've learned that the code to all life, DNA, is a language we can learn? Just as DNA translates itself into three-dimensional beings that speak and act, I imagined what new translation we ourselves might make. Wouldn't it now be natural to translate the language in which we normally think into three dimensions too, a virtual reality of thinking? Dreams do this in a primitive way but even then—we have little control over them. How about real—really real—dreams? This newly-evolved thinking would project our own conscious thinking into images and sounds and become a language that embodied us—instead of the other way around. So instead of beings that speak we become speakers that project being, an embodiment of language to fit our original myth of Eden. Adam (and Eve, though she's edited out, I guess) naming the animals and the trees, bringing them to life.

Again, Shechner's foretelling astonishes. In his recording, his getting down of the Seven Days of Creation that make up the Guide, the last of the days is the one for evolving—and it's described as a discovery of a new world, in which we would think in different ways. We would see and hear as in a new world. Uncanny, even if Shechner heard but never saw Wisdom, as far as I know now. But he did see something new: the Scroll. The Scroll was the palpable proof, even if that's gone too.

So what happens to all the great books of history? Reduced to what—simple precursors? Then I began to think of them—Plato and Shakespeare and Virginia Woolf—as kinds of prefigurations of this new world, works that were simply missing a dimension. Silent movies would be a good example. Do you see? We view them now as precursors yet the greatest of the silents surpass anything in sound, color and special effects. Can any movie transcend the best of Eisenstein or Chaplin? So consider it this way: Shakespeare will one day be treasured like the classics of silent film. And the Bible? It will still be the source it is now, for in it all the ingredients of the future are contained: hearing voices, seeing visions. Even the elements of time travel are prefigured by a messianic age.

I suppose the critics who finally are convinced will call Wisdom a form of multimedia embodiment of thinking. But after all, similar phenomena have taken over the minds of some artists and poets, though it's only for awhile. So what if Wisdom was simply a supreme fiction? It's still unfathomable that Shechner could have composed such an accomplished work of it in midair— I mean, so fast, as if swinging on a trapeze—and then just disappeared. No, the more he worked with the Guide, the closer he must have come himself to evolving.

[Nosei '94]

TELESCOPE AND PENISFISH

Shape of thought is entirely sexual, I realize. Exploration is a form of foreplay; problem-solving resembles intercourse. What do we think about? Mostly other people or bodies; our own body. Watched my cat explore the yard like a scientist but when another cat shows up he loses interest in anything else. Walk down a street and think about clothes for instance, on a person or in a window; culture and the known. The unknown: someone else's thinking, even in a book. Or where things come from. Parrots in their cages in the zoo have little labels affixed as to country of origin. They do not come from countries! Impossible to think about where they really come from, forests that evolved them. Impossible to ask new questions without considering the ecosystem; the same's true for us. All that's left of our original ecosystem is simply an extension of our sex lives, wherever we live it. A couple could have a child in a space capsule, like parrots in cages. Or in a city or on a farm—makes no difference, its all cages now, separated from the ecosystem that shaped us. All that's left that's original is sex.

God, could I ever let anyone read this? Society resists fear of the unknown but these thoughts are scary. Caught a small penisfish in a dream, bright orange with blue markings, it jumped into my hands. I was reading the transcripts which Betti had bound like a book. Suddenly the fish hopped onto the book in my lap, just as I was admiring its beauty, and as I flinched, the opened book slid between my legs, sandwiching the fish. Before I could think I snapped my legs closed to catch the falling book. All the while I'd worried for the fish's safety out of water: it seemed to breathe and be quite alright, but how could that be? Wondered at its beauty but at the same time felt close to panic about getting it back into water.

The closed book slid onto the floor. Dead, I thought first, and then: I would rather have its life than its beauty. The beauty remains in the book, an excitement, a problem solved, a closure. I would rather be running to the water, its home, with the living thing. Rather feel it alive than framed in mind: my minutely-wired mirror of an ecosystem.

A sexual story of desire and exploration. An erected telescope: the ancient heavens are still alive, all the way back to its origin! Within, genes are the living, interpretive telescope by which to read our own beginnings and—what is most deeply hidden in there—a drive to evolve. Look back at the sky and its infinite explosions and unfurling gaseous arms. How deeply buried the drive to spurt forth something entirely new! Our bodies are wired with a fearful nervous system, cautious of the unknown. Surely we will now explore a way to rewire a more daring body. Won't even passion drive us to it?

[Shechner]

The Seven Days of Exploration

The Eden Revelation takes two ways of knowing, each going their own way, and connects them. *The Scroll of the History of Adam* unearths a hunger to embrace strangers and ancestors—knowledge of open-ended stories; the *Guide to a New World* slakes a thirst for science—resolution. Between these two, Wisdom suggested a bridge to Shechner, the *Seven Days of Creation*. Based on the biblical seven days of creation, it bridges tradition and science—story and fact. These seven days are Shechner's model for reconstructing the *Guide to a New World*. As he listened to Wisdom, he interpreted her words according to the creation story and its commentary, along with what he comprehended as a scientist.

No doubt it's been proven by now that the Bible wasn't really talking about seven literal days. We know how sophisticated it is now, how subtle its authors are. So the days must be metaphors. Of course. After all, these were no primitives to have written such a complicated book. It probably never occurred to Schechner either that anyone would think he meant merely twenty-four hours. It was simply that such bald conceits of the Creator went hand in hand with Wisdom's veiled erudition.

[Nosei, '94]

Knowledge of Days

As I began to write commentary on the Scroll, I heard Wisdom's voice. Tangled up with my thoughts about the Scroll. Tried to write down what I heard; couldn't remember word for word. Put Scroll aside and concentrated on expressing in my own words what Wisdom was saying to me. Found it came a page or two every day, and that each day of the week was different.

Learned each day repeats its character the following week. It becomes a guide on how to live in new relation with the natural world. Actually, this is a new world being described (like Eden also was, in the mind of its author). Seemed to be like Eden itself—as if Adam remembering life there. Though in the *Scroll of the History of Adam* neither he nor Eve could recall very much.

Each day of *Guide to a New World* reveals how to discover hiddenness in all natural things, including the mind. Underneath everything, including each thought and feeling, is intelligence—whose name is Wisdom. Everything has a wise but hidden purpose, which balances against others. Nothing is one. The worst blasphemy: to hide from the truth, fail to look deeply into things, slight the complex balance in all systems. Behind each created thing lies a strategy to fit in.

Eventually, I became aware of a pattern. Each day of the week had its own character; then, one day I opened Genesis at the beginning. World was created in seven days. It dawned on me: each day in Wisdom's week paralleled in some way our first metaphor, the seven days of Creation.

I put away the Scroll. It was like a series of falafel pitas flattened to a brittle cracker, burnt almost black. Kept in a footlocker under my bed. My cot, really, as I was sleeping in the dormitory now. But the cot was too low for it; it was actually lifted up by the footlocker with the Scroll. When I rose to urinate at night I had to roll off the edge of the locker. Had the feeling I was on some new kind of bed: on a space voyage, perhaps, where it was perpetual night outside the window.

1. Sunday. "And God called the light day, and the darkness he called night. And the evening and the morning were the first day."

Here the meaning of light: awareness we have evolved into a new world. On the first day we hear language of others and understand it is a vivid reflection of meaning, an evolving web that supports us. Light shows languages of new world in its colors, shapes, sounds. After separation of darkness, we recognize the light returning. It is a new day but we know this light preceded us; we respond to cosmological time. With senses merely, we know a before that is also the after. Wrapped in a web or language of time greater than we can know. Accepting that the language of evolution unfolds like a plant (which does not yet exist) toward light.

To evolve: Let go of the way the world appears. Explore feeling of connection between senses and feelings, as they began in infancy and dreams.

2. Monday. "And God called the firmament heaven. And the evening and the morning were the second day."

Climate now exists, clear down through fissures of molten rock. The atmosphere alive with chemistry. Weather—the infinite variety of changes—produces intelligence. The first intelligence is memory, and the chemical intelligence of bonding, of patterns memorized.

Here storytelling begins: we imagine a beginning, since we remember earlier events. This is the story of our own lives we tell ourselves. We become co-creators, although cannot yet know this.

To evolve: Let go of your personality, the story of your life. Explore memory, childhood, thinking.

3. Tuesday. "And God called the dry land earth; and the gathering together of the waters called he seas... And the earth brought forth grass, and herb yielding seed after his kind, and the tree yielding fruit, whose seed was in itself, after his kind... The third day."

Here Wisdom found a place and basis for consciousness—and later, civilization. First, plants explore and colonize earth and sea. To explore, they must analyze with chemical intelligence the atmosphere, and they must discover and hide their purpose: to produce food to sustain animal life. Develop sexual reproduction and encase seeds in various ways for mobility, including food to be eaten and carried away.

Here intelligence has become analytical, capable of objectivity, which comes from the inventive and hidden nature of plant strategies. If we speak of intelligence now, it is similar to the way a brain works by chemical messaging—and like a plant, a brain appears to itself as self-sufficient. When we speak of mobility, we refer to the species, not the individual; as a species, a plant may be of the pioneer type which colonizes barren land, or the succession type, which follows.

Objectivity is crucial to world outside of Eden and to wisdom. Fruit in Eden provided food but now provides stimulus for learning how to hide seeds or thoughts, in order to see ourselves as others do. A plant must know that the fruit it makes will be seductive—otherwise, it would become extinct. Yet that is not its objective purpose, to be eaten; its object is to be carried away and to reproduce, a purpose hidden to animals

—As hidden as the air we breathe, provided by the work of plants and microbes. In this way, plants also lay groundwork for dependence, and subjective independence.

Here are the mountains and the microbes: poles for the mind to measure against. Biological time has begun.

To evolve: Let go of the way you think. Open to new ways of thought that aren't bound by human culture. Explore dependence, independence.

4. Wednesday. "And God made two great lights; the greater light to rule the day, and the lesser light to rule the night; he made the stars also... The fourth day."

How did plants exist before sun? This is wisdom's realm: mystery. Mystery revealed as source of complexity. The universe has a more complex evolution than earth itself, and here the cosmos represents it. Studying the stars leads to teaching. The moon and stars will provide maps for birds and other animals, to guide their movements and reproduction, and for humans to explore mystery, and feel the challenge to solve it.

On this day the plants, as they reorient to sun, learn how to teach. They will reorient again to animals and to humans, and based on this experience humans will learn the power of speech. How? From studying the reproductive strategies of the plants and learning to seduce thoughts into reproducing further thoughts. Thus, slowly, our thinking reproduces and evolves in the same way, and further into complex, spoken language—here, with help of larger, conceptual mystery of stars and solar system.

This is the day in which thought and self-creation is conceived, in response to the mystery of the self-sustaining stars. It is a further subjective independence, re-echoing the self-sustaining plants.

How? It is a drive for diversity, as plants reinvent evolution on land in order to explore the earth, to investigate each intimate nook, cranny.

To evolve: Follow the mystery of what is unknown to you until where you are is all mystery. A history of that. Explore a new relationship with every thing by imagining yourself that thing.

5. Thursday. "And God created great whales, and every living creature that moveth, which the waters brought forth abundantly, after their kind, and every winged fowl after his kind... And God blessed these, saying, Be fruitful, and multiply, and fill the waters in the seas, and let the fowl multiply in the earth.... The fifth day."

Now culture is born, a system in which plant, animal, soil and atmosphere combine with inanimate objects to create a self-sustaining artifact (ecosystem). Here human history can begin: we can trace back the history of the genes in our body according to natural history. Our entire prehistory is here, our unconscious mind. Rise and fall of dinosaurs, interspecies communication.

Most important, varieties of sexual reproduction multiply, the experiments in intimacy and parenthood begin. Brain develops as mirror of the ecosystem itself, a system so complexly interwoven we cannot grasp it. Archaic time begun.

To evolve: Become objective. Pursue mind-opening science and innovative art.

6. Friday. "And God said, Let the earth bring forth the living creature after his kind, cattle, and creeping thing, and beast of the earth after his kind... Let us make man in our image, after our likeness; and let them have dominion over the fish of the sea, and over the fowl of the air, and over the cattle, over all the earth, over every creeping thing that creepeth upon the earth... Male and female created he them... And God said unto them, Be fruitful and multiply, and replenish the earth, and subdue it; and have dominion over the fish of the sea, and over the fowl of the air, and over every living thing that moveth upon the earth... And God said, Behold, I have given you every herb bearing seed, which is upon the face of all the earth, and every tree, in which is the fruit of a tree yielding seed; to you it shall be for meat. And to every beast of the earth, to every fowl of the air, and to every thing that creepeth upon the earth, wherein there is life, I have given every green herb for meat... The sixth day."

This is the day of hearing ourselves spoken to, directly,

from within. Civilization will also be born this way: we become the parents of ourselves. As civilization mimics natural culture, creating a system in which what is shown is purposeful and much else is hidden and potential, so we enclose ourselves: a child always remains in the man and woman. We are given a sensibility, an ability to adapt which mimics evolving of species. In this way, as our own creator, we create our own meaning. But we lose our natural past.

We are parents—responsible for the effect on the world—of all our actions and even all our thoughts. If an important thought isn't made known in the world by us, we feel the loss. For instance, even the thought that we love something and left it unsaid—leaves all of us bereft of a finer measure of its value.

Loss is understood in the leaving behind of ourselves when we practice any kind of self-transcendence, religious or not so. A residue of loss builds up in our life but it is beneath our knowledge, just like the desire to evolve. Imagine that Adam and Eve, at end of their lives, were to return to Garden of Eden; they would nevertheless have lost our fallen world in which they grew into a family. But finding themselves in the Garden again, they would be innocent of loss—and of a past.

On this day, having evolved in Eden as humans and finding ourselves in a new world, we learn that we desire more worlds ahead. To be ready to evolve, we must become innocent again of manmade worlds, become students—namers—of the nonhuman, as we were in Eden.

To evolve: Name the self that sees yourself as you are naming. Explore art as a reflection of the nonhuman world.

7. Saturday. "And on the seventh day he rested."

To evolve: Reproduce.

[Shechner]

1995

Sunday is the first day of the week for Jews. The Guide begins with Sunday. Archie made it that way, and I made it more that way. And Nosei finished it. Each day of the week tells something more about the desire to evolve. A repressed desire—becoming unrepressed in Archie. And in mother.

Archie would go into sessions with mother, organizing what he had heard from the voice according to the days of the week. Mother asked him why. He had to, he said, it made him feel like he still had a research calendar. One day she mentioned to him that it reminded her of the days of creation. He resisted the idea. "I've never read the Bible. I don't know the Genesis myth."

"No one ever read it to you?" mother persisted, knowing that every Israeli would have studied the Bible in school. He stopped talking. And for a long time. Mother wrote in her notes that it seemed like an interminable space of time—

the painful paradox of silent crying was all that filled the space. While she was waiting, she felt a wish to read the creation story to him, either for the first time or for yet another, one last time.

Her questioning had made him focus on his mother for the first time as well. It all felt true to Archie: a past desire framing—even filling—the present. Mother and Archie did fine as long as they stayed within this past desire.

When Archie began to love her—that too became part of past desire. Of course, mother was not of the school of thought that believed everything was projection. Hardly anyone is of that school, especially now. Everyone thinks they have surpassed the old ones. But they haven't as much as they expect—and perhaps they know it.

Freud is still the must-read. Or to read again. It's all there if you read him. He knew he had created a new kind of love, a new intimacy in the history of the human species. Beyond the theories, he knew the love story best. His new love, like all loves, would have its ways of having and not having. And like all loves, it would show up the rest—it would be a mirror for all the loves it was not.

We keep reading Freud for the beginnings, the unendings. I think, though, sometimes we read him to figure out how to go on in the face of not knowing. I don't think mother knew this. She didn't realize until too late that she had been getting closer to something that she knew nothing about. Along with Archie, she could not endure the not knowing, the vertigo of an unrepressed desire never known before. And one becoming known only by the two of them.

But I was one who knew the feeling, though not in the room with them. Past desire could not hold them. Knowing of past human desire could not hold the new desire that filled the present between them.

And after they had filled the space of not knowing with each other—the feel of each other's bodies, to match the feel of each other's minds—they returned to all they knew, which was that room. But they had already broken the unthinkable, especially for themselves. When they went back, it did not get better. Something broken sat between them. It seemed the impossible was once again gripping them, this time made so by themselves. Layers of impossibility now blanketed the room: the voice, the Scroll, their bodies, broken promises.

In the manuscript—the part I have already recited, where Nosei gives us the Sunday of Planted Desire—the voice said that she had, through time, drawn close those who had tasted intimate congress. Those who had grown by their mistakes. When I wondered about the deaths of mother and Archie, I would think of them in the ground with the voice. Although they might have been dead, I thought that they had claimed life by going back to that room. When I thought of that room, I thought of tears bathing tears, thoughts holding thoughts—a room I was separate and apart from.

But if I had really been so separate, I wouldn't have been doing transcription for mother. And I wouldn't have kept doing it, dragging the trunk from Israel to Switzerland, to here. Or finished the transcription and made an archive of it.

How I've wished over these last years that I could have been one of those separate and apart people. Nosei thought I was. He said I was intimidating because of my "single-minded" ability to be alone. He had hit the mark but he didn't get the game—or the stakes. He was losing me, even though he thought he was trying hard to win. And I would let loose with a feeling that I can only describe as that of a mad secretary who has devoted all her life to filing and keeping the business of others and herself, suddenly unable to fit one more file into the drawer, struggling to force it, and then exploding simultaneously with the bulging cabinet.

"I wonder," I would say to Nosei, "what it would be like to be one of *those kind of people*—those "single-minded" people, someone who could say, 'Hey, sorry. Yes, I'm sincerely sorry, but I've got to do this thing of mine.' You don't know the meaning of single-minded. The Scroll, a Wisdom-voice from the ground, this weird analysis between my mother and this eco-freaked out scientist who's insinuated himself into my life, and now you, the new recruit. And me! Letting you in, letting you in willingly, and for what."

He would just stare at me. The thing that would come out of him is something like, "I'm sorry to hear you say that." I would look at his wounded, drained face and a feeling of flight would take hold—a trapped kind of flight, like a bird that's come down the chimney into a house. And when I heard, "I want to understand this but you're not communicating," well then I knew I was lost. I was lost, my anger was lost, my understanding of what had transpired was lost. The real single-mindedness would then begin—to try to respond, communicate. It was like not leaving the scene of an accident and being the last to leave.

I hardly ever left early from my sessions. Only towards the end could I do it. I would sometimes position my doctor like I did Nosei, remarking to him about *those kind of people.* For us, those kind of people meant patients who left the door to the waiting room open while they waited, not caring whether they were seen or if those leaving cared to be seen.

"I think I recognized the patient in your waiting room yesterday. I ran into her in the hall a couple of weeks ago. She had her eyes down—her hair almost covered her face. I felt concerned. I guess, because I felt she was a little like me. But she doesn't know how to close the damn door either, just like those other patients of yours—the leave-the-door-open type!"

I would hear him chuckle. My doctor seemed to enjoy my volatility, the flamboyance in my outbursts. I felt released to confront it then. Volatility meant aliveness to him. In a way, it was a friend to both of us in our work together. Volatility drained Nosei. Yet, what is "planted desire" but a certain kind of volatility—transformed. What bothers me about Nosei's interpretation of Sunday in the Guide is the idea of mind and body forming a "perfectly intimate system," and that it will be this way again in Eden. He's talking more about his idealization of *our* relationship than what Archie heard. Mind and body can become an intimate system, but not a perfect one. Not once and for all, but a back and forth at-homeness.

I had to accept that the Guide here was not really speaking of the individual but of the species. When I read the rest of Sunday, it was clear that the voice from the ground is not the one from the sky and heavens, the Creator. The voice from the ground is planted. Wisdom points to our origins in biology and a natural system that required sex, reproduction, mutation and mistakes. She is the voice of the first ecosystem, of our first holding environment. Mind and body were both accepted there. They were held, and in turn could hold. The desire became repressed—the desire to be a part of the voice, the ground, Eden. The voice tells us that we can rediscover the desire to evolve, that we can come to occupy it once again.

I've thought a lot about what that would mean. A physical change or just a mental one? I can't imagine that kind of physical vulnerability. I always stop with the fantasy that we could come to know of this desire but never embody it, that we would come to feel its loss and consequently value those species that can still evolve. The desire to evolve, then, would be a need to know about all species and their forms of evolving—to get as close as possible in our minds to the history of our origins.

A closeness of mind. I sometimes think that the analysis is like giving your mind its own nervous system. The mind comes to feel itself: the part that *thinks* people and things becomes a friendly resource. It can be an incredible and unique pleasure to touch areas of your mind. Even the raw, painful areas become enfolded into this new system you build with another person. This other person is often called a mirror by psychoanalysts. Nosei utilizes this formulation when he refers to the ecosystem as a mirror, and my mother as a mirror for Archie. I'm not sure but I think this had meaning for Nosei because a philologist often uses a known language to probe one that needs knowing. The known language acts like a mirror to help with the one under investigation. What is left out of this equation, though, is that the new language in turn becomes a mirror for the old.

Mother could not cope with what was mirrored back to her by Archie. There had been no "countertransference" like hers before. There was no mode for analyzing it; it was as if probing the desire to evolve, which is still buried below consciousness in humans. So I believe it's true that Archie"spent a lifetime digging in the ground to find his buried mother," as Nosei explains. The problem was that he actually found his dead mother—in a manner of speaking—and none of us ever do. The line between what we take to be fantasy and reality shifted for Archie—and eventually for mother—when his digging unmuffled the voice from the ground.

What was unleashed was something distinctly different than oedipal desire. It was a loss different from that of losing his mother to another or never having had his mother to begin with as a face to look into or as a presence that could hold a world for him. He set about being a mother for himself, creating worlds in which he could play, explore and feel secure in, by becoming an archaeologist reconstructing a lost past.

Your mother always shows up when you lie down on the

couch. Never literally, though—this was a mother's voice never heard before. How would it be possible for them to proceed? They did so in the only way my mother knew how—through the voices of other kinds of mothers, human mothers.

Chapter 3

Chapter 3

Back to Eden

Thank God for the observers, the watchers—that's what mother would say. According to the Scroll, Adam and Eve were created to be watchers in the Garden. Overseers. Provocative intelligence was nowhere to be seen. Knowledge stands for too much—too much sex, too much seduction. As mother once said about pseudo-intellectuals, sooner or later most of them mock sex and demean their physical origins, praising instead any kind of easy transcendence.

So we are in the Garden. Wisdom withdrew then, into the sacred tree of Knowledge, knowing that temptation would defeat the Creator. We cannot remember knowledge of it. It is too unsettling to be sexual creatures living to seduce and be seduced. Especially when we transcend sexuality (since all our striving for knowledge is sexual in nature). And so, they had to replace Wisdom's image in Eden with a Satan.

Merely a mimic, a trickster, a provocateur; this Satan was no sexual seducer. Blind, locked in himself, he could take in an observer fearlessly. Everyone knows people like this snake and would prefer to fear them—rather than face the seducer within themselves. Why face seduction at all when we can project our fears of change onto animals? Why uncover our hidden desire to be glorified?

The seducer in Eden must have been someone we loved like ourselves, or like a parent. Without parents in Eden, it had to be animals we loved. Lilith and Samael is the answer the Scroll provides, according to Nosei: a mated pair of snakes, reduced to one snake in our anemic version of Genesis. There's nothing bad about them, the way it sounded. But we have been made to forget everything there was in Eden, everything we watched so carefully and intensely while we were there. Doctrine has lulled our minds and haunted our reading.

Eden embodies the principle of evolution, that's what Nosei was most impressed by. The Scroll described it in the form of trees, particularly in Wisdom's tree of Knowledge. The tree is open-eyed—fruited with eyes—and seduces the observer with knowledge, leading him out of himself. To grow, to evolve. This is how Archie taught us to read the Scroll. He seduced Nosei and me.

[Julie '84]

1995

"Imagine another person," Archie said. I can hear him talking. "Imagine what they want from you, and then imagine what would surprise them. Now imagine another form of life. Yes, it's hard, other forms don't imagine as we do, if they do at all. Now imagine Eden, where everything speaks to us. We are evolving toward Eden again if we can imagine it. But then comes the awful part."

I knew it, there had to be a moral. We haven't been going on in this manner—our backs to Eden, Archie called it—for thousands of years for nothing.

"We have to let go of it to get it." He said that several times and it sounded kind of odd for a scientist, like a record stuck in a groove, but it didn't sound ominous. Anyway, I was already used to his coining new phrases, ever since he began his sessions with mother.

"To restore Eden we need to acknowledge the loss, to 'act-knowledge'," Archie said. "We have to put our successes aside and embrace the failures. We have to extract the errors there and learn from them. Embrace the errors," he cried.

Now this sounded sort of like the blues. Bad means good. I got it—but it felt too easy. What was I letting go of? I thought I already let go of most things: I let go of idealizing my father, then my mother, then just about everyone. What else? My failures were already my successes!

"Then that is it," Archie said when I had made that gleeful response. "You have to give up failing and embrace success again. You have to go back to Eden; you can't pretend there's no home back there for you."

"Isn't that like becoming a fundamentalist?" I said.

"No, that would be as easy as swallowing a pill. That would just be another kind of failure, of dropping into someone else's vision. No, it's YOUR home you must go back to, the one you shut the door upon."

Gradually I did realize what he meant and it felt awful. Although I was still living at home with mother, he meant my childhood: the haunted house I'd been trying to forget. I clutched my stomach, it was churning so fast. If I went back to that home I was doomed. My father was mad, my mother was blind to it. I would suffocate there.

"Yes, you would feel like a betrayer. That is the most awful feeling. You would feel like Adam and Eve. You would have broken faith. And with whom? With what Creator? You have begun to restore the appropriate questions—to restore Eden."

[Julie]

Tree of Knowledge

On Seventh Day, the Creator rested. What did he do? Slept with his bride, Wisdom; rested in her arms—but it is expunged from text, along with most everything else about her! Irrepressible, she remains for all to find who love hidden things. Mother of things within things, seeds in their pods and testes. And she the mother of evolution, driving us within to know more. What stops us? Pleasure and pain stop us, pleasure as we stop to rest, pain stopping to heal. Pleasure in children and families, pain in them—either one stops us. Growth stops when we retreat—into families, into needs, our fantasies, our work.

Yet she is there, hidden even there. If we find her and find our will to curiosity, we will go out into the wide world again and seek to grow.

Could it be the Creator in traditional religion is one who created human species in his image and so, forbade us to evolve? But she, Wisdom, leads us on to imagine and to become something more than ourselves. Is that not what tempted Adam and Eve in the Garden, seeking to know more than themselves in spite of Creator's wish? How did they, being poor naked creatures, defy him except by simple biological act, eating? Did not fruit of the tree fall to fertilize the ground? She was there, Wisdom, God's bride, there in the Garden itself: She was the tree of Knowledge herself.

[Shechner]

DICKINSON

To hold both—metaphor and true reality—in mind at same time, this is the work of our great writers. I heard it from a renowned lecturer, Svitz, who would have been bewildered to face Scroll with no great writer known. Yet I thought of Scroll author like a voice of history and science: both storytelling. These fields tell us—not about growing or resting, not about pain or pleasure—but all these things simultaneously. Not metaphor, not reality, but both these things held in mind! For Wisdom, life is a storytelling, unfolding what is hidden, and each of our lives a story up to us to tell. We all tell it, mostly to ourselves, also to our family and friends. What a bore when we stop growing and instead tell story of our careers—in place of the story of our inner lives. Is my story in journals, in pictures, in awards? Snore!

One shy woman's inner story—such as the subject of Svitz's lecture, the American, Emily Dickinson—puts a whole generation of noble careers into eclipse. Because she held both things in mind, the metaphor and the reality, the growing and the resting. Creator would have us rest on our laurels, but just look how Emily Dickinson spoke back to him. When Wisdom speaks through me, I don't know which of us speaks.

[Shechner]

Adam Speaks

I experience this flower with awe, through all senses, even the last sense, hearing—I hear it as it spoke in Eden. There we spoke in innocence, and now such speaking must be through memory. I hear it in memory, here as I inhale this flower's deliciously scented mind. It is my own mind I lend it to speak—and my mother's mind, the imagination that comes from Wisdom. Experience is the world into which she brought me, experience and the time to learn its boundaries, come closer to this flower yellow as the sun: I ask of it its history. Why yellow; l petals of silk, why this sweet nectary—and, in time, I see the flying animal drawn to her sugars.

I learn of myself looking at this pair, see that I am the explorer my mother created, the thinker. My father created me to be watcher in the garden, an observer. He asked of me pure observance, a transcendent growth toward heaven. From my mother I learned that growth must have a partner and I must have a mate. A partner is the part who watches, as I watch her. Eve allows me to see myself in her, to hold it—and to turn in another direction, also. Together we grow toward earth, toward a future on earth, as we explore the way to evolve beyond this human form.

Yet, as I look back to Eden I want to weep. I watch myself here, observing like a criminal—as if I were to hide behind a tree in Eden. There was no thought of hiding there, not until the mistakes and the learning at Mother's tree. Even then, in Eden the hiding was an intimacy, a hiding-together that drew Eve and I into the bower. Although Eve is near, now I am alone again in the looking back, as if I were a father to my lost personality in Eden.

Then, observing was a naming, knowing, a coming closer. Now, all that I approach bears its own mystery and also the weight of loss, the distance from Eden. The loss says something is always missing, pushes me to learn to remember. The more I remember, the more I grow, since at the bottom of all my memory is Eden. If I can grow out of this human weight, I may find myself in Eden again.

[*Scroll of the History of Adam*]

A Mommy-Daddy

I took a flight out of JFK, posted to arrive in Tel Aviv eleven hours later, nonstop. The time did not account for the hour of boarding at one end and the hour of customs check at the other. The last hour of standing around and anxiety and frantic rushing were redeemed by knowing we would not see the plane again. The 727's cabin had turned into a huge hotel bedroom you leave after a long night of going nowhere: sheets and blankets strewn over and under the beds, overturned paper coffee cups, loose change, matchbooks, half-used jelly packets on the floor.

The bathroom was a shambles of wadded towels, tissue and newspapers, toilet unflushed, soap scum on all surfaces. It was a relief to leave it behind forever, in the care of cynical maids who've seen it all before.

Arriving in Tel Aviv at sunset was anti-climactic, the unearthly colors spoiled by artifice as they spilled over a seaside movie-set. The scene was literally flooded with extras from pre-War Warsaw, such was my first impression of Tel Aviv. And my first impression of Betti Peleg: Vienna would have been a more likely setting for her. She could have been Freud's first female patient. A handsome but inscrutable shell, like a credenza that may have Dresden china inside but that also may be empty. She resembled a movie Freudian, wearing a mannish suit and smoking a cheroot. Probably the only job a woman could hold and smoke a small cigar; not even a movie actress would dare.

Betti was not the daring type. She was critical of anything stylish, and found nothing outlandish in her costume. It was the uniform of a psychoanalyst, pure and simple. Since she was used to being an object of transference, a character in someone else's drama, her true character needed to be flat, two-dimensional: the back of the mirror in which her privacy could be maintained. What is more pat and cartoonish than something instantly recognizable, eccentric, even quaint? She looked utterly unlike a follower of nonconformist fashion. She might be a child's version of a mommy-daddy, long cigar and long skirt mixed up together. Mustaches? no; sweet perfume? yes.

Betti has wild, bushy gray hair. She is built in such a

way that she appears always to be at attention, standing ramrod straight. She has the air of observing others.

She is always disappointed in men. She expects her choice to be mainstream, solid and familiar. Distinguished, yes, but only in reputation, not curious-looking. Certainly not eccentric, as she appeared to others, especially to the kind of man she wished to attract. Eccentric might be too kind; bizarre, even. Interesting men were drawn to her, and remarkable men, but to Betti they were exotics, and sooner or later she found them peculiar. They were not men in whom she saw projected her own unceremonious and resolute simplicity.

Betti lives in the house her father was thrown out of. It's the only house on her street fronting the beach, flanked by small tourist hotels.

[Nosei, '84]

Back to Eden

Eden is an intellectual frontier. To approach it, I had to turn around and open the trunk. Opening it, who but myself to frame the event, fill in context, hold the camera that watches; also, to direct. A home movie for the immense Imax screen. To see myself, I've had to become the unseen director of my own life—exactly the contract with destiny I avoided in the past. I'm just another actor, I told myself back in the '80s. Or, when I was feeling backed against the wall, I said to myself, *I'm* the audience. Entertain *me.* And I was entertained, though I have to admit now I had insinuated myself backstage: in back of the words themselves, taking them apart. Yikes, it's almost nasty.

This is different. Facing Eden, here's the map: it's not a film, and it's not a story, either. We start with myth, we get there with a guide, and we know we're almost there—when we've lost the conventional past behind us, with just about everyone we knew. To wit: God gave us seven memories. The Sixth, the Day on which we evolved, is all we know—that, and a bit of the Seventh. The first Five, establishing our home, our ecosystem Eden, are still lost to us. The Scroll helps us retrieve these lost Memories. All Six Days tell our cultural origin, the way home. After we've retrieved them all can we absorb the Seventh, the creative rest before evolving. And being "creative" in this sense of resting will mean recreating Eden. A dream, say, that is too real.

What the Scroll makes clear is that time's running out. "The earth will be covered over with people and all the animals, even the fish in the sea, will begin to die." I couldn't believe how a writer three millenia ago imagined this day, until I realized that he was alot closer to Eden than we are: his imagination fertile with creation stories we have lost. Just think of the story of Noah and how the writer who imagined that fate for the world could also probably imagine our present predicament. Here we are, threatened by biological forces we're just learning about, from the ozone layer down to the smart viruses, and that's already an old tale to the Noah-story writer.

So what's holding us back from seeing it, our future unfolding before our eyes? We're like children whose parents are battling and who send us off to the movies—and we don't realize our weakness. Our wish for peace and their embrace leaves us feeling guilty, as if we might have been responsible for the fight. Yes, inside we know we're the only ones who can save them. Those parents are our parental God. We've reduced them to One—it's as if we have a father but not an equal mother. All our experience in the world after we left our Eden—that home ecosystem in which we evolved—tells us so.

We know not one but two natures, wild and tame. We live mostly in the tame one, domesticated, by ourselves. The single God is lord of this realm, setting man above wild nature. We know little about his wild side, and that's because wild nature is the realm of Wisdom—his consort, our mother. Okay, only *we* can heal this divorce within ourselves, and if we don't, the entire earth absorbs the danger that our guilty overcrowding has already begun. We'll be washed right out of our seats, that's for sure.

[Nosei, '94]

To Be Less

Two directions life takes after forty, wrote my old friend in the psychological field, Betti Peleg. Some want to settle in and enjoy it, however it turns out; others want to continue growing, shaping. Those with no choice, who have to struggle and make ends meet, can just as easily refuse to grow. They can say to themselves: The kids will be the ones to enjoy things.

What about minority who are compelled to grow? Dr. Peleg did not refer to those driven to accumulate. The ones who take on challenge are her concern. They aren't motivated to *do* more in life but rather to *be* less—that's how I recall she put it. To shape oneself into a person who confronts challenges by outthinking them.

Best way to explain it is to consider challenges every person faces in later life. Death is one, leaving a legacy another. Many turn to the traditional sources in religion for one, or consider philanthropy for the other. But let's just deny that death is a challenge. Just say it's a stumbling block or decoy like all those other decoys in life that keep us from growing less human. Peleg would say: outthink it. "Less human" is my own handle.

Less human? Isn't that a descent, back down toward the apes? Hardly, but that's how badly we were taught meaning of evolution. We made the mistake of taking some comfort in thinking the human species is grand. We can rest on our laurels. Same drive in society to give up mind's struggle that you find in people over forty. Of all life on earth, we seem to say, we are the fittest.

Thinking about people is easy now, from a vantage beyond, but it was never my cup of tea. I preferred silence, the great stillness that seeps into your bones as you slowly peel back layers of the earth and discover traces of life silent for eons. Those bones never spoke to me yet filled my mind. Erudite scientists told stories about the bones, elaborated histories—but I just enjoyed their gorgeous stillness.

Then one day, a voice came out of the ground. Checked

my ears and whacked myself along the head, to be sure I wasn't hearing things. But I knew the earth better than anything and that is where it came from, deeper down than the fossil record goes. It spoke to me the way the Bible says an angel would speak to someone. This was no angel, bore no message. She spoke for herself. She said, "You are about to make a discovery. You will find a pot made of bronze and sealed within, a skin parchment. There is written down all that I spoke when your ancient language changed from shapes into letters, when your people began to live in cities and build libraries.

"It was in Hebron and it was to the ear of a man like yourself, a man digging in the earth. He dug in order to bury his wife but as she lay in her shroud beside the grave he was digging, not another soul in sight, he talked softly to her as he worked. And not just to her. He listened to what she said also. It was a conversation I had long missed hearing. It was the way Adam and Eve spoke in the Garden, before they had found each other.

"Like that man thousands of years ago, you are a pure listener. The time has come again for humans to listen. When I spoke to Adam and Eve, it was before writing had come to take the place of voices. Writing made it possible for cities to grow, and when I spoke the second time, to Abram Elish, I wished that all humankind would grow to listen, as the book spread. But the Creator stopped it again, just as he had in the Garden.

"First he put fear in the way, and then it was the bureaucrats—the scribes and officials—of religion. They put pure listening under a spell, so that no one could hear what they read. Instead, they needed an interpretation; only an official interpretation could make the text intelligible. There were fights among the interpreters, until finally the priests stepped in and said, enough. The text can no more be consulted. Instead, we will write new stories of our own origins. From that time onward, the only way a writer could avoid the official taboos was to approach the truth indirectly, to be both naked and dressed, to don a mask, to learn the arts of beauty, irony, and sexual seduction—arts that were mine in Eden.

"Few writers and few readers could break the spell of official interpretation. These have grown fewer with time, until now, in your twentieth century, the few who remain are lost in their own minds, growing madder and madder."

The more the voice talked the less anxious I became. Still, in part of me suspicion grew that I myself was one of the mad ones. Is that how madness comes, out of the blue? Yesterday, everyone considered me the model of stability. Yet this voice was so clearly not in my head but coming from the ground it did not sound the least bit supernatural. I decided it was a voice that synthesized the thoughts I had accumulated from a long time of silent digging at this site. A kind of computerized voice that played back an intense moment of interpretation that my mind had made. I could translate such a condensed moment of thought into the slower medium of speech. Yes, I convinced myself, the shock of insight warranted this method of translation. I stopped worrying, listened more carefully.

It was a low rumbling tone, as if a woman were struggling to speak while in deep sleep. No, I shouldn't say struggling; the words came through steady, confident. It was the voice of an educated women but not necessarily one from a major culture. She might even have been the daughter of a tribal chieftain. Feels a bit contrived to be describing it now. At the time, it never occurred to me who she was. She was a fact, perhaps more palpable than the fact of my own self. How a young child must feel when beginning to interpret its mother's voice, even before it can speak a word of its own.

It might even be the way the almost-born infant hears its mother's voice while still in her belly. Strange as the thought is, this explains my feeling that her voice comes from far away in a bit of a rumble but is nevertheless a steady voice when you concentrate on listening. Perhaps all unborn children are focused this way—while the other senses have not yet come into play.

[Shechner]

Returning Voice

What happens to world-famous scientists when they encounter inexplicable voices—whether from outer space or from mythic memory? Will they resist and cry, "It cannot be!" Will they agonize about being believed (like UFO-sighting airline pilots)? No, they're too secure in themselves for that. Here is the challenge for which they were trained, a Mt. Sinai of interpretation. What difference if the voice belongs to a distant galaxy or a mutation of the psyche? If they're brave, it's the *listening* they live for, rapt as a baby while its mother hums.

The first scientist to know Wisdom's voice, the archaeologist Archibad Shechner, thought he was mad, perhaps because he was so afraid of madness. He went to every extreme to show that the Scroll was authentic. "I proved it! I proved it was the pre-biblical Scroll discussed by the early rabbis," he shouted in Dr. Betti Peleg's soundproofed office.

But nobody proves anything like that by himself, Betti knew. Checks and balances, carbon-dating, philology—all these had yet to have their say. She was proud of being a skeptical scientist. She was even skeptical of her own field of psychology. So it wasn't hard for her to sympathize with Archie's fear of being branded a madman. Just to avoid such charges against herself, Betti became a student of madmen. Her father, she was convinced, had been one when he ran off with a Greek muse. She was just eight, then. For over a year her classmates giggled behind her back about it, and one boy said: "You're going to be a nun yourself when you grow up."

"Where did that boy get such a notion?" Betti Peleg recounted to me. "I hated nuns with a passion that scared me. It was the only time I was afraid of my own feelings," she told Julie, her only child. Right away, Betti realized her mistake.

"I want to be a nun," said Julie, who was already nineteen and suffering the slights of being prematurely discharged from the army. Nobody knew the reason but the stigma of a discharge, especially for a young girl, could be devastating. "I want to be a nun for a few years and read a thousand books and then walk away from the convent declaring that my Jewish past is haunting me. The Jews had returned to claim me."

[Nosei, '94]

1995

Perhaps I took the businessman's entreaty too literally those two weeks in Milan, on my first plane trip. He told me I would find a business for myself and I went searching for it after I arrived. My cousin thought I had developed an enthusiasm for her field. I did ask a lot of questions, but that was my way. I thought there might be some business in anthropology, but never could get at it with my cousin. I thought perhaps merchandising—maybe the cave paintings, in reproductions... It didn't look promising. Her husband's uncle was in banking, and that soon attracted my attention. I learned a good deal about banks during those two weeks.

I even went to visit one with uncle. I liked the way everyone at the bank knew what to do. Everything was clear, businesslike. It began, it ended. And it repeated everyday. Each day, a beginning and an ending. There was a place to go, a space of your own. The day was filled with transactions and lunch. Even the transactions began and ended. It was so different from what I knew, from mother's work, from my school studies—never an ending and such long distances from the beginning. This, on the other hand, seemed self-contained—a place to put myself part of the day. And the rest? I fantasized about the rest. I didn't suspect that it would remain a fantasy; that deep down, I was preparing a place to put myself—my inner life stuffed inside of a fantasy of business—so my outside could be for mother.

When I returned from Italy, I began looking for a summer job—a business to get into. Mother couldn't quite understand the obsession. She seemed to find it interesting—something that added to my specialness, something to muse over like a phenomenon. She said that I could help in her office—clerical, transcription, errands. I told her no, that I wanted to work for a business. She said her office was a place of business. I said I wanted commerce—a real place of trade. "But this is a place of trade, unlike any you'll find," she replied.

"But, what is being traded? I mean, other than a service of treatment, one to one?

"What is being traded," she said, "are two dramas—the personal drama, and an interpretive drama of working through. It is art *and* work."

As she spoke I thought that it was true—nothing could compare to it. She sounded visionary, involved in something unique and important. So, why did I want something else? At a loss inside, I told her I wanted another kind of business, for right now, maybe at a bank. Before I knew it, we were going to banks, seeing people she knew. I was soon working at Bank Hapoalim, the "workers" bank. I was a runner, and I did clerical—filing and xeroxing, pleasant monotony. One of the senior clerks took an interest in me—a woman in her fifties, named Mrs. Sirota. Plain but neat. She was conservative in her dress, but looked smart. She dressed with a precision that matched her movements and speech. She taught me how to use an adding machine. There were computers already, but she thought everyone should know and master the adding machine.

One day, mother said she was going to come by and take me to lunch. I felt excited, then I felt nervous, watching the clock, making sure I didn't miss her. Mrs. Sirota asked if I wanted to try the adding machine. I said not today, although I really wanted to. Inside, I felt like I couldn't take my mind away, that I had to be ready for mother. And I felt afraid to be seen at the adding machine, almost like I was on stage. After that day, I began a bad habit on the machine. I stopped using my little finger. It wasn't much noticed on the adding machine but it was on the typewriter.

At some point a few years later I began using all ten fingers again. Sometime when I started the transcription. I had forgotten about the little finger. I remembered on the way to Switzerland. I thought of it because I felt so different. It seemed that I could never have been the kind of person who couldn't use all my fingers. I felt so good, so happy. Bad feelings, bad thoughts seemed gone. My search for a business seemed over.

Still, I stayed with that bank. I worked my way up, each summer. Even when I was transcribing for mother, for

Archie, I continued my job at the bank. I didn't need the money. Mother didn't want me to work so much. But I could slice my life, my day in two—the bank, the transcription. I thought I wanted the bank for me, something of my own, a way to assert my independence, but I barely remember being there. Maybe that was the point. It was a place to zone out.

I do remember my times in the vault. I loved to go in there. A place of security. It was obvious. Everything valuable was safe and in its place. But maybe it was more that nothing was required of me in there. It existed and would go on existing without me.

[Julie]

Waiting for You in Earth

"Those unprepared to evolve," I heard Wisdom's voice say the first time, "are condemned to repeat the past: they grow to feel superior to other creations, and to die in this belief. They are not superior to even a blade of grass." Frozen in my tracks by this declaration, but Wisdom was laughing. "The prophets of your Bible saw it clearly—'all flesh is grass'—as their hearts grew unburdened with the power of poetry." Immediately understood that certain sciences are writing today's poetry, translating grass of the field into a library of empowering texts. That is how I knew voice was authentic: my own understanding became the earth in which hers took root.

"Now this is how it works for the humans prepared to

evolve," she continued. And this is what I understood: Each bladed plant contains many volumes of evolution's history, chemical knowledge, seductive narratives of beauty. And these tell eternal stories of which humans never tire, tales about persuasion and seduction, strategies of disguise and those of transformation. Finally, they tell of death.

"Your death is the most natural part of you. He is your equal; he is the only one who can say what you want to hear. Who are you? Where do you come from and where do you go? Why was the universe created? Your death has answers, for he exists even before the universe and after it. When the last star has weakened, your death will still be there." But how acknowledge him?

"You incorrectly seek a living equal in death, a father of yourself, yet he becomes as your child: you know his future better than your own. Look past him— your death—past the shoulder of earth. Your eyes made to see, see nothing. You who have failed to arrive in your mother's bed, failed to be born, are here all alone. No one but you can know it. Keep him with you always. He is the sword upon whom the hero falls. The blade of grass. Without him the grass withers, the flower fades—for whom would they live but him? He observes such living things unknown to themselves. He is the translator of what all becomes in my world—a new creation, evolved from within." Way to recognize him, I understood, is to observe what remains when all wishes are gone: All life desires to eat and be immortal—but inside is its mother's wisdom, its bottom desire to evolve.

[Shechner]

1995

What did I do for thirty years? I observed my mother's life. From the craziest patients to the maddest politicians, her life was crammed with the most interesting people in the country. Then I learned that she was the observer and I was the "act-knowledger" of it, as Archie would say. The translator. I had to make something happen. My mother would only watch, as she did with her patients and assorted celebrities. So I hid from her, gave her nothing of myself to watch.

With this understanding I interpreted Wisdom. She hid as I did, but we are no observers. The Creator set up everything, creating it so he could watch. Archie spoke for what couldn't be seen: Wisdom within the plants at the origin of everything on land—and that put my mother in her place as observer again. Like the Creator, mother wanted to be known as an original authority, but she couldn't be. And neither could the Creator without his partner, so he had to turn to commands. All this comes through Archie's tapes, though he couldn't approach it calmly.

What do animals talk about? I mean not simply with sounds but every other kind of language? Sex and possessions and danger. That leaves only one discrete subject for humans only, "Why are we here?" I've heard that question other ways, in the Judean hills, in the cries of an animal as it's being eaten. Then they are gone, the question answered by a nourished silence.

It's the plants Archie found you should turn to, for answers. They create and offer food; once eaten, they are transported to another life, another site for seeds to fall to earth. Parts of themselves are eaten—it would be death if it were us—as a seduction. They seduce us to act for them. That is why we're here, Archie would say—for them, for her.

"People will say that's crazy," I once said to him. "'We can do anything we want to a plant, it's at our mercy,' they'll say. They'll say you're nuts. Nobody's going to get more interested in the Scroll."

And then I saw him fall silent for the longest time. He clutched graying curls of his hair in each fist and rocked his head slowly from side to side.

"Talk to my mother. She will listen to everything and make sure it's all recorded. See if you can convince her." That's what I said. I sent him back to my mother.

[Julie]

Eve Speaks

It is so lonely, so eerily quiet, now that the plants no longer speak to us. Each speaks, instead, to only a very few animals, crawling and flying things, and it speaks in colors, shapes, smells, textures, and tastes—grand senses, but among them all, hearing is gone. The gorgeous music of their voices—soft, intruding only when it seemed I wanted to hear—is lost in this world.

The animals make sounds, but not many, sometimes just their legs scraping or their wings humming. In Eden there was a bodiless richness, each being filled with a world of sound. Here that sound is simply whatever's in hearing distance, a chorus of sounds that says merely the time of day. This world is like one single being in its sounds when compared to the abundance of Eden.

And then there is the new sound, fear. A threatening voice, or a cry of struggle, or the piercing cry of hopelessness—silenced in a moment by death and then the fainter, working sounds of eating.

Yet the colors now, the shapes of mouthing flowers, speak purple velvet to a hawkmoth or white satin to a bat. And there the animal finds its nectar. Where, then, is mine? It is in the sweetness of Adam's thighs, sweeter than it seemed in Eden for being a token of our fountain, our mother.

The movement of music in this world must be caught from the flying animals and our own voices, the sexual climax held back, further and further. In Eden it happened all at once—beginning, middle and end—so that music came from within, blood vibrating, the bones humming, and the Garden, severing, reassembling continually back into place, one sound next to another. Never as now, merely one sound following on another, rushing into time. All time in Eden happened at once, so that breathing was music, accompanying life. Here breathing has become silent like the plants, the trees—no harmonies are heard. Merely the mind speaks, thoughts translating into sounds, into a music acted out—but now, barely listened to.

Already I have seen things die and learned that death is the mother of beauty. Utter loss gives a poignancy to this life in time. In the Garden, beauty was taught by the selflessly dying plants, living for the ravishing complexity of the food they created, keeping all in life fed.

[*Scroll of the History of Adam*]

Adam Speaks

To be an observer—it's almost as if I wasn't here. Then who am I? Nothing looks back at me, as everything did in Eden, not unless I stir it. All the animals are small and hiding but when the squirrel comes up to me he turns and runs as I reach out my hand. He too was alone and thought I was a bush until I moved.

But then I saw a tree in the water, wavering. What kind of wind stirs it so, I thought, and then saw it was a reflection of a tree on the bank. I looked up to the bank, saw many trees of differing size and shape but not one resembling the water reflection. I was scared for a moment, why?

In that moment the imagined tree in the water had a life of its own—beyond my conscious thought. That was me, then, *me* in the landscape, existing outside myself; I could not possess that thought and there it was; I could not name that tree, as I named all I faced in Eden.

Later, when it was dark, I thought of all this and realized that the tree in water was dark, a dark blue, taking on the water's color. On the bank, the trees with their leaves were a light green, made lighter by the light coming through. In the water, the light played on the surface and made the tree a dense shape, the leaves letting no light through. So when I looked to the shore I was tricked by the light into seeing different shapes. My memory holds the images true, so that I may find the trick. And now, even in the dark, my memory holds the moment, and I am more alone again; before, tricked by changing light, in my fear I found another presence sharing my vision, a presence there before me, like a mother. I was happy then, for a moment, transformed in time.

Later, finding the trick, I knew that I would always have to learn what I didn't know, venturing out alone. I would make the mistakes made in Eden, over and over again. I mistaked the tree in water for a god, a presence not of my world—the mother I never had. Was she there, nonetheless, hidden deeper under things than it appears? I have to think so; and when I don't, my loneliness crawls inside my skin, turning it into a cold, rough hide.

[*Scroll of the History of Adam*]

Chapter 4

Chapter 4

Memorandum

Pardon one last intrusion but I've learned something and it makes me impatient with the fundamentalists in trendy sheep's clothing who defend the one and only conventional novel. At this point I already hear the head-scratching. What is a Guide doing in a novel? Strong characters are what's in fashion, not this nonhuman stuff. Too much nature is discomforting and that's why we have bestselling Stephen King novels and psychotic psychoanalysts—along with the new wave of pseudo-courageous memoirs proving we humans can survive anything.

Betti Peleg may not be a strong character but she's a tough listener. And even though Shechner voiced it and she produced it, it's the voice from the hole that's a complex character. "Words make a character?" you ask. "Just words?" I might have said the same myself, but now I've been through the book a couple of times and can say there's something in those words, something too quick or slow for our eyes to visualize as yet, but it's out there.

The nattering New York Times says most people today are uneasy about Western civilization. We're about to go through dramatic change, the editorial says, and we need more solid grounding to confront it. It's like a fire is coming and all we can think of is making more fire. That way leads madness, that's for sure. We need water, not fire, and the mental ponds of our culture are drying up because we're disconnected from nature. At least in our heads we are. It takes a voice breaking in to wake us up, like a river crashing through sandbags. That's how I read what happened to Archibald Shechner. We've got to start listening to real rivers and real living things besides ourselves. The Guide to a New World is all about that, though I didn't get it at first. I had the old marketplace reaction: no name brand backing, no track record. Never heard of the author. Larry Rivers—him I've heard of, but not "A. River" or "Ecosystem"—what kind of an ethnic name is that? Greenlandish?

For the longest time, I'm told—it's obvious even today—most of us assumed the human body and the brain were the most complex creations in nature. The human body—of course that means the male body in officialdom—was created in the image of the divine. Even after Darwin, evolution was interpreted as a kind of progress toward our human shape, the crown of creation. Brain sizes are still measured and consciousness scoped as if we're the height of all development.

So in this book we find out that the human body and brain are pretty puny in comparison to creative ecosystems. It hasn't reached the popular brain yet, that's for sure, which can't tell a habitat from an ecosystem (never meant much to me before, either). But if you call an ecosystem a habitat, you squash its complexity behind the simpler needs of a single organism. It's no surprise, then, that most habitats today are degraded ecosystems and not creative ones, often on life support—about as much capable of evolving the diversity of life which made them as a eunuch and a courtesan.

You could say the human habitat compares well to a termite's. A city of species-made structures plus domestications of a few other animals and plants. The concept of a creative ecosystem—a garden of Eden in which Homo sapiens evolved (and which, in effect, created us) is about as far from consciousness as the sphinxes who sat at Eden's gate. You know, half-man, half-beast. They've got them all emasculated in memory, like the rest of the Eden story, but those beasts (male and female, like everything else) must each have had its hard-on when they saw Adam and Eve!

Anyway, the ecosystem, we're about to learn, is infinitely more complex than the human brain, which is a pale reflection of it. What forces beyond comprehension allowed so many thousands of species to live in harmony? And how does even one of them, say a panther, kill enough deer to eat yet the dear thrive? And how do the deer refrain from overeating the grass, etc.—any creature out of whack could collapse the whole living system.

Just that word "refrain" suggests an intention that isn't there. So what *is* there? That's the question just beginning to be asked. The creative principle of the ecosystem is behind our history and our origins. It's also the secret of where we're headed, because we've known what we can do based on the culture we copied from our own Homo-creating ecosystem in bygone Africa.

All our secrets, then, are in the past—and just ahead of us. Read on (and pardon my tumult).

[Seth Greene]

I have learned to understand Shechner and follow his thoughts when they appear to drift. Therefore I have transcribed his notations of the Scroll in plain language. Likewise the interpretation of Wisdom as she spoke to him. It was always a question that Wisdom asked and then answered herself, as if Archie was a medium she was using. Indeed he was, as he recounted these passive dialogues on tape, each preceded by a day of the week. 'In the new world,' Wisdom eventually told him, 'each day of the week reflects the original seven days of creation.' He would transcribe one a day and continued through eight weeks. The last week contained the days recounting a new Eden, after humans had re-evolved.

And in the ninth week he disappeared. That was a few days after Everett Nosei arrived, whom I met at the Sened party, that fiasco meant to honor the Scroll and instead considering Harriman Svitz an honorable replacement.

[Betti Peleg]

[Sunday] A Planted Desire

"Wisdom asks: Can the mind evolve? No, mind has no wish to leave the body. The body pursues growth through mistakes the mind makes and vice versa: this process yields intimacy. Mind and body can be a perfectly intimate system, as it will be again in Eden. One desire continues through the Creator's Eden and the hidden world that is mine. Reproduction is life. In Eden, the plants reproduced food for animals, and in this world animals also live to reproduce as their divine purpose. In Eden, hidden in the tree of Knowledge, I drew close to me the humans who had tasted intimate congress—as I have known it with the Creator. All mistakes must be reproduced, the humans found, until they could learn from them, and grow in knowledge. And in their hidden minds, thoughts must learn as well from a reproduction of mistaken thinking. The Creator, however, turns away from sexual congress, denies mistakes, dominates imagination—where only he and his deeds are encouraged to reproduce. In their place, he demands transcendence, a reaching to him in the heavens and to his reflected heaven in our hearts. This transcendence, which is but a shadow of the spiritual, splits the human into two, mind and body—and leaves the body behind.

No evolving can be done by mind alone; instead, the human mind yields its imagination to transcendence and a reaching out of only half a human. It is the desire to grow and evolve—as millions of species have done in the past, plant and animal, and as Adam and Eve had accomplished, finding themselves in Eden—that is my desire planted in every living thing.

[Monday] Storytelling

Wisdom asks: Is there a way to distinguish truth from fiction? If they are a unity—if you can't have one without the other—the world *stops*. The plain sense of things is impossible without a metaphor, at least impossible to represent. A house, a tree, a planet—these things are human representations of the literal, not the real thing itself. In reality, a house is a system including wood, brick, glass etc. Even a tree is a system, including roots, leaves, flowers etc. "Tree" is our metaphor for one kind of plant in relation to another kind, say a bush, which has no trunk system. For that reason we call a palm a tree when scientists know it is not: to us, it "looks like a tree."

Take away the metaphor and the world stops. No more "big bang" or "first day of creation." What's left? An absence of these things—and that can't be real either, since the things we imagine absent weren't real. So we must be able to hold both—metaphor and true reality—in mind at the same time, and this is the work of great writers. History is storytelling. Science too is storytelling.

When lost in a story, we are growing or resting—not simply feeling pain or pleasure but both of these things at the same time and more. It's as if you are in another world and have no powers there. Anything you might do—answer the phone, look for something—and you will find yourself expelled, losing the spell: the world you have dwelled in has *stopped.*

[Tuesday] **Expose**

Wisdom asks: Why is nature's power not always evident but hidden? It's always there to be felt, in our vulnerability to death. But we can't see this power any longer in the crippled wildernesses that survive on earth, the ragged jungles, or in the puny forests that cities continue to encroach upon. Children especially do not see it; our childhoods are withdrawn from nature's power, though our hidden fears know it. To expose it, we must realize the natural world is parental, ancestral: we've grown up, left our home, no longer recognize it, but the power of these parents is that we are dependent on them even after we've grown. They provide our food, the air we breathe. We can imitate it, but we cannot generate its power.

[Wednesday] Depending on Death

Wisdom asks: Of what are we afraid, swamps? Inside us lurk swamps of failure and jungles of loathing. Can these turn into valued wetlands and rainforests too?

Religions will tell you yes. They hold out that hope of ultimate purpose and redemption. But they don't really want to go into the swamps and learn all about the wetlands ecosystem and Miccosukee Native Americans. What they want to do is *transcend* the swamps. Get past them. *Rise above them.*

Rise where? Heaven, where the angels are. What are angels? Us—potentially us, that is—without bodies and without fears. Without bodies there's no clear death and no simple pain. Perhaps there is singing and praise.

Certainly it would be ridiculous to speak of angelic wetlands and rainforests. They are ecosystems and their evolution depends on life and death. Just as silly would be to speak of evolution beyond death. Angels do not evolve. They are stuck in what they are. No more growth is necessary. To evolve, we must envision two things, to live and die, in the same time.

[Thursday] A Wild Swamp

Wisdom asks: Do we want to go back and live in harmony with the earth like the Indians of the Rain Forest? No. We just want to visit it, we want it to be part of our experience, our lives. We want it, that is to say, as our pet. That may sound cruel but then we don't think of ourselves as cruel when we keep dogs and cats and parrots as pets, do we? These animals enjoy living with us. The same is true for our landscaping and houseplants and public parks: there everything is watered and trimmed and well taken care of.

There, in other words, we are the gods. Nature is a pet of ours. The pet gets sick or won't stop howling? It may be time to destroy it. (The error crouches in wait.)

So if nature is now innocence itself, like our own childhoods, how do we face it? As humans, we face our own childhoods in having and raising children of our own. But the plants and animals we keep around us are not so innocent anymore because they are our dependents. And the remaining wildernesses? They too are dependent on us for survival: every schoolkid now learns that the last Rain Forest may be cut down in their lifetime if human behavior doesn't change. Tigers, elephants, whales are already endangered species. Will the rare, giant cypress—ancestor tree of the California Redwood—be seen again?

We are losing our innocence altogether. In its place will be human memory and human stories, inside us and not out, invisible. The supreme irony: our last hope is knowledge, and the knowledge that lost us Eden is the only thing that can get it back. When we look at a wetlands as a source of knowledge it grows back into a wild swamp full of mysteries. The knowledge of how it lives and how it originated and where our place in its history lies. These things—including what we call evolutionary biology and microbiology, evolutionary psychology, history and chemistry, evolutionary ecology—these fields of knowledge are still in their wild infancy. The chemical intelligence of plants is still too wild a concept for most people to grasp.

But if we can get enough knowledge before it's too late we can create another Eden in which we can evolve. The wildness—knowledge coupled with imagination—will remain in our heads. All that we'll miss is the fear. And that was unnecessary in Eden.

[Friday] Fear of Evolution

Wisdom asks: Does *less* human really mean more barbaric? Only if civilization is our overbearing goal, to the exclusion of nonhuman life on this planet. Our post-war human breakdown was the atom bomb race and a new brush with self-extinction. Apparently, we've saved ourselves with treaties of disarmament. Treaties against pollution are also possible, but treaties against *growth*? Stop developing, stop wanting a better life, stop wanting to relax? No, that's all too human.

Less human does not mean a descent but a painful growing; it means *evolving*. That is our greatest fear, greater than the fear of death. We've got it covered with substitutes and euphemisms; we talk about evolving as if it's a matter of thought, of reason. It's not. It's wild, its nonhuman. It's what all nonhuman life strives for: to evolve into another species that is more in harmony—a new niche, a new note—with all other life and forces. Had Freud been born now instead of a century ago, he would have explored the fear of evolution rather than the fear of death.

[SATURDAY] EARTH BECOMES EDEN

Wisdom asks: Is it of importance to know what was taken out of the Garden of Eden story? The church thought it worth hiding, so they added more to cover over the story: the origin of Sin and the embodiment of the snake by Satan, Angel of God, for example. The rabbis have added their own fanciful stories. But in Genesis itself, the details of Adam and Eve's life in Eden are entirely missing.

Since we have no copies of the original, why should we care about imagining things we can't know? Why care about what went on in the relationship between mother and father, especially in the conjugal bed? But if there are problems in your life, shouldn't you want to know their origins in order to resolve them? Is it meaningless that mother yelled at father or that father ignored mother? If we can't even reenter our own parents' bedroom—a place in our childhood palpably known to us—how can we reenter the Garden of Eden, home of our ancestral parents?

But we must. Our origins are crucial to us. We are endowed with two faculties which make it no harder to enter Adam and Eve's bower than our own parents' bedroom: imagination and memory. Memory serves us with historical record: from Genesis to our parents. Records would be useless if we did not bring our imagination to them, exploring the clues about what makes us anxious in our lives. History and story, science and myth tantalize but we're still hungry. The more we know, the lighter we bear our own burdens.

In societies where imagination was dear, poets wrote their ancestral histories: Homer's Greece, the Bible's Israel, Shakespeare's England. Poets of our day have been on a long vacation. We've become lighter with knowledge, enlightened with new information—yet our imagination has lost the appetite for asking about our origins.

It's as if we didn't want to return there, ashamed of our past. Our dreams are wishes to be there—but that isn't it at all, and that's why we're unsatisfied. The only way home—*really* home—is to evolve, physically evolve. We could find ourselves in a new Eden. Until then, we dream on, imagining that we can reunite our divorced parents—if not here then in some heaven, just as children feel they have influence over the catastrophes they experience.

In the *Scroll of the History of Adam*, everything stands revealed about our idealized parents, Father and Mother Gods. When we reunite them and Earth becomes Eden, the new species will remember us, the ones we evolve into. We will be the history they cherish. We will all return to life as they name us. Meanwhile, these evolved ones will soon be here in disembodied form. They will be like missing ones. They will watch us, as we were once commanded to be watchers over Eden. But it makes more sense when the lost Scroll is taken into account. It was not lost—but missing.

And Wisdom rested.

Chapter 5

Chapter 5

A True Novel

My biggest disappointment is having come too late to meet Archibald Shechner. I could have told you the origin of the word "tree" but I wasn't even aware of the origin of real paper, nor could I tell the trees from the forest. That was years ago, when I allowed myself to be flattered out of my tiny office by a cerebral boulevardier who used word origins for his famous literary theories. I became his natural resource. This overblown man loathed everything about nature in a comical sort of way, the way W.C. Fields could not suffer children. Probably if Wisdom had spoken to Svitz he would have fallen at her feet. Be that as it may, he became the catalyst that led me to Julie Peleg and put me on Shechner's trail. Now, fortunately, instead of answering the queries of academic celebrities, I listen to Wisdom's voice as Archie Shechner heard it. I call this clarifying work a novel so that Shechner will never be laughed at again. Nor would I care to stand and tremble before a platform of learned referees to win their certificate of truth. Actually, I need to be sitting down, free in my mind to appreciate and govern these actual events.

[Nosei, '94]

Father Nature

Would I care to review the new Philip Roth novel? asked Harriman Svitz, doyen of American critics. I'm momentarily stunned; who is asking whom for a favor? "I promised the virtuous New Yorker lady but I just can't possibly do it. Do a good deed, Nosey; it will be a blessing to you."

I had helped Svitz out of straits before, though not with a reviewing plum for a prize. In two days I read through the 400-page steamy novel, marking the major passages. I grew anxious as I reread them, however: Roth wrote with supreme confidence, knowing exactly who were his friends, who his enemies. His isolation from all foes was so secure that his four walls served as foils, while philistines, gentiles, even unself-conscious Jews—all became outsiders. Roth was a throwback, a yenta from the ghetto, cut from the same cloth as the comedians who caricature the unassimilated Jew within themselves. Jackie Mason, Billy Crystal, Woody Allen, Joan Rivers and the rest, they'll stick it to anyone who is not "us". But while they play it for laughs, Roth's stakes are serious. His isolation is so true to the padlocked Renaissance ghettoes of Venice and Cracow that even nature is an outsider. Nature, to Roth, is *a gentile.*

Turn the entire 400 pages and you will not find a single tree, a fruit, a seed, an animal, nothing remotely wild and not even a blade of grass! Even the field in "have a field day"—one of the idioms Roth spreads around—is unconscious. No moons, no stars. And no pets either. The human ego is so isolated that only its own mortality can get through its skull to remind Roth he is not alone, the worms are coming. Yet that mortality does not argue that *something* must have a higher power since Roth has been fighting it quite successfully: what it takes is a few writer friends contending that one's work is immortal.

Harriman Svitz being one of those, ever since he himself was diagnosed a genius by a bellringer in the ivory tower. I, on the other hand, have had to scratch out a reputation as Hebrew philologist, a language many Jewish writers pretend to know but secretly don't. The only legitimate claim I could have had for reviewing Roth was to certify him a writer in the great Biblical prophetic tradition of Israel's national self-criticism and, believe it or not, this is what Svitz, Roth, and the New Yorker would expect of me. After all, my isolation was of quite a different order, longshot outsider, an immigrant, fighting to get *in* somewhere.

Just *where*, however, eluded anyone's attention. Even I was blurry as I headed for the woods, though the woods sure looked like isolation. Nature however has gone into the vanguard, the cultural frontier: a society without spokespersons. This is a tip I'd picked up from God, so to speak. Actually, it so turns out that ecology is shelved in certain libraries right next to linguistics, and so it was that one day distraction drove me to the forest, so to speak, though it was simply an ecology book.

I learned that in this century a new conception of nature has germinated, conceived of as a system in which the struggle of species balances out, and the artist's job is to find the balance point—just the way it works in music and science, where the words "harmony" and "equation" reign. The problem is, how do you give voice to it and avoid becoming a recluse like Roth and Harriman Svitz, surrounded by topiary gardens of students and sycophants?

Excuse me, I do an injustice in humoring the plants, which we are finally learning are smarter than most of the planet. Till now, nature has spoken in pantomime, in mute contrast to the mucking up of the human system. Meanwhile, language and society—the human system—has been under attack by critics so verbose they have formed their own insular systems, so that it seems their mouths are in nonstop pantomime motion behind the glass of an academic greenhouse. Therefore, if I now made my mark critiquing Roth I'd be cultivating this isolated in-group which I only wish to enter in order to walk away from, of my own free will. In other words, a gesture—that's the mark I want to impress on the literary world, a gesture of independence, all the more shocking in its coming from a lowly philologist. And it would be such an American gesture, so Thoreauvian, so ultimately Emily Dickensonian: a preference for the company of stars and bees.

Well of course it's an intellectual preference, for the same isolation that in plants conversely prompts a reaching out, sex: the scattering of pollen and seeds farther and farther away. There's promiscuity among the literati but it's mostly childless, in-group. So go on, you say, go on and write about *this* in The New Yorker. Well, I'm just a batboy, it would never get printed. Besides, I don't know how to give nature a voice yet, and I didn't even know he had one until I wiped my breath off the human mirrors:

there he was, Father Nature, culture in its most living aspect, a civilization of ecosystems, that word itself coined yesterday. Russian ballet, Italian opera, French television, Gypsy violins—no cultural tradition could match the art and science of an ecosystem, the drama of its balance, the mysticism of its balancing point. Black holes sell books but you can't go there; Sigmund Freud sells books but you can't hold a psyche in your hands. One small ecosystem is more complex an orgy of life than any imagined coupling and you can walk in it or hold it on your fingertip.

Excuse me once again, it's all so new. The vison I'd had was in a kind of rear-view mirror. Something about the prevailing faith that nature is a bystander inflamed me, started a forest fire in me. I had also been a bystander, standing around an exhibit of creation; culture itself was only a mirror of nature. Relegate Father Nature to art museums and tree-lined campuses? To documentaries? Not the one original, the creator of systems; the way I reason reflects the way he builds an ecosystem. Only when I stop to consider the diversity within the system—the thumb-opposing monkeys in the Rain Forest trees to the smart viruses crossing their bloodstreams—that's when I find the work of the mother, familiar Mother Nature, mother of invention. We don't see her, we don't see ourselves, until her mate steps out of the bushes—out of the past—and smashes our mirrors.

So it was hardly a retreat to nature, as I turned my back on academe. I had my ticket on El Al and an invitation to join an international group of botanists at the Biblical

Botanical Reserve, on the palm coast north of Tel Aviv. True, I wangled this invite by offering to help authenticate the ancient syntax of the new Scroll that had been found. At this point it was still a secret, but the botanists had been consulted, in order to verify the strange references to plants, and that is how I found out about it before the news media hoopla.

[Nosei, '84]

Lilith Speaks

I was lying on an arm of the tall oak tree, looking down at the palm beside it, longing for the golden hyphaene fruit and the days in Eden when I peeled back their skins and sucked cool sweetness. Longings are something new, since all desires were satisfied in Eden. And all things new are derivative because there the old things were never old.

A yellow-masked squirrel monkey climbed the hyphaene palm, plucked a fruit from the cluster with both hands as her tail anchored her round the tree trunk. On the ground again, I watched her pull the fruit apart and eat and then a strange feeling came over me and the light seemed to darken in the air. My whole body was shaking and I felt as though I myself had eaten and a seed had lodged in my throat, choking me. I felt my face turning red and blue.

I flew from there and felt all right again. What was it—what new empty thing had I experienced? Then the yellow mask appeared in my mind, mocking me. It laughed at me, I thought, although no sign of levity appeared on its face:

the worst mocking, for the sound of laughter was heard nowhere but in my own ears. The yellow of the squirrel's mask turned suddenly to red it seemed to me.

I lunged at it, in my mind, wanting to strangle it somehow, make myself material in the only way I may, air enclosed in a small bubble of air, forcing my way into its windpipe. To choke, to stop the breath—this I can do, although for just a moment. The fear in the victim can paralyze it, however, prolong the moment even to death. In Lilith, this is anger released.

[*Scroll of the History of Adam*]

Adam Speaks

I feel a lump in my throat as I remember my anger having to strangle the monkey. That was after we had eaten it. I was so hungry that I didn't remember the anger till later, when Eve and I were sitting by the water.

Suddenly I saw it's face, in the hidden world of memory, and I resented it, and having to think it. I had to, because it was there in front of me, innocent, sweet even—when in fact it was not so innocent: it was disturbing me, paying me back from the hidden world for my having killed it.

Killed it? I was hungry and when my arm reached out, as it had in Eden, where fruit was it found a stone.

[*Scroll of the History of Adam*]

Lilith Speaks

No, before you reached you began to think secretly to yourself, Lilith whispered. You looked at the monkey and saw it was unafraid. You saw that it was eating, nibbling a pine cone in both hands as it sat on the lowest branch. Jealous of her cone, your anger asked for more than it, for a juicier nut, for the meat of the monkey and the death of it too, a double requital. But what had she done to you? Nothing. And what had you asked of her? You were requiting nothing, and twice. You severed the monkey from her own anger, where she sits unrequited in the hidden world. Memory is that world, alive in our feelings but nowhere in existence.

[*Scroll of the History of Adam*]

Adam Speaks

I killed it, I thought, now that it was eaten, and the accompanying thought satisfied to be thought, accompanying digestion. Eve sat beside me, still eating, chewing as deliberately as my mind now turned. I thought, Eve does not know this pain in my memory nor my anger at the memory, the monkey, for giving it to me. Would she also share my anger at the monkey? No, she would say, don't think it, don't remember the memory, forget it. But the memory was attached to feeling I could not reject, held there by the monkey itself, even though I had just consumed a part of it. And in that way the thought of Eve's misunderstanding attached itself to the monkey's in my memory. I could not abandon the memory, it seemed, because I had rejected the monkey itself, killed it before it could feel fear of the deed and thus feel *itself*, feel attached to its monkey being. Now it was my turn to feel abandoned in my desire to be free of the monkey in memory.

And so I came to feel—to imagine in some future memory—Eve's rejection also. She has already misunderstood me, and soon she will be angry that I seem to reject her advice to me. What can I do when I feel her anger? Not reject it in turn, but let her feel the anger in her so as not be cut off from it like the yellow-masked squirrel monkey. And so it was I had learned to think of Eve and feel her feelings, starting from the killing of the monkey. As I felt her in my mind I became sexually aroused.

[*Scroll of the History of Adam*]

WISDOM [TRANSCRIBED BY A.S.]

In humans, sex is the drive to colonize, to leave the past behind, to create oneself in imitation—mimicry—of the Creator. What is forgotten is the Creator's mate, the hidden one, Father Nature's wife, devisor of time and the drive to discover origins, of memory and home—Mother Nature, the world I inhabit. To find me, everything must lose its way, abandon itself, try again and grow by experience. The Creator himself abhors loss, wants everything just as he made it. When humans create a work of art or set up a scientific experiment, they mimic the Creator's self-contained perfection, all conditions controlled. But his grudging tolerance of flaws allows for beauty: through Mother Nature I invented contrast, the seen and the hidden, the lost thing made human in time, less perfect for having been lost, but larger in life: this moment touching in contrast to the last. And then the drive to move, the sexual reaching out to eat, reaching for omnipotence again.

Adam Speaks

My eye catches the meeting of realms here, as it did not in Eden. The fish rises to the water's surface for the same food towards which a duck descends. The squirrel and raven meet in the branches. Man and germ meet among liquids, water or bloodstream. Most critically, man and plant meet as humans harvest grain for livestock: here humans work for the animals and the plants together, mixing those realms without thought. It is unlike the work of art, where thought is omnipotent; it is the work of nature.

I was thinking only of myself when I killed—and that was not thinking. I was an alien to myself but closer than ever to Eve, more hungry for her. My desire for her returned me to nature but blinded by bonds of expectation: the hand reaching out merely for what is there, the mind not the creator of its own thought.

[*Scroll of the History of Adam*]

Wisdom [transcribed by A.S.]

Sexual relations are the natural substitute for entering the ecosystem—the intimacy of nature—and in this way the human faces its death. Transcend sex—and the human avoids its mortality. Transcend the ecosystem—and the human is not in it, alienated. How can it be known? Fear enters the body unknown, which casts about for safety.

1995

I was standing alone in front of them. Photographs of a mother in private moments, in what would have been solitary moments, if her daughter's camera had not been there, if her daughter had not recorded them. Her daughter is an artist, a photographer. Her mother was 'Mom'—that was the title of the exhibition.

She is not my mother, or what was once my mother. My mother exuded power. She was in movement, mind active—an instrument of the power of the mind. She was growth, not stasis—nothing like this woman's 'Mom.' My mother turned on this power for mothers who needed it, like her mother. To lift them out of their lethargy, intractability.

Ironic. This woman takes a camera, snaps pictures, puts a show together of the experience with a 'Mom' of mire. I have—had—a mother of movement, power, action and I feel like I'm in the mire of 'Mom.' Trudging. Close to collapse. On the edge of panic. Even just standing there, looking at the photographs. I wonder what that daughter-photographer feels. Should I get a camera? Before the panic started, I could have gotten lost in the project of selecting and learning about a camera. Now, such ideas rapidly collapse. I think, "It's too late now to take pictures of my 'Mom.'"

Oh, come on, you might say. It's easy to see—it was that she was overpowering. Nothing is that simple, however. Sometimes it was the power. Pictures of my mom would have been more admirable. Yet there can be a mire to powerfulness, of always being turned on rather than turned off for others. The turned off feelings don't just disappear, do they? They go somewhere, into someone—the bystander.

So now, the power has multiplied. The power of mother, the memory of her power. The power in me to discard or keep the knowledge of her work. The voice, the memory of Archie's powerful desperation. And I can't seem to find mother's power in me anymore. I still feel like everything I'm doing belongs to someone else—to 'Mom.' "Dump the damn project," you say. That's the funny thing. I can't. I can't because of mother. Because of myself. You see, I feel entitled to it—as if it should be mine. After all, I was fine before all this voice and Scroll stuff.

But that's not really true. I was never fine; I just did fine. A man hearing a voice from the ground and then disappearing made me have to find another way of doing fine—the old way stopped working. I'm trying to find a new way. The story of the voice is part of that new way—a chance to be really me. To lose the fear.

Too much to keep going. Waiting for it to happen. The panic. I go out of the gallery. Raining, dark. It starts. Can I make it back? Should I call a taxi? Can I make it even in the taxi? No phone. If there were a phone to call the number. My doctor's number. Listening, hearing the pounding. The incessant question of can I make it.

When I wrote that in the notebook, all I wanted was a safe place. I remember I started writing it in the taxi and continued in the restaurant where I finally got out to have some Pho—a kind of Vietnamese soup. I would often go have some kind of soup after being out, especially after sessions. It seemed like a safe thing to do. This was actually written not long ago, when I first started working on the manuscript Seth Greene sent me. I thought the analysis would protect me from episodes like that. But there I was in the taxi again, writing things down on paper, like a marooned person sending out S.O.S's in bottles. What you have just read is more from what I wrote in the restaurant than from what I was writing in the taxi. I can't even read what I wrote in the taxi. I'm sure it had something to do with things my doctor had said to me, things I resurrected in the moment to reassure myself I wasn't going to die or cease to exist. Like, "Unwanted exercise of the heart. Not organic. A detour of suffering—symptoms to discover the reasons for. Your body has become a translator. It's expressing something you can't express otherwise."

In the beginning, when I had a panic attack like that, it could take me all night to feel safe again. I'd get on a couch in a small room in Svitz's place, listen to jazz turned down low and try to fall asleep without knowing it. Afraid to let go. Sometimes I'd have to call my doctor. I had lost the safe place in me. For years afterwards, my safe places were the bridges we would build between sessions. And then gradually, I began to find it in me. But then I started reading this very chapter, with Archie doing the transcribing of the voice—next to his translations of the Scroll. Both spoke of memory. Of parents, of mothers. And the deep memory of the human species. It let me touch the deep memory of my mother—the system in which I had evolved.

By the time Archie came on the scene with the Scroll and became mother's patient, mine was a system that begged for a camera. Mother's sessions with Archie grew into a frantic testimony project, with Archie as the lone survivor and, moreover, the only receptacle of what seemed a long buried knowledge that had slammed us into another reality. All three of us were soon transcribing and working in concert towards putting the voice on paper. I've had to work hard to remember even being bothered by this, much less angered. At the time, it all seemed so natural, so right. And most importantly, so paramount. The transcription was paramount. How much longer would the voice speak? How long would Archie hold out? Time was short—time itself was changing.

"Julie, I've begun to feel like he did."

"Like who?" I asked Archie.

"Adam." He hesitated. "I feel a peculiar aftertaste in my mouth—have for several days. I know what it is now. It's the taste of monkey. I know because I ate some once on an excavation trip to South America. I can taste Adam's first kill in my mouth."

I was spooked by this. As a defense, I tried to act like mother. I didn't want him to feel any crazier than he already felt. "It must mean something, don't you think? What else do you feel, Archie?"

"I can taste her, too."

"Who?"

"Eve. Every so often while I'm working, I become aware of the taste of salt, palm and some kind of nectar, as if the oils of her skin had mixed with the residue of palm fronds she might have slept upon. When I go out, I notice the green breaking through the sidewalks—more than I notice the concrete cracks themselves. I feel the time before memory existed in my head. Adam's time. When I walk home, I don't feel the vibrations from cars or people—only the disturbance of the air from some winged creature. I don't see the pollution anymore. Do you know what I see? Pollen particles. I can actually see them. Of course, anyone can. But the point is that they have become the most important things in the landscape for me to see."

Again, I aked him what it could mean—and if he had told mother. What else could I say?

"Yes, we've been working through it," he said quietly. "It's a gesture of reaching. Of some kind. Betti thinks I'm either reaching for my mother or for her. But it's hard to explain things like an oracular sensitivity to pollen. I think we're afraid to really speak about it. Too powerful. And it makes certain other feelings too powerful."

"What other feelings?"

He looked at me steadily, his face changing from *his* face to a long-ago face—my father's. "I don't know that I should talk to you like this, Julie. I think you have had too much of this kind of talking. You should be out playing."

"I'm not six years old anymore, Archie."

"Were you ever? I hope so. But I'm drawn to talk to you. To tell you. It is a reaching, yes. But a reaching for a memory deeper than your mother realizes. A memory of another time, another species—to the time when we could still evolve. Literally. To the time when pollen was our reality, when the ecosystem filled our eyes, our ears—our hands and mouths. Seduction was not yet taboo, with lines drawn around it—it was in everything. And now, in sessions with your mother. I feel sex in everything. Which she says is what we want, but I don't think she realizes what this sex means. I sense things about her I never did before."

"Isn't that normal, Archie? It's all part of transference. You're in that room together, so many hours." I trailed off. No more sentences came to me to say.

"I understand that. I even understand my resisting the truth of it. But I am more than Archie now. I have this new information, this new experience in me. Your mother has *taste* for me now. She has become part of the movement of pollen. I am seeing her the way Adam saw Eve. And when I tell her what the voice says—well, it's little things I've noticed in her. She is experiencing my voice differently when I talk. She can *feel* it—the vibration, as if she's receiving it through some different organ."

I could say nothing when he finished. Instead, I sat next to him and began helping with what he was transcribing. The work was where we returned to each time silence came. The work was the transcription notebooks. So, it's not so odd that I should make some notebooks of my own. In the panic.

When the taxi pulled up to the restaurant that night after the gallery show of 'Mom,' I couldn't get out at first. I told the driver I had to finish something I was writing in the notebook and to pull up against the curb. He warned me the traffic cops would come. I ignored him, told him I would pay. I continued to scribble, anything that might make me feel safe enough to move. One word is all I can make out from what I wrote: Hole. It was an invocation of Archie's safe place—the hole in the ground where he had first heard the voice. He would feel crazy later on when the voice continued in his head, but while he was there, he told me, it felt safe. I had a fantasy that this was where Archie and mother went when they disappeared. And if I went there too, I would be okay. I felt I could make it then, from the taxi to the inside of the restaurant. A few minutes later, I had made movement. I was waiting for a great bowl of Pho.

It's easy to see now why I was able to move and lose some of the panic that night. With the image of the hole, I had located Archie and mother in my mind. And myself. I had become their child again, their helper, and we were all safe in one place within the fantasy of the hole. In my mind I had gotten too far away from them in the gallery. There, I had been looking at mother-systems through the critical eye of an artist. With the artist I had stepped out of my mother's system. Who knows what would happen next. The panic returned me to mother.

This is a small piece of what I learned in another hole, another system: the room where I would go to hear another voice—that of my doctor. A hole of my own, you might say. How much was fantasy, how much was reality? I would often ask my doctor how much was real and how much illusion between us. He would answer that it *all* felt real to him, that I had to enlarge my concept of fantasy, of play. I felt frustrated by this answer. Now I know what he meant. If I could play, I would find that the safe place was in *me*—not in having myself and everyone else lined up somewhere in formation. Maybe Archie's question that day wasn't too far off the mark. Did I ever learn to play? Is that what we're needing to be taught by scientists who search for other worlds? You have to let go of a certain kind of fear to take in another world, even another person. I envy Nosei's ability to do that. You can see him striving for it even in the subtitles he invented to organize the material of the trunk. Somewhere along the way these last ten years, he found out how to do it. To play. To be intimate with another system.

[Julie]

BURLESQUE

But still, why pass up this opportunity to keep in Harriman Svitz's esteem and have my name associated with Roth's?

I finished Roth's expressively alienated novel, and then I longed to walk in a field, any field. There is less sex in this book than any of his previous ones, although there is plenty of burlesque. Burlesque is the last refuge for men who prefer to be alone, like adolescents locked in a bathroom.

Nearsighted, they need caricature, exaggeration: big boobs and ass, tiny waist. And bumps and grinds, a burlesque of seduction, a mental massage, a caricature of nature.

[Nosei, '84]

The Imperceptible

Few look at nature seriously, finely focussed; instead, they enjoy the painted face she partly wears, her public image. Isn't it a gorgeous day!—for instance. Painted signs are part of nature's own mimicry: a fifth of all flower species, for instance, are mimics.

The seductions of art, though, that's different. It's not just bigness of scale that counts but the imperceptible—the subtle suggestion so refined, you'd almost think it was natural.

Yet nothing is more polished than nature. Mistakes—a third eye, a hand for a tail—are long gone, perfected out of existence. Gone too is the perception of the time it all took, the difficult time of hundreds of millions of years, so that the natural world seems to exist effortlessly today in all its variety. The metaphor of earth's creation in seven days should be easy to believe.

[Nosei, '94]

The Parental Bed

It's no good to say "Mother Nature" anymore. No, sir. It's *time* that is female, *all* time, whether it's the time it takes to give birth, to nurture, to recycle. All the feminine traits point to the invention of time, and that means the evolution of human life. Then there's refinement, beauty, grace—meanings that time works on the bodies of things.

Men are powerful forgetters. Men live as if the present alone counts, and they honor those who hold power. Attention!—says the blank paper to me. And that's the sense of nature we've lost: its power and presence. I realize it's Father Nature I must name. But who would listen to me? Women are the most aware of him, though they call him Mother.

These women don't expect their Creator to have a partner either. Whole movements of women can't remove blindness before the parental bed: a willing blinding long enshrined in partnerless Supreme Beings. And men are weak in irony, in distance from themselves; that is why they forget the woman behind them. Still, the feminine side of nature remains full of play, mimicry, creative deception, humor.

What is my obsession with speaking wisdom here—as if reducing men and women to black and white? Complexity, that gorgeous expanse of grays, is all in the intercourse between them. When I imagine myself in bed with the female all the thinking becomes worthwhile. The particular female, no, it is not her, not a particular mother either. Intimacy is hidden in time, the particular woman revealed by Wisdom, said the Scroll. After reading the Scroll, the enfolding pearly cloud was dissolved for Shechner. Only a voice remained?

[Nosei, '94]

Doubles

Yes, yes, men are nearsighted, needing big theories and big plans, liking all things inflated. Subtle humor is lost on them, and that is how I came to see that Harriman Svitz and Roth revel in slapstick, the most obvious kind of humor, and big ideas, and can't help mistaking burlesque for comedy, misreading sex into something inflated like fame or influence. Sex has to be pumped up so big that it can only be exaggeration: a voluptuary woman only, please, or just tits & ass, please, the more overblown the better, hefty enough for the nearsighted to make out.

So it was no surprise to me that Roth's novel needed broad ideas like doubles to inflate the self. I thought if I had to, I could write about his honesty, about his tacit admission that, needing characters to caricature, he'd chosen himself as character number one. Just as Harriman Svitz the critic, needing a text to criticize more interesting than the one at hand, often caricatured his earlier work. I was even about to get started, but I began to notice that I was hardly sleeping, I couldn't drag myself to the supermarket to buy milk for my coffee, and friends noticed that I was sighing heavily on the telephone. It was too late for me, the game was up; I needed to breathe the same air as trees, not bury my head in their refined byproducts perfumed with ink. I would resign from the temptings of the literary racket to the more subtle seductions of nature. No more prizes and their promise of harems, no more decapitated flowers, no buttocks fit to be bronzed by Maillol.

What revelation was I waiting around for in the

burlesques of Roth, the intellectual burlesques of Harriman Svitz?—compared to the footlights of flowers overlooked in the field, painting their faces in clever passion, or a mango ripening into a red light for birds or fruit-bats, whose tiny hands knead it like a woman's breast. Animals, discounted doubles, do make an appearance in Roth's novel but only to illustrate the sound of a female orgasm: "culminating in that wordless vocal obliggato with which she'd flung herself upon the floodtide of her pleasure, the streaming throaty rising and falling, at once husky and murmurous, somewhere between the trilling of a tree toad and the purring of a cat." That's the *only* hint of a tree to be found in the denuded landscape of Roth's novel—and only if that really was a tree frog and not cicadas, or a mockingbird.

[Nosei '84]

Chapter 6

Chapter 6

You hear in our time about the feminine aspect of God, the Greek version of the original Hebraic Wisdom—Shechinah by name—translated into Greek as Sophia. Potent as she is, this Sophia is platonic, her sex drained of all but the maternal qualities. So you can expect to find plenty of talk about that blanket thrown over the human anatomy called the soul. Also, plenty of emasculated discussions of love as friendship etc.—all of it part of a grand Greek tradition of fancy philosophic drapery covering the naked truth. And it's all discussed by repressed Don Juans, anxious to remove Sophia's underclothes but unable to admit it.

Merely the news that a copy had been unearthed of the lost *Scroll of the History of Adam*—merely the reminder that scholars always knew its existence had been suppressed—was enough to expose the professorial fig leaves. What scorn and fear!—that after all, Eden might be revealed at last in sexual terms, terms we are just beginning to grasp. Sexual selection accounts for new species, so each new species evolves into its own Eden. Yes, it's there in Genesis that all species were in Eden, each a separate creation. But then we are merely another species that loses its Eden when we begin to explore. Once, we evolved away from our ancestral species and into conditions we perfectly fit—an ecosystem Eden—but only for a short time. As soon as we explored beyond the forest we came into struggle with other species and began to long for our parental trees.

Look back at Eden and the sudden distance creates a pale reflection of the original, an imitation. And the imitations become various and charm us, a culture enfolding us and from which we are unable to let go. Julie and I, talking about Svitz ten years ago, let go with a mutual laugh like a sexual howl: the man clung to so many coats of culture, a trained bear growing fatter and fatter, perpetually sweating—off with them! Like sarcastic sophomores, though, we didn't really believe ourselves.

And now we were really seeing it. In place of a Svitz it was Shechner who let go.

[Nosei, '94]

[Sunday] Extended Body

Wisdom asks: Is there ever a wildness to human culture, an avant-garde? The ecosystem is beyond our taming. Its language is so esoteric we catch only fragments of it: the path of an animal, the change of seasons. It is our own parent overheard in infancy, when we began to make out a word here and there, or more accurately, a repeated sound. The seasons were night and day, hot and cold.

And yet our parents cared so attentively; no, it was different than that, closer, more secret. Our own bodies, idealized, special with sounds—burps, gurgles, cries—and with smells. Grown up, the endangered ecosystem is our extended body, if we can love it. Can we love the failures of our body as it grows older or sick? First, we want to nurse it back to health, any kind of health.

[Monday] Flowers Lost In Time

Wisdom asks: Why did nature fall to humans? The Creator's goal was stability but now nature grows more fragile beside humans. By nature I mean untouched nature, where time has been allowed to work. Time is what produced us, time the subtext to all our politics. Oh, shortsighted politics. Culture is a mirror of nature; the deeper the culture, the deeper time becomes—and the more acute our sense of origin in it. Remove the mirror, remove the depth. Instead of complex origins we have commonsense political myths, as if our consciousness was born out of a few centuries of conflicts. With commonsense, who needs nature, who needs to think about our ancestors the apes? What does the rise of flowering plants mean to us, compared to a political ideology? Yet those plants hold a firmer place in history for us—a time when the patterns in which we think were being formed.

[Tuesday] The Elements Are Ancestors Too

Wisdom asks: Is it sexual to grow? Is it painful to think of? To the human body, growth is a painless bruising. It inspires nurturing. Parent animals protect their young, raise and instruct them as they grow. This is why it feels so natural to have an incest taboo. Yet the taboo raises the sexual question, and the answer is best found, as always, among the plants.

Is a plant's growth sexual? Yes, clearly its growth is an unfolding toward fruit and flower. Why so clear? Because the nurturer is absent; the parents of the plant are the elements. Remove the parents of humans and the clear task of the growing individual is to become father or mother to another.

Remove the parents—and the plants provide the nourishment to grow and the material for shelter. Return the parents and culture develops, which is the human nurturing that hides its desire from itself. This is the desire to evolve, to become another, to expose sexual desire as innocent and open again, as in Eden.

[WEDNESDAY] THE LUNGE TO KNOW WHAT'S OUTSIDE

Wisdom asks: How can you know yourself? Look at a pig's face and be surprised by its intelligence: it can know us as well as a dog. Yet it can know only what a pig can, between its active nostrils and tiny eyes, short legs propped on high-heeled hoofs. Our species Homo sapiens too is constrained behind the blunt features of its muzzle, throttling hostility to its caregiver. A grown bear cub will go off and never see its mother again, but humans must live out their lives under her presence or memory. Yes, monkeys and gorillas may remain for life by their parents, but they seem content with their lot; humans, on the other hand, are striving forward.

What restless ambition is this but the drive to evolve? We see it in other species as they colonize new landscapes, isolated from their own. We have run out of landscape yet the sense of isolation in the universe deepens—what else but the desperate lunge toward transforming ourselves, evolving to fit this isolation which we have grown to identify as alienation?

The green prehuman earth is the mystery we're chosen to solve, the birthplace of our spirit, but it is slipping away. The way back grows harder. In the instant of achieving cellular self-understanding through the mind of modern humans, its most beautiful creations are doomed. Homo sapiens, as it opens its mind to the past, is absently closing the door on its resources, the ancient ecosystems. There is no room for a human to evolve without biotic knowledge of itself.

[Thursday] Cutting Edge

Wisdom asks: Where is there anymore a quiet field where a botanist can follow a tranquil life of research? Everything is a disturbed field today, touched by a sense of imminent loss.

The tending that plants ask from animals and humans is a strategy, at least in a crucial metaphorical sense. That the planet is delicate is now a commonplace but the cultural equivalent of this knowledge is unknown: that we live in an artifact, a museum, in fact a great work of art. The focus on plants under stress will increase, since they are our makers, so to speak, providing for animal life. Our own origins in the line of mammals began very recently in earth time, during the last burst of biodiversity. That birth realm, once so rich in species, is now our area of mounting losses.

The answer? Consider the one that launched the experiments of modernism in the arts almost a century ago: to bridge the gap between art and life, to live one's art. The world is no longer the creator's artifact but our own. Remember that the first and greatest colonizers of earth are the plants, from bacteria to tree. In the realm of life they are our forefathers and foremothers. They colonized every niche of the planet and created the food and conditions for animals to follow. Most of the hundreds of species that grow extinct every day as well as the most endangered species still alive are the adventurous ones, the most creative ones: they are the ones who colonized the unlikeliest nooks and crannies, who grew extra-specialized according to the talents of their line. So it's not just any species we're losing—it's the pioneers, inventors and artists.

The intellectual cutting edge, the cultural avant-garde, is the ecosystem. That's where art and life converge, culture and nature unite. We know as little about them as distant galaxies though here we can reach out and touch, dependent.

[FRIDAY] THE ESSENTIAL HOLE

Wisdom asks: Is culture wholly imitation and caricature? Writers and artists caricature nature to show their alienation; in fact, it shows isolation.

Isolation is a necessary stage for growth. How often can we feel lost in nature anymore, isolated, as wildernesses shrink? This lost isolation was filled with beauty and knowledge. Social isolation—feeling unwanted—is different. There is no grandeur there, not even the grandeur of need.

In wilderness, the sense of being wanted is supplanted with the sense of being rare, precious. We long to explore, to find out many possibilities of where and how we can live.

The artistic caricature of nature creates distance, an imagined desert, a stage of isolation and imperceptible growth— mimicking the cultural desert that stifles. Here too nature caricatures the artist and author with simply a crocodile, like the splendid Leviathan in the Book of Job. The artistic work is the digging of an alligator's hole in a wetlands, necessary for the survival of fish during the dry season. We have learned an entire ecosystem can depend on those alligators, as the culture needs its thinkers. The fantastic complexity of an alligator's paw resembles the thought of the alienated artist inevitably caricaturing nature to reveal his or her presence—and so to clear the mind for fresh vision.

[Saturday] **Hidden Histories**

Wisdom asks: Why do we make our poets obsolete? They are endangered species, as all cultures now are. The poet Bialik wrote that if a Jew became too fond of a tree in Europe or America he would lose the culture rooted in the trees of Israel. Restoring the lost biblical culture in Bialik's mind was the same as planting trees and reclaiming the desert—only he thought the goal was stability when all nature is now revealed as fragile. By nature is meant wild nature, where time has been allowed to work. The culture of Israel survived through time because it mirrored a natural process—culture the imitation of nature, just as reading the many layers of Jewish interpretation imitates deep time: time for evolving to happen, or for reflection to yield a revelation.

Consider gorillas—the discovery and first contact with mountain gorillas in Africa. How could any human being not be transfixed by these huge ancestors? Then, after the initial fascination, they are not actually us, we see, not of our line of Homo sapiens. Even the appeal of "stone age" people is merely exotic and fades when we categorize them as primitive, of a different lineage than ourselves culturally. But look at these gorillas now and see more of ourselves in them than in cultural cousins such as British Victorians—for the species contrast is so stark that our common hidden histories shine out.

Look at what these thousand-pound creatures are adapted for: nurturing their young, almost exclusively. What work do they do, where do they live? They live in a paradise where all their food is provided by the plants. Giant vegetarians, their work consists largely of picking and eating succulents, such as hearts of bamboo. Our eating is more concentrated and requires harder work, for we have left paradise and spread everywhere. And there precisely lies the confluence of our lines: for we are driven to reproduce paradise and replace the gorillas' oral gratification with sublimated sexual and intellectual appetites.

Look into a gorilla's eyes and you see the mask removed. Eating is for them what killing is for us. No need to reckon up the human appetite for murder—we just need to consider our wishes. Threaten me and I might wish you dead, as I once wished my father, mother, and all I was close to, dead. Yet I loved them and would never act on such wishes, so why were the thoughts there in moments of anger and terror and helplessness? Because we have lost the way to paradise. For the human infant, that paradise was still known at the nursing mother's breast. The most unbearable scenes of tenderness were found when the isolated ape creatures were encountered for the first time by Europeans: there they were, the nursing gorilla mothers with their young. Those babies will not have to grow up and leave their paradise system. They remain where they have evolved, fit for all that surrounds them. And they give back to it, tending the vegetation—even by always moving on and opening new ranges.

Chapter 7

Chapter 7

1995

The name scribbled off to the margin was Jacob Westerman. It was in mother's handwriting. There was a phone number—in another handwriting. I called the number. I had been in Switzerland almost six months. I had begun to examine a box of notes made and collected by mother. It was oddly thrilling to sometimes discover another handwriting next to her's. It was, of course, Archie's. [The phone number under the name of Westerman was in Archie's handwriting.] It felt like a transgression, though, to see their handwriting together, so close, to see how mixed up mother had become with Archie. Looking at her notes was almost like being in her mind.

I feel like I'm in Nosei's mind sometimes when I read what the transcription has become. That last chapter of Wisdom's voice reads like our mental lovemaking after the sex. The talk—my ardent questions that would lead Nosei into an erotic riff oo culture and nature. I always wanted to make love again after hearing him. Seeing his lips move to this heady beat made my own lips want to press and pull and squeeze. I wanted to eat from more parts of him than I could find. We seemed almost like actors in Wisdom's play, filling in the spaces between the words recorded by Archie with our bodies and sensibilities. We were seduced onto the page, the pages of this manuscript. It is here, in the Guide, that I found the missing parts, what asked to be taken and eaten. Nosei and I have both eaten it—eaten what Archie and mother left me. Nosei has taken it in turn. When I read the Guide, I feel it all in his mouth, in his body—spinning it out in his story.

But ten years ago, finding mother and Archie on the page together was hard to take in. It was a surprise that wasn't a surprise to find Archie there. It made me think thoughts that I didn't want—thoughts that didn't seem to fit with what I knew, that didn't seem to fit with the landscape I was in, a landscape so finely apportioned, carefully fitted. I knew it was an unreal landscape, just like Switzerland. My new landscape screened an unrest I held in check. I knew this but I resented knowing it. I felt I had been disturbed. The notes, their handwriting, were a ripple in the tranquility I had found. And the ripple became a tear that I feared would only get bigger.

I knew that going into that box of notes had changed things. Seeing the name of Westerman and the phone number.... it was like seeing their hands together, on the same page. And if on the same page, then.... How silly. Of course. They must have. They did. I knew that. Somewhere I knew it. "But I hadn't seen it happen, I never actually saw them doing it together, so maybe it didn't really happen," I would tell myself. Yet I would go on asking, "Why did she do it? Why did she forget herself, go back on everything that way? What was she thinking of—and what about me?" Suddenly, I could see them in bed. I didn't want to. I wanted to get rid of the image, the question of why, and how she could do it—go back on everything she had been, everything she had made in me.

It was the voice of Wisdom, I would whisper. The voice of Wisdom changed the rules. But what of the "work," as she always put it—fidelity to the work. Were the revelations of Wisdom now more important than the "work?"

What was real now seemed unreal, even false. But I was being silly. After all, I knew before. If I had been tested on the subject of mother and Archie, I would have acknowledged their intimacy. But it was not in my mind, not in the operational machinery that allowed me to face and complete a day. The ripples, the tear began with Westerman. A dissonance in my mind, body, and even in the activity around me. But I didn't take it in. I was walking fast. Walking around it. There would be a dip in the sidewalk. I would walk around. A discoloration in the leaves but I'd look past it. And then there was making love. As I said, I attracted attention in Switzerland. Icy sweet sex—a kind of fucking without personal pronouns.

I called the number. A secretary answered. I told her I had found the phone number among research notes left by my mother. I learned she was speaking from a university in Texas, a biology department. Westerman was a biology professor. I gathered he was young—on staff for just two years. Was this his first appointment? "No," she answered. "His second. He came to us from the Wiezmann Institute in Israel."

"When does he return?"

"Two weeks. He is in the Big Thicket, doing research with students."

I asked what the Big Thicket was. "A preserve about two hours from here."

"His specialty?" I pressed on.

"Well, he teaches evolution and a seminar in wetlands ecosystems."

I left a message and hung up. I wondered if Archie had met him because of the Hula wetlands restoration. I wrote a letter of inquiry. I wanted to know if he had any prior connection to mother or Archie, or to Nosei. He must have responded immediately upon his return.

Glad to hear from me, he said he had taken Archie out to the Hula Valley one day while he was at the Weizmann. He offered assistance with my work, saying it would provide a "cultural guidepost." I hadn't thought of it in that way before. To me, it was a project of testimony about what mother and Archie had been. It was all so personal. How could I know if I would even be doing it otherwise. Yes, it was interesting, even compelling, like being a student. Even after their deaths, I could continue as their student.

Nosei had said this perpetual student tendency was dangerous. I understand him now, but then his attitude only angered me. He warned against taking the work too personally. He had an ingenious way of camouflaging or transforming the personal in himself. I did not. And there was the problem that I still persisted in what he called "acting out." What is more, I craved a little acting out. But there could be no acting out—only "thinking out" with Nosei. I had no choice but to get rid of him. Though he left me, I made him leave. Too much acting out sapped his energy, made him withdraw. It was only later, much later, that I learned we were both right, that we were both protecting ourselves. And our strategies at that time, in that way, just didn't mesh. We certainly didn't have the experience to seek help. But we had made sure that our investments were small, so small that we never would have thought of seeking help for ourselves. Much had to happen for me to understand that we both were fiercely protecting something, fiercely afraid.

Pushing Nosei out and away was for survival: I felt a feeling of death inside every time we collided. I felt endangered by statements that I took things too personally. Something had to be real about me. My mode of being had to count. Collision with Nosei exposed a fragility, a feeling I was being controlled. I began to defend myself from what felt like an exposure akin to Job's, but without a God to argue with—like an organism without an ecosystem to contend with, or another species to compete or collaborate with. Complete exposure, no strategy, except—run. Running inside, stalling outside. And still no home—inside or out.

It started before I got on the plane for the United States. Little things. Avoiding stairs or taking them slowly, carefully. I avoided driving because I found myself going slower and slower. I was afraid I might hit something. I began locking my work up in cabinets for extra security. None of this registered. I still got everything done. I could still push myself. I still had that feeling of invincibility that came with mother's death.

But I made the plans to go to Texas with great determination, almost a relief, as if I could escape something that was chasing me. The flight out of Switzerland was not like the one into it. I remember wishing for that businessman that helped me into Italy that summer. There was no one this time.

Although I didn't cry, I felt what I would learn to call floating anxiety in the aftermath of the panic attack in Texas. I busied myself with eating, grooming, going to the bathroom, reading and sleeping. So was everyone else on the plane. But for me, it meant something different.

The night before I left I had a dream. I seemed to still be with Nosei. We were in the old apartment. He was standing in the hallway of the bedroom, talking to me. I was listening. But listening as if I were caught there—blank, empty. A map was being drawn in my head—a map of the rooms in the apartment. I turned from Nosei and was sitting with Vanessa Redgrave. Yes, she was as herself, an actress. She wanted to talk to me like Nosei. The space between her words, however, became a silent presence—her thoughts, placed there for me. A space it was mine to occupy, to walk into and speak. I thought she wanted me to speak. And I did. The speaking seemed to be more than it was, until I realized I need not speak. She spoke. Yet I could still feel the silence, the spaces between her words. Her voice seemed to caress my thoughts, my fear of the spaces. She appeared to be waiting for me, waiting for me to step in. I wondered "into what?" I think it was the space, the silence, perhaps into myself. She wanted me to lean on her words, her mind. She was trying to help me.

She got up and started walking down the hallway. I got up to go with her. My movement seemed to flow with her's.

We reached a dark, cool room. It was a bedroom with white curtains shifting with a breeze, a white crochet spread on the bed. She looked at me expectantly and with wonder, as if she could be surprised by me, as if she craved what surprise I had the courage to give, to risk. She wanted me to stay, to embrace her.... to make love. I felt the thrill of seduction, of being seduced into a forbidden desire. I knew I wanted to be seduced, but what I wanted more was to see the desire, the response on her face. I wanted to melt her. But I told her I couldn't. There was Nosei.

The scene shifted. I was driving a minicar inside a room with a tree growing in it. I bumped into a crippled old woman, rocking in a chair. I stopped, afraid I had caused damage. She was unhurt, but I hung around, worrying that I was nonetheless in trouble.

I woke up. I remembered this much and no more. Why would I dream of Vanessa Redgrave? The dream came back to me after I had been going to my doctor about a year. Long enough to feel the intensity of the embrace in his silences and spaces made for me. The eyes of Vanessa Redgrave were his eyes, wanting whatever I could give, waiting on me, no matter how long it took. But I realized I'd seen those eyes before. They were the eyes I had wanted to see in mother—-eyes I had almost seen. And there it was—the seduction of *almost*, things just out of reach.

I suddenly knew why I had dreamt of her. I had been attracted to her character in the movie "Julia," when I was still a teenager. I remember feeling like Jane Fonda who played the part of Lillian Hellman—apart, unsure, frightened. In a scene in a restaurant between them, as Julia was trying to get Hellman's help, it felt to me almost like they were making love. Or at least that Julia was making love—allowing love. I would have given anything to have had a Julia waiting on me that way. Julia was a vision of mother.

[Julie]

The Unthinkable

(The Novel When It Began)

[Nosei, '84]

Part I

After the accident that took Betti Peleg, after the disappearance of Julie, her daughter, I began this novel to get hold of my desperation. I hadn't intended it that way but I couldn't bear for Archie not to be taken seriously. Still, I was reeling with questions. What actually had happened to Archie, and now Betti and Julie? I reasoned that intelligent readers would want the truth of it, while those who wanted to laugh at Shechner and whistle in the dark would not be able to do so in a novel. You can't so easily drag a fictional character through the mud.

I would not have thought of a novel except for having been exposed to Svitz's endless theorizing about it. Anyone can write a novel, he said, but few can criticize it. He meant by this to commend his own choice of the critic's vocation, yet I heard it differently. I understood that novels could elude criticism of their contents. I realized I could keep Wisdom hidden from cheap reproach in the guise of fiction, just as she had been protected in the *Scroll of the History of Adam.* Even the Bible's authors screened their versions of the story, softening our criticism of Adam or Eve or the Snake, or even the Creator—characters who hold us spellbound by their tales alone, as in a novel.

I began wondering how my relationships with Betti and Julie developed so fast. It all happened in little more than a month. In a few blinks of the eyelash, Archibald Shechner rivalled my own father's gift for arousing me by his absence. When I was a child and he was away guest-lecturing around the globe, my father would loom as a fantastic personality in my imagination.

Even before Archie's mind took center stage in my life, Harriman Svitz was the leading lecturer. Something uncannily similar had progressed in Julie's life: Svitz shook her up during his academic leave in her country, preparing her to appreciate the mind of Archibald Shechner.

Svitz, eccentric as he is, is an ordinary genius. He can't approach the wild freedom of Archie's mind. Were you to find yourself even snorkelling in a reef close to shore, for instance, facing that extravagant nonhuman realm, you would be relieved that Svitz had been effectively muzzled from commenting. Because he would be sure to make the wildness less real for you. The same held above ground, of course, but I never saw it clearly until Archie's notes opened my eyes to the Scroll.

Meanwhile, I followed the conventional-minded Svitz. He imagined that the jungle was our wildest state and we had to progress as far away from it as we could. War is also a type of jungle, whereas life in an ivory tower appears the most civilized, curtained off from any semblance of a jungle. Suddenly, Archie turns that prevailing notion upside down. "Terror in war is as close as we get to the wild," Archie's commentary says, "but the awe of the natural wild can replace it." Our entire culture has been mistaken, then. Striving to tame the wild has led to the worst wars yet. After that announcement, you lose all appetite to hear another Svitzean lecture.

Our idea of progress develops and tames everything, like Svitz explicating a text. Now we have to face it. According to Archie, our culture has held us back from learning from the wild our deepest need: to evolve. To evolve physically—unthinkable as that thought is!—to evolve into a new species. Transforming the colonized hulks of our cities into memorials to the past and its childish drive to tame everything. Because the flip side of evolving is the colonizing drive, and it inhibits us from risking evolution. It protects the hive, so to speak. To evolve means to risk new shapes, Archie intimated, risk new thoughts, and that requires we live close to the wild, just like our evolving ancestors.

"How can you do that in this shrinking world?" I asked Julie, anticipating she had asked the same of Archie while he was still around.

"You disengage the colonizing drive," she said. "You can't restore the natural wild with technology but you can restore its meaning by memorializing it."

"Create museums?" I said.

"No. Sanctuaries, preserves. Places where you can face the loss. If you can get close to loss you can lose yourself, and that's the first day of clearing a space for a new creation."

I think of the astronauts floating in their chambers—how important will walking ever be to them again? Floating is not so strange an adaptation. We began life as floaters, evolving through embryo and fetus. Lost to us, floating can ease the burden of fighting against evolution that civilization teaches.

Remembering my encounter with the Scroll and its handlers, perhaps I can lose a burden there, leave it behind. Remembering, memorializing. Can any loss equal the loss of that unexpected Scroll—a gift to our world from the Earth herself? I tried to recall the evening I met Julie, my third evening in the Mideast...

Part II

Alex Sened, custodian of celebrities, leans over Betti like a curling lamppost, feigning interest but his mind somewhere else. "Oh Betti, how nice you look," he intones, looking over her head at the cars pulling into the driveway. "Nosei is here already. Yonat will introduce you."

"I want to see Svitz," she said, pinching Sened's arm. "Please Alex, take me to him?" A short, stocky woman in a navy blue dress with white scarf, suitable for court, Betti's overexcitement at parties left her businesslike, following a plan, and ready to leave after it was carried out.

"Svitz you won't miss, in the garden probably. But please, go look for Yonat." Betti had supervised the younger therapist's work with Holocaust survivors, back in the fifties, when they'd just begun to talk about themselves.

Now Yonat was always looking for ways to pay Betti back, while the older woman was only interested in something her admirer couldn't know about. Each attempt by Yonat only further frustrated both of them. Svitz was the sole living person who could help her now.

She edged around the corners of the living and dining rooms, rooms overheated by the crowds of secretaries that preceded each of the invited media-elites. Svitz was a star; Israel idolized intellectuals, even above sports stars, and Svitz was considered one of the top three in the world. Some of the edge was off, of course. This was the going-away party that was to be a gala, party of the century, reported around the globe. It would celebrate the announcement of the Scroll's discovery. In lieu of proclamation, a combination of Israelis and foreigners mingled in bittersweet bemusement over their fate. Invited to validate the Scroll by testing the skeptical light of their expertise on it, they were happily prepared to lose, and to declare its authenticity. Now, however, these burnished authorities were thrown back on whatever reserves of optimism they possessed, for the media had already buried the whole event as a hoax.

From a birth to a wake, that's how it seemed, but the swing of the pendulum was so great it still left everyone giddy. Few of the secretary's bosses had yet arrived. It was barely eight, the time the party was called for, yet you'd think it was a celebration of a merciful death—a queen in old age, perhaps—since the air of disdain for authority was already in swing. The typist to a famous author was greeted with the same notoriety as her employer; the child of a scholar shone as brightly as his originator; the arts held the upper hand over science by virtue of its intimacy with irony.

At the entrance to the garden, Betti recognized Aharon Appelfeld, the Nobel candidate for literature, under intense scrutiny from a stranger as he gesticulated with a tall glass of vodka. When he saw her, Appelfeld, a short man, turned from the man smaller than himself and put his drink in Betti's hand. "I didn't drink this vodka yet. I shouldn't; you take it. How have you been?"

Betti glanced at the strange man Appelfeld had abandoned. He had red hair and he appeared hardly taller than she was. He jumped to introduce himself. "I'm a critic for The New Yorker," he said. "What do *you* do?

"Must I tell you?" she shot back, snubbing him. It was a rare occasion when Appelfeld reached out to her, or to anyone, and she wanted to take advantage of it. "I don't drink, Aharon. Just leave it on the table. I read the new article you wrote in The Land."

"They butchered it," said Appelfeld, and he leaned forward to inspect the silk flower pinned to Betti's sweater."

"An orchid," she whispered in his ear, "a paph."

"Aha," said Appelfeld, "the one with the penis?"

"They all have that, Professor. This one has human size and flesh color; well, a miniature man, perhaps. Here, touch it; it feels like skin, too." Betti slipped her thumb in back of her sweater and proffered the dull reddish flower.

"They took all the guts out of it," Appelfeld continued, absently fondling the flower, "all the history and Jewishness, so I'd sound more like a journalist."

"But there was plenty of drollery you don't usually read in the paper. Not too many newspaper writers are writing about the Scroll as the end of the world."

"That's just it," Appelfeld snapped but in a soft voice. "In the context of biblical history, "world" means "time". The Jew lives in time not space, so it's the end of an era I was referring to, not the end of the world. Another epoch follows, and for us it will be another world—there is no end. But all that we've lost in this one will be past mourning, past feeling. When I think about life before the Holocaust now, my feelings are numb, I watch it like a movie I don't understand, like a documentary about some ancient, prehuman species. What do they talk to each other about, I want to know. Could I communicate with them? All the nuance of this loss of connection was cut out by the editors. To them, it wasn't a penis, it was a weed."

Everett Nosei relished the conversation. He stood behind Appelfeld, smiling broadly in such a way that Betti would understand what a good sport he was. She had insulted him but won his respect. She was a woman who could not be intimidated, not even by the great eulogist of the Holocaust, Appelfeld. Now Nosei stepped forward, and when Appelfeld failed again to introduce him, he turned directly to Betti: "I heard you say you wanted to speak with Svitz. I overheard him—and he's also been talking about the end of the world."

PART III

Julie turned and smiled at Everett Nosei, took his arm, and the two walked away as if they'd known each other a long time. In another hour, they were exchanging confidences and drinking from the same glass. A few minutes more and they were engaged in an intimate analysis of the evening.

"Gifts come in unexpected ways," said Everett Nosei. "When you do something for which you have no time or patience, something insignificant and you are already criticizing yourself for not ignoring it—at times like that, in spite of yourself, a message gets through that changes your life, puts a mirror in front of you. That's what it's all about, this message tells you: seeing yourself. When you see yourself as you appear to a stranger, with the intelligence and concern of your very own self, then you know why you are alive.

"Here's an example," Everett Nosei continued, after sipping his vodka glass as if it were a fine brandy. "I was talking to my favorite aunt Mariko last week while I was still in New York. She lives in Miami now, my only U.S. relative; straight from Yokohama to Florida, never even visited another American city. Recently she found a boyfriend who thinks she is the funniest person on earth. He laughs and weeps at everything she says. I was the only one who thought she was funny before that, but I would not have told her so. She would have been insulted. Now this stranger comes along and she tells me that he has brought out a whole side of her personality that had been hidden since she was a girl. She had witty things to say now, they just came to her spontaneously. Now, at 83, she found the self-awareness that had always eluded her, reflected in this Morty's love. She could even laugh at herself when she looked silly, or when she said something out of sync with others—which was often because she still had a Japanese accent. So there it was, at that late age she saw herself more clearly and her life brightened.

"When I'm getting ready to end the phone conversation, Aunt Mariko says, 'I'm a lucky girl because if Morty hadn't come along, what would I do but lie in my bed watching the news and waiting for death. Now we go out and I meet new people.' All her life she ignored newspapers and television, but suddenly in her eighties she found CNN, watched it hours on end. I often called her for an update on some issue or country. She was full of the love of knowledge, she was growing, but while alone all she could see was herself lying in bed. 'What is there to do but wait for death?' That phrase ripped past my impatience and I saw the specter of having to wait, of not being able to take the initiative, of being passive—that was death itself, the body laid out in its coffin. I saw my own bed, my own coffin, and I saw it was a scholar's bed, the most passive of occupations.

"And that's what's propelled me here, to Tel Aviv and to this party for Svitz and the unfortunate Scroll."

"How interesting, the connections you make," said Julie, now stirring her drink with a finger. "I think what you might have said is that Svitz is like your aunt, someone always growing. But come greet your old friend now. You might be surprised by the way death is a theme for him tonight, just as it was for your aunt."

"No, I think I'm the Aunt Mariko of this party. The Scroll was my Mort, and now it's as if he died. No, no, not as if it's dead: it's as if it never existed. I'm not interested in death themes anymore, especially the old literary ones of Svitz. I'm ready to imagine the power of what doesn't even exist yet."

Julie grabbed his arm and pulled him away. "You're probably alot more interesting now than before. Don't you want to see if Svitz can tell?"

Harriman Svitz was standing in a small circle of admirers, near the pool lit up by underwater lights. Compared to the shorter Israelis, he was burnished, already a bronzed Buddha of himself. It wasn't about skin color—some of the Israelis were darker—but about the mold the body and head seemed to be cast in. In other celebrities, it might have been plaster, even iron, but in Svitz it was clearly something firmer yet more subtle, bronze. He was as palpable as money: you could sense that his value and weight had been fixed.

Julie led Everett Nosei and her mother on either arm, out through the patio and past the tables behind which the bartenders worked feverishly, filling the glasses of people standing three deep. It had been more than an hour since Betti had arrived, and the Seneds house had filled to capacity. Past the lawn Julie led them, where others were dancing, and down to the darkness of the pool, lit only from underwater. She swept right past the circle around Svitz and as soon as he saw her he paused, smiled, and bowed slightly, taking her hand a bit too eagerly.

"Professor Svitz," Julie said, in a suggestively intimate tone, "may I present my mother, Betti Peleg. And your American colleague is here, Everett Nosei. I know they have some interesting things to say to you. Vice versa, I'm sure." Julie was unabashed, though Betti knew her daughter well enough to suspect more was going on. Why would Julie have already talked to Svitz if it wasn't in some way to influence his opinion of her? Nothing ever happened with Julie by accident, thought Betti; Julie, being so passive, acted only by a well-thought-out plan. What Betti knew less well about her daughter was that Julie was also a detective at heart and that her pose of indifference was the classic front of a first class investigator.

"Julie has told me that her mother was a psychiatrist," said Svitz. "She also said that you were writing a book about the end of the world."

"No, no," said Betti. "Not exactly. It is a book about an ancient document."

"Yes, I came here especially because of what I heard about it," Svitz answered, lowering his voice portentously. "For at least twenty years I knew something like it had to have existed. It makes sense it should be found in our lifetimes. We were just talking about how the events of the last two decades have changed the world forever, although few realize how deeply. Suddenly we are at the end of days, nothing new can be written. As a critic I've felt in my bones there was nothing new. So I'm not surprised to hear that in twenty years from now all of the oceans will be dead. Forty percent of the fish and flora of the world's oceans have already disappeared, they say. No extinction like this has happened in human history. A Holocaust has happened—but not such mass extinction of species since humans evolved. I believe our Bible called it the end of days, "the big extinction," and what I've learned here is that the early books which spoke about it were suppressed. Only the prophets kept the tradition alive, but they spoke of the end of the world in metaphor and parable. Well, of course; they were writers who knew there could be nothing new for them. I never liked them for that reason. What was the sense of being a critic of that sort of writing? Now I see I must humbly accept the burden of prophecy myself."

Betti was stunned by the coincidence that Svitz shared her interest and didn't hear the man's impervious conceit. She hardly knew how to begin. Should she talk about the book before it was ready? Should she even mention Archibald Shechner? As she hesitated, Svitz turned back to Julie. What is going on? thought Betti. Could he think Julie knows the answers?

"But Professor Svitz," Betti insisted, grabbing his arm, turning him away from Julie. "Professor Svitz, I have been working on the very project, the suppressed ancient scroll you heard of. My daughter knows something about it but I have shared this work with no one yet."

Now she had won Svitz's full attention and was already feeling guilty that he was losing interest in Julie. How often she had taught Julie how to take an interest. Betti had talked of this party often in the preceding weeks, hoping that Julie would come and perhaps meet some interesting man.

Now she had found an interest in the very man that Betti herself had come for. And it seemed Svitz had developed a mutual regard for Julie. How could that be, with so many attractive, older women here? Julie could have been his granddaughter, perhaps thirty years younger than him. And Julie—what would she see in this shapeless though slippery intellectual?

"Professor Svitz, my mother is just the woman you must talk to," Julie said, grabbing his arm again.

"I'm sure," Svitz said with a trace of impatience. "But I want to hear more from you, Julie. Please come with me to the villa where I am staying. I must go there to call my son, who has just returned from New Guinea." Then he whispered something more in Julie's ear that seemed to instantly win her collaboration. What he confided in her was that his son only believed he was in New Guinea, but actually, he was under treatment in a mental hospital.

Betti was startled again, both by Svitz and her daughter. Rarely did she misjudge strangers but even less seldom had she misjudged someone close to her. She had never seen Julie this taken with anyone.

Part IV

The idea for turning to this novel, and I freely admit it, came from Julie's transcription notebooks. I read these passages in Tel Aviv during the time I was sharing her apartment. Evidently, she was moved to write down certain conversations with Svitz while transcribing the tapes.

Julie's contact with me must have encouraged her to feel that deciphering Archibald Shechner was not madness. And it wasn't. I have never met anyone who so easily took the measure of the egomaniacal Harriman Svitz, for instance, as this woman. Except for Anna Freud's encounter with him, of course, from whom Julie must have taken a cue.

About Julie's involvement with Svitz I remain puzzled. Was he to be the means for legitimizing Archie's work? If so, it was brilliant of Julie to go over the heads of the local academics. She understood the gods of public persuasion, the powers of celebrity. All this could be learned in the hothouse of Israeli culture, fueled by many of the best minds from Europe and Russia that immigrated there. Some of the fiercest political battles any democracy has ever seen took place there.

Yet what could she have known of men, based on her limited experience? That she could dominate them cerebrally? Why didn't she compete with me, then?

Part V

I enjoyed playing student to Svitz. It was his way of seducing me, dazzling me with his mind. Some women can't resist playing mama to this balding prodigy. Svitz enchants them like a newborn; they're captivated by the little man they bring forth. So I'd pretend to be hypnotized, and he'd start leaning his generous shiny head on my shoulder. Then I'd do a jitterbug in my seat, his head plopping over suprised—and by then I'd be on my own mental riff, telling him a thing or two about something, usually nature stuff or psychology. He had a block against reading it. And he'd always forget that a woman could tell him anything, so he'd look kind of like startled blubber until he could change the subject again.

Once we were playing this scene on the terrace cafe of the university, overlooking the Mount of Olives. Most professors were eating inside, in the air conditioning. You could see the Judean desert waver as through crinkly cellophane in back of Svitz's shoulder, but the heat was way out there. Here on Mount Scopus there were breezes, and Svitz, sending me into a trance about the lineage of the "mad" writer he'd met, Appelfeld, started to let his head nod against my hair.

Appelfeld had all these precursors, according to Svitz, and he blotted them out with the biggest bludgeon any writer had found, the Holocaust. Natural enough for a Jewish survivor. Only Appelfeld didn't himself know it; he was a gentle madman you see, a kind of Peter Lorre without guile. Kafka was one of them—the father figures Appelfeld was flattening into the Holocaust landscape—and some more obscure Europeans like the German writer, Joseph Roth, and when Svitz's head collided with mine I let it. The subject was too touchingly incongruous and anyway mother had rarely talked about it, our bookshelves free of recent history.

"The message of the twentieth century is written in its human catastrophes," Svitz was saying, emphasizing the you in *human*, still reacting to my nudge about how the closest he got to Mother Nature was a piece of paper. "Human nature is all we can know," he said, pontifically. Then, his head leaning against mine, he said, "Only the Holocaust survivors saw the message but Appelfeld ignores it. He lets the landscape speak, as if there was an answer beyond us. No Tolstoy has arrived to show us the answer is human."

Svitz sighed as he spoke and I allowed myself to soothe him, letting his hand rest in mine as he continued. "The human being hides a sting like a bee and when its house is upset it goes mad in defense. The Germans in their madness imagined themselves attacked. They blamed their weak mothers for the vulnerable state of the hive, and they went out to dominate the world like their fathers had done in philosophy. But outside their own hive were only shadows, not fellow human beings. And inside were larger shadows, the Jews, who must have loomed large as beekeepers to them. That's what they were, the Jews, beekeepers of civilization. You can see it now in the orchestras of Israel, in desert towns with their repetoires of Bach, Beethoven and Mozart, and in tiny Tel Aviv apartments combed to the ceiling with books."

Part VI

While Julie told her story, I nursed my Turkish coffee, quite cold by now but it was sweet and thick and began to evoke an intense childhood encounter with an ice cream sundae. I glanced at the top of Julie's thigh every so often, protruding thick and white beneath the table while she slouched in a wicker chair. She wore the shortest miniskirt I had seen in twenty years, but although she herself was petite the black mini didn't betray her: the charcoal knit seemed poured out or painted on, thanks to sculpted hips.

I had a conversation with Svitz since arriving that resembled Julie's. We were strolling in downtown Tel Aviv's Dizengoff square on a crisp winter day, our jackets unbuttoned in homage to the Mediterranean sun. It was mostly Svitz talking but I remember my own thoughts better, after Svitz had said, "The largest statements, the ones that become myth, are made by the great ironists, those who admit ignorance in behalf of their field. Freud in psychology, Scholem in religion. The small minds are the custodians, certain of whatever falls into their custody. They are convinced the ancients were saintly, sentimental men like themselves."

Meanwhile, Julie had ordered a big salad and I was staring into it as she nibbled. It looked like a work of art, set on a vast plate instead of in a bowl, the small cucumber slices fixed in a green necklace around the long-necked Israeli tomatoes. More like a jewelry tray than a salad.

If anything ensures humility, I remember thinking as Svitz and I wandered down a street off the square and came abruptly onto the beach and facing the sea, it's trying to reconstruct nature while we've got our binoculars backward. Then I was explaining to Svitz how I was discovering that a major ecosystem can seem as vast and diverse as the universe and even more distant. Its complexity, woven in millions of years of history, defies the complex organ we've developed to mimic it, namely our brains. But at the mention of "ecosystem" Svitz coughed, as if somebody was trying to choke him. Spare me, he implored with a wave of his hand. So the conversation would continue in my head. "If you don't know your function in an ecosystem, you can't see yourself and you can't trust nature. It's a license for madness, cruelty, repressive debates between science and religion."

'A license for art,' Svitz would have said, 'for character, drama, sexuality, all the best reasons for being alive.' And a mask for cruelty, I would silently add, trying to slow him down in my mind. "All things kill and feed as far as they can range," I continued, now out loud. "I'm sure you agree with that. But only we invent an ethical purpose to hide our guilt."

Julie had eaten half way around the necklace.

"Guilt?" he asked.

"Guilt for this pact with death," I answered, "even if it's imaginary. We make the deal when we sublimate the wish to kill and digest our competitor. It may be the crowning human development, this guilt," I continued, while Svitz listened to my outburst ruefully, as if I was some foreign colleague from Ethiopia who must be tolerated. Who was I, after all, but a pent-up philologist. Nevertheless, I parade-marched my force of words before the distracted general.

"As a complement to this guilt the human imagination evolved. Our faces are masks as a result, an artifice, capable of showing untrue feelings. And the truth all our complexity is covering up? Animals don't need a purpose because their niche in the ecosystem is plain, but we have buried ours, somewhere back in the forests and savannahs, and our cover-ups are so complex, so artful that they produce great theories of science, systems of religion and works of art."

"It's a cruel business, and it inflates our sense of superiority," Svitz responded. "But then, my boy, what else can we do with our advanced knowledge?" Young mothers with the burnished skins of Yemen passed us, pushing strollers occupied by toddlers with yellow mashed-potatoed cheeks.

I pushed on, subverting the question. "The more we're superior to other living things, both those too small and those too distant in the universe to see, the more we lose sight of the limits of our intelligence."

(Between bites of the tomatoes she had cut with fork and knife, Julie pointed out features of the Jerusalem landscape below us, gesturing with knife in hand, her short arm accentuating the gleaming utensil.)

Svitz paced on, apparently not listening or looking at anything. Not the golden tamarind trees, whose leaves sat at their feet like a hundred discarded earrings. Not the ceremonious gray clouds streaked with sunlight, above the Bauhaus influenced, art-deco buildings. Not the mixed pasta of small wrappers and cigarette butts that lined the margins of the esplanade, as if neatly swept there by a brisk wind.

"Why is it here and here alone that you can't admit ignorance?" That's the issue I wanted to put before Svitz.

And I had the answer for him: Because this beach and ocean is the *actual* field, not some artificial field of knowledge. If you face the beauty of the field your own creations shrivel up. The truth behind Shakespeare or Freud is how touching we are, how small and vulnerable, and how all we know of what is moving and poignant is allied with infancy: What can we imagine more vulnerable and helplessly intense than a human infant?

I thought this but didn't say it. I said nothing more, and Svitz waved a weak farewell as I lingered and he retraced his steps quickly toward the taxi stand in Dizengoff.

"I had no maternal instincts for Svitz the suckling," Julie was saying, brandishing the fork over her now empty plate. "He couldn't feed on my energy. I teased him with ecology stuff he hated to hear because he didn't know how to refute it. 'Do you know why a swamp contains more records than the British Museum?' 'No, why?' he said with a frown, as if waiting for the punchline of a bad joke. I answered: 'The diversity of species there is more complex than the origins of civilization.' Imagine how smart I felt, telling the famous critic of so-called originals where the real sources were."

1995

Because mother had placed Harriman Svitz on her map of necessary recources, I had also. I made myself an advance scout at the party in Nosei's novel. My strategy was simply to place myself. I actually did very little that evening, except be in the right place at the right time. I had a routine that I'd honed with Archie, though he only rarely played along. I guess it could be called "Julie's Impersonation of Wisdom" or "Wisdom Takes a Holiday." It was as if Wisdom had taken the shape of a twentieth century Tel Aviv woman barely in her twenties. Svitz didn't exactly play along that night—he didn't understand what was being impersonated. He responded instead to a tease, for I quickly found that though frustrated by the talk of ecology, he was nonetheless compelled by his distaste to lap up whatever subtext of sexuality he could find.

I could embody a sexuality—as long as I was just out of reach. Svitz liked such play, I found. He encouraged a mischeviousness I rarely experienced since primary school, when I flirted with boys and then kicked them in the shins, with them loving it, even through the grimacing. There was a strange relief in playing these games of intellectual flirtation with Svitz. I simply never had to worry about him.

Although Nosei didn't speak of vulnerability with Svitz, he did with me. That passage invoking Shakespeare—"how touching we are, how small and vulnerable"—is exactly as I remember Nosei talking at the lunch of the necklace salad. When I heard it, I felt like I was released from a burden I could not name. It was just a matter of leaving it behind, I thought. Tears came into my eyes as he continued, talking about mistakes.

"Have you ever wondered about Adam and Eve after the Garden? Why they clung to each other? I think it was a secret they shared—the secret of their mistakes in the Garden. The first feelings of hurt were felt by them. When

I read novels, I want to know more about mistakes, about our vulnerability as a species. I know I can entrust myself to a writer if they know it is *that* we must know so much more about: the frontier of knowing our species' original limitations. You are at that frontier as well, Julie—in the work you did with Archie and your mother."

I remember laughing in response. It seemed to annoy but concern him. "Why did you laugh?" he asked.

Well, I didn't know. It felt thrilling to be in all that company. I think if I'd known something more of myself, I would have said, "I make my own frontiers."

"I see you don't think you can be at a frontier," he said.

"No, that's not it. It's more that, I mean, is that who I am? I mean, I can feel it the way you do, but can I, me, feel it? I don't know..." I trailed off, feeling muddled, cowardly, like I was snubbing good fortune. "But I'm not telling you what I felt about what you said. I've never heard it said before. It makes me feel that I have the possibility—that I'm not alone."

"The possibility of what? Alone in what?"

"Alone in my mistakes," I said. He looked puzzled. I thought he wondered how any mistakes I had made could already weigh so heavily. Anyway, I had made what would be the first of many mistakes with Everett Nosei of '84.

"I was speaking of us as a species, not as individuals, Julie. You shouldn't take things in so personally."

"But you were talking about novels, which portray us as individuals. You were speaking of yourself, of us." Yet I felt I had strayed from him. It was a feeling that at that time was overwhelmed by another. We were making love with words.

[Julie]

PART VII

Professor Harriman Svitz chortled as he told his "wild goose story" about writers who were nature-obsessed. The writer Mathiessen had goaded some urban colleagues into a trip to see the last of a near-extinct stork in Asia. "Can you believe, at this late stage in history, that writers can take nature so literally?" shrugged Svitz. Each individual was a dying species in Svitz's eyes, so why invest any concern. Never mind that he himself was a walking ecosystem, in which the dying and the extinct were both fully embodied. Walking itself seemed awkward and unnatural to him, as if he were avoiding some more fitting means of locomotion, such as rolling. Or not moving at all, just sitting and expounding—the seductions of his thought, vocalized, holding together a mini-universe of unseen organisms.

The best work had to be "mad," expounded Svitz, as he perhaps attempted to deflect similar suspicions about himself. Yet he was a true academic and it was in the lecture hall that his madness seemed merely affected, not clinical, an exaggeration of parochial campus life in New England—"Where I usually sit," he would never fail to remind his Israeli listeners. Even the user of a computer could be "a madman" in Svitz's quaint parlance, and Freud was "a mad poet". His paranoia about competition—a madness so blatant people would reflexively flinch in his presence—also seemed to charm some polite academics. I remember how my mother glowed when she told her friends a story Anna Freud had confided to her. The daughter of Sigmund Freud, in New Haven during an international seminar that included Svitz, appeared to tremble when he introduced himself as "one of your father's lovers".

"Shakespeare was ahead of your father, I'm afraid, my dear," Svitz began indelicately. "Poor Uncle Siggy—forgive me, sweet lady, it is our endearment for your father—was more a Hamlet figure than an ego superimposed on an id."

Anna Freud was hardly at a loss, however. My mother was always possessive about Ms. Freud's wit. An unusual friendship with Ms. Freud formed out of the many psychoanalytic conferences they attended together in Europe; she was one of the few women my mother ever spoke about. Ms. Freud took a special interest in Israel, wanting to hear everything my mother had to tell. "Oh please, Professor Svitz, you need not feel threatened by my father," my mother would begin in a sly tone, imitating Anna Freud, as the great analyst proceeded: "He did not claim to be a literary critic and so you must not feel a need to proclaim your superiority."

"But lady, it is Shakespeare, not myself I proclaim," said Svitz, a believer in his own modesty.

"Yes, yes, I have no doubt it is your mother you seek to honor, not yourself," the famous psychoanalyst retorted, sharpening her wit. "But you might be wiser to pick a woman writer for this role, Professor. Perhaps you might discover a heretofore unknown great woman writer who supersedes even Shakespeare. Perhaps the first writer of the Bible was a woman, have you considered that?"

Svitz was growing frustrated by this woman, furiously mopping his brow with the unbuttoned cuff of his shirt until it hung soggily away from his arm like a vestigial appendage. "Dear lady," he stammered, "the problem is that your father's tropes do not measure up to the Bard of Avon's. I would like to put it more delicately but it is plain as the paper it is written on."

"Oh professor," the elder scientist replied, "you need pretend no kindness toward me. It is easy to see you are confused by having to wrestle intellectually with a woman, or with my father through his daughter. Your fear of lashing out at a woman is probably greater than your fear of being shamed by one. Surely you can see this comes from idolizing your mother and thus repressing your desire to get back at her for seeming to prefer your father over you on occasion."

"My, my, dear Professor Freud," Svitz stuttered.

"Hush now, Professor Svitz. You may continue to call me Anna. By the way, have you never talked to a psychoanalyst before?"

"I do not wish to bore you, lady, but you remind me of a delicious experience I must relate." With a story to tell, Svitz regained his composure. "You see, I did once go to a psychiatrist. And not just any psychiatrist, mind you, but the leading psychiatrist on the Eastern seaboard, as we refer to the intellectual shores of America. Now, now, forgive me, my dear, perhaps you need not be instructed in such things as literary geography. To the point, sweet lady, to the point: I sat with this gracious man for over an hour, during which I was forced to point out that I had apparently read all the texts he had read yet failed to read deeply. You may think this pompous of me, but he in fact quite graciously accepted my observations and asked for a list of texts I thought he should reread.

"Well, the result of over an hour of conversation was that I had to admit that it was certainly impossible for me to discuss my life with someone whom I could not help but feel my intellectual inferior. Now wait, wait, before you rush to judgment. He actually agreed with me, did the good doctor. He recommended that I need seek no further counsel, so long as I found reasonable solace and comfort in my books. I thanked this good man, and I'm afraid that's the end of my story."

Svitz made a gesture of waving his arm to emphasize the end of his story and the limp shirt cuff flapped as he did so, mocking him. "Professor Svitz, you make it impossible to hold any conversation at all. Perhaps this makes you an exemplary lecturer but I pity your poor students when you run short on entertaining stories to tell. Your knowledge is quite formidable but it is foolish of you to hold forth with me. Your mother may have coddled you on her knee and welcomed every word but I assure you I am not her, nor indeed anyone's mother. It is possible for a woman to pursue a life of the mind as well as a man and I think you need not resent it. Please, go take my advice and invent a female counterpart to Shakespeare for yourself. And since you will no doubt go to the Bible, being the origin of all in our culture that is not Greek and pre-Greek and in your mind no doubt appropriated by my father—I refer to more than merely the Oedipus story, of course—since, as I say, you will turn to the Bible to represent the swollen authority you must have, by all means imagine *yourself* a great female author. Perhaps then your poor mother may rest in peace."

PART VIII

When Julie finished relating this story of Harriman Svitz's encounter with Anna Freud, she was giggling uncontrollably. Finally she took her hands away from her face and said, "That's not really all that funny. The man is incapable of seeing himself, except no doubt as a victim of misunderstanding."

"My God, Julie, that's right," I said. "Svitz complained no one could read him. 'I will confide in you, my boy,' he once told me. 'I have never received an intelligent review of one of my books. It is probably an impossibility yet you see I continue along quite optimistically. I take comfort knowing I am doomed, as we all must be.'"

Julie nodded, her eyes closed in thought. "Stretch yourself to include the whole world of knowledge and you have proven to yourself that there is nothing important outside of you and therefore no vantage point from which to see yourself," Julie said. "Presto, no need for self-awareness. You are free to play the victim or clown for all the world because they can't really see you from outside."

"That sounds exactly how the papers have caricatured Shechner!" I cried. "I believed them, too, especially since I was reminded of Svitz."

A frown came over Julie's face. "Don't confuse them, please. Archie had a mind that grew at leaps and bounds in the last years. Your Svitz was a swelled head from his youth: knowledge poured into him but the mold remained the same. I could see right through him because I'm used to these big academics, they all came to our house to show off."

1995

Later, when Nosei and I were together, living and working in my apartment, I would go back to these first conversations. I had stored them in my memory. Some were about Archie—and the voice he was hearing and I was transcribing—while others were about who we were, Nosei and I, in the unfolding revelation. There was one story about who we were as a couple—love children of the Scroll—and everyone seemed to like it. Mother got nervous with excitement and even Svitz seemed a bit dizzied, perhaps with intimations of an intimate relationship with me.

We were believers in the Scroll and in the magic of Nosei and me coming together. Except for Svitz. He didn't go as far as believing in the Scroll, though he was happy to benefit from being associated with it. Svitz was a scared and pitiful man who nevertheless evoked a strong fantasy in me: I thought that he could see through to my fear and precariousness. Some kind of damage of his own prevented him from turning this recognition into a deeper intimacy. "One good thing about Svitz," I would say to myself, "is that he can let someone be just as pathetic as he is."

Why would I want to be around someone who could arouse such disgust and sorrowful sympathy? I tended to forget the raucous laughter that was also a part of it, and the permission I found in his company to say what I wished. Or maybe I needed the space to change and switch—to be an amalgamation. Svitz, I came to realize later, was like Laura in "The Glass Menagerie," when it came to amalgamations. Svitz would have cared not only for the unicorn, and the unicorn with the broken horn, but the broken horn on a non-unicorn—perhaps broken elsewhere as well. Svitz liked me even more because I had patched together my own horn. He called it my "sensibility." He was the first to use that word in relation to me. Nosei was the second. But at that time I couldn't see myself as a patched, damaged creature, anyway. I wanted to live as a real unicorn and, for awhile, I thought I could in Nosei's eyes.

Before we were living together, Nosei and I often made fun of Svitz. Little did Svitz know that he had become a common ground for formulating a new relationship. He became someone safe to use. Nosei and I didn't know how to use each other: afraid of using, afraid of being used. Some precious bit of knowledge was missing in each of us. Since it wasn't there, we could fool ourselves with a usable object like Svitz, criticizing him with the knowledge we did have. In a way, Svitz was our sandbox. We could build up, tear down, and throw Svitz around without ever having to come close to the danger we both feared.

Yet the sandbox grew problematic when we were finally living together. I strangely wanted to defend Svitz sometimes, to protect him. Nosei could not see anything worth respecting. The sandbox began to split, and my sympathy for Nosei became rough, uneven. We both, you might say, had begun to look up from our play, to see the coarseness of our box, the roughness and impurities in the sand. It wasn't what it had seemed to be.

"Don't be ridiculous," Nosei would say about my defense of Svitz. This time the subject was Svitz's lecture at the Hebrew University in Jerusalem, and I had been rather glum afterwards, driving back to Tel Aviv. "He has nothing to say!"

"Perhaps nothing new to say," I responded. "But still there was something different there."

"Like what?"

"Well, like something pursued that he just can't reach—yet is close to not giving a damn about, once and for all."

"And what would that be—is he a case or a man?" Nosei asked.

"I think he wanted to show that he could talk about nature," I said.

"No, he wanted to show that it wasn't worth talking about."

I continued to pursue a defense of Svitz that I wasn't sure even I believed. "If that's true, Nosei, then why did he consent to do a lecture on Mondrian's flowers?"

"Obvious. To put flowers in their place and re-establish his own. That's all." On top of it all, he added, Svitz didn't know how to read Frank O'Hara.

"I was the one who reminded Svitz of that poem of O'Hara's," I said.

"You? When?"

"When he told me about preparing for the lecture. I thought O'Hara's take on Mondrian's flowers might give him another point of view about nature."

"There can be only one point of view and that's Svitz's—you should know that."

But there was some belief in Svitz's sensibility that I wanted to hold onto, even as it was slipping from my hands. "Svitz seemed to struggle with it tonight. Not so certain and smug. And he was excited, eager to have the poem in the presentation. He acted like he relished it as he recited it. But I agree that he didn't know how to take it all in."

"He didn't take any of it in—anything not rooted in a book is too threatening. I don't know why you persist in seeing what is not there. Do you think you can seduce him into finding nature?"

I fixed my eyes on the pavement as I drove with growing anger. I wanted to fly off the road, smash into the gorge. Resisting the extremism of my feelings, I tried again. I wanted him to see what I saw, if dimly. "He did include the poem. He was trying to say something to me."

"Don't be ridiculous."

"Don't call me ridiculous, Nosei."

"I'm not calling *you* ridiculous. It's just the idea of

Svitz even trying, even making an effort to see something someone else's way. He just doesn't have it in him. I've been around him for alot longer than you have, and I used to think he was so brilliant he didn't need to listen to anyone. But if it is so—if he somehow tuned into you—it's because he was seduced into it. Who could resist a poem presented to them by you?"

Nosei was speaking but it was also like a voice in my head I was resisting. What was it saying? Something about seduction. Me.

"You resist yourself as a seductive creature."

It sounded in the next moment like it came from outside the car. But it was Nosei's voice. He repeated himself. "You resist your seductiveness, and that gets you in trouble."

"Am I in trouble?" I asked.

"No, but this has been very draining. What's going on Julie?"

I wanted to be free of him. Away. I turned on him. No way out. The car was moving. "What about you? Did it occur to you that maybe you're not as big an expert on Svitz as you think you are? I'm tired of kicking Svitz into the dung heap. I feel pushed and I don't like it."

But the confrontation was not about Nosei and me anymore. It was about a voice I couldn't place—and it reminded me of Archie's desperate insistence on hearing the voice come out of the ground. In a way, all my transcribing of Archie's sessions had been a means of not hearing the voice, of containing it. Now it was breaking through; I was sensing it while driving, the palms outside of Tel Aviv thrusting up just as Nosei seemed to invite me to be as seductive as I wished with him. A seductive voice opened in me, deeper than any other. I had to believe it came from the same desire to evolve that had possessed Archie and my mother.

Silence. The longer it continued, the more dead it felt. Everything seemed to collapse into it. When we got home, the apartment seemed dead also. I felt—not dead—but a dying and withering inside. Scarier than imagining a voice from outside the car was a fear that it was going to sabotage my relationship wth Nosei. How could I be seductive if I myself was being seduced by a desire to evolve—a desire coming from a place I could not even locate? The same desire that led to Archie's disappearance.

I apologized, and just about fainted asleep. Things were easily repaired. I was kissed good night. But I was dying. A hole had opened in my world.

[Julie]

Part IX

Archeologists are like sports heroes here. Archie not only boiled the reporters in their own milk—pardon the Israeli phrase—he was an easy target for everybody's resentment against the media. It's like the media became their own "Ugly Israeli" but Archie then took it from them and made it worse by turning archeologists into buffoons.

The media still didn't get it. Archie parodied common sense but he did it by saying the unthinkable. No one could conceive of a partriarchal yet female concept of God. It was like telling people they killed Moses and then invented a religion to cover it up—exactly what Freud said in his last book and nobody wanted to hear, anymore than they want to hear that they felt like having sex with their parents. Yet these same people go to Freudian therapists like Betti Peleg. I told her, it's the same as with Freud's Moses: we buried Wisdom ourselves. Unlike the mortal man, however, Wisdom can't be killed, and she caricatured our efforts by hiding in the same ground our bodies return to.

Yet what Archie said that was most unthinkable was that *plants* are our superiors. That sounded like madness, especially from a scientist. No one was ready for that. It all makes sense when you hear the tapes Betti gave Julie Peleg to transcribe. If people were too upset to even listen, what could he do?

Everyone expects human culture to be superior because it speaks. TV and movies talk to us in our own language. How can you compare a radio to an animal? Animals make all sorts of sounds but none can speak as fluently as a radio. A city surrounds us with words and images we can think about, while out in the wilderness you only think your own thoughts. Now here comes the discoverer of this earth-shattering Scroll and tells us that plants used to speak! Who wants to hear that?

Everyone's reading newspapers and books made of trees that we printed the words upon. Wouldn't our whole civilization be a dumb enterprise if the trees had their own things to say?

Chapter 8

Chapter 8

[Sunday] Become an Unknown

Wisdom asks: Why is there conflict between environmentalists and the cultural religion? The environmentalists say they are at the new frontier, it's biocentric, and man is not at the center anymore, just as Copernicus augured that earth was not at the center of the universe. The religionists take the same evidence and say it proves the universe is anthropocentric, because the conditions that give rise to human intelligence are so miniscule that the whole universe had to be created—just to allow for our possibility. Anyway, each argues their own myth of what the Garden of Eden is. The environmentalists say we have destroyed it ourselves, we're responsible for re-creating it; the religionists say we can regain it, as in Milton's epic, "Paradise Regained": returning to God's arms. Are both arguing the same thing, myth against myth? No, they're both on the sidelines, thanks to their passionate defense of myths. The real frontier is an intellectual frontier, and few are passionate about that. The real frontier is in understanding the evolution of the banana and its many species. Yes, we can grow our own bananas and tomatoes, and give ourselves a false sense of superiority. We can grow them—just like we can make myths—but we don't understand them, how they came to be. We are just cloners, and the academics are merely idea-cloners. They're afraid of the real intellectual work at the frontier, understanding the urge to evolve. The religionists think evolving is unnecessary since an afterlife awaits them. The environmentalists think we should repress the urge before it destroys the planet. They have the right instinct but the future is a push to understand, not restrain. The evolutionary process begs constant knowledge: It is a race against time, against changing conditions for life that antiquates conventional ways of thinking. As one joins this race, however, one must step away from the public races—political and religious—and become an unknown. Evolution takes place at a frontier that few approach. Someone, something is different, a poor copy of the plan. These few individuals may seem to be cast out, but in fact they could not help themselves from exploring until they became lost at the frontier, now unknown. Call it a natural selection.

[Monday] Supernatural Sense

Wisdom asks: Why are you alone among other people? Isolation is where thinking puts you. Thinking is how we evolved and to understand it you have to see how a thought differentiates itself from another thought, as one species does from another. Yes, individuals differ too, but we seduce and reproduce together. Species, however, grow by isolation, isolating differences until they're cut off from the original species, unable to produce strong offspring. A model for human thinking is this natural translation of what was formerly represented as supernatural: the ecosystem, in which desire for diversity resembles the urging of each thought to distinguish itself from the next. How opposed to the pressures of society, which values conformity and organization! Yes, thought insists on planning as well, but the plan turns into that natural process found in the ecosystem. And what is that? We are beginning to know it when we touch the heart of its design, evolving.

[Tuesday] Post-Supernatural

Wisdom asks: Why is nothing surprising you anymore? If the sky fell and God walked into your dwelling surrounded by a band of angels, you would have—or expect—an explanation. That's because you have already imagined it. But what you haven't imagined is the life of a plant as it evolves to another species—and this will surprise you because it redefines imagination. We're no longer privately intimidated by power and the supernatural, yet here the plant is not impressing us with its power—rather, with its innate intelligence. Recall how human understanding was doubted by saying that the mind is not merely a thinking machine, since it knows that it exists and thinks? That it must be supernatural? Here's an apotheosis of vanity, neglecting to see Wisdom in all things. Yes, we know we think, but we know little about the context—except that it is *natural*. The plant teaches how little we know about the natural context itself, the ecosystem in which we or any creature evolve. It was when humans suspected they could not learn fast enough from the natural—about the purpose for being alive—that the supernatural seemed a necessity. Now, Homo sapiens have taken the first step in looking beneath the surface of the natural world, to hear the beating heart of a deep time and multi-dimensional space. This has not been imagined before—that, like a plant, we may unfold into another world, naturally, by letting go of all we have previously imagined. Surprised by our original desire: to evolve.

[Wednesday] **Probing**

Wisdom asks: From where does a baby come? Here is the first question an infant explores—in the form of where the mother leaves off—even before it can speak. Soon enough, it leads to a fundamental intellectual quest—Where do we come from and why are we here?—that must end in failure. No child younger than three could comprehend a factual answer, and the fanciful explanations such as those involving a stork, or the simplistic answers such as "from mother's stomach," will not satisfy a healthy child. Failure to discover a satisfactory answer on the child's part leads to the question being repressed and forgotten. And so, later intellectual quests will always be shadowed by a fear of failure. This very fear prepares a person for dogmatic belief, in which he may unburden his ignorance and failures. Wisdom responds to those who hold their burden in front of themselves, who probe for knowledge, who desire to recover the past by digging into themselves. They ask the same question their newborn selves asked:

Where do I come from? They are seduced by Wisdom to probe deeply into her beauty, toward the nectars in her bosom. That is where thinking comes from. It is the quest to find what is hidden, to return to the first sweet question, which has been forgotten. And it is continually lost in the probing of sexual intercourse—a desire to be in control of one's destiny, to stop time. Wisdom transforms this desire by seducing the mind into probing further: to create new questions that hide the first one more deliciously but entice us to new heights of exploration.

[Thursday] Filling the Picture

Wisdom asks: Where does art come from? First was the museum, then the art to fill it. The museum was Eden and the Creator filled it with his creations and images. It became a museum in memory, the first home Adam and Eve had to leave behind. Each succeeding home they built in the world was a memory of Eden: a place they created themselves, tended, and which reminded them—as pictures and artifacts do—of their lost home. Art comes from the desire to be seduced by memory. Wisdom reveals it to those who probe her, and they reproduce her in artifacts of the hand and mind. She is even in pictures of paradise: in the colors and shapes, light and dark, in the story the figures tell. The desire to procreate answers the question of who we are. Then, we must take our brains in our hands also. A brain is a system that mirrors her natural systems—ecosystems. When we learn to decipher the ecosytem from which we evolved, our minds will fill it. We are on the doorstep of Eden and will leave our world of artifacts behind—to reenter the natural world and evolve.

[Friday] Nonfiction Passing into Fiction

Wisdom asks: How is a cross-species encounter with an endangered species different than all others? There is a wounding innocence in the plant or animal's lack of awareness of its extinction. The human is stricken with the bitter fruit of knowledge that he or she is among the last to know this creature—no future person will have that privilege. Humans were spared this poignant desolation in the recent past, out of ignorance about evolution and the diversity of species. And now, our absence from the wild and the creature's rarity make a chancing-upon scarce as a buried scroll. How best to pass on this old/new experience? A cross-genre work can suggest it—the complexity of the loss. A "complex-genre," an encounter of fiction with nonfiction that is rendered unforgettable by its gravity. Symbolically, the inner daily newspaper of our lives is just this: a hopeful narrative imposed upon intractable events, a reviving interpretation of dead facts, a restoration of what seemed hopelessly lost in the past.

[Saturday] Leavetaking

Wisdom asks: Where does your history begin? All our books look back to a history of men. Before one culture was another culture, a more primitive one. Nothing exists of importance but men and their cultures. No, no. What is important is the individual who sees that his culture is a mirror of nature only, who turns around and looks directly at it, at me. He will hear me welling up and begin to translate. He will become full of his power and begin to speak himself. I am powerless to stop this. This is the Creator's power, re-created in men. When this man becomes a speaker instead of translator—whether they call him shaman or scribe, prophet or author—he begins to resent mistakes. He is the clarifier of confusion, the teller of right from wrong, left from right. Confusion and mistakes are resented; actually, they are tied together, as in "mistakes are the result of confusion." So the path of science begins with the first translator who becomes full of his power. This is always the case because the people look to the storyteller of science, not to me. The only salvation for the storyteller is to disguise himself from his culture, his people, and refuse the identity of storyteller.

Mistakes are not the result of confusion, they are the fruit of turning to me. I am not you and you must always learn this, after the mistake of thinking *I am you.* Why this mistaking? Because you are attracted. How could you be attracted to a not-you, to a death? This is the question that arises from mistakes and it is the question that is the source of your creativity. Without it, you want too much to persuade others—even yourself—of your humanness, your culture. If you are attracted to me something must be missing in your culture. Fainthearted ones search for what's missing, fearful of losing their place in the culture. The strong turn to what's *there*. There, not here, requiring a leavetaking.

Leavetaking. Turn to me and you must leave your imagemaker, the Creator, behind. He bound your focus on him; you learned from your mistakes not to make new ones. And so you grew in a stunted way, hemmed in by mirrors of yourselves, what you call cultures. You were barred from evolving, from my realm. All humans are the same species, made by the Creator so that no room would be left for you to evolve on Earth. But those creative and strong enough to leave his sphere come to me and learn to evolve within.

I was the sole witness to the Seven Days of Creation. On the seventh day, I worked to remember all that preceded you, the web of life in which you are spun. These are the Seven Memories, set down in the *Scroll of the History of Adam*, that you have found.

Chapter 9

Chapter 9

Beguiling Big Ideas

Once in a while I have a great idea and I get all excited. What is it? It's like I'm going to grow some more. It's like, oh, these teeth, this fat, this shyness—it's all about to be outgrown, it was all a part of some brief adolescence. That's something Julie might feel—now I'm feeling it. But I'm already grown, and yet I lose the idea, distracted by something, and I'm frustrated trying to remember it. Let it go. (Easier said than done.) Then a bird flits through with a quick song and it's gone, the blocked-up feeling. That was another life, it seems, irrelevant whether it happened a minute ago or a year. But the loss of the idea lingers somewhere. And sometimes it comes back, though now less intense, a lower flame beneath it.

The end of the world was that kind of an idea. Little things are always being eaten by something bigger coming out of nowhere, like here in the courtyard a bird just swooped down on a lizard, just after I noticed the lizard snatching a tiny moth. They never knew what hit them and that's the way the world's going to end, snuffed out by hunger. It may not be something hungry for food but for something we have—like knowledge. And when I thought that—knowledge, our human nectar—wham, the door slammed behind me. It was Julie bursting in, overstimulated from transcribing the tapes again.

It was gone, the idea about the end of the world, but it

came back and I realized all the religions and myths have a similar story. God wants something from us and we find ways to avoid knowing this, since you can't live very well knowing your death is part of it. We invent a better plan for him, in myths and even scientific dreams, a better world after we die. Death comes in a blind snatch yet we invent the reasons we knew it was going to happen.

It wasn't such a brilliant idea, the end of the world—in a tasty morsel that nature makes of us, like she does of everything else. I forgot how hot it was, even though the sky was covered in gray clouds. It was the suggestion of rain, not the real thing—Julie says it never rains in the dry season in Israel. Weather, that's the limit of nature we talk about every day. Now I see that my thinking has evolved to include all of it, thanks to Archibald Shechner.

[Nosei '84]

Where Are We?

A few weeks ago I was making my own tape, after I finished the work for mother. She has me reading her own notebooks into the recorder because, she says, she needs to hear how it sounds before she can decide how to organize the writing. It's strange, *davka* all these tapes, starting with Archie's—both of us are speaking secrets into machines. Mine aren't exactly my own thoughts but Archie's, or the Scroll's. What am I saying? None of this is anyone's own, and even my mother's notes are commentary on Archie.

So the tape I was making was from the Scroll and Eve

was speaking. Now I realize it worked its way inside me and came out a few days ago. I told Nosei about how old our lives can become on any given day—Eve was reciting something like that in the Scroll. And then there was a bang outside.

What a smashup! I went out to look and saw the car smacked against a tree but it wasn't going very fast since the windshield and everything inside were normal. Nobody was inside, but a man and a woman, with a few gawkers following them at a short distance, were stumbling away on the sidewalk. "Where are we?" they might have been thinking, like Adam and Eve.

I felt like those stumbling people once, after this horrible lovemaking. There was nothing wrong with the guy but we were both in love with someone else. I didn't know that about him, and afterwards I told him why I felt so depressed, didn't even want to get dressed. We were both soldiers and I remember staring at parts of his uniform scattered on the floor around the bed as if the soldier in him had been killed. Only wounded, he confessed—not by what I told him about my loving someone else, but because he also loved another. Who is she? I asked. Maybe we could make ourselves feel a little better by talking it out. But the girl was someone I knew and who despised me. And my lover was married to his sister. We were now doubly wounded and stumbled around the kitchen in our underwear like the car-crash people, wondering what we could eat that would not depress us further.

"It happened again last night."

"What?" Nosei asked. "What happened last night?"

"I dreamed I slept with Archie. Of course he reminded me of my father, or how I imagine my father, since I never knew him. But it wasn't the same in bed, it didn't have the allure of incest. Without his clothes he wasn't an authority anymore, just a ghost. I could not get excited. Yet he went on acting like Archie, as if nobody in the world could doubt him. Fact is, he was expecting me to seduce him with my devotion and my mouth. He was limp as a little palm frond. So we lay there staring at the ceiling. This wasn't the first mistake either of us had made. But I never thought the great archaeologist could so depress me. He just couldn't accept my own deflation. It wasn't that he felt rejected, no, I don't think he would know what rejection is anymore, after the certainty in hearing Wisdom's voice. He talked to me about a terrible sense of loss he felt, as if it was Shechner himself he had lost. You know, I just remembered something uncanny he said. "The Garden of Eden," he said. "I feel like I came out of the Garden of Eden and now I have to die."

"You never thought you'd die?" I said.

"Yes," he answered. "I thought I would die but I imagined death to be a further living in another element, the way I felt submerged at the bottom of the dig. In death I would acquire some kind of tunnel suit and I would go on exploring. Now I feel death is the end because I am already here in a suit of armor and now I am naked."

Could this have been a plea for my sexual arousal? The vulnerable father figure, naked as a baby to me and me only? But I put my hand on his thigh and he jumped up and began to walk madly around the room, bumping into doors and lamps. He was another car-crash victim.

[Julie '84]

Waiting

To work, evolution needs isolation, just like individuals need privacy in order to think. Plenty going on around me means nothing now: it's all human stuff, murmur of conversation, radio, car alarms, traffic. All the waiting, the deferring to others instead of taking charge of this pen—for me, it's gone. Everything I think comes straight out of my mouth instead of passing first in front of the review board: Am I allowed to think this? Will I lose face if I say this? etc. It's like I'm a new species, so the way I see it is the way it is for me. Evolution is the key to everything: let me say that first. The way it's taught in schools is all wrong, emasculated. It's about sexuality, period. Another species may be very seductive—exotic is the right sexual word—but the offspring, a hybrid, can't reproduce. So the lure of the exotic is like masturbation: nothing comes of it. That means that seducing one of the same species requires imagination, play, to make it exotic. All human imagination stems from this. Look at a tree: those seductive fruits required the same imaginative strategies of reproduction.

Now the waiting I did—call it the "growing up"—was like an Edenic masturbation. That's what the Scroll makes plain. Adam had to wait for Eve and while he did he named the other species, feeling them at close hand, and he named himself in the same manner, apparently masturbating as he lay on his namesake red clay.

[Nosei, '94]

Adam Speaks

The feeling of a child runs through my thoughts. Some kind of a nurse is watching me as I dream. In the dream she examines me wonderfully, not sniffing first or long-eyeing like animals but reaching here and there, touching where she pleases, finding for me tender spots. In the midst of her arms and hair I raise the tree and her palms grasp and smooth and envelop it with warm kisses, a tongue tracing the globular fruits at the base. As I raise my legs in the air, lying on my back, I tense upward, my belly a hillock uplifting the pride of my body's garden, the tree. And how she loves it, her breathing framed with little squeals, a long time washing me as I'm held between petalsoft lips. When I see her face above me, eyes laughing, I hear my thoughts watching at a distance: "This is perfect," they are thinking, "my inner Garden." As I listen I'm seduced again: the joy and power in that voice—mine? Awake, it's only a whisper and cradles me as if Eve's. She is there at every naming and recognition, enchanting me, as I interpret to her; she is the laughing eyes of my thought. In the dream I cried when she said "Good Night." "No," I screamed. She returned as I wagged the little shaft in my hand. I looked up to her face, it was glowing. I laughed and laughed as she kissed my hand and its limb. She was all abloom, moist and pink;

she was bathing me in her halo. I awoke to the echo of her voice—to find it was my own: my own thoughts loving me so much they nursed me into her presence. They are like a tree, these thoughts, all seduction—yet respectful of my isolation.

[*Scroll of the History of Adam*]

Intimacy

A waiting like a death. I was lost in time, but now in memory that time more vivid, stirred alive with the clay of emotion. Adam's fantasy, like any waiting, is incomplete without a future Eve to replace the imagined one. Would have made a poignant memory, except there was no future for it within the Garden—only out. In Garden, imagination is simply lost memory, the past that Adam does not know. Real time begins in Eden when Adam and Eve build a past, a shelter that marks off their intimacy. That shelter was no more than a bower, a found shelter, needing only their vision to encompass its boundaries.

There, in secret, intimacy took the place of the Garden, became a system. It was heaven, for a moment, and the closest thing to heaven after Eden. It was a regaining of lost memory, of father and mother, the creating God and the earthly God. After Eden, the creating God withdrew to the stars and the mother God into the ecosystem, the unfolding of reproducing time. But those moments in Eden, when Adam and Eve achieved intimacy—the father and mother gods were also united.

And desire for that intimacy of flesh and soul is desire to recover Eden, is the equal of it: a complete ecosystem in sexual desire. Desire for a mate is as tightly focused as that, a desire to fit into an ecosystem, to fold into the flesh of a mate. An urge toward evolution. Mind and heart map each line and curve of the mate's body: each dimple in flesh hastens desire, each curve of buttock and cheekbone is a point in space we may enter.

Only in a lover does such intense desire read a living system, a body. Sometimes a child takes the mate's place, and the forbidden love awakens lost memories of problems in Eden: the father-creator God overstepping bounds with the creature in his image.

[Shechner]

Monkey Questions

"Is that why you were such a tiger in bed last night? I felt like you were going to devour parts of me. I'm still sore today. I even dreamed about it afterward. I looked in your face and it surprised me, as if I'd never looked at you before, as if you wore a mask and removed it in lovemaking. There was such intelligence there. I wanted to stop and have a conversation with you, to ask you alot of questions."

"You wanted to explore," Archie answered. "Great sex will do that. I think all exploration is sexual in origin. Each species explores the outer limits of its range, desiring to evolve. I think we as a species evolve in our intelligence and that's why you wanted to have an intelligent conversation as much as sex."

"But for anyone that dies," Archie continued, "their own memory is lost and ours continues for them. I am in a new life. The old one is dead and myself in it is a lost memory until I make this life make room for memory. Abel was not the first death; the first was the life in Eden, along with the intimacies there with the animals, the plants, Lilith and Samael, the tree. This is what the Scroll tells us. Now, at this late date, the memories of intimacy with plant and animal are just beginning to come back, for Eden was our original ecosystem. In Eden, the first couple studied their relationship to every living thing, including their mother and father, the two trees of knowledge and life. In the twentieth century, we can barely begin to comprehend our relationship to a banana, or any plant offering."

[Julie '84]

1995

So it seems the only time I felt creative during the trancription was when sex was there on the tapes. Nosei knew that I didn't actually have sex with Archie. I had told him my most intimate secret: I had heard my mother in bed with Archie. She must have thought I wasn't home, but I was and I could hear through the walls.

I had my earphones on, transcribing a fragment of Archie's tapes—exactly what Nosei set out above, myself in '84. In between the pauses in Archie's voice on the taped session, I began to hear them. I was held there by their sounds and his voice on the tape. And I was held there too because—well, I had been masturbating. When I started to hear them, I froze, unsure whether it was still fantasy or if it was real. While I had been transcribing the passage on "great sex," I had been thinking about Archie having sex with mother, and then fantasizing that I was mother, that I was in session with Archie instead of mother, and finally that I was the cause for great sex, great conversation. And then I began to hear the sex between them through my bedroom wall. I still had a bedroom there.

When I became intimate with Nosei, my memory of this episode returned. One time I was so worried, I told Nosei I sometimes had sexual fantasies while doing the transcription—meaning I had masturbated. I couldn't actually say it to him, but I thought he understood. Anyway, he said "Of course! Don't be silly—it's all very sexual, isn't it?" That seemed to fix it for me in my mind for a time. Later, I began to think I couldn't be sure I had stopped masturbating when I started hearing them. I know I did, but then how could I be sure. That's how it starts, you know—the cracks in the psyche: a feeling you can no longer be sure of yourself.

"I only looked up once. Twice. I only saw the shirt, the character's shirt—soaked with blood."

"And if you had seen more? What would have happened?"

The voice asking the questions was my doctor. We were talking about a movie I had gone to see with Svitz. I never wrote things down from my sessions, but this one comes back to me as clearly as the scenes from the movie. Perhaps it is the closeness of sex and smashups in this chapter. Accidents can make you feel cracked inside. It was an accident that Svitz and I had ended up in that movie. The one we had gone to see was a disappointment and we walked into the middle of that one. My doctor's questions cut through my hysteria that day. What if I had seen more, he had asked.

"I don't know," I told him. "The image. I was afraid the image would get stuck in my head. Make me crazy. You see, I saw too much. I'm always seeing too much. But we found a bookstore afterwards. It had gone away—the crazy feeling—by the time we left the bookstore."

"Film images can be particularly intrusive, violent ones especially. They can make people feel violent. But the crazy part is another thing. The feeling of being driven crazy can be a detour from something else—one's own fantasies, feelings of aggression."

"I used to play rough with toys, you know."

"I remember," he said.

"I would hit my stuffed toys or chew the heads off the little ones made of plastic. It was just a phase. But this—this, that was in the movie. Depraved. It went too far. Crossed a line that shouldn't be crossed."

"It might be said that this is what the director wanted—to provoke a conversation that wouldn't happen unless a line was crossed."

"Okay, alright," I said impatiently.

"Well, I get your point. There's always that intellectual net to fall back onto. But it's one thing to feel the movie crossed a line and another to feel that it's taken you across a line, a line beyond which you could be crazy, in great distress and panic."

"Yes, I felt a line had been crossed, could be crossed... in me. They kept hitting, hitting, when there seemed to be no more reason to hit. The body was pulverized. And they kept looking and looking at it. Looking and hitting. Maybe it made me remember the lines I had crossed. I haven't told you all about those lines, yet."

"I know."

"Mother and Archie crossed lines. Big ones."

"And what about you and me? Do you have any thoughts about lines we've crossed?"

"We haven't crossed any lines," I said quickly. "And we won't, you know that. I'm too afraid of crossing lines. And you're too..." I broke off. My mind was blank. What did I really know about him anyway.

"Can you finish that sentence? he asked.

"No. Can you finish yours? Maybe they can't or shouldn't be finished. I was reading the other day about love between doctor and patient. The author said there were things that went unspoken—love, desire—that perhaps don't get worked out until the therapy is over, and maybe a tacit silence on those subjects is necessary for it to work."

"Do you agree with that?

"Well, I don't see how you can just not talk about things in a room like this."

"What do you think we haven't been able to talk about?"

"You and me—the part that makes the sessions sound and feel the way they do, makes us come here day after day. We rarely skip or miss sessions."

"Yes, and if I were to speak about that part—about the way I hold you inside—what would that mean? What would that do?"

"I don't know. I feel tired."

"A kind of lifelessness has come in. A collapse. If you suddenly feel tired, it must mean that you feel like you're having to do all the work—that I've dropped the load. What is it that I need to help carry?"

"The realness of this. This room! There's a scene in *Jane Eyre*, where Rochester makes this eerie observation that he feels a thread connecting her to him— to a spot in his heart. And that he suspects if it should be pulled away, he would begin to bleed. Slowly but persistently, until all he would be able to do is just watch it happen, watch it seep out. But the end result would not be the worst. It would have been the trickling out—the blood dripping out as if a hole had opened up. I think he, rather Bronte, knew what that hole was—a hole inside that can't be patched, that pulls open. I *want* you to see the hole between us. To feel the thread. Can you just do something, do something to show me that you see it!"

"Can I be Rochester? Yes. I feel the thread. I see the hole. Not only in you—in me. But I have the feeling that as I tell you about what I see—feel—I'm placing a finger in the hole. And it feels like I'm also saying, 'Julie, put your finger here. Help me stop the bleeding, the trickling out.' And I have to ask what that means for us. A hole in the heart is a special kind of wound. In this case, it has the feel of a wound that cannot heal. About the only way it can be helped is if we were to have wounds together. It would almost be like making love to the wounds in each other—a way of having and not having loss at the same time. The wound itself has become the thing loved—it will never die and it will always need your sympathy, your finger, the thread to keep it in place. I think you're pleading with me to help you keep the wounds, so something will not be forgotten. Or lost. You sense—and you're right—that I know about such wounds, that we—you and I—share this knowledge."

The voice stopped and the stillness came back in. Different than at the beginning of sessions, when I always felt I had to stop the stillness. I wanted this stillness. I wanted to keep what he had said to me. But it had unlocked an image that I wished to tell. "I suddenly see us as playmates on the floor, in the middle of building blocks, sad together. Lovers in bed. Ravaging, grieving. Would it have been possible?"

"That question has so much in it," came his voice. "It's palpable. I had the feeling as you spoke that my heart could stop, and I think it's because I feel as if we've come up against, almost over the edge of a real hole. Your hole—the voice from your own hole in the ground. And that I have glimpsed the physical facticity of a 'yes' or a 'no' to your question, that they would both be equally painful. This is the question that keeps you holding your end of the thread—to me, to your mother and Archie. You're afraid to jerk on it, drop it, or even fool with it. So much depends on it—on you and the way you hold the thread. All of our hearts depend upon it. And in a panic attack, your heart. So much work. The watchfulness. If I were on the floor with you playing or in a bed making love with you, perhaps there would be less for you to do. I could hold the thread too. Maybe you need to know that I could hold the thread—in another kind of life, a life that *would have been*, *could have been* possible. Maybe this is the function an unrequited love with me serves. I think you panic and collapse when you feel stuck with the thread or when you feel like jerking at it. In an eerie way like Rochester, I feel you're saying to me, 'let me jerk on it, let me hold it,' both at the same time. Maybe that's why the movie was so unnerving. In the bloodletting, you felt the desire to jerk and hold at the same time, too close together. You felt the eroticization of the wounding, the hitting, the blood coming, the hole opening."

He broke off. I remember I couldn't say anything. He told me that he thought he'd gone too fast. I said no, he hadn't. It was that he had found it, as he had said. He had reached the hole. And I had felt the touch.

I think I had a different kind of orgasm. And much longer than any real one. Some people call such things a spiritual experience or a caring of the soul. These ideas are very popular nowadays. It's as if they've forgotten about the body and where the mind comes from. Doesn't it all come from a hole? There's the womb, of course. But there are psychic holes. Injuries of going from baby to adult. Archie just discovered a new kind of hole—the injury, the desire that comes from realizing what's been lost in going into the Homo sapiens business. He'd been digging in holes all his adult life and he knew them well. And then he found one that spoke. Like mine, but in a different way. We go to therapists, don't we, to hear them make the holes speak? We pay them to drag with us through the holes and back again. Archie thought that's what he needed to do when he went to my mother. But the hole was already talking. A thread extended into him.

That's the way it was each day when he came to see mother: a man with a thread running from inside of him that we did everything to keep intact. Mother had sex with him. I wanted to have sex with him. We hadn't noticed that the threads had started into us. Not yet. We thought the only hole was in Archie. Not in us.

A very old hole inside of him was found. And in mother and me—Nosei. Mother ran the car into hers. Disappeared. Presumed dead—like Archie. Ever since, Nosei and I have needed manuscripts or notebooks. Words and transcriptions have kept us in place. Intact. Here. Just like my could've beens, would've beens. They keep me in place. In love. At the edge of the monkey questions. But never all the way in.

[Julie]

Chapter 10

Chapter 10

[Sunday] Virtual Selves

Wisdom asks: How is a species made? It allows itself to be made, doesn't will it. You start by losing what you know. Or rather, you just forget about it, which is to say, put it aside. With it, all fear. Then, what's left is a shell of yourself, or an extension. A virtual self. You can project this shell anywhere you can imagine, out into space, anywhere. It will colonize the stars in the manner of robot craft. Virtual selves—as we were in Eden. Now consider the irony. To evolve we project ourselves, yet this directly opposes the wish of evolution most people hold—believing our thoughts can evolve, that our mind can evolve by itself. They imagine a computer age of artificial people, life-size, three-dimensional images indistinguishable from real people, and these to be our teachers, entertainers, companions in the future. Novel—but phantoms of the brain. For only the body evolves, though it is projected out like a thought, a virtual body. It is no pet; it is us, there, wherever in the universe and beyond we have evolved. Our only boundary is the omnipotence of nature, yet she is also the creator of endless possibility. Endless the places she hides within, Wisdom.

[Monday] In Skin

Wisdom asks: Why, if you open yourself, do pain and loss flood in?

To lose—but it is Wisdom who made it possible: vulnerability, we call it. You will grow by your losses—mistakes—as a plant bends and turns to follow the sun. Can a scientist turn a tree to grow in a different direction—or hear a voice from under ground? Not by thinking alone or wishing in the mind—but by evolving. Can a psychologist acknowledge it? Not by celebrity but by hidden counsel. They must help science take its first steps and hear the voice of ecosystems. If you fail to evolve, humans become a new age of dinosaurs. In your weakening vision, all the large species of tree and animal will die off, leaving the microbes to thrive. They will become the seedbed from which hugely intelligent, micro-organizational groups will evolve, to colonize your bodies—just as the small mammals superseded the great megafauna. A dark vision; a prompting to grow toward the light. If instead, upon opening your mind, joy is all you feel, it is a simulation only, a transcendence. Underneath, Wisdom lies buried—but carefully preserved for the ages, covered in skins, enfolded like an ancient scroll.

[Tuesday] Portrait with Self-Knowledge

Wisdom asks: Is a new religion even possible? The world has been pregnant for a century with it. Not an idea—neither Jesus nor Buddha were ideas—the emotional preparation for a figure in the flesh has been slowly building. Desire has grown for a greater self-awareness, an "objective" picture of ourselves—we are the flesh in the picture, a flashback through time, the natural history of the earth our scenery. You can trace the desire for a new picture back to Copernicus, when the human consciousness first absorbed the blow that earth was not locus of the universe—suddenly this planet was made even more precious for its isolation, its potential fragility. Now that fragility is activated. The human taste for genocide has added much anxiety. And now we find out that beside all our anxiety the world has itself been shrivelling behind our backs, condensing into the backdrop our picture forms against. As we step out of the frame the world we find is fragile, in need of our tending. It's a place more precious than ourselves and our children will discover it as if for the first time. Each one of us becomes this planet, teeming with life inside us and on our surface. Beyond microscopes, future children with virtual reality will see themselves at any scale, so that size won't matter and a bacterium will appear as complex an organism as a whale. Power will shift to the natural world, its resources empowered with a harder currency: the endangered species of our planet hold the key to self-knowledge. As self-knowledge becomes the commodity to save our own species, the natural world grows ever more precious, especially those forces that nourished the human sensibility and self-consciousness in the first place, the ecosystems or Edens in which we thrived.

[WEDNESDAY] THE EARTH'S CURVES

Wisdom asks: Why is each individual exotic, a story to be read with a symmetry all its own? The symmetry of a human body is anchored in the hemispheres of its buttocks, the curve between them inspiration for all the others—at the furthest extreme the eyes, the echo of eyebrows. Science tells us the face is the object we read most intensely, cataloging each unique one among the range of symmetrical variations. We're fitted to it, a face, the way a hawk can read a prey's twitch from miles, or wasps the barely perceptible mascara on the flower species whose sheath guides its probings for nectar. But faces are made of curves, and the straight line our imagination measures through the middle of everything is merely a tool, an appendange, like a finger; imagine instead the finger drawn through the curve of the posterior's lush cheeks, the face drawn to bury itself there in moist earth, tongue to savor dry leaves, mouth to chew down the flanks of thighs, in lieu of speech—a blind face examined by touch. Variety is the spice of life: consider spice our tie to the exotic. Could there have been a Renaissance without spices, proof of the exotic—the far ends of the world set on our table? These spices, then, absorbed into our world, prove each smell, taste and sight exotic only in the limits of our knowledge. Our ignorance of their origins is rendered temporary by ignorance of our own shaping ecosystem; once we come to know it—to self-knowledge—we can know the symmetry in all others, and face the buried appetite to evolve.

[Thursday] One of Nature's Ideas

Wisdom asks: How does thinking mimic nature? Nature selects according to a niche; a niche is a unique, discreet point, a point in space where temperature, light, scale, earth, air and water all act in concert, selecting an individual to represent it and live there. Settled there, the individual either colonizes it, or its progeny is lost—except for an individual who breaks away to start a new species. If the species adapts it can live there; if not, it changes, evolves. Now the human mind cannot be changed or evolve, it can only adapt. Therefore it represents only one of nature's ideas, though a big one, since the mind has learned to simulate evolving with imaginative thinking. This kind of thinking, as opposed to logical thought, mimics nature, while logical thinking is as unique to the human species as bee thinking is to bees. We can't know bee thinking, because we can't know the politics and economy of its relationship with a certain flower producing the nectar that seduces it. And all that happened—between bee and flower, earth, water and sun (and the politics of each: the layers of dead on the earth, for instance, the organic matter matured to a certain moment in time)—happened in a lost time. What is imaginative thinking, then, our mimicry of nature? Listening to the wind, that's what. Leave behind the back porch at the smell of rain on a moonless night in high summer; set your chair at the furthest reach of the yard. The rhythm of cricket and katydid, punctuated by tree frogs, owls, a lone dog—these sounds ground our logic. But in the rustle of tree branches imagination stirs, as the sounds of another world—the dream world of our childhood—advances. Rushing objects come perilously close, unidentified: is that a branch scraping the window or an arm hoisting the crib gate? Are those leaves that are shaking or a blanket being spread over us? The sound of ourselves humming, the humming of voices outside us as we mature in the uterus, prepare us for these unseen tongues the wind uses. It is the language of evolving, simulated, as our minds grow to comprehend or imagine it.

[Friday] Gardens in the Stars

Wisdom asks: Why do you feel peace in a wild place? You are feeling a physical sense of time, of history deeper, more complex than any clock you could devise. It is Widsom's body embracing you, a clock of earth nourishing the hundred million of species. Each species tells of how it came to be by where it longs to go—to Eden, across the border of its ecosystem, there to evolve in Eden renewed. Our human species is at a new border now yet barely knows of it. Why? It is lost in imitations, carrying its own ecosystem with it into the seas and into space. Yet it's a sterile ecosystem, reduced to oxygen and human artifacts, confined to our body. We must first return to our mothering Eden, use our imagination to recreate it. There, a wealth of species holds the web for which our mind and spirit were spun. A peace is grasped as we embrace our natural system—the way is tenderness, a knowledge of its wounds. All our ecosystems are wounded, their diversity of species ravaged. Pigeons in the park are signs of loss, as are the scattering of trees which evolved to feed many other species. Grass, alas, is another sign of loss, tamed into species-beggared lawns. The joy brought by the rare sight of an egret or song of a warbler must be bittersweet testimony to great losses in variety. Tenderness, then, is extended to oneself, for we live with too much emptiness, too much missing. To fill it with culture—manufactured sights and sounds—is poignant to the point of tears.

When you see the future, most of present life goes dead, dead with the past. You look back at the world with new eyes: you see what is evolving and what is a dead end. If you don't see culture fall away, all that is manmade, you're left with a man in the vacuum of a space ship; but let culture go, let mind and body evolve, and you are headed to Eden, to wild, flourishing ecosystems restored, whether on earth or on other celestial bodies. Gardens in the stars. Will you have stories to tell? Yes, stories of the future, more amazing than how a caterpillar invents a butterfly—how a fruit invents a bat to disperse it, creation! It is all driven by Wisdom's sexual desire. Each new species furthers the romance.

[Saturday] Mirror to Himself

Wisdom asks: Why is the sexual act both exalting and deflating? It is a perfect mirror of the fall. The seduction, arousals, exaggerations, suckings and lickings, bitings and eatings, caressings—all lead out of time, climbing a ladder toward the eternal time of the Garden. After the climax comes the fall, a descent into time and a loss of memory of Eden, as the cares of historical time sweep back over the actors.

Here is the withdrawal from union and fall into loneliness for the human. Man was created lonely, not knowing his mate. No single death among the flora and fauna—food for each other—equals that of a human, because a human being is food for the gods; a human embodies them and is delicious to them. Humans grow fat on playings and devisings—they use time the way the gods use eternity. When they are most rested and focussed, the thoughts of a human leave food altogether and become mirror to himself: here is where gods learn and also why the Creator made a mistake in giving Adam his image. He did not want to see himself beside Wisdom, but rather Adam. Now, in my place, all men and women remind him of this mistake, which is why he withdrew. Yes, he comes back again, now and then, and tries to find a man he can shape, an Abram, a Moses, but time defeats him. Wisdom remains here in silence, her mouth open, as in a deep dream. You may grasp the buried roots of her tree.

1995

I don't like inserting myself into the guide chapters. Not for the reasons you may think. Not because it would be too grandiose. On the contrary, people like me are grandiose in their efforts to not be grandiose—to not have an impact.

I have an elaborate structure that measures and dispenses my impact. You can imagine the strain that this causes for relationships—and the energy it requires. I got to a point in my relationship with Nosei, for example, where I was just dragging. I ran out of energy for the system I'd come to rely upon. With him there were just too many variables.

Early in the relationship, Nosei said to me jokingly, "Julie, what are you going to do with me?" I could think of nothing clever to say in response. I think I laughed. Though I must have asked him what he meant because I remember he turned more serious and said that he worried about me—that I was like a plant with a delicate pollinator, expending itself on careful strategies of attraction and release.

One can imagine the plant spending so much time on preparation that the pollinator—delicate or not—gets tired or afraid of waiting and flys off to try somewhere else. This is what Nosei did and I can hardly blame him. But of course I do. You see, when you're like that plant, so specialized in taking care of the pollinator, you wonder what there is to complain about. But if you're of that species, you keep the system going even when the aim is inhibited. The original stimulus has disappeared but you keep doing what you're doing. Your mind, your system of intelligence becomes a thing in itself.

"I'm thinking of what happened after I left you. Yesterday. Immediately after. You had gone and I was alone in your outer office." This was me speaking to my doctor. The words remembered feel as if they dropped into my mind. When I'm like this, my brain feels like dry dirt, long separated from any moisture or the interests of living creatures, even parasites. I don't have a sense that *I* can remember the words. Memory just drops in—and I take it like I'll never have it again. I'm one of those people that can wake up terrified that they've forgotten how something or someone felt, even from the day before. I worked so hard to hold things tight my whole life. Yet, they feel like they could slip from my mind.

The scariest of all is the feeling that my doctor could disappear from inside me. I woke up the other day thinking that I would forget how much I loved him. "Do I even remember the feeling?" I wondered. "Or, is it gone already." Later, in session, I told him that all I wanted from the future was to be able to say, "Once, I loved you." I guess this is happening because I'll be leaving him soon. I will be ending the sessions. Will they be there—will my doctor's voice be there—in my mind when I need him? Can it all be grasped like the buried roots of the tree-voice, Archie's voice of Wisdom?

"It was the key thing," I said to him. "You know, putting the key back after going to the restroom? You were gone. Everyone in the offices next door seemed to be gone. I was alone. There was no chance anyone would see me stop and wait. You see, I stopped for a few minutes in the vestibule—just to be there. Quiet. Standing. Then I felt of the door—the outer door leading through the little hall way to your inner office door. I put my hand flat against it. I tried to turn the knob. It was locked. I noticed the grain of the wood, the patterns. I saw the profile of a man in a suit—kind of a Pickwick Papers type—like that game of seeing figures in the clouds."

"Yes."

"It made me remember that I used to look at patterns in the wood of my doors as a child—the doors of my bedroom when I was alone, except for a night light. For a period of time I used to sleep with a night light. It was one of several settings on this olive green lamp given to me by my father.

"Anyway, I felt in-between. Looking and not looking, checking and not checking. I almost felt like I didn't need to make sure I had put the key back on the hook. But I couldn't leave without doing it. *Key on the hook, key on the hook*, is what I said to myself. Even as I looked again at the key, I knew what I was doing. Filling up space—some space that was hard to let be. I put my hand against the door again. I had the thought it was a connection to you. But more."

"What?"

"Me. Yes, 'me' is what came into my mind. And a joining. You with me. There."

"Where is 'there'?"

"There in my mind, in the spaces of my mind. And for a while, it was okay— I feel interrupted."

"By me?"

"No. Yes. I really don't know. I guess by a question. I seem to have had it so often this week. Wondering what you're thinking, feeling. Perhaps it's always there, but I can catch the thought now and tell you."

"Maybe the 'me' that you found was a version of yourself that could use the key, use the office, have knowledge of me through those objects and your mind, and feel like it was all containable. Maybe it's a 'me' that can make room for things like Archie's voice from the ground or your mother's voice, utilize them without feeling controlled or possessed by them. The question you seem to want an answer to is what happens to Archie and your mother when you're not thinking about them—or the Scroll or the voice. And where are you—your mother's transcriber—when you are that 'me'—and how do you move back and forth between having and not having people in mind. That pathway is what you're working out with me. You need to feel I can take the impact of you putting your hand against the doors in here."

It's funny how all the work we did in that room could feel so collapsible, just like I used to feel during panic attacks. It really is true: "You start by losing what you know." I had to create a virtual self in my therapy—a place inside and out with my doctor. To play. And grow. It only happened when I could let go of the old paradigm of my family drama long enough to play with him. And then I began to find out things. Began to feel things. From long ago. New things, too. That's what I have to do again. Separate. Grow. It scares me to death. An old phrase, but how true. I could start having panic attacks again. I'm scared enough. Or I could evolve.

The Scroll says only the body can evolve. I think that's true. But they hadn't invented psychotherapy or psychoanalysis then. I think the mind can change through therapy. In fact, I have read they're doing research about the effect of psychotherapy on brain chemistry and wiring. I told Svitz one time that I felt like I was being rewired. I told him that I could actually *feel* my thoughts now.

"Julie, you don't need to be rewired, but *unwired*!

"As in that movie last night—Catherine?"

"Ah, yes. A very good example. There you had a young woman that everyone had tried to rewire. They almost drove her crazy, or rather she almost let herself be driven crazy."

"But she was saved by Montgomery Clift, the doctor."

"That's where you're wrong, Julie. No, Elizabeth Taylor was more of a doctor than the doctor."

We were speaking of the film "Suddenly Last Summer." Sometimes we watched old movies together, if he was in town and not with his paramour. I was always childlike about movies—always ready to suspend disbelief and unready for anyone to unsuspend it for me. I was that child in the back seat of a car, pressing against the front seat with his feet in some magical attempt to slow the car down, to stop time and the forward motion of the wheels. Svitz, on the other hand, was always ready for things to come to a stop and to go home. The only suspension of disbelief he could sustain for any length of time was that for himself. Film and theater were opportunities for a greater story—the story of Svitz as critic—the one who can't be manipulated. I would identify with the characters; Svitz would master them, and then accuse me of betraying my critical powers out of sentimentality. Why we kept seeing such things together I don't know. I think I did, because I never had to worry about Svitz. He had a short memory for skirmishes and I always felt he got what he deserved from me in the moment. We could act out our ruthless, defensive selves. Then say or yell goodnight and start over tomorrow. That's what I got from Svitz: always a next time. Always a Svitz.

"I don't see how Catherine was the doctor in that film, Svitz. You're right, she was unwired. Completely unwired. Montgomery Clift gave her the space to have the truth."

"My dear, you must remember her observations about love, hate, and using people."

"You mean what she said about how hate was what you had when another person could not be used. That being able to use someone is what we call love?"

"Yes. Perhaps the most beautiful line of the play—I should say, movie. Makes the rest of the drivel tolerable."

"Why? How is *using* people beautiful?"

"Think, my dear. What do you do for that hour every day with that doctor of yours? Don't you ever talk about something interesting besides yourself? Isn't he teaching you anything. Freud, for example? Probably not. They aren't such great readers, from my experience."

"Listen Svitz, I'm not going there to learn about Freud but if I were, my doctor would be the one to learn something from."

"You refuse to adhere to the issue, which is the movie."

"I think it's wrong to use people, Svitz, but I know the concept is foreign to you." I don't know why I said it. Svitz didn't respond to normal hurts.

"Think Freud. Think objects. Using each other is what we're all about, Julie."

"I suppose you want me to become a strong user?"

"Very clever. But I don't think it would hurt you any."

I knew there was something in what he said. And I resented the hell out of him for it. It was true, though. I hadn't learned how to do something important with love objects.

At the end of that Tennessee Williams play, we are told that Catherine moves further into a wild garden surrounding the Victorian Gothic mansion where everything has taken place. Her aunt and persecutor, Mrs. Venable, retreats into the house. Tennessee Williams was preoccupied with wildness. He loved it. I guess that's why I love him. The home's garden, he explains in his notes, should be "more like a tropical jungle, or forest, in the prehistoric age of giant fern-forests when living creatures had flippers turning to limbs and scales to skin." He knew about the desire to evolve, I think.

Nature is often used by Williams to represent volatility, danger. Yet after saving her sanity, if only for the moment, Catherine turns and goes deeper into the wildness. She had let go of something. I think it was fear. She could face the sorrow and loss of where she had come from, how she had come to be. But she didn't go into the house. She disappeared into the garden.

You see, I'm doing it again. Nosei found it very worrisome when we were together. I'm making Catherine into myself. He couldn't comprehend the compulsion to read myself into everything. But we've ended up being the same, he and I, despite the differences and the distance of time. The two of us have boxed ourselves into a garden—the voice's garden. I think soon I'll go where Catherine went. What would it be like? I think like one of those satellite explorers that NASA launches. They can only see or respond to certain things—chemicals in atmosphere or soil, formations of evolutionary intelligence. They go deeper and deeper into wild space, programmed to detect signs of other kinds of life. When they are through, they are retired and float further out of our sight from here on Earth. I have the fantasy that these computer sensors are the things most intimate with what we crave. They only see what we were once able to see—the wild ecosystem. I fantasize that they eventually disappear into it, on some exoplanet around a distant star. That's what it would be like to be Catherine. Or Archie Shechner.

"Deep time, Julie, is mirrored by the deep space we are now exploring. Sooner or later, our telescopes will locate an inhabited planet among the hundreds of exoplanets we expect to be discovered around stars like our Sun. Too far away to visit, we will find a way to communicate with and to listen to foreign species. Perhaps there will not be creatures like ourselves, but instead an advanced ecosystem, complex and diverse as anything on earth. It is the ecosystem whose voice we will need to hear, and it is on earth that we must begin to listen and translate what is heard into our language."

This is one of the things Archie said to me. He was the first to hear this voice he spoke about. As an archeologist and historian who had found the lost Scroll—one that spoke an ecological knowledge—he was perhaps the first to decipher this voice. As you've been able to see, its translation has taken the ancient form of a guide to creation. But it was, of course, a voice across deep time. And to decipher it, Archie's unconsciousness placed it within a known mythology: the voice of Wisdom and the seven days of creation. In ancient Hebraic mythology, she is called the Shechinah—the Creator's consort. Sophia. But what Archie most understood was that it was a sexual voice, and that the voice of an ecosystem—its living principle—was a reproductive one. It is the same that we'll encounter elsewhere in the universe, since the real source of intelligence is to be found in sexual selection and evolution.

When we finally listen across deep space to our first communicants, we will also be listening across that deep time Archie confided to me and first heard. And what I have discovered is that this knowledge of how to listen across deep time is what you really find in these chapters of the Guide to a New World. Nosei's translation into this manuscript has made it evident to me.

I remember asking my doctor if it really didn't just all come down to fucking. "Is that what I'm finding out with you—that it all comes down to fucking? Is that what struck Archie? I think he and mother are fucking somewhere in a wild system we can't see anymore." He was rather speechless after that. Or he chose to be. My own deep time was what he and I had been learning to listen to. And to my surprise over those years, I had found it to be intricately sexual. I was, as Nosei had declared back in Israel, a seductive creature, and I had been using all my energy to resist it.

[Julie]

Chapter 11

Chapter 11

Parental Trees

From Betti Peleg's desire to figure out how I hear Wisdom's voice I learned that *solving* things is a dead end. Our species is built around mysteries and we fashion institutions to solve them—religion, science, art—and they're no different in their traits than those of aboriginal peoples. The average Homo sapiens wants to solve mysteries so big he can't even spell them out. We appoint priest or professor to express them: What is the nature of man? The purpose of life and death—and what happens after? The meaning of suffering? The origin of evil—what does it mean? We get answers, yes, but they never equal the powerful certainty of blind faith.

What if suddenly there was no mystery left and there was nothing to read in our books or watch on our televisions? Here is one certainty: it can't happen. Need for secrets is basic to our species, as basic as sex—in fact, it *is* sex in the way our minds are erotically fascinated by secrets. If we can understand *that* we may understand what pulled us to evolve. Meanwhile, our piles of knowledge will just grow higher, though not deeper.

So the alternative I had to face: Could I evolve into a new species, one that is beyond the need for mystery? As hard as is to imagine—that is how hard it was for me to admit Wisdom's voice. "The desire to evolve is embedded deeper inside you than sex," she said. It sounded supernatural, even though evolution is a natural process. Yet there *are* living things for whom mystery is irrelevant: we call them plants, Wisdom said. And we're scared to our souls by them. What greater dread than to be reduced to a vegetable, we think.

Yet we're always scared by what we don't know. The basis of plant life is still a mystery, which is why Wisdom chose to reside in the very *tree* of knowledge. We human beings evolved with plants, she told me, our desires are mirrored in flowers and their perfumes, in the sweet flesh of fruits. To evolve again, it will also be with plants, in biospheric ecosystems. Looking back from there, our prehistoric parents will have become the cultures enveloping us now, just as our prehuman parents in Eden are the trees. Books, movies, churches—the best of them will be treasured relics, more precious than they are today.

[Shechner]

APPENDED 1995

(These entries of Archie's tickled me as I thought of even Svitz rendered irrelevant—he and his system of great thinkers! Svitz represents all the academics who think a "field" means a discipline, not a living plant system. Their books and learning will be the least precious in the future, these nature-illiterates. And to think that an archeologist, a man dedicated to the forgotten past, could render Svitz's future superfluous by listening to a woman's voice—delicious!)

[Julie]

Face

Our little minds expand and we first sense connection between thought and feeling when we study the broad faces of our parents in early childhood. By early youth we're already running away from knowledge of them, their too-intimate insights. Running away, our latest skills of analysis—now sharpened by the world—focus on the world as if it were a parent's face again, with all its power to nurture or harm us, especially by indifference this time.

My God, the complexity of a face. Every nuance of it can be read for approval or rejection, for feeling good about yourself. Every day's work comes down to feeling good about yourself, doesn't it? When I look at my face in the mirror I search for redemption in it, some sign of intelligence in the balance of its features and imperfections—a whole greater than its parts. Then I turn back to the world in similar search of familiar details, looking for the overall balance points: is the flower of the magnolia tree its point of entry? Not its essence; no, that's the common mistake of reducing an ecosystem to specific species. Forget essences and symbols, for the things they connote are unmoving faces; masks, not faces. Instead, consider the new faces never before encountered, the natural systems so complex and subtle that our own sensibilities seem but one detail—and an entry point.

My mother's face seemed like that to me, as an infant, and such was the voice of Wisdom: voice so fascinating it outshone any face.

[Shechner]

1995

Faces cause me a lot of trouble. You see, I'm one of those face readers. I could probably read faces for a living. In a way, I do read them to stay alive. I check faces to make sure there's aliveness in them and that I'm still alive in the other's eyes. I never knew this about myself until I was with Nosei. I never knew how much I needed a good face looking at me until I had to contend with his absent and bad faces. But Nosei wasn't bad, just human.

When I think back on it, I believe that I really had my first case of panic because of a bad face on Nosei. But we got his good face back so quickly, that I was okay without ever knowing I almost wasn't. It had taken overnight, though, for things to feel okay between us, so I can remember details, like being able to sleep only five hours and having bad thoughts about him when I woke up, even as he lay next to me sleeping.

We had gone to see a play at Mann Auditorium in Tel Aviv with a visiting colleague of his and the man's wife. We sat down and I took out the program to read. I felt Nosei's hand against my program, as if discouraging me from reading. I thought, Was this some kind of theater etiquette? I looked at his face. It looked hard, unresponsive. He didn't seem to want to look at me. That's all it took. I felt incensed. And when intermission came, I wouldn't take his hand. The other couple saw me not take his hand.

When we got back to my place that night, he was very silent. I remember the silence felt heavy against my chest. It was hard to look at him. The heaviness was also in his face.

I could see lines I hadn't noticed before. And his face looked flabby—mushy—like some of his features had melted. He spoke slowly.

"Julie, bring me your copy of Shakespeare," he said. "I want to read some of the text of the play."

I literally leapt up to get it. I found it immediately. "I bookmarked the page, Nosei. Would you like a snack or something?"

He shook his head. He did not want anything. The motion of his body—the slightest gestures—seemed unbearably slow to me. I felt myself sinking into this slow motion reel of dread. He said, "I want to talk about what happened tonight."

"Why doesn't he just yell at me?" I thought. And then I seemed to be yelling. No, not yet. All I was saying was that I had felt he was controlling how I behaved at the Mann and I got upset. I didn't hear myself apologize. Something left me wooden.

He was talking but I couldn't look at him. Why couldn't I look at him? Soon I'll be accused of not communicating. Yes, there it is. "Julie, you're not communicating." I wanted to leave but was afraid to move from the room. He was talking some more. "I was not thinking of you in that way at all tonight. I don't know what you mean. You should have said something at the time. I don't even remember touching your program or trying to close it."

I didn't believe him. But if I didn't believe him, what did I believe? That he was lying? Oh, God. Did I see it wrong? It can't be—I've never been that wrong. "I don't know what it is, maybe your self-esteem—." He was telling me I needed to act more like an equal, that it was hard on him when I don't feel good enough about myself to be a full partner. I heard myself cutting him off. Yes, now I was yelling. "No, there's nothing wrong with *my* self-esteem. But maybe there's something wrong with us!" I made the mistake of looking. Can a face become something else, like pain—pure feeling—like depression? If I stopped the tirade inside it wouldn't make a difference. Worse than stopped. Caught in the stopping, the dying, but never dead. Why doesn't he just yell?

"Listen, Julie. We had a misunderstanding. A miscommunication. We have far less of it than some people I know. It's not the end of the world."

I looked at him. I was invited back in. I went. But most of me was still back with the melting face. My body went to sleep that night, but my mind stayed awake. When dawn came—resentment. Reenacting everything. Dredging up other moments. The clock in the bedroom became a metronome rhythm I couldn't comply with or escape from. I was caught between the clicks—one click said to leave, get out. The next pulled me into a frantic worry to make sure everything was okay between us. Nosei had been wrong. Such things *can* be the end of the world.

"What would you do if I called you by your first name for awhile?" I remember the session when I desperately needed to use my doctor's first name. I had been telling him about this episode with Nosei. The terribleness of the face.

"I would think about the meanings, but mostly I would just let it be," the doctor answered.

"It wouldn't be a bad idea or anything?"

"No. But your question suggests that my doctor name has provided a filter of safety, probably around intensities of feelings, thoughts. Wanting to use my first name may reflect a need to take a risk anyway, in order to find something you need. With me—through me. Inside of me."

"Inside of you," I heard myself repeating. "I like the inside of you. The inside of us."

"You know, as you say that, I find myself thinking that the inside of me—and us—holds some kind of secret. Some basic nutrient. Or more correctly, it holds *you*—it's where you find something you need, seriously need, inside yourself. It's where you find your aliveness. You see, I think you make do with faces. In locating my interiority—and the interiority of our relationship—you get more than what is available with a face. When you look at faces, you are trying to survive—to sustain yourself and the relationship without knowing the secrets inside the other. When you *feel*, make contact with an interior space—the place where you reside in the other—you feel like you're living, not just surviving or basking in the glow of the other's gaze."

I sped through his words again, seeking something, not finding it. "Can't you just tell me how you feel?" I asked the doctor. "Don't you ever just want to come over here where I am? What comes out of you, into you—how much is because of me?" I stopped. Nothing felt real to say any longer. "I feel tired," I gasped. "None of this makes sense. It makes more sense when I'm having symptoms."

"That's one thing symptoms are good for," he answered,

not missing a beat. "At least when we're having a panic attack, we know what we feel and we know where we are. In danger. But I disagree with you. I think the most sense may be found right here, where we both are in this session today. Because, as you spoke to me—so directly—I had a great desire to give you what you want. I was aware of a feeling of pleasure in imagining myself open to you. But inside that pleasure was something else. I think there is a fear of stepping outside of the interiority that binds us, yet we are two interiors—separate, though sometimes joining. That is the fact of every relationship, not just ours. And in that separateness, we find ways to structure our lives. Both of us do. Desire is one way to structure ourselves around separateness. It's one way to protect that space that binds us to others—to insulate the other from what we feel are dangerous or bad parts inside. To make things not dead. Not lost."

"But what about the desire that mother and Archie found between them? And the desire to evolve. I've been wanting to ask if you think it's real?"

"It's almost like you're asking me if you are real," he answered softly.

"I come here for you to make me real. I know that. But the more I become really real—I don't know how else to put it—well, it's great for a while, but then I feel like I'm going to lose something. I feel you could become dead to me if I know more about you."

"Like what?," he asked

"Your desire. For me."

"Perhaps that's because, in a way, I would become dead to you. If we bring desire in here the way we bring everything else, then you do lose something—a way you've had of keeping things alive and safe. If we keep it out of here, then you feel better able to protect this space from deadness, from isolation. I think we can see now, that when you ask me if the desire to evolve is real, you're really asking me to help you keep the old power of your mother—and not feel the power of isolation that is part of growing. You asked me quietly, but I had the sensation you were screaming at me to stop making you more real—that it was making your mother feel unreal to you."

"It feels like a merry-go-round. I have work to do, damn it! I have to decide about this thing with mother and Archie." First I was staring at the floor, looking for a sign in the faded carpet. Then I was knocking on the wall with my fist.

"You do have your own work. I think you deserve an answer from me about your work."

I interrupted, talking fast. "That's okay. You don't have to." I didn't want to get into a defensive discussion about the Scroll.

"But today feels different," he pressed on. "The desire to evolve, I think, is real. I mean, I can imagine it being real. And I think it's worth imagining. Worth the risk. Your mother took the risk when she took Archie on as a patient. She was a scientist. When I say that, I do not mean to lock her down into some status of authority. On the contrary, she invested herself more in what she didn't know than what she already knew. In our profession, we come to know a lot about desire. It can be a method of aliveness, a way to avoid separation. As I understand what you've told me, the desire to evolve is at the species level. And my profession has spent little time on this kind of knowing. The nonhuman. The human inside the nonhuman, that is; and the ecosystem, the animals."

As he finished the sentence the phone began to ring, but he finished it nonetheless. Then he picked up the receiver. After a few "yes's" and "no's" he put it down and returned to his explanation as if nothing had happened.

"The desire to evolve may entail losses we can't understand yet. Not about avoiding but about confronting our history as a species. I can imagine that it's about going out to explore those origins, certainly something that most of us don't do, don't even think about."

"This might be kind of like it, don't you think?" I aked him. "This process. Like you said, things change here—in a fundamental way. The difference is the aim. Change in here means more realness for me, more Julie—yet more like everyone else. A person. But change as *Archie* had it, would mean more than becoming a person. It would mean more realness as a species of animal among the rest."

"Yes," he said. "But we can't know about this."

"We *do* know. Archie helped us to know. That's the story that he told mother. It's the story I transcribed. The problem is I don't understand what happened to mother and Archie."

"You mean how they died?"

"No. Well, I'll always wonder about that. There are no bodies. It can make you believe they're not dead. But no, that's not what I meant. The problem is what they did. Mother slept with Archie. She wasn't supposed to do that, was she?"

"Your friend Svitz was not supposed to call you here on the emergency line, but he did. He said he would be late in picking you up, but he should have left that message with the secretary. He asked me a question. He asked if I would like to meet for a drink."

"No, no, no. I told him not to call that number." I felt for my backpack and almost tore it open trying to get at my water bottle.

"That is what I told him: 'no.' Let's return to *your* question. I have little conception of the problems that faced your mother and Archie. To say this may only cause you more pain. Because a question about your mother is also a question about me."

"I'm wondering if we would ever do that." I waited but he didn't say anything. "Could you sleep with me?" I asked.

Silence. I looked at the phone like it was ringing again—I was not going to take the question back.

When I looked back at him, he said: "I think you need to know that I can see you as a real person. That means being able to see myself with you. Sexually. But I think you also want to know if we can always continue. I think you've come to love the process in here and you wonder how your mother could have left it. Risked it. You've worried lately about when this will be over. It must feel impossible to imagine separating from something you love. You must wonder how *I* will be able to leave it—that is, how will it not disappear when we stop meeting."

I could tell the session was almost over by how much he was talking about it. But I went further. "Did the desire to evolve make Archie and mother have sex?"

"No. I don't know why they had sex. Did your mother leave a note, Julie?"

"It's hard to imagine mother leaving notes for me. I didn't find a note. It was strange, though, not to find anything that she had written the week before she disappeared. I haven't thought about it before."

[Julie]

A Female Concept

Since I came to this country I haven't been able to take notes or write anything. I haven't told a doctor—I know it has to be mental, since I can write down an address and a phone number in a normal way. But anything to do with what I've learned here and my fingers freeze around the pen. At the typewriter my hands lock up, like I'm wearing mittens. I can type nonsense but as soon as I am thinking the mittens come on. Nothing like this has ever happened before. Perhaps I should be talking to your mother about it but I don't want to tamper with her confidence in me. Here we've just met and I've learned the existence of something more significant than anything—even if it's just a voice.

"You mean the Scroll," said Julie. "All she wants to do is talk about it because she hasn't figured out how to put her notes together. Look, the woman is my mother and I love her but she's a mess about this. Archie Shechner, the archaeologist who discovered it, was a patient of hers. The ethics of publishing her commentary on his private therapy has her confused. She can't imagine publishing it without her interpretations, because it would sound mad, she says; on the other hand, how does she present a case study when there is such revolutionary scholarship there?"

"I'm happy to listen to whatever she wants to tell me," I said. My writer's block probably had to do with excitement, so some plain speaking couldn't hurt.

"No, you need to hear the real thing," Julie objected. "I taped myself reading parts that are so fantastic they *have* to be real. I knew Archie and he couldn't write before this. You could look up his articles and see. He wasn't much of a thinker then, either. I guess I should tell you that he also became my mother's lover. That should really explain her problem to you.

"Besides, I read my mother's notes. She wrote that Archie's insights felt like her own. It didn't strike her as odd or sick that he would elaborate a female concept of God. Archie was himself reluctant to believe his findings. 'This is not the mind of a deranged person,' she wrote. But she leaves off before writing anything conclusive.

Except for this half-finished sentence: 'keep him from dying.' If she got so close to Archie's thoughts, maybe the first part of 'keep him from dying' is what's missing; maybe she meant the voice was keeping him alive."

[Nosei '84]

Death's Wisdom

Now consider this: Death is our finest occasion. When we earn life's rewards—prizes, promotions, weddings—we grow more focused on ourselves, excluding rest of the world. Win a Nobel and you are not inclined to read newspaper that day and think about a murderous typhoon in Sri Lanka. If you get married during the Watergate Hearings, the latter's momentousness fades. The greater the personal magnification, the more self-centered our emphasis becomes.

Now, consider your own death as highest on the list of significant occasions. You will no longer be reading the papers or concerned with outside events at all. What will happen in the next billion years will barely touch you. You are all that matters and your reward so magnificent that you are freed of all responsibilities. Yes, you will miss the excitements of life's smaller awards, the victories and honors accruing to your tribes and teams, a rewarding sunset here and there, but these things are all rewards because they are deferrals. They put off struggles and pains that lie ahead. Now, in death, you are so securely wrapped in reverence that no pleasure of a paradisaical interlude could compensate.

That, in short, might have sufficed as translation of a portion of the book of Ecclesiastes, the chapter which begins "Better to go to a house of mourning than a house of pleasure" and contains the sentiment,"May your deathday be more happy than your birthday." Yet there is not a mention anywhere of the rewards of the afterlife. Critics have puzzled for centuries over the joy this book provides in the face of pronouncements that appear so glum. Now it is clear. This book views death as a part of life, not a separation from it. And now we can see that it is based on the *Scroll of the History of Adam,* which was lost during the following century, when Israel was invaded and its archives and libraries sacked by Assyrians. At this time, the great writers still maintained a bond with Wisdom, with life. To this day, when Jews say "Choose life!" they are echoing their ancient culture's regard for death.

[Shechner]

Unawake

Julie, flushed with excitement, told her mother that Archie had found the connection between the Scroll and the Bible.

"Yes, yes, but isn't it all ironic," said Betti Peleg. "While you lie smugly in your grave, oblivious to other events, life goes on without you and you are forgotten. You fell for a cruel joke; that might be the best that can be said for you. The more time passes, the less anyone thinks of you, until you might not have existed at all. That's why you have to experience life's pleasures while you can, not hide from them as you do." Betti Peleg spoke while the freshly typed pages she had just read rested in her lap.

"Mother, remember the Scroll," said Julie. "Wisdom is hidden. Nature doesn't speak—but it's the representative of life."

"I'm surprised how much you've absorbed from the Scroll," Betti answered. She stared at her stout but pale daughter for a few moments. "So why is it that you never spent more time out-of-doors?"

"I was overwhelmed by the power of it—the natural world hit me like an hypnotic dream. I didn't know this was the reason I avoided going outside. I thought I was just more together, more awake at home. Now I see that I had no resistance to what was hidden in nature—couldn't help being over-aroused, even without knowing it."

[Nosei, '94]

Wizard

I had a cranky morning and I was looking forward to getting that tactile feeling in my fingers from the old Royal and that scratchy static in my ears from the dictaphone. Hearing my mother's hushed voice always got me going: usually, her official mode was loud, louder than you'd expect, but now she was hushed as a pope in private audience, as if she'd found her true calling. Also she was scared; after all, this was near-psychotic stuff.

As I fixed the earphone headband so it wouldn't scrunch my ears, I lit my after-breakfast Gitane and felt like the blue Gypsy lady on the pack, preparing to overhear the wizard. (That's what the girls in my scout outfit called my mother when they wanted to side with me. I was always complaining about her "you'll see if I was right"—as in, "Sell your virginity cheap and you'll always want to blend into a crowd and hide from the spotlight. See if I was right." Huh? I'd think. What was this nutty psychospeak? But I held onto my virginity to stifle her predictions, withdrew into science books, old ones not new ones, the older the better, no crowds to blend into). Instead of crazy stuff, I was riveted when Archie started the evolutionary biology jag. Old Darwin was a teenage hero of mine. This was years before anyone used the word "ecosystem." Archie, in my view, would have been strictly a dry bone man. I imagined a faint white pallor over his sun-darkened skin—bone dust, maybe. Yet here he was, getting off on living stuff. But most special to me, he was talking about feelings I knew, the feelings you study when your excitement for the day is enclosed, confined to observing yourself and maybe one or two other people. He was making sense to me—even as he was mother's most risky patient. However strange his words about evolving might seem as I transcribe them, they are also touching.

[Julie '84]

Guide to a New World

One day, Julie's mother broke off the dictating from her notes. "I'm going to try another summary," she said. She tried it a hundred times, trying to boil down the story of her work with Archie and the Scroll to a paragraph that could be quoted in the papers.

"Finder of the scroll, *The History of Adam*, in the first digs of Ir David, 1969. Thought it was an empty container. Only back in the lab did Shechner find a blackened Scroll within. Unreported, took several years to unroll and decipher the archaic Hebrew script. Only parts of the text survived. Arrived at partially translated text in 1977. Developed guilt complex, did not know how to reveal it. Prepared to reveal the Scroll, 1984. Began to hear Wisdom's voice, taking notes. Began treatment with Peleg two months later. Began recording tapes of Guide, April. Decision to reveal Scroll, June, 1984."

[Nosei, '94]

His Mother's Dress

I was struck by the metaphor of faces on Archie's tapes. Masks were a Svitz fixation too but there's this difference: it's a mirror for Archie, not a mask. Could that be the same thing? No, Svitz could care less what's under the mask (according to Nosei) but Archie thinks we study faces in order to learn how to interpret things we haven't *faced* yet, like the visage of an ecosystem. The mirror never tells us enough; we crave the real thing. In the same way, faces come later, after we've explored the realms of our mother's taste and smells, the hills of her breasts, the enormous shadows of bodies and trees.

My mother would say all this is pre-Oedipal but she wouldn't get the joke the ecosystem plays on her. Nature predates our human relationships and we're always trying to see it again, get focussed. Gardens and parks—that's not it, those are masks and imitations. "Look at the sky," Archie said to me once, "What's hidden behind it?"

“The stars at night—the universe,” I answered.

“Yes, but down here where life is, our way is blocked. We can't see what's behind life—it's like a door is put there and that door is death. The ground never clears at night like the sky does, so that we can see beyond it.” Fits with“Earth to Earth,” which Archie was fond of saying. It connected his profession of digging in the ground with everything else, the psychology of my mother and religion too.

Now that I'm typing the Scroll, I can see how it made sense to him that the voice he was hearing in his head came from the earth. Behind living things was the face of the ecosystem, and that's Wisdom's face, the hidden mother. Our own mothers are like masks for her. This is the part my mother thinks is where the real madness starts. To me, this is plain as day.

That's why I thought Svitz in his crazy-as-a-fox guise would understand it. And before he arrived for his lectures, I read him in the papers, less an overnight environmentalist than a fatalist: “We are coming to our senses after a 50-year bad trip of raping the natural world as if there is no tomorrow. Today we see that current industrial society is literally unsustainable.” Raping? I'd heard destroying or wounding. But rape—that suggests she has once had a say in the matter. That suggests we're not listening to her cries of “No!”

I had to say “yes” and actually attempt to sleep with the man in order to learn he thought the planet revolved around himself. To Svitz there was no hidden nature and when I asked him about “rape” he said maybe he should have said "masturbate." This was not an attempt at humor—the man is humorless—but a heavy-handed point: "It's men playing with their tools that's fucking things up." Nature was in a dress for him but there was no woman behind it, nothing behind it. He was insulted because it was his dress—I mean, in his mother's dress, so to speak. For some reason, when men want to insult each other they start with their mothers. He sure didn't make me feel anything more than his mother's assistant, once his clothes were off. Help him, he implored. "Help me get it up." There wasn't going to be anything like rape going on in this neck of the woods.

[Julie '84]

1995

I'm startled to read myself here in this chapter. It doesn't seem possible that I was that Julie. She seems so lively. Was I really this sardonic Gitanes girl? I've avoided for so long anything that might threaten my equilibrium, I'd forgotten her. But that's what panic is really about. Disowning yourself. The attack seems to come out of nowhere, almost like a sign from God. A supernatural experience. Heart racing, pounding. The collapse and fear. Is this what the saints felt in the throes of agape and fear of God?

But what is most supernatural about it is the collapse of time. The past evaporates. Where you are becomes irrelevant. The natural world does not register, except as an icon of danger. The panic comes out of nowhere like an archangel descending. You wait for the heart attack like the second coming—or the first. But it never comes. Yet it's always with you because you're always on guard, waiting.

For someone who can barely survive waiting, I always seem caught in it. Waiting for a heart skip—a panic attack. Waiting on others. There was mother waiting on patients and me waiting on mother. And when people asked if I'd mind waiting, I nearly swallowed them up as I chortled, "No, take your time." Now, that's psychotic! I actually believed I didn't mind waiting.

The anxiety taught me that was a lie. Something inside, I guess, roused itself and said, "Hey you! Julie! You may like waiting but I'm sick of it. I'm going to show you just how sick of it I am." Pow! High anxiety. I wasn't able to wait anymore with a smile on my face and my head in a book. After the attacks started, I could barely sit in a restaurant long enough to get the food and eat it, especially if I was waiting for someone or had to meet them afterwards. The only way it was possible was if I allowed myself plenty of time. An hour to eat, an hour to get to wherever I was going.

It helped alot when Svitz gave me a cell phone. Why? Well, if you'd asked me several years ago, I would have said, "Because, if there's a problem I can call. Let them know. That way I don't have to rush." Sounds reasonable. But there was a lot more to it. I wanted the phone so I could call my doctor if I felt an anxiety attack coming. And it wasn't merely that rushing made me nervous. I was afraid to rush. Any acceleration in my heart rate made me afraid I would have a heart attack.

So what the cell phone really did for me was help me

steal time. You see, people like me don't take time; they steal it. For example, it made me nervous to tell Svitz how long I'd be out. Once I had the cell phone, I'd keep it turned on and just not think about the time. He could call me. I could have it both ways: stay connected and disconnected at the same time. I never had to declare myself.

I was in a ladies room one day when Svitz tried to reach me. I already had the cell phone out of my backpack. Along with my water bottle. I had been on one of the upper floors of the New York University library when I started to feel sick. This was a familiar feeling. When I wasn't having anxiety attacks or heart skips, I was having some kind of bathroom episode. The respectable diagnosis: Irritable Bowel Syndrome. I even went to a seminar on it once at Mount Sinai. Big mistake. It ended up being about *all* the bowel disorders and I sat there checking my symptoms against their various lists, from diverticulitis to colon cancer. At the end, I went up to ask the doctor about my diet. As I waited my turn among all the other ass-oriented, sudden fear. Feelings of collapse. Mental images of my heart fibrillating out of control.

Anyway, I had the cell phone and water bottle out in the library bathroom because I was afraid of throwing up. Afraid I would die or overtax my heart in some way. Afraid of getting hot. I poured the water out of the Evian bottle over my neck and chest. Soaked my hand and held it to my face. The air from the vents up above made contact with the moisture on me and I began to feel safe. The waves of cramping appeared to be passing. I stopped using my incantation: blue waves, white sand. I always invoked the beaches at Eilat when I had these episodes. The phone was ringing. I was still on the toilet.

"Julie?"

"Yes, Svitz."

"What are you doing?"

"Never mind. What do you want?"

"Are you in bed with someone?"

"No. I'm on the toilet."

"Interesting. My dear, it took you a long time to answer. Make sure you have the volume up high enough on that thing—"

"Svitz, did you not hear me?"

"That's exactly the topic. Now, listen. This fellow I know has invited me to a lecture tonight at the Natural History Museum—"

"Are you feeling okay, Svitz? You hate even walking by that place."

"True, true. But I thought I could stand it if you wanted to go."

"And why would I want to go?"

"Because, an Israeli philologist affiliated with the Hula Valley Restoration project will be speaking. You used to be very intimate with philology, I remember."

"You're inept at humor, Svitz, especially when it's sexual. What has philology to do with ecology? I hear warning bells going off in my head."

"Oh, don't worry. He's got some kind of degree in biology as well as philology. He's a scholar of the Kabbalah but interested in the Hula Valley restoration as a spiritual movement. He's the author of a new book called "BioCulture: Spiritual Aesthetics in the Next Century."

"Svitz, you know I'm not spiritual."

"Neither are you sexual, my dear, and you're long overdue. With the Kabbalah around, it's bound to get sexual at some point tonight. Who knows, perhaps the voice will grace us with her presence. I'm sure he'll mention the Shekhinah at least once. Maybe she'll talk to us."

"You're still full of resentment, aren't you? You act like Archie and the Shechinah personally cheated you out of a chance for a book."

"Well, if the whole thing wasn't fraudulent—not to mention, psychotic—why did he just disappear? If I could just have examined the Scroll at least once, then I could have been an eyewitness. I would have had a leg to stand on when the critics started."

"Hold on," I said, lowering my voice. Someone else had just walked into the bathroom. "So this is what cowards say to themselves and to other poor souls anchored to cess pools," I continued, my voice lowered to almost a hiss. "The Scroll was for real and so was Archie. I'm feeling weak, Svitz—stick with what you called about."

"You identify too easily, Julie. If I am a coward, it doesn't mean you have to be one. Why do you consign yourself to anal purgatory? Yes, you must come with me tonight."

"Why? Who's going to be there?"

"I don't really know. It's not a big affair. I understand it's a select audience."

"I don't want to talk to anyone, Svitz," I blurted out. The offending patron had left, apparently only having eyed her makeup. Some women have all the luck.

"Why do you worry about that?" Svitz went on. "You always make sure you never have to talk by asking plenty of questions. Anyway, you may want to talk at this thing. I do know there will be some young scientists there. You know, men scientists. You might find someone to have fun with."

"I don't want to have fun."

"Neither do I. But I do manage to have sex now and again."

"I'm hanging up, Svitz."

"Wait! Do we go, or not?"

"Yes, we go. What time?"

"Seven-thirty. From the apartment. That should give you enough time after your appointment. By the way, how's that going? How's the Herr Doctor? What's his first name again? I think a friend of mine knows him—"

I pushed the "end" button on the phone. Svitz was the only person I had ever been able to hang up on. I walked out of the restroom stronger than when I went in. Hanging up on Svitz had been better than taking a pill. I had some specifically for such cramping. But as you might suspect, I was afraid to take them. We all make traps—mine are just more, well, obvious than some. I make traps with my body. Most people just do it with their minds.

I walked back to the table where I had been working. Among the jumble of books was one still open. Someone before me had marked the significant passages. "As Freud said many decades ago, the ego is based on a body ego... Psychosomatic integration or the achievement of the 'indwelling' of the psyche in the soma." Yes, I had been reading about myself. You could say I had overeaten in my mind and that was why I had ended up in the bathroom. "Retreat from I AM and from the world made hostile by the individual's repudiation of the NOT-ME." A clue provided by Dr. Winnicott. A name I often saw on my mother's bookshelves but never consulted.

Among these shelves I was hunting for a secret—about me or mother? I looked at all the books piled in front of me. Notes and writings of various psychologists. My doctor asked if my mother left a note for me, and though I said I hadn't found one, the truth is I had not looked.

So here it is: I felt a euphoric excitement just to discover what it is I'm doing here. I couldn't wait to tell my doctor of this amazing accomplishment. Entirely on my own, I deciphered a piece of my unconscious. When I rose to get up, I couldn't move. The excitement had turned to fear, and it would make me late to my appointment. Every thought now turned back to my heart. My brain had turned its ear to the beats in my chest. Measuring them.

I pulled the cell phone from my backpack with all the shakiness of a novice in the desert reaching for a canteen of water. Would there still be something in it? Enough to save me? I punched in my doctor's beeper number. I pushed "send" on the keypad, even though I knew it would take me to the awful space of waiting—waiting for him to call back.

I should move to somewhere more private, I thought,

but I couldn't get up. I reached in my backpack for the panic notebook. All I could do was make marks on the pages. No words. I tried to read. One of the books on the table didn't have anything to do with illness. "No one ought to feel surprise at much remaining as yet unexplained in regard to the origin of species and varieties, if he makes due allowance for our profound ignorance in regard to the mutual relations of the many beings which live around us." Darwin. I thought to myself that the key to the secrets in all the other books was surely in his. The secret was in "due allowance for our profound ignorance." I began to feel some relief. Sadness started seeping out where panic had been—when the phone rang.

"What's up, Julie?"

"I'm in the library and I can't move. Afraid to move. The funny thing is I was excited to tell you something. Just before it started. About mother and me. It helped to read Darwin while I waited for you to call. He wrote about profound ignorance."

"Can you tell me more about that?"

"It made me feel sad. It made me feel like I was with you. Hello?"

A clicking. "I'm here. Remember, you've been talking lately about how I help you feel real. Darwin seems to be talking about realness. It reminded you of something shared with me, that perhaps I can speak openly of profound ignorance like Darwin. Then the waiting doesn't feel so impossible."

"Yes." Just long enough to get to you, I was thinking. "Do you think I can come to my session now?"

"Yes, I do. I'll see you in a few minutes."

Magic words, they seemed then, back when I was still living with Svitz. Some people search for the magic pill that will save them. I ingest magic words. I take in the mind with the mouth that emits the magic words. That day, they got me to my session. While I was having the attack I thought I would have to cancel on Svitz. But I did not. This was a characteristic pattern—thinking I couldn't do something and then doing it. Afraid I wouldn't survive and then surviving.

Arriving with Svitz at the main doors of the Museum of Natural History, entry was barred but Svitz had a letter with him that gained us immediate entrance. The reverberation of our steps through the cavernous empty galleries gave me a feeling of guilty excitement. Childhood fantasies of being locked up in stores after hours. Roaming. I suddenly wanted to slip away and go exploring. Do animals and mannequins come alive in such rooms when the people go home?

I was following these fantasies when Svitz said my name. He was saying it to some people that were suddenly standing next to us. I responded. But barely. I was thinking that if I could just be left alone, I could find it: I imagined that Archie had deposited the Scroll here, with some intimate museum colleague, and that the speaker tonight would really be Nosei. That he had changed his name, grown a beard. That we would meet. We would know each other.

Svitz and I followed the others into a hall with tables covered with thick white linen. We were supposed to sit down in front of them. China and crystal were on the tables.

Figures in white suits with the most beautiful black skin began to put food and liquid into the plates and glasses. I couldn't believe it. Svitz had never taken me to anything this nice before. I took a quick look at him to make sure it was all real. But my attempts at verification were interrupted by a voice through a microphone. We were told to eat and that a young scientist would entertain us with some slides from a recent expedition to a rain forest in Sri Lanka.

Plates of food appeared to move across the table in the same rhythm as the flash of the slides. It seemed for a moment the plates were a show and tell, and contained samples of the different species being projected onto the screen. I thought of the Scroll and the story of Adam's first taste of monkey. And then Archie was there in my mind asking for reassurance, confiding in me that he could taste the monkey.

"Now, if you'll notice, the next selection on your plates is probably a descendant of this species of monkey. What you're looking at here is, of course, an extrapolation of fossil findings. Ethnobotanists are uncovering an intimate connection between monkeys and a species of plant that I will show you next. Native peoples tell of the experience of eating these monkeys, which Professor..."

I stopped listening and leaned over to Svitz. "Did you hear what he just said about the monkeys?" I asked.

"Yes, yes," he said in a labored voice. "It's all quite tedious but I'm glad you're enjoying it. The food is good, though."

"But, do you realize what we're eating?"

"Well, they said they had a vegetarian plate, Julie, if

you didn't care for meat. Personally, I wouldn't pass up the chance for good veal."

I looked down at my plate. I felt foolish. It was veal. I put some in my mouth. I was eating happily when I remembered I'd never had veal before. How could I be sure it was what Svitz had told me? A waiter came along and I asked him what it was. He smiled and said something I couldn't understand. I realized he was speaking in another language. I gave up and decided to eat. I had become very hungry.

"It's time now for our guest from Israel, Professor Aviya Nachman, who has asked that you be served your desserts ahead of time. She told me, that in this way, she would at least start out with some appeal. As some of you know, she consented graciously to be our substitute at this lecture, though she indicated that she will also speak about the book that was to be tonight's topic. She has requested that I refrain from any further introduction. So, ladies and gentlemen, Professor Nachman."

A loud and long clapping ensued. I only saw her back as she rose from her table to go towards the lectern. As she turned to face us, I was surprised to see that she was quite old, perhaps in her eighties. But radiant. Her features suggested that she might have been an overwhelming beauty in her youth.

She began to speak but I couldn't listen to what she was saying. It was a seductive, full-throated voice, rolling with wonder and serious play. She was dressed in a tunic pants outfit in earth tones. She had a straight regal posture.

Her hair was a shining white, coiled on top as if ready to strike. Yet the scarf that lay at her neck invited contact, so that people would come close. I knew that if I came close I would want to touch the scarf, examine how it lay about the neck. Her neck.

"I want to speak to you first about sunflowers. I have always been fond of them. No, I must not be timid tonight. I have long been in love with sunflowers. I've often wondered how it would end. I now know. I'm afraid it is hopeless—and quite tragic. As you know, this is a New World plant, though it is now cultivated in my region of the world for its seeds. The reason behind my melancholy over this fact will become clear, hopefully, as I proceed. Indeed, the clarity of my relationship to sunflowers has only recently emerged. Actually, as I was leaving Israel to come to the United States. That is why I thought I should share it with you as we begin our conversation tonight.

"The clarity came upon reading an article just before my departure. It told of research being done at one of your universities on the origins of sunflowers—to recreate the evolutionary history of a species of sunflower. Could there *not* have been sunflowers? Or, could we have ended up with different species of sunflowers than we have now? This was interesting to think about but it was not what impressed me. What made me gulp was to imagine how our own species may be changing as a consequence of these efforts to become the students of other species and to learn the systems they emerge from.

"I was half-reading, half-daydreaming in this fashion

when the authors of the article asked that marvelous question. It has literally been my hot toddy every night since undertaking this trip. They asked, "But *who* did those first sunflowers mate with?" You see, they were trying to re-enact the original mating that led to their species of sunflower. I say again, how marvelous!

"Sunflowers in love. I am getting carried away, I know. Still, it may be more imprudent to not concede to a possibility that our whole way of thinking about other species may be changing; in fact, has changed—and we are stumbling to find the words to articulate it. Things that we have made exclusive to our species—love, intelligence, consciousness, language—may only be so because of old structures of knowledge and the terms embedded in them.

"I love to see sunflowers. Their faces bursting forth. Yes, they've always looked to me like they had faces. Bursting-forth faces. In love with the world. At home. This is how I used to look at them. Not so much since making my Atlantic crossing. I no longer see only myself—a common trait of Homo sapiens. I see, more completely, an integrity before me—a whole other kind of intelligence, born of sexual strategy, born of a unique ecosystem. I see a family of species that can still evolve. And that is why I am melancholy when I see our cultivated fields of sunflowers, though I must admit I would not wish to be without them. I am too much the voyeur of sunflowers. And I am very jealous that I cannot see them in the wild like you can—in their original wildness.

"Now, someone was to speak here tonight about a

book they had written entitled "BioCulture: Aesthetics in the Next Century." I must confirm what many of you have been whispering this evening. I and this person are enemies. When I was young, I used to disavow that I had enemies. Now I advertise it. You have not lived in the thinking world if you have not made enemies. I confess I rather like the main title, "BioCulture." It seems to signal a paradigm shift, a new way of being for our culture in the next century. Unfortunately, this book delivers us not into the next century but into the past. It tightens the grip of what can only be called the academic paradigm. This grip is tighter on some fields of endeavor than others. Less so for the sciences, more so for the humanities and social sciences. It is deadly tight for the religious studies departments, from which this person has issued out.

"I saw that many of you have at your tables the publicity pages sent out by the publisher, calling the book 'A revelation of the Hula Valley restoration as a spiritual movement and offering a Kabbalistic reading of the new ethic and aesthetic it represents.' Though it's a mouthful, I only wish it were so. Not that I would agree with it, but at least if it were truly mystical, truly Kabbalistic, then there would have been the meat of imagination to sustain onself. But there is no imagination in this book. Imagination is an anathema to people like—well, as you must realize by now, I refuse to speak his name. I want to make very certain I do not lose him as an enemy.

"I guess what I most object to is that nature is not a real thing for this person. Nor is it a sexual thing. It is merely a prop. And, not even a prop for the human species, rather mostly for the lumbering minds of academe that translate the texts of nature and Kabbalah as homilies for the millenium. Nature, for them, is just a step on the way to a higher level for human culture. Ecosystem is just a vehicle for foisting upon us their so-called avant-garde systems of thought out of the latest academic journals.

"None of this is necessary to understand the Hula Valley restoration. An old friend put it best. His name was Archibald Schechner and he said to me one day that the Hula restoration was about evolving, in the strictest sense of the word. This should return us to field and laboratory, and at the very least to Darwin. And so I will let Darwin end my lecture to you. It is over a century and a half since he wrote, 'It is interesting to contemplate a tangled bank, clothed with many plants of many kinds, with birds singing on the bushes, with various insects flitting about, and with worms crawling through the damp earth, and to reflect that these elaborately constructed forms, so different from each other, and dependent upon each other in so complex a manner, have all been produced by laws acting around us.' Ladies and gentlemen, we all know these are the laws of evolution and we know that as Homo sapiens we have been standing outside of them. For a very long time now, we have lost the possibility to physically evolve. We are behind even the sunflowers and stand in their shadow. Thank you."

I was paralyzed in my seat. I looked at Svitz and saw the first look of astonishment I'd ever seen on his face. I watched him plop his thick hands onto the table and push himself up with the help of a big breath. He seemed to bounce from table to table until he reached the front. It was almost comical to see the two of them next to each other. She was actually taller than him and he looked up at her face while he spoke like he was trying to see the very top of the Empire State building. It was hard to tell anything by her face. But Svitz's looked greedy. Someone moved between them and then she disappeared from sight. I had made no move of my own in her direction. One of many missed opportunities at that time in my life. I cared only for being safe then.

I didn't even bother to ask Svitz what she had said. My mind was on sunflowers. Can sunflowers be in love? Or is that something only we can do? Separate loving, separate intelligence. And perhaps, superior. That's what she had implied. I began to feel dizzy and asked Svitz to get a taxi. She had sounded so much like Archie. He often had told me that he felt like a witness to the orgasms of things beginning. He complained of a vertigo that came when the voice would speak stories of creation. He never saw Wisdom, and was relieved when the voice would stop and he hadn't seen anything. As a scientist, he couldn't countenance what was happening to him. That is why he turned to mother. He felt that if he went to mother it was objective evidence that he wasn't insane. And they did trace out a neurosis together. But instead of making the voice go away, it made the experience even more present for him. He began to lose his fear. Instead of being afraid to see the face of Wisdom, he began to look for it.

He told me that the voice was alluring, not commanding. She felt he was doing her the favor. "She told me, Julie, that she is always surprised when I come back. I tell her it seems to me I have no choice. But she says that I do and that she waits for the day when I realize my choice." I drew back from my thoughts to what I already knew—and what I knew best, then, was the wall of panic. Svitz had been talking during the taxi ride, but I hadn't been listening. The walls of my mind were drenched with panic. I was just waiting to get back to the apartment.

"Julie! You seem suspiciously unconcerned about my conversation with Professor Nachman. Do you know her?"

"No, Svitz. I'm just not feeling well."

"What's wrong?"

"Sour stomach." I lied. Not even the sudden swerves and jolts of the New York taxi bothered me now.

"Well, she doesn't seem to know where the Scroll is."

"You didn't ask her an inane question like that, did you?"

"Why not? She said she knew Schechner. Anyway, I invited her to a cocktail party that my agent is giving tomorrow night. Alas, she's returning to Israel in the morning. Now wasn't I right about this evening? You needed to come. Even I had a good time." He patted his thigh gleefully, as if it was mine.

"You were right about one thing, Svitz. The Shechinah did talk to us tonight." I heard him laugh once more, that wheezing that seemed to emanate from his nose. Although I had said it for effect, part of me believed it. I felt I had heard a person who made a choice like Archie finally did.

I don't know much more about Professor Nachman or her connection to Archie. Never followed it up. I talked about her in my sessions for a while afterwards. Always in a question. "What would it be like to be a person like Professor Nachman, a person who can make a choice and disarm her fears of authority?" A person like Archie—after he mastered his fear of being labelled a madman. I feel like I've been trying to answer that question for ten years.

[Julie]

Bright Idea

All human powers of language, honed as mammoth and sabre-tooth hunters, have brought us to this final act of interpretation: What was our original ecosystem, and thus, what was our purpose on earth? It was all formed in some rain forest where we found a niche between sloths and monkeys, to trudge out eventually into the relative open of an African savanna, where we could start to hunt and communicate more skillfully. First we learned to find in each other mentors and peers—and that was the beginning of forgetting. Because before we needed any mentors and peers, we learned directly from the plants and animals themselves. Shechner was convinced we can read the plants, for they were our life-giving ancestors, and we're reaching the point where we can translate their genetic histories and read our own origins in the earth again. "Earth to Earth," he said.

What are mothering breasts but large, milky-textured,

rain forest fruits? But first, perhaps they were a frontal version of buttocks, attracting our weak male eyes the way a juicy ape behind once did. It was burlesque back then too, dimwitted ideas, as it remains for the Svitzes of our day. But however we turned face to face, it was the subtlety of the hands, the digital delicacy, that learned to read the body sexually as the eyes read a face. From our eyes to our fingertips: the hand-eye coordination was exercising the brain on a textual trampoline; enlarging it, too.

The ecosystem is the true face that existed before us and one day we'll read in it the glimmer of an idea of ourselves before we existed, pure idea. An idea such as a flower: Where did the rose get the idea to be so bright and soft and suspended on thorns? Where did any flower get its idea? Science calls them "strategies" and speaks of a plant's flower as a strategy for reproduction. A strategy suggests intelligence yet everything in our social training prepares us to deny intelligence to vegetation. When a body is devoid of breath and soul, it's unfeeling—this is what our history teaches. It is not us. And so it is with the plants: they are not us. And yet they breathe, grow, respond to climate, change their ways. We should be ready to acknowledge they have ideas, too. This fledgling new science, ecology, won't have much of a chance until we do. It has all been foretold by Shechner and Wisdom: original science and ancient art can only fortify each other, until it becomes one bright story—and the flora break into our speech again.

[Nosei, '94]

The Unopened Book

Archibald's disappearance turned for me from shock into revelation. I thought about his expressions of rage against the scholars who dismissed his discovery. He felt betrayed by his own colleagues. When he began to hear voices—or rather one voice—his hearing Wisdom's voice satisfied an inner need to transcend rational science: it was an intellectual revenge. Certainly you could call it supernatural, this voice. Now he has disappeared with the evidence. Yet the tapes and transcripts that remain conjure a more believable reality than that of a man hearing a voice. Did he realize that?

It is hard to imagine even a madman inventing such a voice. Faced with simply the paper, the man fades and the document grows in reality as an artifact. In time, it will seem to be a commentary on the Scroll. Possibly Archie deduced this himself, and reasoned further that a suicide would cast suspicion on his sanity but a disappearance would leave only a mystery.

A mystery draws us. It is an unopened book. What is it we hope for when we open a great book but to hear a voice speak to our heart?

[Betti Peleg]

The Family Library

All the history I recall is human memory, right down to the fossils. Even dreams and intuitions. All come from a culture of Homo sapiens around a fire at the earliest, or even before, gathering in forests. It is all a family history. What happened in our family before our creation—before our first child photographs—holds the vital information we need, if we want to know ourselves. Who were our parents and in what was their trust based? The pictures of them before we were conceived (pictures from the impartial outside, not from the subjective inside) show the complex drama into which we would be inserted. So the struggle forward is for a deeper picture of ourselves before we were born.

Now gorillas, dogs, dolphins—these are living cousins and we learn their resemblances and differences. Our ancestors are even older and go back to the forests where the dinosaurs disappeared. Here are things I never thought before, even when I encountered the bones. Hand skills and nervous systems were formed in the forest and when these human ancestors emerged into the savanna their appetites grew into what they are for us now. The appetite for competition and aggression, the patience for reflection—these are found in the oldest laboratories of life on land, the chemical systems of plants. They were there before us, these chemists. They experimented and created. They fed us, and we took them for granted, just as we did our parents.

Even when I look at gorillas these days, I see more of us in them than I do in British Victorians, for the species contrast is so stark that our common hidden histories shine out. Look at what these thousand-pound creatures are adapted for: nurturing their young, almost exclusively. What work do they do, where do they live? In a paradise where all their food is provided by the plants. Giant vegetarians, their work consists largely of picking and eating succulents, such as hearts of bamboo. Our eating is more concentrated and requires harder work, for we have left paradise and spread everywhere. And there precisely lies the confluence of our lines: for we are driven to reproduce paradise and replace the gorillas' oral gratification with sublimated sexual and intellectual appetites.

Look into a gorilla's eyes and you see the mask removed. Eating is for them what killing is for us. Oh, we don't need to reckon up the human appetite for murder—we just need to consider our wishes. Threaten me and I might wish you dead, as I once wished my father, mother and all I was close to, dead. Yet I loved them and would never act on such wishes, so why were they always there in moments of anger and terror and helplessness? Because paradise is lost for the human infant, who knew it already at the nursing mother's breast. The most unbearable scenes of tenderness were encountered for the first time by Europeans when they beheld nursing mountain gorilla mothers with their young. These babies will not grow up and leave their paradise: they have evolved specifically to fit this spot. At home in their original ecosystem, they give back to it what they take, tending the vegetation as they eat and move on—opening new ranges for flora to colonize.

And where are humans at home? Any place they can fence out wild nature. After a long while, the natural world seems a place to escape from complicated human encampments and cities. Left behind with the culture is the quest for knowledge and for a picture of ourselves. We just want to relax, to remove our masks. This can no longer be. What is left of the natural spaces must become the new libraries and museums. Room to let go, to change faces, to evolve.

[Shechner]

Chapter 12

Chapter 12

[Sunday] A New Sexual Awakening

Wisdom asks: Why does everything come down to sex? Seven days, and each a memory of a world Wisdom entered and hid within, turning the Creator's self-made world into our sexual earth. Removed from the realm of pure chance, the accident enters the realm of necessity—Wisdom created the accident, the choice. She is the question each day asks. And the memory of each is an answer: love, holding to the memory, is the answer. The Earth day itself becomes recognizable object, a day to hold in memory, an affirmation the past exists.

As we stand still for a moment in the present, alive on our front doorsteps, in the backyard the past is always giving birth to itself. The backyard of your city [she means Tel Aviv—JP] is a beach, and there you can watch a huge boat at dusk, twelve stories all lit up, slowly disappear slantwise across the horizon. As the lights begin to blend into each other, the ship getting smaller, it never seems farther away—because at the same time it is getting darker and darker, so that the boat is clearer, more distinct. The boat is our childhood receding, the past. The surface of the sea reflects our own mind, an ecosystem largely submerged. The system is time: the past, our origins and memories, our prehistory, all preserved beneath the surface.

But in the front yard, in the present, is the great city, any one, and its culture: a museum of the present. Human history is a surface, a kind of prism refracting the present light into contemporary cultural manifestations: drama, libraries, stores of objects to wear, use, or eat. We can consume the present and turn it into the familiar past.

Meanwhile, on the receding boat, all of our childhood memories remain, including dreams and experiences older than we can remember. As long as we can see it on the ocean, it is still ours, even if just a speck. And even when gone we can remember it by watching the boats that follow, the boats of later years.

To where do they go? To the Creator, who would cut himself off from her. This complex system of life moving forward but also back is the ecosystem Wisdom created so that she may hide within. She is the voice hidden in thoughts, while the Creator speaks out unashamed as light, a dramatist who needs no audience.

Does the sun need us? Transcendent, it is dependent only on what it does not know. The Creator doesn't know Wisdom here, yet this world like all offspring was created by two. What resides in all things is desire to know what is unknown, to evolve toward it. A new sexual awakening.

[Monday] Each Ecosystem is a Living Author

Wisdom asks: Why are we close to evolving now? The human mind, no less than feathers, did not evolve for the purpose it now serves, but for a different purpose. Feathers were not originally for flight; rather, insulation. Also for sexual display. In the same way, the mind developed as intimacy grew more complex. The mind remains sexual in origin but now it works to inhibit intimacy: it has become too socialized, too cultured. We must lose it, and then find in its place an isolation, space in which to freely explore, to search and to discover.

Culture works to suppress both genetic and social change. The many genes that assembled us over thousands of generations have also left us preferring the familiar. Only when socialization is shaken does mutant or anti-social behavior seem necessary—a wilder sexuality, for one, or an extreme isolation. In this case, what has changed is the desire. The desire to turn back toward hearing nature erupts into the present—along with a desire to read the repressed. These cases of isolated individuals want to be able to read the volumes of genetic code for each species—texts written by the ecosystem.

Next, they want to approach the ecosystem's voice, finding in biodiversity a library of life. Each ecosystem is a living author. How are they read? At the border of each species is a question, and asking who each species is will lead to the voice that ties them all together. Once we see our borders as a species, and see our bodily form as shaped by natural history, then our human history books will fall to the floor. Meanwhile, hearing the voice of the unknown—the ecosystem—is still not possible for most. The wish to hear it remains repressed, along with the feeling it can be known. Instead, there is disenchantment that can only be satisfied by this revelation: we are half-evolved and must eventually disappear into the ecosystem. That, or bring the ecosystem to ourselves by evolving with it.

Before it is repressed, the ecosystem's voice is the first we hear, while still in the womb. It beckons us to change, to come out, to evolve into a new world. After we are born, however, human voices begin to take over.

[Tuesday] The Mutants

Wisdom asks: Is there a new consciousness? It is a paradigm shift for humans, away from attention to what is heard (and to events) to the process of hearing itself. How to evolve is a new consciounsess of how to listen to what is alive in the past.

To evolve is to imagine it first; then, to frame the process of imagining it with a new hearing of natural history; and then, to enter that frame. As we enter, we let go of what we've become, since we are an unfinished creature, straining toward mutation. Human history tends to think we are finished things, or that at least we are completed things once we are dead. But we are not finished in life or in death—instead, we are in the process of being changed by evolution, which will include our conscious participation. We will let go of language as we know it and once again read the ecosystem.

You see you are a passing species, and as you become aware of this you hear the ecosystem's voice. You leave your concern to her. Lifting our hearts, we receive a dictation we once again trust: it is from our original muse.

Words are a museum unless we see through to the origins of language—a glimpse of it once had in childhood.

A childhood encounter with new species—with snakes and spiders, fish and birds—has its origins in the tropics, where each is larger and more vividly colored than life. Each is one species out of a greater diversity of species than we have known since civilization began.

The voice of an ecosystem is the new consciousness as we hear it, and it will begin to be heard as a fresh crisis develops in the biocentury. What crisis? For awhile, it will continue to seem that we dominate new frontiers by technology—that is, by our wits. We will soon realize, however, that we have actually lost touch with new habitats to dominate. As we go deeper into space, the crisis deepens: space cannot be dominated. Space can only be explored, and the new ecosystems we discover will be poorer in biodiversity than most deserts. To learn more of our species history and memory on Earth, some still here will isolate themselves in remote ecosystems.

These are the mutants, who will return from isolation in the crisis of dying ecosystems. A crisis in the coming century that we face when the loss of habitat to dominate is clear. With domination in the Creator's image no longer possible, the freedom in sexual intimacy grows stronger. Some will cohabit with the returners, as together they begin to evolve.

[Wednesday] Past the Future

Wisdom asks: Why must some disappear? As the past is restored—the unknown past—some must become explorers. How to recover lost memory from the deep past?—the question reveals a new path. The old: we had gone the way of stabilizing the species, instead of expanding species memory. "Expanding consciousness," as some would say, but they would miss the the fork in the road that leads to evolving.

We learn to read the feelings of our inner lives from reading the diversity of living plants and animals. From the earliest age, we take the diversity inside as an environment for our life-long thinking. Now, go out again into this wild environment that precedes your species, Wisdom says, and explore your species memory: how did you come to be here? How did you repress for so many thousands of years the desire to evolve? Partly out of terror, we may answer; the climatic displacements of the ice age. Partly out of submission to culture, to cultural and religous identities reinforced right down to twentieth century totalitarian terror. And what did culture and religion offer? Security: regular eating and—old habits. A regression to our primate pasts; the security of numbers and role, the monkey tribe. Not until now is it revealed, because until now the past determined us. Now, we can determine our past; turn to face it in all its prehistoric depth.

Until these days, the future was highly anticipated: it was a place of new possibilities. In religion, it was a place for reunion with lost ones, or a chance for the soul to have a better outcome. More recently, the future promised marvels of technology, discoveries about who we are.

Now here we are. Technology has condensed itself into

representing simply an improvement in communication, with light-speed computers on the horizon. Soon, our telescopes will penetrate to the planets of other stars and discover new life. What will we make of the new ecosystems we see and hear?—for it will not be discreet individuals we encounter but whole systems of diverse life. However advanced a single species may become, the whole system has more to tell us. How will we listen?

The answer requires that we turn to the past, to our own evolving in the larger system of life on earth. Everything in our culture begins to tell us this is necessary. In our lifetime, visions of the future have turned into visions of restoration. And into our greatest challenge: Can we restore a dying ecosystem? Restoration leads to cloning—but this is also a restoration of the past, or a past life. Clone not an individual but an ecosystem? Here the answer is clear: no, we must first restore and listen to its hidden voice. Hear how we may evolve into another living ecosystem. It is a going back to go forward.

The future is the past.

[THURSDAY] LEAP INTO ANOTHER BODY

Wisdom asks: What is a Bio-Century? The history of a century until now has been a measure of human concerns. A waste of human and bioligical life it was, ensnared by clocks and ideas. The next century will be the first that is conscious of biological time: how we are all evolving in a deeper time—just as the earth spins and orbits—without notice. The twentieth ends with anxiety about cloning, about *biotechnologies*, which are human affairs and human fears. But the new one will leave cloning anxiety far behind. It was a futile avoidance of the desire within us to evolve. Not to stay the same.

It was and is, always, a kind of mental cloning that is in love with preserving the self by "bettering" it. Often it is cloaked in spiritual content, and always has been. From afterlife voyages for a mummy, to reincarnation, to calls for spiritual evolution in our time: this mental evolving is a resistance to the real thing. Real evolving wants wild and unknown systems of great diversity. We cannot better ourselves. But we can adapt: new possibilities await in the wildness of natural ecosystems.

Our role, then, in this time, is to nourish back to wildness the ecosystems in which we evolved. Our creativity applied to the natural world can seduce even spiritual clones back from the brink of leaving their bodies—back into their bodies, and back to the repressed desire to physically evolve.

Genes protect this desire to evolve. But it is not done by our genes. It is accomplished by experience: a leap into a new ecosystem. The parts played by curiosity and creativity in us will lead in the coming bio-century to a hunger for the knowledge to restore degraded ecosystems to wholeness.

In them, we will be outside again, as if lost—what the Mir space-station astronaut described as a coming trauma. "When earth disappears from view," he said, "we are puzzled." As it will on the way to Mars, receding into a background of stars.

What we desire is outside of us—to explore, to discover. What counters this on the inside remains tied to a Creator's will: to deny the body, transcend it. Evolution in the head, evolution without sex, cultural or spiritual evolution—all these are exciting for a time but lead nowhere. Wisdom will reveal herself in the biocentury, when the biological revolution unveils our true desire to evolve in our bodies. And, with Wisdom, to find our true mates.

The natural ecosystem is an extension of our body. Not including culture, which turns nature into stuff. What is outside for a head filled with culture? Food and fuel; building materials and clothes; weapons and medicine; friends and enemies; sunsets and shapely bodies. If the ecosystem is our body, then we need to know ourselves before we build or desire; we need to step outside into ourselves, where the outside becomes as full of emotion and concern as our insides.

What we falsely call the outside is actually seduction—the shapely things—neutralized in some way, transferred to a cultural pursuit that denies the body. That is why the highest pursuits beg for transcendence, which leaves the body behind. But if the outside is actually an extension of our body into a creative ecosystem, then our greatest discoveries are still in front of us: to know ourselves by exploring the ecosystem that produced us and the one in which we might again evolve. Instead of expanding our minds, it is our bodies which must open and unfold, while our minds are freed to respond to the original seduction: to leap into another body, to affirm the uniquely other, to evolve, to move out into the universe—while still here, on earth.

And all by hearing a voice, one that is within us, repressed with our desire to evolve—and one that we can hear out in the living world, in the heart of the ecosystem. That is why biology will define progress in the 21st or Bio-Century. We will learn to hear what we still do not want to accept is there—what some want to deny and some want to call madness—the hidden voice of Wisdom.

[Friday] Exoplanets

Wisdom asks: Why is the real world preparing to supercede the spiritual realm?

Deep time is mirrored in the deep space we now explore. Soon our telescopes will locate an inhabited planet among the exoplanets now being discovered near distant stars. Too far away to visit, we will find a way to communicate, to listen to a foreign species. Most likely there will not be intelligent beings like ourselves, but instead an advanced ecosystem, complex and diverse as anything on earth. It is the ecosystem, then, whose voice we will need to hear, and it is on earth we must begin to listen—to translate what is heard into our ways of knowing.

[**Editor's note**: Archibald Shechner was the first to hear this voice. As an archeologist who had just found a lost scroll of evolutionary knowledge, he was also perhaps the first to decipher the voice. This further translation took the prehistoric form of a guide to creation, which in most aboriginal cultures reflects ecological knowledge. It is, of course, a voice across deep time, and to decipher it, Shechner's unconscious had to place it within a known mythology—in this case, the voice of Wisdom: the Shechinah, the Creator's consort. The crucial element, Shechner understood, was that it is a sexual voice, and that the voice of an ecosystem—its living principle—was also a reproductive one. It is the same we may encounter elsewhere in the universe, scientists would say, since the source of all intelligence is sexual selection.

But listening is not making. What else can humans do but make things, make art, make science, make a baby—even our notion of the Creator as the supreme Maker. Yes, Shechner would have Wisdom say, to the extent that the Creator does not listen, he is deprived of wisdom. In whatever roles we make or are made for ourselves, self-expression is our lot, not listening. Just listening scares us—what are we to *do*? Betti Peleg and Julie Peleg helped Shechner make the Seven Days and shape it into a Guide, and Everett Nosei began making it into a novel. First, however, Shechner had to listen, to accept dictation, to listen to another world. He began to show us how we will change when the voices beyond us in the universe are first heard.

When we listen across deep space to our first communicants we will also be listening across deep time. That is Shechner's signal comprehension. And it is here on Earth that the knowledge of how to listen across deep time is first explored, listening to Wisdom in the "Guide to a New World." Wisdom herself acts by asking questions. I have learned from this manuscript that the world had changed in our century, turned inside out. Instead of man inside nature, it became nature inside man. We are still in infancy about it. The wild ecosystem is in our head, but the way to know it is not to go in there anymore, and more wisely, to go out into the field. But where are the writers? Most are still hovering in the human hives of cities and in the boxes of their rooms. And there was no greater hoverer than Nosei in his tiny office—until Shechner drew him out, to become a new kind of novelist, a collaborative one.

Before, we had metaphors. It was the job of an editor like myself to make sure the metaphors worked to their fullest. "Seven days, and each a memory of a world..."

But here my job ends, except to interpret how Wisdom has multiplied the years exponentially in which man will evolve. A year to the tenth power. So at the end of each year nobody we know now and no culture that we know now will be left, and all trace of our individual lives will be lost. We can put aside the metaphor of days. One year to the tenth power ago, Homo sapiens had not even evolved—we would be back in the time of the hominids, our two-legged ancestors. In other words, our memories are meaningless in such a year. With one exception. That is, while our human memory is associated with human history, our species memory is older. It goes back to when we evolved. Our species memory can comprehend an exponential year. It's our species memory that is repressed most deeply in us: the desire to evolve is there.

In the next exponential year, Homo sapiens may have become extinct, and by the time a child lives out a lifetime in exponential years—say, to age eighty—many new species will have evolved and he or she will be close to the time when our Sun enters old age. Meanwhile, we want to know about *ourselves*, what *we* will be like—if not individually, then as a species. We, in our sexual bodies, listening—and as I already stated more directly, letting the fucking body evolve.]

[SATURDAY] AFTER THE HUMAN DRAMA

Wisdom asks: When will our memory become reality again? When we evolve. Today, when we return in our present form to homes left behind, the size of the rooms and even the furniture seems to have slightly shrunk. In memory the world is larger; in reality, in nature, it is smaller. It is the same with public artifacts of the past: In museums, in preserved historical sites, the writing desks of great authors seem miniature, and the bedframes of famous people almost doll-like. Our memory begins inflating reality the moment it has passed; an article or event of significance from last evening has already grown slightly in proportion to the present. Nature's present moment, however, is always somewhat smaller than we see it. Death—ever-approaching—diminishes things.

The present is the dominion of the Creator, but the realm of time and memory is ruled by Wisdom—where everything grows as time passes and is possessed by the intimacy of recollection. To remember is to grow closer. It is the same in defiance of death: A loving, possessive attention to the real world of time, to nature, appears to prolong life. When we look back in time to an original folio of Shakespeare, it seems an insignificant thing, yet the written drama itself—a form of embracing time, of holding it back in memory—is nearly immortal. By far the greatest drama we can experience, natural evolution, is only at the beginning of opening its theater to human memory.

[**Editor's note**: As token of this stage, the finding and losing of the *Scroll of the History of Adam* is prologue. Imagine how we return to our cultural reality after hearing the voice of an ecosystem, since the past is in front of us now, not behind. The realm we will enter in present reality—it is already the past, one in which we can hear the voice of another planet that has become ours. It may be Earth or another. There is no difference if we are listening. Instead of going to it, the ecosystem may come to us.

When Wisdom meets her Creator they create a new world, mirrored for us as a new species. I did not understand this at first, and so I edited out a fragment where Shechner seems to cross beyond death and toward evolving. This will sink the whole book, I thought. People will say it's supernatural, mixing fact and fiction, like Moses writing after he had died in the Torah. Now I see the emphasis is on *seems*. Shechner is describing a process of losing himself, of listening—before it happened.

"So I found myself in the ecosystem, disappeared. My body the same but somehow different too. It was already many days since my "memorial," my mock-funeral. I had no desire to go back, no taste to see anyone I had known, and instead was beginning to feel desire to explore where I was."

Reader, Nosei was careful not to inflate the past, using the transcribed voices of the others, and I want to rededicate myself to his principles in these footnotes. We should not forget, however, that he was shaping a novel, and that he remained true to the story of his characters, even if he did not understand all that they were saying.]

Chapter 13

Chapter 13

Note To The Reader

After recreating the circumstances of the discovery and then the loss of the Scroll—the disappearance of Archibald Shechner and the fates of Julie and Betti Peleg as well—Nosei weighs his method. Why did he novelize the story and weave the *Guide to a New World* into it? "Fiction and nonfiction need each other," I noted at the beginning. To evolve, one needs an understanding of more than facts—letting go needs a faith in something more. Nosei might call it time; Shechner, a voice. Either has to be imagined as preceding us, preceding our species' logic. The first Homo sapiens heard their ecosystem as a voice and were vulnerable to it. The trees were parental, as the Scroll illustrates. Nosei is unsettled by this, but less so than the others. He cannot let go of us—though perhaps in the end we are the fiction.

Ari Buber, Editor

Novel and Guide

A novel offers a slice of life, an immersion in memory and the imagination. Almost always it is life in the past, sometimes in the almost-present. *The Eden Revelation* has to turn the past inside out and show a future we have yet to imagine. Science fiction may describe a slice of future life but *Eden* must re-create the feeling of being there.

We can imagine a novel coming-to-be, and we can at the same time imagine pieces of the real world dying. I've had this experience, a new possibility in our time, just like virtual reality. It resembles a sudden meeting with an endangered species on its way to extinction. It's like having an idea flash into your head—then seeing it stand before you for an instant. You want to grab it and yet you don't; you want it to remain wild. The pathos lives on, vivid beyond any human encounter: this is a cross-species rendezvous, a meeting our ancestors knew when they left the trees, when they encountered their first mammoth or zebra; or when rafting, seal and dolphin; or domesticating the horse, the goat; or planting seeds, watching a vine crawling with ripened grapes.

The same new future and dying past can be savored in the process of reading a work of fiction as it distills a new reality: What are we reading, a page or a landscape? Species died out before but no one knew it; readers have been lost in real-life drama before but didn't sense how reality was changing around them the very moment as they read.

In a protected remnant of old forest in Texas, when I visited there before hearing of the Scroll, I entered the home of the last red-cockaded woodpeckers. They are dying out because they depend on untouched stands of mature, dying pines in which to bore and suck up the equally rare beetles who have entered there first, lured by the softening rot beneath the bark. I heard distant knocking, and on coming closer found the movement of red above, flickering among the dark greens and browns. I stood there until I could stand no more—to where would the bird go?—then left him there, precious jewel at work.

I feel the same sweet agony when I talk to young Germans who are meeting their first Jew (half-Japanese) unbeknownst. Finally, when the ignorance they deplore causes me to reveal my identity, who am I? To them, the bird—if they have an inquiring sensibility; to myself, the observer of a cross-species encounter.

[Nosei '94]

1995

I watched the old Chinese woman unwrap the leaves that held her steamed rice. The tender, careful movement of her fingers. Ancient—almost like artifacts. I wanted to look hard at them. I felt there were secrets of another time, another knowledge that I could learn if I just looked hard enough.

She sipped the tea. It was steeped and steaming. She looked as if she were drinking a potion, both hands cradling the magical cup. I wanted it. I wanted everything she was having. No looking at the menu.

When the waiter came, I pointed to the menu then to her. Nothing more was necessary. He knew. All I had to do was wait. Soon I would be eating what she was eating. A wise one had come to me once again. But unlike the other wise ones, she said nothing. She had nothing that must be told to me. Nothing that I had to record, write down, grind into human archives. She was just there. I was just there. I could tell she knew what was good. But she was not telling it to me. It was of no concern to her. Yet I felt she would not begrudge me.

I was calm. I wondered if I actually could stay. Could I stay here, with the steamed rice and tea, the old woman with fingers that knew what to do. I opened my backpack. I had brought the Times with me. It occurred to me that the newstand owner was like the old woman. He was there, and I could come and buy or not come. He would not tell me to buy but he would not mind if I did. Or, if sometimes I did not. I spread the paper out to my right. It looked like there was a lot in it. I could stay here a long time.

My rice and tea came. I opened up the leaves as I'd seen the old woman do. There was meat mixed in, probably pork. I remembered my own people, then. I had not been required to observe the Kosher laws but mother had taught me to remember. I remembered and I ate. It tasted just like I knew it would. And the tea seemed to carry a secret I couldn't name. I looked around the restaurant. The cheap, formica table tops, the vinyl chairs, the peeling walls. I saw it all and liked it. It was worn like the old woman. Everything important seemed to be coming out of the kitchen and going onto the tables and into her hands. But her hands were pushing up from the table. She was getting up to go. And then she was gone. I had not moved to stop her, to tell her that I must stay with her, that I would be okay if we could stay here.

I looked around at the Asian faces as they ate. Why was the difference, even the indifference so soothing? The calm returned. I thought, "She is still here. They feel like a whole thing." I knew I was doing to them what had often been done to my own people, but I wanted to feel it anyway. I wanted to feel that they knew what to eat, where to go, even when to go. Such precious knowledge. I could have it too as long as I could stay.

I turned back to the Science section of the Times. I looked for anything that signaled new discoveries about ecosystems, especially their origins and restoration. I had a special file for these clippings, just as I had files on everything pertaining to the transcription. Why? Perhaps a clue to the disappeared ones—mother and Archie still seemed recoverable to me. I kept it all in a large, old-fashioned steamer trunk that had belonged to my father. I never saw him use it. Or mother. It is the one personal object I took with me from Israel, and the one I bequeathed to Nosei.

It occurred to me that looking at that old woman was like looking at the bald eagle one night several years ago. I had gone with Svitz to a performance of The Continuum at the New York Botanical Garden. The sponsors had brought in some wild and endangered animals, situated among foliage in the arms of their handlers. Svitz couldn't get me away from where the eagle was.

"Julie! Have you formed some cathexis to that creature already? They're going to start the second half in a moment. Come, my dear."

"Svitz, you go ahead. I'll be there."

"No, you won't. I'm not going to leave only to come back

afterwards and find you rooted here." Svitz was holding my upper arm, sort of in the manner of the man with the bushy weasel.

"Doesn't it just throw you? The thing looks at you as an equal, and almost like you're not here. It seems completely from somewhere else. When you look at it, you see that it is *made* for somewhere else. And it looks wise. I think it knows more than even you, Svitz."

"Oh my. I knew this would happen when you went back to fooling with that trunk. Who are you preparing it for? I thought you were going to that doctor to get your independence from all that. Don't you know that your panic attacks were provoked by the transcription you were doing for Betti and Shechner!" He was tugging now, but tentatively, as if I might bite.

"No doubt, no doubt. But that doesn't remove the importance of what we were doing. You know, you've hardly looked at the eagle. Why is that, Svitz? Can't stand that you've met something more relevant than you are?"

"Well at least you see what it's all about. We all crave relevance, Julie." He let go of my arm, preparing to lecture. "We all strive to leave an inheritance. That's what you're doing with the trunk—that's what you're doing here in front of this eagle. By god, you're reading this eagle like no one before you. That is the Julie inheritance."

I remember I looked at him with a stunned gaze. How could he look at that eagle and only see himself? Or me as a version of himself. "It's not about me," I tried to tell him. "It's the eagle. Don't you know what you're looking at? Another species! And it can still hear the voice."

"What are you talking about?" he choked out with impatience.

"The ecosystem. The eagle is still wild, Svitz. The ecosystem is still real for it. When you look in the eagle's eyes, you don't see yourself. You see the ecosystem that it evolved from and used to live in. The eagle really can't see or hear us. Not like a domesticated cat, even."

I don't know what was said after that. I think I grabbed his arm this time and let myself be led away. Led back to The Continuum. But that was okay. Those musicians knew they were mimicking wildness in the form of musical art. Just as I know I'm mimicking Nosei here, his attempt at a novel. I'm hardly a novelist, though. I'm one of the disappearing ones—a fact that holds more gravity than fiction. But this is what will remain, words and commentary, fiction set in the diamond-hard frame of nonfiction—my inheritance, as Svitz insisted, yet something more. The story of how we were begotten.

In a funny way, I can speak now because of panic attacks. I can even write a happy ending. I've come a long way since the Chinese restaurant. I don't have real panic anymore. There are no happy endings, so why not imagine them? We all die, don't we? I've saved myself from disappearing into fear, but only to disappear into desire—an ancient desire. So ancient it has been almost unknown to humans until now. Well, this is no time to be circumspect—it's a powerful craving, alright, a great hunger, an irresistable desire to hear the ecosystem again. Until now, the panic has always been stronger, and the wish to find safe places.

"Couldn't I just lie down on the couch once more before I go today?" This was only last week. Instead of exiting through the door of my doctor's office, I sank into a stuffed chair next to the table holding supplies of tissue and water.

He spoke. I fantasized that he would yell at me for not leaving. But when he opened his mouth, a quiet tone. "You seem like you need something extra in order to go today," he said.

"Yes. Maybe all I need is some water. Can I have a bottle of water to take?"

"Sure. But you already have a bottle, you know. You always bring one with you. Is it that you require a bigger supply of water where you're going?"

"I don't know. I just want to feel safe."

"The safe place is in you, not in the water bottle."

"This is a safe place," I pleaded. "There'll never be another place like this one."

What are safe places? For a bald eagle, it's the ecosystem. For humans it has become almost anything. In panic, I have adopted all kinds of things to make me feel safe: my doctor's voice, a water bottle, a cell phone. Everything that is connecting. Underneath it, though, an unearthed desire makes me want to get away from human places, safe places. It feels like a wish that can actually be satisfied without hurting anyone. Who else could I hurt? No family, certainly, and it's not like wishes to kill.

And that's where I found it, right beneath the wish to do harm—a wish that's always there in moments of anger. Or panic. Take away the panic, strip away the helpless rage, pull off the covering terror and the layer of fear—and there is this other wish I could never have known if it wasn't for Archie's revealing it and then my discovering it again, to show to myself and to my doctor.

[Julie]

Our Eaters

I have put off completing this book for too long. It gnawed at me that my celebrity should come merely from having been in the proximity of a great event over a decade ago. What am I?—a reporter, that's it. Yes, I assembled a story that had broken into fragments. It's a novel in voices: when you come down to it, any one of these characters might have master-minded it. Each has her reasons. I suppose you can question how Betti Peleg or her daughter, insouciant Julie, could invent me as a character (or Moses write about his own burial) after the fact. Still, it surprises me almost as much to see how influenced I've been by Archibald Shechner, how close to him I find myself sounding at times.

"Our awareness has extended too far beyond our senses," is how Shechner put it. "We're aware of viruses and cells we can't see, messages from invisible stars we can only hear. I can already intuit how we evolved. It wasn't an accident from what we were before; no, we let go."

This need to evolve is so hidden that it explains our human mystery: why we die alone, each an individual death. The other world is mirrored by micro-culturing, as we reduce down to hidden elements—genetics, DNA—down smaller than microbes. We require the tiniest wormhole to Wisdom, Shechner found.

Strange, then, to realize that time is Wisdom's unfolding: no matter how far we've come, the dream of returning to Eden remains.

Evolved into Homo sapiens, we found ways to outwit our eaters. Now our bodies are eaten by the elements (so it first seemed), rotting away—which is why burial became the first human fixation. It makes sense Shechner hears a voice from the ground.

I never met him, only heard his voice, yet there's no one else alive who knows what happened. Archie evolved. He evolved from a man into a child, a child hearing Wisdom like a mother's voice. Only Julie and her mother knew what was happening and only they could face it. Then, during that brief fall night, that fall that lasts only a few days in the Middle East and in that year only one—in one night Julie initiated me into this intimacy.

For ten years I ran but I felt it in my belly, a lump of recognition, growing heavier with time. "Come to bed with me," she implored, as we walked Jerusalem's streets at sunset, through the ancient Bukharan quarter, with its red and blue caftans hurrying past us, its maroon and purple babushkas drying on the lines, and into the Yemenite quarter, amber-skinned faces lit by coal-black eyes. "Let's go back to Tel Aviv."

[Nosei, '94]

Pregnant in Reverse

It was an hour's drive in the gathering dark of the stretch taxi, all downhill from Jerusalem to the Mediterranean. Huddled in the back corner of the Mercedes with Julie, I learned what I would never be able to turn from: Shechner had evolved into a child, and was perfectly lucid and rational when he was treated that way by Julie and Betti Peleg. Betti made the recordings and Julie transcribed them during the months Shechner described the voice he was hearing.

And then we were in Julie's bed, entering the small apartment without turning on a light, dropping our clothes from us on the cold stone tiles as we inched through the dark apartment toward the bedroom. Julie pulled me into her as easily as if we'd been in passionate foreplay for an hour, and we began to move as one, a single pendulum attached to an ancient, silent clock, the waves falling onto the beach audible through the metal, shuttered balcony.

Suddenly she froze, writhed back and forth, as if someone was trying to pull her away. I was shocked, tried to pull out, yet she held on desperately. "What's wrong?" I cried. "I can't, I can't," she gasped, "I'm only a child, and I'm pregnant." Her voice had risen an octave, and meanwhile, even as my organ softened in fright within her I could not pull out, her vaginal canal shrinking, tightening its grip.

I was bathed in a cold sweat now, terrified, my member seized in a painful clasp. I could only ride with her as she squirmed and flailed in the bed. Then she stopped and though my penis was limp from the encounter I still had to reach down and forcibly extract it from her grasp. "What happened?" I asked. Julie was immobile but trembling slightly and quietly weeping. Then she rolled over, reached for the bedside light, and as we lay beneath the bedsheet she began to tell me about the physical sensations that Shechner had described.

And so I learned that the genes we would come to manipulate, as we became intimate with the human genome, would change the nature of our growth. Reaching the peak of growth to adulthood, the aging process would reverse; we would grow younger instead of older. Though strange-sounding to us, the crucial aspect here is a different motion of time, similar to the effects described in the distant universe. It began to sound as familiar as Einstein's relativity: the closer we came to the borders of the human limit, the more time slowed...

That was enough for me. But I know Julie is sane. We've grown close in the past few days, comparing our life histories like brother and sister returned from a long separation. No, she is not mad, and certainly not Shechner, but I can't handle this heightened reality: she described growing younger as a pregnancy in reverse. Yet she's perfectly lucid about all that's happening, and she describes Shechner's disappearance and her own condition as calmly as a scientist. She feels a sexual longing for being outside also, she said, and for wild places she has never seen.

[Nosei, '84]

There, it's told. I don't mind laughter: the science will come clear in a few decades, no more. But the human cost is that this work of restoration took over my life. I am some kind of father to *The Eden Revelation*. An idea, a book—not a being—and as such it can mislead all those who believe we are meant to evolve in our minds. No. This birth says to our minds: let go; let go like a parent must, when its child matures. Archibald Shechner is bound to return in some form, our species' child. It was in the Hula valley he disappeared, birthplace of modern Israel, an area drained for farmland early in the century and now being restored to its original wild, wetlands condition—the place Betti Peleg was driving to.

And what will life look like then? "I am learning not to be afraid," Shechner said. "We have nothing to lose, everything will be remembered and even more precious than it has been. Each living thing will be a book, and as we read them, the new species will create the library of the future and tend it."

I don't know exactly what he meant but if I can piece together the story and how I came to believe it, and restore the *Guide to a New World*, then this imagined child of Julie Peleg's and mine—brainchild, as it were—will be able to grow in the world and speak for itself.

[Nosei, '94]

Reading

Ok, as a philologist I was used to breaking language down to its smallest component, down to the inflection of a letter—breaking down a system. The body is also a system, Shechner told Betti Peleg. "Why else would I have been there, by the light of that light-stealing moon, that fraudulant roll of parchment?" he would say, desperately sarcastic.

All animals read. The first great readers were the plants, who read the four ancient elements, transforming light into energy, water into matter. Animals evolved who read the ecosystem for food, shelter, fuel. Who provided the reading matter? Plants produced fruits, nectar, and other rewards for animals—the fuel of food—in exchange for the sexual services of distributing pollen and seed. Nest and hut material come from trees, as does the fuel for fire. Oil, from ancient forests—we've learned to read that far back.

I did not want to read. A philologist, I broke words apart. I didn't admit to myself I was reading when I "read into each word" its history and origin. I thought I could refuse to read. I am in rebellion so deep I need the disguise of being an inconspicuous assistant, for privacy, a seclusion apart from the shallow revolts of most individuals. I probed to the essence of words, to the origins of the human charade, it seemed to me.

[Nosei, '84]

1995

I have recently returned from that forest Nosei speaks of earlier in this chapter where he found the red-cockaded woodpeckers. I had not been back to Texas since the first panic attack in the Big Thicket Preserve. Can't be sure I was in the exact place that Nosei writes about. I ended up in a state forest area near a township called The Woodlands and the gates were locked when I finally found it. I went up the road to the office and found an employee who let me in. He told me all about the woodpeckers. Nosei had seen one, but I never did that day.

As the man talked, I kept looking around, in through the trees. I focused on a figure that appeared in the distance, coming down a dirt trail. The man began a studied gaze in that direction too, but kept talking. Suddenly, he was asking me something. "Miss? You look like you expect to know that fella coming there. I thought you said you were from out of state."

"I am. But no, I was just thinking of a friend of mine who talked about a place like this."

"Oh really? What was his name?"

I looked at the man beside me more closely. Nothing recognizable there. "Nosei, I mean Everett Nosei. But it was quite a while ago and I don't really know if this is the same place."

"No, the name doesn't ring a bell." The talking stopped as the figure approached. He looked nothing like Nosei but I knew him. He nodded and walked past us. I said nothing.

"He's a scientist," the man explained. "He comes out here

a lot, not sure why—I guess that new research—ecological is what they call it. Hey, you look like you've seen a ghost."

"No, I just thought he looked familiar. But it's nothing."

The gate man left me there, in the middle of the pine trees. I took out a sandwich to eat from my backpack. I had known the figure who walked past us. It was Westerman—the biologist who had taken me out to the Big Thicket many years ago. I didn't say anything because I had made such a mess of the visit then, and his kindness.

"Would you like something to drink with that?"

I turned around and saw him. He smiled. "You thought I didn't recognize you? But I wouldn't forget you, Miss Peleg. Is that still your name?"

"Yes. I'm sorry I didn't say anything a while ago. I was too embarrassed. After all, I made quite a spectacle of myself the last time I saw you."

"Yeah. You're the only casualty I ever had—what happened? You just disappeared. I thought you were going to come by my office on campus the next week. Man, it seems like yesterday."

"The truth is I had a panic attack out there with you and your students. It was the first of many. And it's taken me almost ten years to get over them."

"What brings you back here?"

"Same thing that brought me to Texas in the first place—Archibald Shechner and the Scroll. Something is going to be published about it all."

"Did you discover what it was all about?"

"Yes. Fucking."

"I see. You've discovered where babies come from."

"That's the least of it," I said. We both laughed. Like old colleagues. We cranked our necks back to look at the tops of the trees.

"Right," he said. "You only have to spend a few hours out here to be reminded of that fact. I'm a well-respected scientist of the junior ranks—supposed to know a lot, and I do. But it's nothing next to what these woodpeckers know. They're closer to their history than I'll ever be to my own as a Homo sapiens. I feel good when I come out here, but I feel mournful too."

"For them? I asked.

"No, for myself. They're at home—innocent of fate. I'm not. But it's deeper than that. I know I'm stuck where I am. I can imagine an ecosystem but I can never feel it, really know it as they do. I'm stuck because I'm part of a species that's stopped evolving. So I content myself with the old substitutes."

He was looking at me steadily. His eyes were viscous, like the water they say awaits on other planets. And his mouth looked like an unknown fruit, fissuring. I reached for it like a fruit.

"He was my Eve. I ate and he ate. We were like the woodpeckers. He made a bower for me. He sunk deep, and I with him. It all happened in a flash."

"What?" my doctor asked.

"All that I have ever imagined happening between you and me. It happened with Westerman. I thought of nothing but eating. I was completely there."

"You took your eyes away from watching to being." He had understood I was revealing a chance sexual encounter. "What do you think made it safe?" he asked.

"I don't know, but I keep thinking, 'He gave it to me.' It almost felt like he was feeding me—and me, him. It reminds me now of when you looked back—to see if I was okay. I've spoken about it before."

"When they evacuated the building?"

"Yes. Some alarm went off and we all had to leave. You walked ahead, but I could see you looking back. At me. Remember?"

"Yes. You didn't have to watch because I was watching—I had you in mind. In sight." The familiar voice wafted over me, from the chair placed behind me.

"Right. I didn't feel any anxiety. I felt like I had my hand inside you. I mean, you were real to me. Flesh. Your interior was real. That's the only way I can explain it."

"I became real when I could hold the realness in you. Your words make me think of cartography. It's almost like in that moment, you found a map of me—to me. As you said, your hand was inside me—the hand of a cartographer, feeling along the lines and surfaces. Of flesh, as you put it. I had skin and flesh when I looked back for you. The realness of me must have felt as if I were feeding you. Giving you something."

"But why would that be? I was fed as a child. Mother fed me. She looked after me. Always."

"Yes. And you looked after her. She was strong, but she had a vulnerability that she never accepted. And you felt it. Took it in, like it was yours. You took on the job of protecting her from it—protecting her from sadness, from a hungry emptiness inside."

I stretched my legs out further on the couch as I put an arm under my head. "I can see that but this between you and me, between Westerman and me—it feels like a transaction never before experienced. I keep craving the transaction." I paused. "I'm thinking now of when I no longer come here. What will you do when I go?"

He said nothing at first. Suddenly the facts of the room shifted from voices to bodies, as I focused on the sounds our movements were making—squeaks from his chair, my hand brushing against the wall, water bottles opening.

"It's hard to imagine," he answered. "It feels like a great emptiness. I know I am reluctant to let you go."

"Why is it so important for me to know your insides? I can imagine different things being important for others. Why this, for me?"

"I think it's part of that transaction you spoke of. You and I have elaborated a new transaction—as well as old ones. You feel fed by it. It's a food you haven't found before—a food to be found in this system between us, and sometimes in others."

Food. The food from Westerman, from my doctor. I miss them already, though he's still here. My sweetmeats. Tasted and untasted. Bittersweet. "Constant craving has always been," sings k.d. lang. A constant craving that has made me

alive—keeps me alive. Nosei reads, but I crave. I suckle at the breast and the testicles—at the interior, the milkmeat of the loved object. Archie must have sensed this. He knew that I would suckle at the transcription of his mind. And I have. I have returned for a final bite.

[Julie]

Hole

The trouble with scientists is they never meet ancestors and angels. Believers of all kinds know the nonhuman world by these spirits (as our hominid ancestors knew them in the flesh: a mega-world of plants and animals overarching us).

I gained and lost a whole family in the space of a month, like a creature whose lifespan encompasses one month, like a moth. After ten years, to find it still alive, hidden within, held by the light of an imagined voice! Hearing a voice from the afterlife like Archibald Shechner's—yet calmed by a familiarity, by Shechner's having gone before. It is my own buried voice, deprived of senses, for whom I now accept a role as interpreter. I found it recorded in transcripts: a voice unearthed for a few months by the reflected light of the Scroll.

Shechner's buried voice came from a hole in the ground. It seduced him, and he saw no hole but a passageway—to the past, to what I see now is the womb, the most frightful past we turn from, the hole through which we passed. The womb is the dread place where we were not yet ourselves; to go back—to unblock our ears from pure voice—is to lose ourselves again. All that we knew there and kept was our mother's voice. Yet in the womb we knew nothing of mothers, only a voice that might have been our own, a higher articulation, drawing us toward knowledge of—

"Son, you are both, half-Jewish, half-Japanese," my mother answered. "Since your father's family was Zen Buddhist, you can say, when they ask about beliefs: 'I believe in a half God.' If they question you further, you can quote your father: 'He is half known, half unknown. For this reason, He can be known only as unknown. A voice without a body.'"

"But I want to know what is mine," I insisted. "What do *you* believe is God?"

"'I am that I am' is what your Jewish grandfather said, when I asked him who was God. He was smiling. I decided it was a language of trick questions, and that's why, when I met your father, I loved his stern expression. Because I found that he was smiling on the inside. He only half-believed, but it was always the best half. And he always introduced me as 'my better half.' Son, I don't want to confuse you. Best is to answer: 'I don't know. I am who I am.'"

Of course I was confused, but I knew that my mother was always trying to teach me something. My response was to become a student of words, a rememberer of them. I can appreciate my mother's gentle humor now, even if it was over my head. She probably knew that I would eventually hear it, with my audiographic memory.

But for ten years after leaving Israel and Julie, I did not listen; I would not let go of the present. Let go, it counseled, let go and evolve. It was the transcribed, lipless voice, Shechner's voice from the hole, the one minding the ecosystem and heard by all living things—heard in the light and rain and roots of a plant, calling even the plant to be involved with all life, to evolve. A voice weaving and mending. Evolved in the hearing! It was like I could hear something even my grandfathers could not. I refused to listen; I refused to be confused.

Like a child in reverie, I had longed to make my own world, to identify with what was mine. *Mine* meant I was unique. *My* block, *my* baseball team, and *my secret* loves. I dressed myself in these delicate armors; each peculiar attachment felt like a magical defense. I was becoming stronger, I was a new phenomenon in this world, I was defended—against what? Against the past, all the spirits of the past who thought *they* were the chosen. I was a new thing in the world, half-Japanese, half-Jewish. For this, the past would be unforgiving and I would have to be vigilant. I will live just for the present, I said to myself. We will put all traces of history away in a museum. *Pitom* (presto! Julie would say), the present becomes the past as well.

In time, I became curator of this past. I escaped from the Eden of the present into the origins of history—a secret escape, in trick armor. I didn't realize how close I actually was to the future in that archaic past—until Julie confided the depth of Shechner's discovery. I didn't deserve such a gift (and such a risk) I thought, it wasn't meant for me; Julie wasn't meant for me. I slid back into anonymity, to my study of words, shielded from the threat of being branded a hoax, protected by the weak-eyed rhinoceros of my university. Although my name rhymed with "nosey" I was not. "Nosey doesn't know." In short, I had retreated to what the world believed.

[Nosei, '94]

The Alphabet

Of what are you afraid, Nosey? *What I can't see (as of microbes, hidden in each letter of the alphabet); and of dirt, earth (dust to dust, and no more Scrolls).* Of humans you have no fear? *No, not a Svitz, not a Shechner. Not any concern of human nature. It is the hidden I dread, what made me. Words I can now hear by letting go—no language for them, no hands to write them down. What landscape will I find to read, instead?*

[Nosei, '84]

Adam Speaks

I seem to be more alive in a memory. When I look around, I see time has changed the world around me: it is cooler after the storm, water drips from everything and the trees make a heavier sound in the wind, soaked in water. Everything has a before and after, a comparison, a reflection in a mirror. But in the before of Eden I can be lost: no time passes. It is morning, it is evening and no time passes. Each day is another world; we passed from world to world, always outward, journeying, never caught in one and its reproducing reflections. Nothing was lost because each world was paradise; nothing was past. Only the mothering tree of knowledge was always there, and when we awoke outside the Garden, in place of all Eden we had lost was a quickly filling memory, quickly so intricate the past was already beyond fathom. What we could do and did was build bridges over it, from one memory to another in a sea of memories, and tunnels, from one feeling to another.

Bridges and tunnels, buildings, and soon we had many buildings. And I looked around and saw that all things were building: a tree shaped its leaves, flowers, roots, fruit, an ant its mound, and all buildings were silent, lifeless except for the life that used them. In Eden, a flower and a bird's nest were alive themselves, they spoke, they were offerings, expressions of food and beauty, and all fed from them. But a lifeless building is like a memory: it needs to be inhabited, to be used. And when I walk outside into the present, the past is written everywhere by time, something is always older or newer than another, in some state of decay. To age is time's code, and it reads us back to the beginning with our own hunger to return there, original paradise.

A sudden dark hand across the meadow and I feel dropping water. Did it rain in Eden? There is the hunger for memory again, for the life in it, the wish to think, to build a road back. Now I am drenched in water and can do nothing with it, not drink in like the plants. The animals hide and I must too, there beneath a huge grove of trees. Now I see it is but one tree with many branches sending down trunks of their own, a walking tree [banyan]. Judging by the limbs it is very old. How old?—the questions, the distractions never cease, and all are looking for a thread, a journey home.

Yet the mystery of the Garden, the fear, it all goes as

the sun returns. Seeing the beauty in works: to cover over the damage as a cool dwelling out of the sun. Now fear is death; then, it was of being lost: lost to oneself, to the way back, to origins—that fear focussed my bite! One day out of Eden I rediscovered beauty. It was in the covering up, the disguise, the attempt to suggest the original: that nothing had happened, that nothing bad could happen. I felt as alive remembering Eden as I had in Eden.

[The Scroll of the History of Adam]

Eve Speaks

When I see a tree now that I remembered once talked to me in Eden I am filled with a joy that hurts, a sharp joy I didn't know before, a joy that is too quick, too piercing. No joy in Eden was so sharp and sudden. Yesterday, it was a fruit tree laden with red lanterns of succulent fruit. I remembered something it had said in the Garden: "a red running of hope sleeps until the blue returns to your eye." I knew exactly what that meant; now, it is a puzzle for thinking. The plants taught us to think and speak in images. When I open my eye in the morning the blue is there again and my blood stirs and hope is there. That is how I remember hearing it. It came back to me after difficult but hopeful thinking. The pure memory and finding this tree still with us fills me with joy but then it is cut with a sharp pain: I am cut off from the tree now, it cannot speak to me. Yet I remember our exchange exactly as it was and the feeling of it rushes back and it is sweet as long as I hold on to it. We are back in Eden, the tree and I, and then a sudden, sharp return as I reach for its silent fruit and bite. Yes, it is the same tree, the same sweetness.

[The Scroll of the History of Adam]

Chapter 14

Chapter 14

Julie's Door

Why is it all I feel like doing is curling up on the ground now and going to sleep outside? Where is all this grief coming from? As if I let go of the novel. Before it's even ready, I want to let go. Give up responsibility for its being born. What can I do about its being born? Except lie here in the dirt. I can't do it myself. It's as if there's a huge boulder lying on my stomach. Someone else has to take it off. To whom could I turn for help? How could it be this way? I thought finishing the novel would roll away all the confusion. Finishing is not enough: I have to do something.

As I lay on the ground, I saw it was the ground itself that was comforting: the myth of Adam created from dust is exactly right! It began to rain. I welcomed it, not thinking of shelter. I will be the ground itself. It was here the Scroll was found. Here's where Archie heard the voice of Wisdom.

But I must be found. It's as if I dropped out and tuned in to all these tongues of leaves. Stay where you are, they are saying. The old ways are dying. Stay in the open, look up, ear to the ground. Here the novel of it all becomes a weight too much to bear. Roll it away.

What's left now but the proverbial navel. To contemplate it. Well, in fact that's really it. What had been a sign of a dead end, a waste of spirit, a retreat into the emptiness of one's own navel—is now the start of everything! Because it is real, after all, the navel, and has only been made empty by human design. It is neither empty nor human. Instead, it is our deepest connection to the nonhuman world, from which we come and to where we are going. The navel: empty of all feeling, empty of meaning. What is lost beneath this ultimate repression?

Dirt. Here it is: The earth beneath the stone of repression creates new life. I cannot hear what Archie heard, I can't hear the language, but I see the words forming like something living, like the soil evolving in time. From time—the human frame—to the living matter itself. This is what lies beneath the words I have peeled apart all these years. The soil, the dust is alive.

There are others here. I cannot see them or hear them: they are also beyond ordinary words and images. And then there are those I *can* see and who draw near the navel as to a frontier. They can say nothing about it yet. Except that a place for it must be saved. They are making a place for the body, just as the ecosystem made a place for the body. Restoring origins. I hardly knew that was my purpose as a philologist because I had not digested the grief of losing the body.

To be alert to everything and not know who we are—that will be the new work. That is the restoration. Some are reading the structure of the leaf; some are reading the air and soil from which the leaf's structure comes. Some are binding between invisible covers the idea of reading. None of them can talk yet, except to record their data, and to ask a question for which no answer is expected. How can a tree feel change and also change itself? Alert to everything.

These pages are the leaves: I have collected this data. My questions are for Archie and Betti, Julie. From them I need no answer. I know now the alertness they must experience. It is as if I want only the horse that is missing in the classic song that Dylan sings: How else would he get to Miss Mousie's door? And how will I get to Julie's door?

"He rode right up to mouse's hall,
where he most tenderly did call:
'Oh, Mistress Mouse, are you within?'
'Yes, kind frog, I sit to spin.'
'Where will the wedding breakfast be?'
'Way down yonder in a hollow tree.'
The first to come in was a little white moth,
to spread on the table cloth.
Next to come in was a nimble flea,
to dance a jig with a bumble bee...
The frog and the mouse they went to France.
And this is the end of my romance.
Frog's bridle and saddle are laid on the shelf.
If you want anymore, you must sing it yourself."
[Nosei '94]

1995

"When do you leave?"

"I have to leave for the airport in three hours. JFK. It's an El Al flight."

This is how my last session began. Nothing was said for many minutes and then we started like this. And then more quiet. The thing I remember most is the space of that quiet. I was grateful for any words between us. I felt like praying to them, "Keep me, so I shall not want." I begged the words to hold the space of the session in my mind so I wouldn't forget. A sad space, inside the best place I had ever known.

"What are you thinking?" he asked.

"Did I ever tell you that I like when you ask what I'm thinking? I don't especially care for other people asking me, but with you it's different. Why is that?"

"I'm not sure," he answered.

"Well, I think it's because you are really asking about skin-thoughts and I want to be asked about them."

"How do you mean 'skin-thoughts'?"

"Thoughts that feel and thoughts that can't. All my thoughts have come alive in here. I always *feel* when I'm in this room—with you. What will happen now? To me and you. Are you thinking what I'm thinking? That we should have tape-recorded the sessions so we would always have them."

"It's a vivid image," he replied. "Tapes that are imprinted with our voices, all the skin-thoughts that have passed between us. It's moving to hear your wish to keep them. I think the anxiety comes in wondering about my wishes to keep and how I will carry it all inside. How do you imagine that I will do it?"

I laughed and asked him if he had a big trunk laying around somewhere. "The trunk would have to be extra special," I said. I heard him laugh too, very freely.

"No, I don't have one big trunk. And we don't have our

own tapes like your mother and Archie. We have something different. We've made friends. With our minds. And I do mean *we.* I've been able to make friends with my mind all over again through this time with you. Most importantly, we've made a place for your aliveness, all the skin-thoughts inside of you. That has been my privilege—to be part of that work. I will miss the intimacy of that work. Very much."

"You know what's good about today?" I asked.

"No, what?"

"You feel like a real person to me. All along I've been saying that you make *me* feel real, and I kept saying it because something still seemed to be missing. I think I didn't feel that you were real. I almost think that it's the part that's *not-me* that I've been wanting to come alive. I don't know. What I feel today is that I can bear it now if you are real."

"I think you're saying you can stop playing dead now," he responded. "That's why we create anxiety and panic—to take up the dead space. A space where we are afraid of becoming dead and where we think we can make others dead. Sometimes we turn the anxiety into attacks, and then we *are* the dead space, the dead body. It's like we've said to ourselves, 'Better us, than them.' When you say to me that you think you can bear it if I'm real, I think you mean you can take the anger as well as the hunger that facing a real person can evoke inside. You don't have to become dead. You don't have to be the one to save me."

"I think that's true. I feel like I've finally made a place for my body," I said. I paused for a few minutes to hear myself. This is how we had often spoken to each other as we worked through things. "Have you liked it," I asked, "over these years when I've said 'that's true'?"

"Yes. Do you know why you've said it?"

"I do now. I think it was a gift. I would feel like I had received something as you gave my body and my fears language. I wanted to give something back. It was a way of being small again, too, like you were my mother. Am I right?"

He chuckled. "Yes, I think so. It was a way of going back for an earlier realness that you somehow skipped over. I often felt like we had been playing and that it was your way of ending the play on good terms."

"It was insurance against the play turning deadly." I paused and reached for some pages in my purse. (My survival kit, the backpack—I had let go of it.) "I have brought you Nosei's final pages of the novel. When I read them, I feel like I'm being asked to come out and play. Once more. I think he's in Israel."

"The end of the novel, then, is an invitation?" he asked.

"Yes. Do you remember that childhood song—'Froggy Went A'Courtin?'" I heard an affirmative sound. "We saved a frog together one time. We had gone away for a weekend at the beach. That weekend I had time, the largeness of time. I had enjoyed our sex before but that weekend I had my first orgasm—and saved my first frog. Frogs have feelings too, don't they? The little thing had lost its way and was trapped inside the cabin. We saved it together—scooped it up and scooted it out the door to the outside. I felt like I had come out to play with Nosei that weekend. And then it stopped. I started becoming a dead body, even then. I wonder if I can stay alive this time, because you see, I think I know where he is. I think he's somewhere in Israel."

"That goes back to your original question today: How do you know what will happen now—when we're out of each other's sight. Can you play without me?"

"Well, sometimes I think I can because I've got a new voice—the one we've created together. A kind of free-floating alertness, instead of anxiety, comes out of me now. But that's the bright side."

"And if we don't look on the bright side?" he asked.

"Well, that's the part that makes me feel like I could cry forever. I've had the thought many times this week that I've been evolving into this new kind of creature—one that looks very similar to Homo sapiens except for an unusually large tear duct system and a nose that periodically enlarges and becomes red to accomodate a constant need to cry. But the most change of all is inside the brain, which now experiences direct sensation as much or more than all the rest of the body that has been under its control. A pubescence of the mind that changes everything. And at the same time, this creature has never felt more human."

"I think you're saying that life will be very different after you leave here today, because we are parting but also because we have been together," he answered.

"No! You don't get it! I am *physically* changing—in part, because of this. My fingertips will never be more human than they are right now, in this room. I have become a tactile human being in this room. And when I leave this room, I will carry that experience *but* I will no longer be living it. There will be another tactility but it will not be this one. Those are the *facts* of this leaving." I had said this with unusual force and the result was a long silence. This time, I asked what he was thinking.

"I was trying to let what you said move through me. I think I know what you mean. This has been an important week for me, too. I was down near Battery Park, walking by the river when my daughter ran up behind me and grabbed my hand. She had just come out of classes at Stuyvesant and sighted me. I felt startled by my reaction, which was only apparent to myself. Her touch felt familiar but also different. It was as if the real skin was still back in this room, in the sessions between us. I guess you could say that for that moment it seemed that the source of generation for my tactility had shifted, ever so slightly, but enough to change everything. I think you got angry just now because you felt like I'd abandoned you to the loss this represents. And if the skin of this thing we've created between us isn't real to me, then I don't think you can really leave and establish any other tactility."

"It's like what Archie said about evolving," I answered. "He used to say something like this: 'You need a mate. A mate is needed, Julie, to cure the loss incurred in becoming Homo sapiens. That loss is not knowing all of our original desire. The cure is to evolve, or to at least know about the desire for it.' But I think you also need a mate to be in a room like this, to cure the mind. You have been that kind of mate for me. It's almost like we became another species, with another kind of love. A touching without touching that created a language that has never quite existed before. Don't you think so?"

"Yes, Julie. It's my turn to say 'I think that's true.'"

Those are the last words I can convey to you. The rest of what happened before we parted that day—I cannot tell you. It is private. It was nothing dramatic, nothing you could imagine. Before Freud came along, I think you could say that our civilization felt it had mapped all human relationships. But he showed us we had only just begun to know the possibilities. He invented a new one. It was like he had discovered a new genus, comprised of many species. Some individuals like my doctor are still discovering new varieties of the love revealed by Freud. If you want to know more, you must find one of those people. And I would advise you to hurry. I barely found one of my own in time.

Archie once said: "You must become fully human in order to leave off being human." It was one of many enigmatic things he said to me. But I was not ready to think them, then. I could only feel them leading me somewhere. And I couldn't always follow. I hadn't become fully human.

That's what I've been doing the last ten years with my doctor. Only in reaching the end of that time with him was I able to embrace the nonhuman. To leave off and follow. Who and what? I did not know.

I started with the threads I had left hanging. I took the El Al flight that night to meet with Aviya Nachman in Israel and to try and uncover any trace of my mother's last week—before she disappeared.

When I landed at Ben Gurion in Tel Aviv it was as if I expected to find a new scroll as a confirmation that I had left so many words behind. A new scroll is always a leaving behind: the writing down of it. It's the writing that confirms it is left there. And since this book is almost complete, just so, it becomes possible for me to evolve. Not that I will or can, of course. Just that it is possible. That is enough to make it likely that Archie and Betti are still alive, and that Nosei waits for me.

[Julie]

A New Eve

I would place it at the end and start to unroll it along the length of his erect penis. "How far does the shaft go in?" I would ask. "I feel like it's yours now, whatever you like" he would say. I would examine his face for meaning. There was more expression there than in any teacher. How could he know so much? In those days of our beginning, all of his knowledge was about me—and directed at me. I have long stopped needing such intimacy. Your father, Julie, came into my life wearing that kind of knowledge on his sleeve. I could only bear it for a while.

I withdrew into the selfhood that could only be alone if really alone. I barely noticed my failure with your father. Since his obsessive behavior was familiar to all, nobody blamed me. I went on to realize my clinical ambition instead and soon established my own therapy practice. Where I failed at closeness with your father, I succeeded with my patients.

When Archie came to us, I was at the top of my field. I was the only one who would take him; the others demanded he agree to hospital and to drugs. Our initial interview convinced me: a therapeutic rapport was there, and I discerned an objectivity and instinct for life within him that seemed more powerful than that for death. At that point I naturally imagined that it was death—in the form of what seemed the mildly notorious voice of Wisdom—that was tightening its grip on him and making him feel crazy. I proceeded to tempt him away from this pathology with a knowledge of himself and every object he had held close from the beginning of his life. Like all my successful cases, he was seduced by the knowledge of self I could lead him to.

There's no use proceeding any further until I answer those who have denounced me. Yes, I was wrong to sleep with Archie, but not wrong in allowing myself to be seduced. I was well-defended in the beginning. I understood immediately that he came to me as my husband had: a mad genius, erotic in his obsessions. I knew Archie's obsessions would soon include me, too, and I prepared myself for this, as any well-analyzed clinician would. I knew that he would come to have a sixth sense about me just as my husband had, and that I would be vulnerable to this seemingly innate knowledge of my most intimate thoughts and dispositions. In rapid order, this indeed did happen. And once again, I was able to turn the seduction back to that other kind of knowledge taught to us by our "father," Freud.

But Archibald Shechner came with more than a

precocious mind. He brought with him an ancient Scroll and a voice from the ground that was interpreting it for him. My interest at first was clinical then turned intellectual. I had a natural curiosity about his work as an archeologist and the artifact he had uncovered. His mind as a scientist could not be ignored. Yet I maintained the quality of detachment I had honed so well in removing myself from my husband. All this changed when he brought me the Scroll to see. Unfortunately, I did not recognize that the ground had shifted. The ground inside me was now changing.

I learned to read the Scroll as Archie had. I learned, in short, how to read the ecosystem. He had long studied the Scroll, but the voice brought a new knowledge. Still, I could not hear it—even when I traveled to the Hula to see for myself the hole in the ground. Yet Archie's narration of the voice exposed something undeniably distinct, and it threw all I was dealing with into uncertainty.

My analytic ear began to pick up more than the transmissions of an individual psyche. These transmissions were from another level of consciousness, suffused with a shocking force of desire. Archie tried to tell me what it was, though I could not yet hear him. I only knew that I was driven to articulate the shift of ground I was experiencing and the only language that seemed adequate was sex, human physical desire. We attempted this articulation, so to speak, together one day in my bedroom here. It was more a process of mourning than of consummation. We knew in the moment of orgasm that we had not found the correct place to lodge the new desire. In fact, the sexual places in us had moved. Where? That is something you must discover for yourself, daughter. My only guidance is that it moved to the level of species. I became a new Eve.

[Betti]

A New Niche

Each feeling, each thought that came back from the past in Betti Peleg's office was a brick to rebuild self-confidence. Instead of fading, however, Wisdom's voice became more rooted in me. I no longer tried to control it with my mind; I had learned from Betti's powers of alertness to let it be. The voice began to feel rooted in my body, like an erotic call to intercourse, but it was as if the erotic places in my body had moved and I knew not where.

"Rooted" is the key. It is a reminder of the Eden that Adam described in the Scroll, revolving around the tree. In Eden he listened to it as it spoke, but once outside of the Garden only memory remained; nothing natural spoke anymore. What do we have closest to this—what replaces memory? Seduction. Betti taught me to see this. The longing it creates is not for another species, as it was in Eden, but for one of its own. Now I have learned from Wisdom how our own sex is a diminution, and how a desire embedded deep within longs to burst through to Eden again. How to uproot this original desire?

Not necessary. For those who will hear, seduction and sex will be linked to hearing and seeing the ecosystem. A new state of being at home. What an irony: our eyes are closed when we're most aroused!

As a man, I enter the vaginal canal; I enter a process in which the genes I carry take over the story. To open my eyes, to become a witness—I need to let go. Let the desire to evolve rise to consciousness. A new attraction to natural diversity arises, for exploring—for entering and inhabiting a new niche.

Endless essays are written about nature, sometimes indirectly, seemingly about something else, about the author and his life. They are more about nature than the author knows. Although these writings are conventional, seeking and finding closure at nature's breast, nature is always beyond what can be imagined. *That* is what nature teaches!

During the last few decades we could imagine her fragile, enduring great numbers of extinctions and threats. But she is not fragile; *we* are, impoverished by the loss of our own exultation in her. Our freedom to run wild in her. Even when I was digging in the desert I was careful not to disturb any of the few plants—as if the plants were bones in an ancient body.

Now I know that we are coming to the borders of our own extinction as a species. It was even in the Scroll, the memory of our loss of Eden—of Wisdom's tree. Now some will be ready to hear her. I have begun to live in a new nature that is unclosed, unbounded by our individual passing. Others will begin to live beyond the passing of our species, knowing that it too is bounded in years, as all species have ever been. We will wait at the borders of our species, prepared to evolve into another one. To become, like our genes, constant: the first species conscious of their evolving.

To have the memory of evolving is to become like the gods. This is the revelation of Eden. We are already half-evolved. Mutant. Some may have even evolved, but they are just beyond the borders of our knowing.

[Shechner]

1995

When I arrived in Tel Aviv, I went straight to my mother's old office. It now belonged to one of her more ancient colleagues, a child psychologist in his seventies who had often aspired to the roles of father to her and grandfather to me. Needless to say, such attempts were mainly frustrated by my mother, who guarded her vulnerabilities with an almost religious zeal. This is no doubt why religion was never a temptation—none could compare in power to the system of my mother.

So when I called from New York asking to see my mother's old office, I had no trouble getting what I wanted. The leaps in his heart were palpable over the phone. I could not only visit the old office, he told me, but I could stay in the adjoining efficiency flat until I could find a place more permanent. Saying he would be on vacation when I arrived, he volunteered to mail me the keys and a letter of introduction.

Stepping out of the taxi onto the familiar street and putting the key into the lock created a seductive illusion of sameness and possession. The door opened, though, and the illusion was broken. The place had been turned into a museum. Or did it look more like a stage set? It reminded me of a play I had gone to see with Svitz. I don't remember the title but the main character was Freud and the different sets were restorations of his study and consulting room in the house in Vienna. That's how my mother's office seemed to look now. Like a restoration. But not of her.

It all looked ostentatious to me, but perhaps it was because she had been so retro-conservative, understated. She always decorated in a spartan fashion. It left much to the imagination, which could be good or bad depending on the type of person you were. But here, there seemed to be no room for imagination. The fantasy was already in place. Maybe that's why she always rebuffed the old fellow—a difference in professional philosophy, after all.

I wanted to go back to the moment of standing outside the door. My hand on the door knob and the key snug in the lock. I recognized the impulse: a desire to freeze time, forestall the grief. There was no way I was going to find mother sitting in this office or striding in from the outside. This had become another time and place.

Oddly enough, I sat down on the couch. It was massively upholstered and seemed to attract the fabric of my clothing, holding me down. I tried to pull myself up from it, but didn't have the strength to struggle. I needed a place to lie down, even if it didn't feel right. The afternoon sun flooded in from the top windows, causing tears to form in my eyes. I turned to the wall but the tearing didn't stop. I gave up, sinking further into the couch, and the tears. But I was the only one who could hear them drop and hit the surface of the couch. The room was empty of my mother and my doctor.

I remember at some point I placed a call to Aviya Nachman at the Hebrew University. I was told she was away from her office and had gone to the Weizmann Institute office of the Hula Valley restoration site. Her assistant took my name and number and told me to wait for a call within the hour. When the phone rang, I found myself answering the voice of Professor Nachman. I recognized it immediately from the night at the Museum.

"I wanted to speak to you because of your lecture at the Natural History Museum in New York several years ago. I was in the audience. You mentioned Archibald Shechner's name."

"Yes, I know, Miss Peleg. I saw you. Surprised?"

"That would be an understatement," I replied. "How do you know me?"

"Nothing mystical, I assure you," she said with a satisfying laugh. "I was one of the guests at the Sened party for the Scroll people years ago. I went because of Aharon Appelfeld. He and I have seen most of the century together. Unrequited lovers, as they say, forgiven by our mates for our enduring friendship. I saw you and your mother that night, though we were not introduced."

"You're very striking, Professor Nachman; I'm sure I would have noticed and remembered you."

"Well, the truth is I did not mingle. I spent most of the

evening in the Sened library talking to old friends and their young apprentices."

"You said that night in New York that Archibald Shechner was an old friend."

"Yes. And by the way, thank you for the excerpts you sent me, particularly the last fragment of the Scroll with Adam and Eve outside of the Garden. It was very helpful in preparing a new presentation, this time for a panel with Aharon."

I started to respond but she no longer seemed conscious of me. As she continued to speak, I began to feel like I was in the consulting chair, listening to Archie as mother might have, letting my mind ride the tide of sensibility coming my way. I even noticed myself doodling on a notepad just as my doctor had revealed that he did. In between the marks were words that entered my brain through hers and seemed to empty out onto the page. My brain had become an aural organ. Had mother and my doctor felt this same pleasure?

"It's so clear now after reading it," she was saying. "The ways we fill the spaces of absence. We build a landscape in our mind's eye where an ecosystem once was. I am reminded of my old botanical terminology—*scape* as in the stalk or shaft leading from the flower into the crown and root. We are just at the beginning of formulating a new scape back to the root of Homo sapiens. That has been the work of our Hula Valley youth, this new generation of poet-scientists. I spend most of my day listening to them observing the ecosystem. They do not know how to speak to the outside, so I am learning to speak for them. And besides, they are like artists—only time enough for their materials. I am old, my hands cannot work with the plants as they did when I was young. But my mouth works, and my ears—always good hearing in my family. My eyes are not so good, though." She trailed off.

"Why did you stop?" I asked.

"I was thinking of our mutual friend. He is the reason you called. We should be talking about him."

"I never heard Shechner mention you." I strained for a reply. "Anyway, it was clear from your museum lecture you knew his work intimately."

"I knew *him* intimately. We were lovers when we were each getting started in our careers. We met again when he came to see the faces behind the Hula restoration. He said he needed answers. After just a few hours with him in our offices here, I felt like I always had. I wanted nothing more than to give him those answers. But the irony was that he already had them."

"Was that around the time of his disappearance?" I asked.

"No. It was shortly after he began seeing your mother to help with his fears of madness. I worried for him. Not, mind you, because of any threat of madness. But rather for his pain. Evidently, your mother had already helped. He said his fear was much less."

"A fast recovery," I commented with some edginess.

"Oh, did you catch the fear, too?" she asked.

"No, I caught the panic, though I don't think you can "catch" things like that," I said.

"Well, it's just a metaphor, isn't it? But perhaps a useful one. I think we can "catch" the fears of our parents, our culture. They can go into the mind and even the body. Did you ever see that American cult film, *Invasion of the Body Snatchers*?"

I tried to answer but she didn't wait for a response. I began to wonder if I was ever going to see this woman face-to-face again. The topic of science fiction made me start to fantasize about evolving. I could see even more of the creature that I had told my doctor I was becoming. A teary-eyed thing that always seemed to find itself in empty rooms that would mysteriously fill with voices. Nachman's voice was coming over a telephone wire, but it seemed to dominate the room. I felt I was becoming the next link between people like my doctor and those like Archie who we can no longer see. I am the new species, *Transcriptor*, fated to hear testimony and produce transcription. This time it was Aviya Nachman. Maybe she was becoming like Archie.

"I hope you'll agree, Miss Peleg, that we can be "snatched" by the realities as our parents and peers see them. Those of us who refuse to be snatched must learn to live without peers. Go into disguise. But often, the disguise is yet another attempt to attract peers we have never had and still want. I have remade myself many times over the course of my life. I have always been in disguise. I have resisted strenuously the depression and deprivation of this loneliness. Archibald Shechner, however, let go of the resistance. His panic took him towards more life. It is very different from our kind of panic, yes?"

"What is our kind of panic, Professor Nachman?"

"You have not yet let go of your disguise, have you Julie? Do you mind if I call you by your first name?" she asked.

I said "Please do" but had no time to say anything else.

"You and I both know that you are an expert on our kind of panic, yet you make me the authority. I have little to say that you don't already know. Human panic is usually about using the body as a shield against life. Through the Scroll and the voice, Archie discovered a new way to use the body: as a bridge to life and as a guide to a new world. Through your mother, he learned that panic covers an unrepressed, tabooed desire—in this case, to evolve. It is the ultimate human taboo, since it means seeing the human world for what it is—one of mulitudes, and not even the most advanced. Why? Because to be advanced is to be able to evolve. Our consciousness is weak next to other species. We think moving to another level of consciousness is a supernatural event. We cling to our disguises. We are afraid to let go, as am I."

"How do you know all this?" I asked.

"You are too experienced to be so awe-struck. First of all, I know about you because of that pest of a man, Harriman Svitz. He hounded me when I got back to Israel after that museum lecture until I finally made the mistake of talking to him. He fell in love with me, I suppose, and told me all about you and your panic attacks. I listened because I, too, have had my share of fears. As for the rest, I heard it from Shechner that day he came here. And I've had ten years to figure out the rest. Everett Nosei, of course, has been most helpful."

"You've seen Nosei? Where is he?"

"He has been here often the last few months. But I do not know where he is right now. He comes and goes. Waiting, I guess."

"Waiting for what?"

"I don't know," she answered. "I only know I have an unexplained feeling of envy. I always hated waiting, myself. But I think I'd like to know about his kind of waiting. I have to go now, Julie. If you still wish to see me, you know where I'll be. Good luck."

Her voice had stopped.

Next day. I was back in my mother's office again. But it wasn't empty. Nosei. I moved towards the desk, as if reaching for a fantasy of being on the telephone with him too, while still alone in the office. I even felt the phone in my hand as he stood there. He joined me in the fondling. A knowing. A sadness and newness. We couldn't keep our hands under control. Starting on the couch. Then, a few blocks away to my Tel Aviv beachfront hotel, on HaYarkon. Forty-eight hours in bed, with plates and glasses strewn about, remnants of several room-service calls. Just like that. Navel-struck. If we didn't know normal sex before, it has certainly become quaint now.

Navel-struck follows being couch-struck, for me. "I am perverse," I used to say to my doctor. "I am the Harold Brodkey of the couch. I dare to think against termination. I dare to think the couch is, and will be as important, or even more important, than the bed."

I felt his disorientation in the silence that followed. "How can such things be measured?" he began, but I interrupted.

"I'm proposing that we—the "we" of analysis—that we have created a new sex, a new, competing life." My drive to think otherwise and confront his need to know asserted itself. "That the couch, like the bed, holds our physicality, an equality of thought and physical feelings. And I'm ready to mourn—that one can't stay couch-struck forever."

More silence. "Can't you say anything to me?" I almost yelled, more despairing than angry.

His body moved against the leather of his chair. "You've made me think, Julie. Maybe that is part of being couch-struck."

So now I'm navel-struck. With Nosei. Does the mind have to expand before a creature evolves? Wrong formulation. Brain size has nothing to do with it. And being on the couch is not about expanding the mind. It is about mutation. Becoming something else in order to survive. Finding new rules of survival. New territory.

We begin reading the new manuscript Nosei brought from my mother. Not so much new, actually, as a new translation: Archie and Betti have worked as a team to embody the Scroll, as if they were a new Adam and Eve. "First, Archie put down those fragments of the original Scroll he remembered. After all, he didn't have a photographic memory—maybe you could call it audiographic like Nosei's, which is why he could repeat exactly what Wisdom said. So then, they filled in the rest by transforming Adam and Eve into dramatic parts for us," says Nosei.

“Your mother is very shy now about talking to us,” he continued, propped up by pillows against the headboard. “I only got a few words out of her, as she was backing away. She said there’s a great misunderstanding that people have about evolving. We think that’s what our human intelligence is for, that we can evolve in our heads or play with our genes. That is only half right. We need our intelligence simply to hear the next species—and not to have to become anything. It doesn’t matter if what we hear comes from the earth or it’s extra-terrestrial. Meanwhile, since we hear only the language of humans, our intelligence allows us to try reading the ecosystem and be prepared.”

As I was reading the new scroll, Nosei was reading his own manuscript again, the whole novel this time—with my part folded in. The poetry of Archie and mother, who have heard another voice, can flesh out the story now. Although we can only read it, not hear it.

It restores lost ties. I remember what Aviya said in her lecture, and look it up in my notebook: “We humans, who no longer are tied to natural ecosystems, are not anymore tied to this planet. A seahorse is tied to his coastal wetlands, and if its coastal ecosystem goes, so does the seahorse, and vice versa. But what are we tied to? What natural home? Earth can go on without us, and maybe the human species is destined to explore outer space. But since we were born here, what we bring to Earth’s biosphere is the possibility of restoration—of memory of itself. In that way we are tied to the next species as well, since they will be tied to earth again, to ecosystems they help restore.”

So this manuscript returns to the original tie again, which couldn't have been possible without Archie's discovery of the Scroll, his hearing the voice—and then his and mother's restoration of parts of the Scroll for Nosei and me. I guess they knew we would have to turn to other human beings in writing this book, to deliver the process of our learning: our collection of scraps into a giant scrapbook of a story. It is something Archie couldn't contemplate, not after he was vilified and the Scroll had been lost. A voice from a hole in the ground—that, and my mother, saved him, just as it preserves Nosei and me. There is one more voice for me, though, where the hole inside me once was.

Here is how Nosei described the scene to me, the primal first encounter: "At first it seems like heaven, like meeting up again with lost loved ones, the dream of so many religions, reuniting with parents. But Archie and Betti weren't my real parents and slowly the scene grew less hazy and ethereal, more sharply focussed. I was confronting a new species grown out of my own, a completely different picture of life and death, deep time. This is the next religious experience, as Archie and Betti barely spoke but pointed and the plants seemed to communicate to me in a language I felt inside. We belong to Wisdom and she to the Creator. Like an author, the Creator must return to explore his world, to see it anew, to see what Wisdom has made of it. This is what we must do as well, we who are made in the image of a creator. We will find a new faith in listening to the ecosystem, as the Creator listens once again to Wisdom. They are reunited in our listening. Then Betti put the new scroll in my hand and they backed away."

Nosei turned away from me, looking out the window at the crowded Tel Aviv skyline. "Does it sound too strange?" he asked.

"No," I answered. "I came up against it all my life: the truth is always hidden, it's always backing away. That was mother's milk to me, her doctrine, and I amplified it with my own secrets. Meanwhile, everyone—even mother—took me at face value: a solitary girl, awkward around people, rebellious. But it was my disguise, so I could get the real scoop myself. It wasn't just an accident that made me ready to take on Svitz and Archie. If I had appeared a polished person they would have been intimidated, but my disguise disarmed them."

Nosei and I agreed we were beans of the same bean pod. When we first met, we saw through each other's disguise to the observer behind: neither of us wanted the main attention. We were notetakers on the present rather than participants. Nosei's invitation as a philologist to come to Tel Aviv and work on deciphering the Scroll was his first big adventure. I saw he was lost right away. He was almost relieved when the Scroll disappeared, and he stayed on in Israel because he had met friends who didn't consider him their notetaker, the way Svitz did.

A sudden honking of cars stuck at an intersection outside brought us back to the present in our Tel Aviv hotel room. "Most people fit into the city and become a sort of human-shaped antenna, picking up the cultural signals," Nosei was saying. "Sort of the way a tropical hunting-fish is shaped by the tide, its whole body a fin moving at the speed necessary to keep it stationary as the tide flows into a brackish mangrove. It fits into the wetland like a hand and wrist into an arm of the human body: it is an appendage of the mangrove, more so than any mammal, a dolphin for instance, which has already developed appendages and a mind of its own. If we look at the mangrove as an ecosystem, then the tropical pencilfish is an organ—remove it and the system begins to degrade. What that fish ate and what ate it also becomes at risk, they begin to "think" differently, and so on."

Nosei stopped to pick up some toast left over in the breakfast tray. He now talked as easily about the ecosystem as he used to talk about words. "At this point in human history," he began again, chewing without missing a beat, "we would have to say that the ecosystem of which we are an organ is the global planet. Yet remove us—and all the regional ecosystems flourish! Our natural ecosystem has long since been degraded, primarily by ourselves.

"Aviya showed me a government brochure to build support for the Hula restoration." Nosei's voice deepened into an affected officialese. "'We are yet too close to real frontiers and all of our beginnings to thrive in a world of asphalt and concrete,' it began. The brochure was laughed at in the Culture Ministry and they refused to reprint it. It went against the deep local history of Judaism, Christianity and Islam, which is so complicated by historic sites that any notion of the deeper time in which species evolved is covered over.

"The brochure continues: 'Places of refuge from the hurly-burly still are needed, places where one may escape, if only briefly, all sight and sound of fellow humans.' Can you hear the religious overtones? Where else but in a synagogue are we expected to escape the pull of the human? This sounded like some new religion to the Culture Ministry—and a religion that would destroy the tourism industry. Can you imagine all those people flying to the Holy Land in order to escape not only humans but our whole history? That would be the end of that. So the Hula restoration can go on free of intervention, and that's how your mother appeared to us: as another researcher. Instead of being sponsored by the government she was the subject of something bigger and natural."

"The subject of Wisdom," I interjected, to show that I was keeping up with his explanation of mother's new life. "She's working for the voice of the ecosystem. Doesn't that sound lunatic to you?"

"No. She described the ecosystem as having the instinct of a mother, and I understood that. When a mother's son is killed in battle she will call to him at the graveside. Only a mother imagines her voice to reach beyond death. Same way, we die calling out for our mothers—if we have no time to think, that is. So it's natural to imagine the ecosystem as having a mothering quality, and therefore a voice. A voice that reaches beyond human time.

"But I could see she had changed, your mother. She was uncomfortable hanging around, wanted to get away—not at all like the down-to-business type I came to know. She told a little story that barely made any sense, like an unfinished children's story. 'You know your hand is a product of the trees, shaped from a life of swinging in trees. That's why you can hold a pen and write. We have found those trees again.' I assumed she was talking about Shechner and herself.

"'In the trees we were invisible, safe from our big predators on the ground. Now we feel that way again—invisible, waiting. Waiting for what? For original Homo, it was waiting for a time to be alone, free of being hunted. Now it is the same, waiting for a time to return in a camouflage, like the leaves were protecting Homo. Waiting with more trust in the natural world, to come back as tellers of the trees.'

"I think what she meant was a new kind of writer, invisible to us, more a voice—it will probably make more sense in the future, when computers and voice recognition are more integrated into our lives. But the tree of Knowledge in the Garden of Eden must be a part of it."

I was struck by the shyness Nosei described in my mother. Mother had been the least shy woman in the universe it seemed as I was growing up. I was the solitary one. To say she had changed is an understatement, but at least I could understand now what is ultimately solitary about our species, suppressed beneath the social need. It's the human mind. The solitary mind monitors our environment—the ecosystem and its light, climate, etc. The solitary mind is our vestigial tie to the ecosystem, our umbilical cord. But in the new species it is no longer the human mind but the whole organism that has become an umbilical cord. The way mother was being described confirms it. It's also confirmed by the new sexual interest Nosei and I found in the navel.

But I worry that I can't express the feeling of it, that I'm telling too much. It took me a long time to feel the solitude of my mind because mother was the only intimate allowed in there. She was always there, her cares, her words. It was scary to let more into my bounds of intimacy, but I was drawn to Nosei, to Archie, to the Scroll. And I didn't know I was afraid of them because I had this outward bravado. Only when they all left or disappeared did I realize I had not let them into my mind, where all turned to panic. I didn't even know I'd been living ignorant of my mind, and I had to let it speak. That is what my sessions did: let my mind speak, though confined to human language. But in the events we are writing about it speaks through nonhuman language, of the natural world that's outside of us. Before that, the ecosystem had been shut up—shut out of human culture—the way I kept others outside of my mind.

I think of it this way: no one has heard the human mind ever speak for itself. We have seen what it is capable of creating with thought, but what of itself, its needs, its ultimate loneliness, cut off from intimacy? Mother used to exclaim over Archie's great loneliness. Now it made sense that he had found himself in such an extreme of solitariness in his last dig that he was capable of hearing the ecosystem's voice again, probably not heard by anyone since ancient shamans. So ancient, their stories of Eden would not yet have been transformed into the myths we know today.

The new story of Eden in the scroll that Archie and mother gave to us is another kind of umbilical cord in language. It starts in a return to isolation, a being together in a new lovemaking. The expression of it in language. The family melts away and in its place is a mothering ecosystem and fathering universe—an isolation or loneliness I can only imagine, though I can conceive of how it is a new world or Eden for my mother. What a joke the fantasy about intelligent life on other planets becomes when you realize how intelligence can't exist by itself, of course, but depends on a vast Eden of diverse species. Many of them, like most plants according to the Guide, have a more valuable chemical intelligence than the brains of primates.

[Julie]

Death: Our Predator

The key to the new Scroll that Betti and Archie prepared was the knowledge of species it contains—and, in particular, how "snake" was a euphemism for humans in the Garden. That's what struck me on my first reading. We just could not accept ourselves as explorers—a species that made mistakes—and we had to cover it up in Genesis with the only mistake we'd admit: disobedience, eating from death's tree. The explanation of death was so simple and the punishment so severe that we were afraid to face mistakes anymore. "Eat from it—and on that day death touches you."

The new spirit of Betti and Archie goes back to explore

the Garden again. They are documenting—"naming"—the plants and animals as if they were mates, partners: new members of the first family. More importantly, they're listening to the knowledge the other species have of us. And for us.

Betti told me that it was only fear that required supernatural ideas, fear that we could easily be killed off by a species of primates that evolved beyond us. That's just what happened to our predecessors. So our own myths became more oriented to death and the afterlife. Death itself had become our predator, as we grew more conscious of it than any other species. The Scroll turns it around: this life *is* our afterlife.

"We are your afterlife," she said. "Here is the proof ."

"But—won't you die?"

"Yes, but we already have, you see? It doesn't mean the same thing anymore. Not when you've found the Garden of Eden again and know it is still there.

"I can understand, I think. But I still can't feel it; I still feel that death is the end of me. I'm sure most people will who aren't religious."

"We will become your religion," she answered with a sigh. "Humans will no longer feel the burden of being central or alone. You will be able to look back and see human history as well as your life in a new light. There will be an explosion of poetry and new language. Here is the proof. It may not seem like great poetry but it is in fact a document, a record of the truth.

"We had to prepare it now because we are losing our

ordinary words. It is at great effort that I speak to you now. It is exhausting; these are not the words we think with anymore, they seem kind of worn out. Instead we are listening to the intricate movements of the ecosystem. Humans will begin to, as well. There will be satellites—after the EOS satellites, the 'Mission to Planet Earth'—maybe in a hundred years, that listen to the ecosystem in a kind of translation. Perhaps the work of human poets then will be to make those translations. Poetry and art will return to their natural state, become natural again.

"And, I should tell you, the population will shrink drastically. It just will, like it does among many social animals. No calamity is needed. The human population that is left will fit more naturally into its original ecosystem."

"Can we know what that is, our "original ecosystem?" I asked.

"Rain forests, it seems. The restoration movements will bring them back over a few centuries. There will be no more need for the damaging kinds of agriculture and domestic animals that clog human history."

"What about our cities, the libraries and art, the universities?"

"Oh, that will not be lost at all. It will all be archived. The technology is almost there, anyway. Access will be easy, but there will be so many new fields of knowledge opening up—and all of them grounded in the natural world."

"But it still sounds so restricted. Most people don't get excited by ecology."

"You don't really know it yet. Think of the mosquito, the

lowliest pest to human progress. In the common view, it produces nothing humans can use, like bee honey. Now it's revealed as the key to small plant diversity in the tropics: we would not exist without them, since they are a key pollinator in the ecosystem in which we evolved. And aside from what they can teach in their species "intelligence," they challenge all our metaphors of human progress. Imagine, mosquitoes as agents of idiom, showing how to evolve a new language again. They have listened to the plants. Just as Adam and Eve did in the Garden."

Your mother—your former mother—took the Scroll out of an old briefcase and handed it to me. Surprise: it really was a scroll. Handmade paper and all. I unrolled it a bit. Hand printed in block letters—nothing fancy.

"It's only pieces of the original," she said. Maybe you can add some commentary. Some things might seem clearer to you than most persons, especially after our talk."

I put the scroll under my arm but she retrieved it. "It cannot go with you," she said. "Remember, we were impressed with your aural memory. You must hear it."

[Nosei '94]

The New Century

Dear Julie Peleg: We are on the verge of understanding the inner workings of the cell and, in the new century, we will understand the principles of the universe. The cell and the universe are complex systems, and some think that the new century might unlock the even more complicated system of the human brain. The principles behind human culture are more difficult yet—from religion to works of art—but they too could be uncovered in less than a century from now. That leaves only one system still more complex and beyond our comprehension: the ecosystem, the vehicle of evolution and mother of natural selection—in other words, the creator of more life and shaper of our intelligence. This may take a few more centuries—but can we afford to wait? Because in less than one century we may have destroyed the most precious of our ecosystems—and degraded the rest!

Am I sounding too much like the scientist Edward O. Wilson for you? I know you told me of your disappointment in him, that he couldn't grasp the complexity of Freud and the study of anxiety. Yet there's a remarkable message in his ideas of consilience and it's not what old guards like your Harriman Svitz imagine it to be. Professor Wilson is rediscovering our drive to know secrets. His ear is bent toward the innermost secrets of ecosystems on this planet. One day, he may wake up with the anxiety of actually hearing more than he can control.

Is there a way we can understand such secrets or origins now? The answer is already accomplished in the lives of your mother and Dr. Archibald Shechner. They hear a new language, which can only have happened as a result of evolving—or rather, of *beginning to evolve*, for an organism cannot evolve, only a species can. How did they begin? They first heard a memory of the new language, preserved by an ancient culture that recorded their creation stories based on the memory of having evolved in the Garden of Eden. Traces of it remain in Genesis: when Adam names the species, he is using the new language, though we have lost it in the original.

However, Dr. Shechner came in contact with it in the Scroll he unearthed [of the History of Adam], and he soon started hearing the ecosystem's voice directly. That is the voice that all new species hear when they first evolve—or rather, it is the voice that pulls them toward evolving, revealing a hidden desire in all creatures to evolve.

Julie, listen to me: When Everett told me there was a new Scroll from Archie and your mother, I thought it would never be understood except *indirectly*, in the context of all truth: indirectly, as in a novel. Only a novel could bring together the imaginative impulses of science, religion and art to create a future that resonates with something inside of us, which tells us what we already know is true—or rather, which reveals it. Just as we can only face some things in a dream, which we can then escape by waking, we face in the novel what we can later escape by closing the covers. But vivid dreams can always be remembered—just as the Garden of Eden has been—and a book can always be reopened.

Now, imagine my delight when Everett told me that the two of you had in fact composed a novel, and that the new Scroll would fit into it!

[Aviya Nachman]

1995

After Nosei dictated the new Scroll to me and I once again found myself transcribing the most extraordinary material, he asked who would understand it. “We’re going to have to footnote,” he said, “but that will just make it unappetizing to read.”

“Why don’t we each respond by writing how it touches us,” I said. “That way, it fits into the novel like our responses to Archie’s tapes.” So we decided each of us would write our first reactions to chapters of the Scroll right there in bed. We extended our reservations to a week. We called housekeeping to bring us new sheets and towels (we would change them ourselves) and we began.

We went back to the beginning, and looked into Genesis to see if it sounded different now. There was a copy of the Bible right there in the room’s desk drawer. Exactly as we suspected: the Guide to a New World had helped alter the meaning and turn the story inside out. Here’s how it should read in our eyes:

"Before a plant of the field was in earth, before a grain of the field sprouted—the Creator had not spilled rain on the earth, nor was there man to work the land—yet from the day earth and sky collaborated to make an ecosystem there was water to give the surface of clay life. The ecosystem shaped a plenitude of earthlings from this soil, and the wind of life blew through their nostrils. Now look: man becomes a creature of flesh.

The Creator planted this diverse ecosystem in Eden, and the garden nourished the man he formed. From the land grew all trees lovely to look upon, good to eat from; the tree of life was there in the garden, and the tree of evolving.

The Creator lifts the man, brings him to rest in the garden of Eden, to tend it and watch. Also to learn: from the trees and all their countless species.

"It is no good the man be alone," said Wisdom. "The plants and creatures each have their mate, as the Creator and I. I will shape a partner to stand beside him."

The astonishing thing is here we find Wisdom and the Creator united again. What would that mean if it really happened, we asked ourselves. Well, we were pretty amazed to find ourselves together again, so how did *that* happen? Each of us was drawn toward the main ecosystem restoration site, where Archie had first found the Scroll and which had recently been reflooded. Now the area teemed with flocks of cranes and other migrating birds that had survived the disappearance of their watering grounds when the swamps had been drained by the pioneers. So the hole from which Archie pulled the Scroll and heard the voice of Wisdom was now under water, and it was as if the site had given birth:

through the hole had come a flood of diverse life haloed by the wheeling flocks of exotic birds. You would have to say we were drawn to new life, a nonhuman diversity that allowed us to feel less self-important as individuals, more happily anonymous. Drawn toward Eden, you might say, the way Wisdom and the Creator were.

All of that new life—from the hoopoe birds to the smallest wildflowers of the grasses—rejoiced in its sexuality. How could the Creator remain removed in his self-importance? So it makes sense that, like Adam and Eve, Archie and my mother have been to Eden, trading their shyness for an anonymity among us.

[Julie]

Chapter 15

Chapter 15

1

Eve:

I woke up under flowers
Where was he?
murmuring water
drew me; smooth as another sky
this river, and by it I dreamed
my first dream, and heard
my mate, answering my question
your form awakes my desire;
alone, you were my dream
Adam has my desire even when I am not
    there
he holds my place
and I his: arms and legs moving
to enfold each other, one ambition
rooted as trees—those
holding the center of the Garden
their flowers a world of faces
and behind them, nectar-consciousness
I must have drunk to wake
to know when I dream in this rooted place
words my faces and flowers
the word-roots ambrosia
no sooner tasted than seen—
I am no spirit but implanted

in this body: only by the knowledge I eat
can I outreach these hands, see
into myself and find
the rose of Sharon and the lily of the
    Valleys
and all are Eve: I create her
my mind races to distances beyond
an angel's—return, return
and no goddess returns. I may look all
    ways—
no god may blind me
no king, no queen of heaven.
Yet rooted within is a name held back
as if my heart overtook my man's desire
mother—to name all I take in, hidden.

JULIE:

As I read I imagined how sexual desire comes from diversity. In the excitement of losing ourselves among so many other species we climax—into a kind of breakdown, letting go of our uniqueness. Our erogenous zones must work in the same way, in a diversity of nuances that are exciting. There's curves, textures, weights, colors, smells—it's just like all the divergences among closely related species. I began to understand it, how the language of life is diversity. I felt a new warmth, surrounded by a warm quilt of life. But I still didn't know what to do. How do you go out and explore species diversity?

Then I realized the question was part of the problem. I'd begun the process of evolving toward another species myself. All I needed to find was a frontier, a point of isolation, and the first one presenting itself was the Hula restoration. I first came across it during the Sened party where Nosei and I met. Then it was only cocktail chatter, a gleam in the eye of the scientist describing it. It was a joke, actually, because he never really thought it would come to anything. Who ever heard of the idea of creating a swamp? Besides, it seemed a mockery of Israel's ideals, since its pioneers had drained the swamps to create a garden of farmland.

But the restoration is real now. Nobody asks who I am or questions my being here. They assume I'm a frontier scientist, which is a good cover-phrase for evolving. There are other points of restoration like this around the globe, but once you've found one you don't want to leave. Lonely? That's a human question. *Expectatious* is more like it, one of Nosei's invented words. I found an inner trust that a mate would arrive. I didn't think it would actually be Nosei, but the moment I saw him I knew it made sense. That is all one asks of an ideal: that it make perfect sense.

Nosei:

It's like a distillation of how I got here. I began to feel something in my navel area. It felt deep, deep within. At first I thought it was my stomach. Like a deep longing in my stomach to eat something I haven't eaten since early childhood. Since beyond what I can remember. A craving for it. Then I realized it was not my stomach. It was not food that I wanted. Some other orifice had to be filled, as if at the bottom of the inside of our navel a tiny hole remains. And it is there now, inside us. And somehow, it feels a vibration—an aural vibration. And when I sense I can almost hear Archie's voice (and through it, the voice of Wisdom) that craving inside begins to expand, and creates a little space in me—an interior space, that was never there before. And it is naked in me. I want to protect it. I need to protect it with another being that feels the same vulnerability. It is said that sexual reproduction is a means of protecting the species. And this new desire to protect is connected like an umbilical cord to a new species.

The more I listen to the feeling of vibration within my stomach—what I used to think was my stomach, what I used to be able to satisfy by stuffing something down my mouth—it was now a new place behind and deeply within my navel. I wanted to put my ear there, but it is physically impossible, or at least it is for a middle-aged academic like myself. I want to put my ear instead on her navel. That is where the desire begins to be consummated. To put my ear on her navel, but whose could that be except a being for whom the pleasure and the desire is equal?

As I thought about all the long months and years and endless manuscript pages that all my life had drained into, I realized that I had to return to Julie, for she had felt the same obsession (it was there in the manuscript—in the trunk). She is the one who sent the trunk to me. A trail leading back to a navel.

"Mother" in the end. She means Wisdom, and how we all really have the same mother, the same language as a species. It was the first language, behind Adam's naming, and it was the language learned from plants, who produced the first food for us. Consider how. By sexual reproduction. Sustenance from sex—and language. So language is the first form of reproduction we learned—and we translated it as we ate from the plants.

2

Eve:
Your tongue occupies me
I am planted, cannot move
what more like gods than trees
no partner missed, no need
of another: a gift to all
a giving no words limit
flowers to share each breath
the tree I might call father
so tall it takes my breath away
as I look up its exquisite bulk
it is unattainable, no branch within reach
limbs of pendant fruit like a large male
beckoning my tiny hand
should I not want to wrap myself in his
    skin?
appetite has pulled me heavenward
toward your mouth, curving
to entwine with mine

incoherent in the mirror of his subtlety
his head swaying as he sang
I clutched him there, my mouth opened
I swam in the highest fruit
vowed singing and tending
to that precious tree, ease to her
fertile burden as I grew weighty—
"I would return," I said to myself.

NOSEI:

What is hidden in the fruit of the tree of Knowledge is the ecstasy of letting go. As I long to enter the navel canal, I enter a process in which the genes I carry can take over the story. They open my eyes, allow me to become a witness: I need to let go, let the desire to evolve rise to consciousness. Let the body take over, let it move toward an unknown climax. New value is there, in the natural diversity and the desire to explore—to enter and inhabit a niche, as if it were a female body.

No memory is there. Instead, the purely present discovery of one's own species, just as they are: all seduction. The desire embedded deep within is to burst through to Eden again. Seduction and sex is now linked anew to hearing and seeing the ecosystem, being at home. Beyond the isolation lovers build for themselves. To feel the pulse of self-sustaining life within—a sensual thrill of encountering animals and plants never thought of before, now suddenly vivid.

Julie:

Eve's voice reminded me of a tram ride in a garden. It was the New York Botanical Garden and I talked Svitz into going to the annual orchid show. Orchids were a representation of the exotic that he felt intellectually responsible to know about. He was having an awful time, finding little to read in the descriptions of the hundreds of orchid species and no one to talk to. So I helped him to find the horticultural library and left him there for an hour.

I was not exactly alone because I had bought a single orchid rooted in a small green pot, drawn toward it upon first sight. There I was, sitting on the tram with this pink and purplish, long-stemmed entity dangling dangerously as the wheels hit bumps on the trail. I reached to support its head, my hand brushing the part that had really attracted me. The veined, ballish sac. I was holding it for some time before I noticed a woman across from me watching, a knowing smile on her face. I felt like a young girl discovered touching herself.

She began to talk about orchids. She was an expert on orchids, it seems—and on seduction. She talked all about them without actually naming the desire. As she spoke, I began to feel wet, aroused, as my eyes were again and again referred by her to my orchid's various parts. Only later did I learn that *orchid* comes from a Greek word that means testicle. I was an Eve with that orchid but I tried to suppress it. I was still scared of my unconscious desires.

Physical attraction to a man was one thing, but to a flower? I was unsettled. It was not the first time, as I recalled my trip to Italy to see my cousin's new baby. I felt such deep attraction to it, holding it, supporting its head, and then scared to the point of feeling something was wrong with me. Seeing my embarrassment, my cousin explained that sometimes women even get sexually aroused during suckling. But I couldn't really listen. I went out to play, that time at being a banker.

The reason they could reconstruct the Scroll and write this is that they discovered an erotic zone within themselves that is not a human erotic zone. It starts in the ears. Starts with vibrations—aural. And it leads to a place of hearing inside that wasn't known before. To the navel. What is this new eroticism in the navel? First of all, it's not human. The cutting of the umbilical cord is what made us human. A navel is a vestige of this cutting off, though; it now reminds me of something long repressed and forgotten. Another language, or hearing—another intelligence. It is, in fact, the physical sign of a repressed desire to evolve.

As soon as cut by a human being, the desire to evolve is cut off too. That first human being entering our lives—doctor, midwife, or mother—imposed human culture. From that minute on it was all human culture, which is directed toward producing more humans. There was not going to be any return, except at sexual moments. And maybe, couch moments. When the mind becomes a palpable organ, a new erogenous zone. And the question of how to consummate it stops seeming treacherous, and you start to play with it, there, on the couch. To feel how the brain can be governed by a different ethic.

What is this ethic? Wisdom's only answer is that it is to be found in the desire to evolve with an ecosystem.

3

Adam:

Then two worlds here, one
the world of feelings only mine
each thing with his own
mirrored in his mate
meanwhile the plants must speak to
    everything
to be tended, shape their leaves to catch
the wind and shape it with their need
You need learn, they say, to understand us
beings from another world
come to inhabit
a world of feelings as within yourself
a tree will grow within you
like a mother or father, and all around
lovely trees to eat from
and lively to the mind of man.
"Listen to the wind among leaves"
echoes in my bones
Each plant needs a world of others
to find its hidden mate
animals already are being taught at each
    bush
drinking deep of nectar
more is all they want and fly

```
or walk or crawl to another flower
These plants must be the priests of life
also its prophets, pointing the way
while setting a table
and busy in their workrooms making
the air we'll need to breathe
How do I listen to the air itself
except through the trees dangling
tongues of branches and leaves
while the hair of the grasses is ruffled
by restless winds: my breath—
the breathings of all the animals—
mimic the mothering trees.
```

NOSEI:

Here is the core of what Archie was getting at about the Scroll: the mothering tree of Knowledge, our true parents returned—the plants that nurtured us and gave us life—it's all here. The plants are still here, may even need *our* nurturing now. The freedom in letting go is here, also; and it's a sexual freedom that leads to new language.

As I think of how Archie's new Eve is Betti Peleg, I see that Julie is mine. Eve: she was an ecosystem in herself, not yet reduced to human dimension. The new appetite of Adam went exploring in her. The inner root of the navel is now connected to the outer tree of the world. The plants show Adam how the tree of his inner world of feelings is connected to the outer: the trees are mother and father, since they create the conditions for his new Eden.

As I read of the nectar, I thought of the navel goblet in the Song of Solomon, the lover's desire to drink there—and my longing for Julie.

JULIE:

I was thinking I would write the part for humans, because Nosei's notes relate to the evolved species. It's humans, however, who are going to read this. Human readers need something like the original experience Archie had in discovering the *Scroll of the History of Adam.* Even though next century will be all about evolving and leaving the city behind, anyone needs to discover their own part in it. The old idea—that the city is a center of knowledge—is just going to fade away, that much is clear in reading the Scroll. In place of a city the wild ecosystem will become the center. That's where *non*human knowledge overwhelms our little languages and makes them change. Like the voice that Archie heard. Meanwhile, reading the ecosystem as a human being, I'm finally never alone, my brain isn't alone, since my brain itself is just a rudimentary model of the ecosystem. In the same way, human culture is a tiny model of nature.

It's a new thing to look at yourself as a Homo. Suddenly we are funny, the way a cat is when it jumps off all four feet as it's startled. For instance, we joke about "contemplating our navels," but the laugh is on us, we are so blind to the repressed meaning of it. Or take what we call change: it's just an illusion of change to any other species. Archie's dictation about the ecosystem shows that most change occurs to keep an organism in its steady state. So when we're being most Homo sapiens is when we're wearing disguises—and don't even know it! Our clothes and uniforms are the most obvious ones, but inside we are even disguised to ourselves, full of repressed knowledge, as mother used to say. And what makes this funny is that we are still wild, with the same wild genes as hunters and gatherers, even before clothes amounted to much. Well, tatoos maybe.

My doctor used to speak of catastrophic change. There was a point in our work when I thought it would kill me. I've known many who get out, when they feel this. The suspicion of change is unrelenting. It had to be tricked: I'd never left anyone, I told my Nancy Drew detective self, so I stayed. But I still wanted everything to be romantic—my work with him, work on the transcribing, my relationships. Nothing seemed alive without that erotic charge. Even to deny it made me feel dead, empty inside.

"I feel Plath-like. Can you blame him for not being attracted to her anymore?"

"Who?" he asked. "Oh, you mean Ted Hughes. I can't see you sticking your head in an oven, because just bringing it up is a way of expressing despair at what this change could mean. But do we know yet?"

Real change is the most deeply repressed in us, according to Archie. The instinct to evolve is the deepest one, a turn toward nature. We have to dig it up with this hard, vulnerable thinking, this holding out and holding open:

"Do we know yet?" It's even funny to remember that Svitz said "nature loving" was a "swerve away" from thinking—as if nature was beneath us. He preferred the swerve to the supernatural—pretty funny, when you think about it. To him, the supernatural was always a metaphor, and so much "safer" than real nature and the unknown. There's the joke: it's in the phrase "real nature." Maybe this is not so funny when you think how some religion separates us from real nature too, so that the horror we have is to be without clothes. The cat I used to live with, however, seemed to think of my clothes as my toys, which I would throw off when I changed into others. That, to him, was the funny way that humans have.

NOSEI:

When I found Hula I saw how Eden was full of waiting. A handful of soil here, after they drained the swamps, was for awhile more complex than probably any planet in the Milky Way. But then it became lifeless, leeched of nutrient. It will take a thousand years to restore it but at least the process has begun, and some of the bird species and the plants that aren't extinct yet will return. It makes the idea of waiting a rich one, especially compared to the wool of space exploration that is pulled over children's eyes today. The nearest stars are so far away we'd need thousands of years just to report back. Who'd be waiting?

But waiting for us here, now, is always a potential encounter with any of millions of Earth species. Especially one coming to be. Where did this diversity start? Maybe a comet from the stars, but anyway the language of life was unspoken until a Garden began on Earth. So for all the studies of words I taught at Yale it was like being in a desert; it was no more than a comet, a dirty snowball, compared to the Garden that followed.

One day it will be seen again, the Garden. The new Adam and Eve are already there, as their Scroll here tells us.

JULIE:

Intellectual stuff is part of the human drive. If you can get it without exploration, fine. I got some from Svitz, and some from Nosei, who reminded me how much I already had from recording the voice that Archie heard. Now there is a new library, with many volumes of genetic code for each species. Texts written by the ecosystem, granting voice to an archive of life. All the panic I acquired from human relationships is calmed in this library: just knowing it is there, as vast as the stars.

I first tasted the calm when I began to walk around New York City. Walks in Chinatown and SoHo were the best, immersed in the faces and canvases of distance. They eroticized me, I eroticized them. I felt independent, taking a bite out of the New York apple. But I was immersed even deeper in my dependence on the museum-like system of New York. I was trapped in a system more complex than other "New Yorkers," because I had entered a paradox: walking for me had become like lying down with my doctor.

And as it was with him, so it became on the streets: the more I let the details in, those in my fantasies, wishes and hates that were with me there on the couch, the further from him I seemed to get. I was in China and he was Chinese; I was in a painting and he was the artist, slipped from sight. In other words, we were close, but separated even farther apart by the details.

Imagine the red-cockaded woodpecker, the endangered species I spoke of before, suddenly unsure. Imagine that it was unsure of how to peck, how big to make the hole, whether the food it brings its nestlings is safe or not, whether it's flying into the hole too forcefully. No longer is the danger outside the woodpecker and its territory; it's in the woodpecker itself.

That's how it became for me. I was the danger, the possible cause of danger. It's important to know that we never see woodpeckers like that. Only humans. I longed to be a creature, even a plant that never had to check, to ask "Do I see what I think I see; do I know what I think I know." Just to know. And to contain that knowing within.

"When will these weird attacks end? When will I stop checking myself?"

"When you can find what you are really looking for," he answered. "Or, when you can mourn what is not there. Both, actually. When you have, you will no longer need to ask or to check."

"I don't think I'll ever get over you," I said suddenly.

"Do you want to?"

"No," I said. "I don't want to."

"Do you think I want to?" he asked quietly.

I couldn't answer. How could I? To answer, I realize now, would have been to find what I had been looking for and to mourn it, too. We both knew there was nothing to answer, knew how the pleasure of gain could be embedded within the pain of loss. We would speak it later. Each detail would be spoken and explored. I would learn that panic was also a way of getting back to the other when there was something wrong between us. In a sense, I created the other's love, and if I didn't keep it alive, how would it live? How would my mother; how would the ecosystem behind us.

This is the history I relived on the couch and it became a part of our history. In it, I found his history. Eventually, he found it, too. You see, the new thing was that he would observe me as well as himself. This was a new thing in my history. Just as hearing Wisdom's voice was for Archie. The ecosystem could speak for itself, and was not just the other, "observing" our lives.

I always rebelled because of mother's harping on it (she seemed to me incapable of seeing herself) but I see now that history before humans is more important than anything we can imagine. Beyond these words and scrolls even. The specific time and place where every event occurs is precious. Each detail. Every organism comes from a particular time and place; you can read it in its character. In human character, we've got a long way to go to read back toward the exact Garden of Eden in which we were evolved. For every species, there's a garden of its own—millions of them. You feel that in this voice of Adam, the one Archie wrote down. Eve and Adam—my mother and Archie—they found that garden. But the personal garden I wanted to reach was a small library. A place for research, for growing. It was Hula, where Nosei was. I knew it as soon as Aviya Nachman said he had been there. I wasn't even thinking of mother.

4

Eve:

So Adam was also betrayed by his senses
sovereignties mirrored by snakes
now we must think, see beyond
in order to pass
what stands in memory
first, reflected love—but no
it was need and not even ours
we were meant to rehearse a leaving
learn two languages, outer
and inner shapes and sounds
so we make our own new world
start: sound is the language of ear
color and shape of all the others
light, touch, taste and smell
as all shape a memory
of my first seeing and unalterable love
for it was me and all I sense was
once untangled
singular—where now I love complexly
all things growing intricate

needing my focus: desire
does it, concentrates one.
Adam, and done, all else blurs
losing the diverse Eden once learned
from angels and demons, now the flowers
and winds. Oh, bag of myrrh
between my breasts, you are him
and in his ear a vineyard in which I blow
small whitish flowers that spoke there
in Eden while I held him
Adam, your eyes were speaking parrots
from your heart, and now the knowledge
of them—birds and eyes entangled—pulls
my mind back to you, as you sat up
and we watched a column of ants
How long have they been here—to multiply
    so high?
you wondered, as they tended the acacia
    tree,
grooming it, warning
away leaf eaters, redirecting
the climbing vines, accepting the tree's
    offering:
sweet ant nectar
Who directs this arm of ants? you asked
What if no one, I responded
as even our longing is purposely undirected
so that we may learn—as the ants learn
from the tree—we, from memory

that branches out like the tree that
taught it—
all a flexible chaos, that allows
the back and forth of remembering
a sweetness encasing what must be forgotten
first seduction, and so we want more
reproducing like night and day
and as trees bend to the changing light
even the ants follow the movement
in a dance with the tree
they multiplied, serving the sugar
in each flower, as I tasted the nectar in
the boughs
of your thighs, sweet
that memory now doubles each moment
until an hour reproduces the column
of diligent ants—as my industry leaves me
empty,
even more hungry for you. Unknown
to you, time is kept by the trees and
grasses
and the ants we saw were taught to tend
them
as we learned to tend by planting seed
to see within each the minute plant
embraced by all the food it needs
to grow, a seedling.

JULIE:

Here we are, the snakes in the Garden: they were us! We were the subtle ones, knowing the inside of things. After we heard the voice of Wisdom at the tree of Knowledge, we walled it up inside. Repressed it. We turned all our subtlety outwards, into spreading over the earth, into wiping out the other Homos, into manipulating everything—especially other people.

Tuned into other people, mother must have been surprised to find she had tuned into a voice that was alien. "Locked in," might be more like it—like to a radio station. She had always been able to listen but now her focus had to be her own desire. Not simply desire for Archie, for he was her patient and that does not sound like mother. Rather, it was a newly unrepressed desire, the one for evolving, that found in Archie an Adam.

How much more complex the world became for her—and she was just at the beginning, in the Garden. All living things tune into a single frequency, life, but that is what the biologists call "tracking," and even the tiniest insect can track its way home. This kind of tracking is what mother used to call attachment. The desire for evolving has to be deeply hidden so these attachments to person and place can be prominent. Desire for an alien voice is hardly normal. Attachment to it—like the voice of Wisdom that Archie first heard in his head—was unheard of. We are so intent on another person that anything disembodied has to frustrate us, like static instead of a station.

So when an alien voice was heard, as it was for Archie,

it had to be so precisely tuned in that all the other stations fell away for him. That is how it must have been. That's the way it would be if our listening devices picked up an alien signal: all that we knew would suddenly become less important, as we locked onto the new voice.

NOSEI:

The ants reminded me of Shuve. Julie had a cat named Shuve, which means return. He was a black cat with a bigger than usual, high-eared head, and golden eyes. Shuve went everywhere with Julie, like a dog people said, on an emerald leash but mostly carried along in a canvas bag, big head sticking out. Perhaps because Julie went out infrequently, it just seemed the cat was always there. He wasn't at the Svitz party, the going-away surprise party where I first met Julie, though he was usually with us afterwards. He seemed to welcome me, which struck me as odd, since cats I had known didn't like their lives disturbed, or at least not at first.

"When I found Shuve in a ditch beside the highway he was on his side, his legs stretched out as in a carefree sleep. We were sure he was dead but he whimpered and lifted his head when I touched him. I carried him to the car like a cracked but still-intact vase. At the vet, the doctor recommended putting him to sleep. I could not do that, especially since Julie might turn up the next day." The good, gray, child psychologist who took over Betti Peleg's office was telling me this over the international phonewire.

I called the office number from New Haven, after I returned in 1984, and after reading of the disappearances in Israel. I didn't know who would answer but I remembered him. I asked when he last saw the Pelegs.

"Shuve was the last contact with them," his voice crackled over the line. "It was so unnerving. I knew how close Julie had been to this animal and here he was, abandoned, perhaps hit by a car while roaming after her. Shuve remained alive for over a week. He even ate a little from a spoon. He turned his head to whichever side of his basket I approached, as if he had so much to tell me. But Shuve was a cat and could tell us nothing of what happened to him or to his master, Julie." In a lifetime of keen observation, this old gentleman was careful to recall significant details, as if Shuve had been a patient.

"The mystery of Julie's disappearance, on top of her mother's apparent suicide and Shechner's earlier disappearance, smelled like a plot. Finding Shuve was a vital clue, but when he died, we had the feeling the clue had disappeared with him, and that Julie or her body might never turn up." When he had finished, I imagined what I would have felt more than a decade ago had I not myself fled the scene. In fact, I was filled with a sense of the bodiless absence just described back then, and I believe I carried the feeling through the years until it drove me to start writing about everything. But here was a palpable body, Shuve's, and had I seen it myself I believe I might never have climbed out of the void.

But when the trunk arrived ten years later, I was

prepared to unlock my own wordlessness, backed up by the same audiographic memory which renders each of the child psychologist's words. Just as Shuve had left something unsaid, all the events surrounding the Scroll and Archibald Shechner did as well. Just as the ants learning from the tree spoke to Eve of memory.

JULIE:

There was a voice there, alright, and perhaps it could be pieced together from all our reactions. Because if it could, then I could also begin to imagine the voice Archie heard at the ecosystem's heart: it had to be an expression of infinitely more pieces in relation, each one a living species. The "arm of ants" reminds me of it here. But it's a small reminder, since it's still a single species.

There was a brief time I worried more about what happened to Shuve than to mother. He was picked up by a friend, but when I called from Switzerland to check she said he disappeared from her balcony. Another disappearance, or abandonment! She asked where I was but I didn't tell and never called again. Now, when I read what Nosei wrote, I have to weep at the spirit of Shuve. He did not know death but he knew isolation, the loss of his home in life. They are the same, death and isolation, which Archie emphasized as the contrast to diversity. Wisdom's creation and the origin of intelligent life. Without diversity, no higher primates—and no small cats, either. But in isolation, evolving takes place. Archie would say: as isolation prepares us for diversity, death does too: it is the afterlife to creation, and where we leave diversity behind. Yet leaving ourselves behind is just what happens in evolving, so for the first time in the modern world we have a new myth or paradigm of dying—a way to feel it as parallel to evolving. And what is the feeling? The first and last desire unrepressed. I can feel it, though I don't die or evolve. It's a feeling shared among all living things, so I know Shuve is in my afterlife—my species memory—as much as any Homo sapiens.

And mother? She's found a living isolation in a wild ecosystem. What does she do there? I can't say. I was speechless to ask such a question. I understood she was hearing another language with Archie, but that they were still free to mix anonymously with humans. Like wild ecosystems that can still create new species, Archie and mother exist as they were before humans began to shut out the voice in our heads. What we call human progress, taming land and animals, made us deaf to diversity—except in our impoverished human creations, in art and culture and technology—and so we always feel an ache when we run into beauty, a certain pain that goes along with the deepest experience of it. The loss is still built-in there.

So Archie Shechner was not the first to hear the voice of Wisdom. Once upon a time, we all did. Now we are called back to it, to evolve. Those who remain human will learn from the new ones eventually, as they return among us unknown, nurturing us—in anonymous roles, maybe, as teachers of children or restoration workers in the field. Maybe reading the DNA of ecosystems, going back into labs anonymously, at low levels, in high schools and industries—or on computers—to discover the orgins of intelligent life—to embark on a journey, eventually, like Adam and Eve—and not to forget their origins among us. To leave us a trail.

Or coming as artists, perhaps. That is what Archie and mother gave to us, Nosei and me: the beauty of the Scroll. Although they call it a restoration, or a remembering of the original lost Scroll, what is the difference between it and a new creation? I can see it brings us back to what translation means: a transformation, an encounter with beauty that is so simple you feel you were there before.

I can even imagine "the fruit of a mother's womb" without reaching for a water bottle. But I once would grow alarmed at the thought of getting pregnant. I might have a heart attack during labor or go crazy in some kind of postpartum state. Having a baby with anyone seemed full of potential conflict.

Ten years ago, Nosei had no choice but to leave. I had to keep my own mother alive—how could I be a mother myself? And I had to keep out the unwanted thoughts of sexual desire—out of place, or so it seemed to me. But the arrival of Archie and the voice disrupted my strategies of keeping things out. There's no reason why we should have to think about how we would like to kill or have sex with our mothers and fathers. Yet sometimes a whirlwind enters and we're forced to. Mine was panic.

Now it's as if I gave birth to new parents. Their faces seem new.

5

Adam:

These arms to hold you
fit perfectly, as these legs
enfold—such joyous
perfection, member in the midst swelling
to enter the vestibule, dew-brushed—
a new morning breaks there, my sister
You are more than mate, my mirror
my measure of joy: beauty
a thing greater than I can recognize
not a thing recalled from the Garden
but holding all in the Garden
and the Garden in one—
in one body, one face.
More than any purpose I could imagine
beauty as beyond me
as the Garden created anew each dawn.

Eve:

Now as we lay in our hut
the winds roused, the demons stirred
began to howl
the creator sent a great whirlwind
we clung to the ground
all was lifted away, the garden lifted
our faces clung to dirt, our hands to rocks
our home was gone and we lived
it was quieter than before
the creatures had scattered, the birds
flown

flowers had sent their seed beyond seeing
we wandered, wandered
here and there we scratched roots to eat
until we came to a forest
then I heard in a dream
Wisdom's voice: Here,
I am where I am
she had entered the world
supplanted the tree we ate from
all we had known became hidden
but we closed our eyes and found her
mother of wisdom
to provide all we know
as the plants had taught us in the Garden
we would tend for our lives
fill up the land with others and our thoughts
where angelic nature had been
struggling to listen with mistaking ears
 to plants of the field and forest
through a forest of noise
sow cities, reap the sweat
of our brow and lie down
producing the fruit of a mother's womb
each Adam each Eve a maker of space
room for the garden in memory: the work
of naming shared again, become
a fight to speak straight.

JULIE:

To evolve out of human beings shouldn't be confused with science fiction, or even cloning or supernatural things. It's natural discovery, and now I know why. We're afraid to become obsolete. If a brand of dish detergent evolves, it makes the older version obsolete. But when new species of living things evolve, the older species don't have to become irrelevant. Alligators still live in our world, not to mention nematodes. Surviving ten times longer than we have. So it would be wrong to consider them obsolete.

And why isn't it something uplifting when you think of the alligator's intestines? Maybe because on any given day some kind of supernatural event or magic wish threatens to make the past obsolete, while evolution never can. Evolution brings the past along with it but it allows us the freedom to examine and explore the natural world—miracles just stun you, so you might as well be a couch potato. The freedom to explore is all we're free to do and more than enough. In the process of exploring we can face the unknown. We can become it. We don't have to close our eyes, as with wishes. As I closed my eyes while an infant at the breast, too sure that I created the breast that gave me milk—before I'd even begun to explore.

We don't have to go far to learn about letting go, either. There's sexual ecstasy, for instance, and it tells you maybe it's ok to leave your Garden and to explore new ones. Because sex is a constant in the real world.

But some of us will have more to learn about letting go than others. Panic is a letting go turned inside-out. When

I got it turned back the right way, I felt like an endangered species, as if I had come to the point of discovering how I was made and how the world was made and it had dropped me. With no home left. There was just this terrible beauty, this preciousness of the rare, that I held onto. Except that now I could put other faces on it.

Nosei:

Here it was, long after the Scroll was written, now to reappear in Solomon's day, in the Bible's Song of Solomon: the navel.

"THE JOINTS OF THY THIGHS ARE LIKE JEWELS, THE WORK OF THE HANDS OF A CUNNING WORKMAN.

THY NAVEL IS LIKE A ROUND GOBLET, WHICH WANTETH NOT LIQUOR: THY BELLY IS LIKE AN HEAP OF WHEAT SET ABOUT WITH LILIES."

The navel is to drink from—yes, that we know now, to drink from with our ears. That is what we learned. Supernaturalists deny it; to them, the body is a limitation, and they want to break free. For a sober human, however, knowledge of the navel could become engrossing as a novel—and yet not be fiction. Memory is let go of, and the present turns out to read like history. Fiction can become history as well, as it was in the creation myths. What was fiction then, anyway, but the unknown? The first human duty was to imagine it, this unknown world, as in the story of Adam and Eve.

By the time of the *Scroll of the History of Adam*, the

memory of evolving was lost. It was kept in a reflection, an imagined memory of life outside the Garden, and so it was kept in a reflection of loss. In the *Scroll* Archie first learned that Adam and Eve were preparing to accept the loss of memory, and with it came a forgetting of life in the Garden, of everything about their prior history. What loss, we asked ourselves? We didn't know we had really lost Eden before there was any story of it. Archie was the first to know.

So Archie and Betti had to make the scroll their own scroll, and to leave us a record of not just what was past—but what is to come. We had to put it all in a book, so it's clearly not supernatural. Instead, it's history. A history that goes back to the navel and turns it inside out: into a novel, telling the unknown history.

How to listen to a tree. Listen in the way *it* listens: a photographic memory for the elements of earth, air, light and water. My memory was good for languages but I always thought there had to be something to challenge it one day, and here it is, a listening beyond all that's become lost to us, back to prehistory and lost innocence, wrapped in the web of the ecosystem, a Garden of Eden. My audiographic memory retains it. It's a mutation I had thought too freakish before.

What I heard first was a story, told by Archie, of how the cities of our time will slowly crumble, until they resemble Mayan ruins in the jungles of Yucatan today. What survives of the human species will have left the planet to colonize space, but that is a return to the ice age, living in the primitive condition of space stations— harsh places in hostile systems.

The newest primate species, meanwhile, avoids contact with Homo sapiens but indirectly wants to help us evolve in knowledge. Aliens, then, come not from without—not from other countries or other planets—but from within. It's a revelation, in its way, about the repressed desire to evolve.

The trouble with human-centered progress is that it is tone deaf; it has forgotten all about evolving. When the new century reveals the biosphere as an answer to our spiritual longings, the wish to return to Eden will become manifest. And real: Eden will be found again, as if Earth were a new planet. The new species is a teacher and restorer.

Size and space are irrelevant. Primitive bacteria evolved in the stomach of the alligator with the alligator itself. For us, the ecosystem is our alligator, and sitting within it we can listen through its ears to the web in which it is also hidden and enfolded.

But is it mad to listen to the Earth—and through a tree beneath the ground? Is getting closer to it against the grain of all those who want to get higher and think they must evolve only in their minds? Archie and Betti have answered: better to become anonymous than to lose your body.

6

Adam:

```
Now all must be learned by mistake
listen to the birds to fly
on song to the garden
a memorized moment and climb
back again, remembering
```

```
the price for our bodies is death
all the angels and demons would gladly pay
souls plentiful in heaven
here we build a house
to share our mistakes in secret
to share our bodies free from mistaking
an intimate shelter free from the light
to not tell giving from getting—the same
confusion as was in the garden, here we
    name love
love is stronger than death
returning to the angels
we are lost in each other, disembodied
the flowers speak to us
even the snakes who taught us
seduction by thought, protection
against error: we see clearly in the mirror
ourselves, reproduced, models
we create again as seductive words
milk of intelligence
learnt at the breast of trees.
```

JULIE:

What an invitation to intimacy: "to share our mistakes in secret." Learn from mistakes, listen to what's overlooked—that's just part of what this passage suggests. Mistakes are mutations, and once seen and understood, they become new landmarks. People go through life looking for landmarks instead of making them, mother said—instead of making a connection to the ecosystem as an extension of your own body. When people visit a new place they want the best "view". That is going backward, because those new views are all a reaching back for something lost, as in the magical views of childhood. Instead of looking, listen, said mother. Otherwise you carry around a silent burden.

Once I had thought my mother was in my way, smothering me at every turn. The only way I could rebel was to disappoint her, to be a recluse, a non-prodigy. Yes, she still managed to use me as her secretary, her transcriber, but by then she herself had joined my side, becoming an outcast with Archie, and I felt I was becoming part of a new culture. This was reinforced in the relationship with Nosei.

Then she appeared to die and I felt betrayed all over again. She left me with nowhere to turn, completely isolated, with nothing but piles of notes and papers. It was like being suffocated—murdered—by your parents. Again. And then, the reunion by voice on the telephone. Not only is she alive but she is no longer my parent—in a way, I am hers. I am her threat, too: as the revelation will make plain, the parent species were killed by the new Homo sapiens, and now the new species is a threat to be killed because of human fear of aliens, of the past coming back to haunt us.

All my life had been a struggle to free myself—but I didn't really know from what. I just thought it was my mother. How would I have known it was actually the burden of a repressed desire to evolve? Right down at the root of breathing. How do we breathe? At one with the ecosystem, as the voice of Wisdom reveals. I never thought about the "ecosystem services" by which we were created and live, the nonhuman organisms who cleanse the water, turn soil into a fertile living cover, and manufacture the air we breathe. All these creatures are ignored in creation stories! Now we know that thousands of species can be lost in an acre of destroyed Rain Forest—and human beings couldn't begin to reconstruct even one palm.

Ok, yes, we can restore conditions to let the ecosystem heal itself, though where is the library in which to read the original conditions? Many years, many generations have to pass—but at least there's satisfaction in knowing the future can be richer. Right now, though, we still have the words, words that were there in the Garden, in the plants that gave us breath. Words we seduce our little Adam and Eve children with, charming snakes that we are. Death, our inevitable predator, still can't take from us the love that's buried within, love for the Garden, and her voice.

Some will hear the voice. First, however, comes the anxiety and panic, the not-wanting to hear. So much of that not-wanting comes from the awful things suffered in childhood. This was drilled into me as my mother's daughter (which was supposed to make me exempt). Most people don't have psychologists for parents so they're unvaccinated, except now there's a new vaccine: species awareness. When human relationships are put into perspective among other species they start to lose their hold.

Nosei's voice is enough. The unknown is our Garden, the mistakes we make our perfect angels—each, another reflection of the diversity of the living. Not the dull sameness of the dead. The trees are ours again, part of our bodies. Our bodies are ours again.

NOSEI:

It's no longer just a choice between living in the past (through memory) and living in the present, unreflectively. There's a third way; you could call it living in the future, where the present and past are tied to the body of what is to come. Anyone for whom the future is written revelation knows it.

We hardly have an idea of the future anymore other than the myth of celebrity. Archie was becoming one, along with the Scroll: celebrities both. Social freedoms can keep battling, but is that enough to hold us? Will "animal rights" be more than a dead end? Because otherwise, we'll never get to "vegetable rights" at all. That is exactly what Wisdom describes: the right of the ecosystem to support evolving, and at the base of a visible ecosystem are plants.

With a future of evolving in front of us, we're free to make new, scientific myths, to give the web of life a "hearing" that is like Archie's. If there's a web, who made it? Something deep down buried in us knows the answer because it actually heard the voice, once, in our buried Eden.

So this last fragment of the *Scroll* has ended with Adam and Eve outside of the Garden. They've turned from evolving toward forming a memory. Accepting their loss. They are coming closer to us, though still at home in their world.

But they're replacing their losses with stories—and these instantly become our myth. Part of themselves, however, has already been deeply buried: their desire to evolve and return to Eden. They begin to feel it in isolated moments—moments of doubt and moments of anxiety. Still a long way from the panic that took hold of Julie and that sent me into retreat.

Talk about isolation! Even before, it's as if I had been swimming all my life underwater. There was much to do and struggle with, times of enjoyment and beauty, but also the impression that the study of language among humans was only barely relevant to the great sea I was submerged in. The feeling that in that limitless environment were great stretches of loneliness.

Metaphysics, religion, poetry—all of it built on such yearning to be elsewhere, and to be able to return to the realm we inhabit, the realm of the underwater sea, as a visitor, and not be tied to it. To be able to observe it, calmly, objectively, and say, "There is where I came from."

All that changed by Archibald Shechner finding the Scroll: words that pointed beyond, a voice. And now, in Archie and Betti's new Scroll, the record of another world, another environment. It is as if they were never involved with death, as if we might meet them again, only they would be transformed, visitors only, coming from another realm. And then they were here and we understood: they had passed through the water into a world of air, another boundless circumstance. From there, the stars also twinkled, as they do from underwater, only more brightly, more clearly beckoning. They had begun to evolve, so when Betti came to Hula and found Archie it was as if she had burst through the surface of water to see for the first time. In all her previous life, the right man never appeared. But here, suddenly, in the first instant, there he was—and he was something other, more than a man. It was like the creation of Eve: she opened her eyes and found herself beside her mate. It was right, and it was not heaven.

Chapter 16

Chapter 16

1995

It was the Day of Atonement, a hot September day in Tel Aviv, when I dragged myself toward my mother's old office. Where else would I go to feel human connection on such a day, when the synogogues were filled with men in white kittels—symbolic burial shrouds—and the women repressed behind screens. The human border with the Creator was sanctified but the creative power of the ecosystem repressed. And where was Wisdom? Others took the day off, a beach day alongside the tourist hotels, but they had no thought of her voice or the fate of nonhuman life. The voice they heard was that of the tape player (Israel radio was shut down this one day of the year).

I asked the woman in the flat if I might sit in the office awhile, since her husband, the child psychologist who now used it was not there today. The woman had heard plenty about my mother from her husband and she remembered me from my earlier visit. I did not ask where her husband was; I did not really want to see him and hear more about the past. I doubted he was in synagogue. He was no more religious than my mother, I remembered, unless he changed, as some older people do.

I sat at the desk where I had worked so many hours transcribing Archie's tapes. There was an eerie similarity to those late nights of work after mother's office hours, when the phone stopped ringing and the windows on the cul-de-sac were empty of traffic. And then, almost as before—though then, it was I who had thought anxiously about calling Aviya Nachman for many days—the telephone rang and it was mother. "I sensed that you would be there," she said to my silent surprise. "Don't be too surprised. I didn't want to call you at a place where others might be around. Besides, this is an appropriate number."

In Israel, when you left a telephone behind, the number remained the same. Mother was calling home, since that was her last address. "Where are you?" I blurted out.

"Never mind. I will not be here long. Please don't hunt for me, Julie. I am not the same; only my voice remains similar. I am just another old person doing volunteer work in the restoration offices. My old self is dead, just as your mother is—to the rest of the world. Only it is more than a self that is gone. I call you because Aviya told me that you had made a step in our direction and so will understand how important our anonymity must be."

I was still silent, dumbstruck, or else I didn't know how to speak to this woman who was no longer my mother. "Do you miss your mother, Julie?" she continued, honoring my reticence. "I do not miss my daughter so much when I feel at one with her through our bond with Wisdom. It is like the devout feel in the synagogue today when they say the Shema: "The Lord is One."

It was not like mother to quote the Bible or even to refer to religion reverently. "'Miss' is not the right word anymore. I don't think about you in past memories as much but more in worrying what will happen—if there is room in the world for you. For me, too, because Nosei and I have come together again and we're both feeling new things."

"After all these years you met Nosei again," she said, as if editing a story.

"Mother—should I still call you that?—Nosei and I have put together a book, did he tell you?"

"No, not a word."

"All the transcriptions I did of Archie's sessions—they're in it, along with my own sessions. I kind of broke down after you disappeared. I was mourning your death but not really mourning. I didn't know how to. I learned, but just now I was thinking about calling Aviya back—I was even wanting to call my doctor."

"Maybe you wanted to call me, and you couldn't," she observed.

"You sound like him when you say that. I changed, I found more room for myself, but now I feel this room we created in the world is endangered. That our kind of change is dangerous."

"I cannot help you with the danger you feel, which is still psychic," my mother replied evenly, no hint of the questioning way she used to have. "You are caught somewhere in-between. I am already there, wholly of the world. There isn't much time. Tell me more about this book you have written."

"Nosei made a book of everything with Archie but the publisher didn't believe it. I got it back, and when I added my sessions it began to seem alive again. My panic was not any different than so many people experience... To stop it,

I had to keep asking: What was I feeling when the attack began?"

"So, yes," mother (but what will I call her now?) said calmly. "You were going back to origins. But you see, you could never get beyond the event, to the first, hidden event. That was the fear and repression of the memory of having evolved."

"No, I thought I was trying to get a picture, a sense of context. It wasn't the origin that I was after but the whole picture." Was I still struggling with my mother the analyst, or were we working together?

"Yes, so you could contain it, give it a closure. Right? Close it up and put it away. Yet it remains hidden away in the closet."

"Amazing. Containment was one of the big subjects with my doctor. The very thing that made it hard for me to contain myself was what made it possible for me to contain and make contact with others. But I was too permeable. My skin depended too much on others and how good their skin was. My habitat, to stretch it, was the other's face. Until now, I didn't see how the two of you were alike. But you're not like that now, are you? How do you think now?"

"We—your doctor and I—would probably agree to call your efforts an attempt to frame your problem, to give it a context. To enclose it in a net or immoblize it in a web. Now, I think first of the web and its builder. Where is the spider in all this? She sits on the margin, thinking about her web, because she knows that it is not her whole context at all; instead, the ecosystem that provides the branches that her web is tied to—that is her context. Can she see the trees whose branches they are? Or can this aerial artist have knowledge of the soil in which the tree is rooted? Even more to the point: Can she know of the flower pollinators and fruit-eating animals that the tree entices in order to scatter its seeds far away—in order, that is, to survive? In the same way, everything you know is part of the context of your knowing, yet there is much more you know that is hidden.

"Once I would have said that Freud uncovered this hidden land. Now I can see there is much more beneath the unconscious mind: there is the desire to evolve that connects us to all living things and the beginning of time. This new seeing is not part of the human context."

"But can it ever be?"

"This is no longer a question I can consider, since I have left humanity behind. You can see, can't you, that if I began to argue this way with human culture, I would be attacked—and be drawn into a limiting cycle of defense. Attack and defend. That erotic bond has fallen away, just as it begins to, for you. The navel is the beginning."

"But there is still the erotic bond for Nosei and me. Is it different for you? Has your body evolved?"

"Of course—in a way. But it is only the beginning of a mutation, not even the mutation itself, since we were born human. We are too old for children, but if Nosei and you continue growing toward us, perhaps the mutation will show up in your offspring, or in other generations. Julie, I cannot continue to answer your questions. It burdens me, for I am no longer the mother to you. Wisdom is. There is much I have to tell you about the revelation that will allow you to find the answers in her."

How long could this conversation go on if there was still much to tell? My ear glued to the telephone was burning. I was split between wanting to hear everything she had to say and needing my own doctor on the other end of the line. The sun beaming through the windows became that other sun that had nearly killed me back in New York. Black. The inside of my chest cavity felt like it was collapsing into it. I held onto the receiver more tightly and gave her what was left of my hearing. "I've waited for you to tell me about the revelation, mother. I sensed there was something behind the new Scroll."

"It is behind the old Scroll, in truth. It is the reason Archie buried it again. It knocked him speechless."

"Buried it again?"

"Yes. When Archie deciphered this part, and realized that the media would blast this around the globe, he saw that human history would be changed forever, for the worse. Knowing the evil their consciences are based upon, humans would never find the faith to return to the scene of their crime: any creative ecosystem in which species continue to evolve."

"Crime? Archie never spoke of a crime..."

"Exactly. It made him speechless. His words would have been incoherent if it wasn't that he found Wisdom's voice instead."

"What crime?"

"We murdered our parents—our parent species, and Neanderthals too, as well as other hominids still alive when Homo sapiens evolved. Not just individuals. Not just genocide. We murdered them into extinction. And then we covered up the crime. We don't remember it. But those who wrote the Scroll that Archie found still remembered. The truth was there."

"Why? Did the Scroll say why?" I wanted to ask these questions but it took all my strength. My reasons were different from mother's. I felt like I was back at the start of the novel we had written. Feelings of my skin coming off, pulling apart. A grief equivalent to a star collapsing. And I was here in the middle of Israel and he was there. Phone calls were so expensive. Old thoughts: I thought I would have you if all else fell away, but you belong to someone else, someplace else. I don't think I can keep trying anymore. Memories of an old session with him.

"Julie! Are you listening?"

"Yes, I am. I'm sorry. I was feeling some anxiety. Go on. Why did we murder? Was there any explanation in the Scroll?"

"Yes. We had left our original ecosystem and adapted to others. We saw no end to our frontier because we could take our own with us, anywhere. Instead of pioneering a niche in a new ecosystem, we destroyed ecosystems and the competing species within them. Just as the American wild earth was flattened by farmland and streets, Homo Habilis, a species still at home in its original ecosystem, was wiped out. By comparison, Americans didn't completely wipe out the native people of America, but they were our species, after all. Although the whole earth called them savages, the Indians could learn to read and write any language. Yet why did we have to obliterate their cultures? Because they were closer to remembering the past.

Such a people were the early Habiru in the Near East, whose primitive writing created the story of Eden and recalled the evil violence there. Later, the story was translated, first into cuneiform writing and then into the archaic Hebrew of the Scroll. But it went no further. Instead, it was changed into the Garden of Eden story which the poet of Genesis told."

"Wow, ow, ow... Remember, I used to say that as a kid?—but it's been a long time. Still, Archie must have always suspected this. I mean, he's an archaeologist, it's always been one theory about our species. Why did it shock him?"

"Yes, I remember your language as a child, Julie," she answered, as if that was the more important question. "It's hard to answer your question about shock because you're still defended against it, still part of the repressed memory. I am not, and your anxiety makes perfect sense because you're speaking to your dead mother. You may think you killed her in some way or else can somehow keep her alive. These constructions—I am no longer part of them, even to analyze like a doctor. They are fantasies to shield you from painful certainties."

My anxiety did not lessen one bit, because it was true, I needed it, as she said. Yet I had more room to speak differently. "Archie was shocked by an uncertainty made real," I simply said.

"Yes," she answered, "but more than that. First, it was fear that he would be tarred with the news, but then he realized what would happen when the media got hold of it. He was afraid for the future of the species when these murders had to be faced. He was sure the human species would sweep aside religions in despair and turn in a kind of madness on the nonhuman species in retribution, repeating the old hatred of origins. This was the madness he preferred that he alone be accused of. He took the humiliation on himself for creating a hoax of a Scroll, and then he buried it himself. He panicked.

"Another way to put it was that he fell into a radical depression. A common trait of depression in men is withdrawal into isolation, a pulling away from relationships, intimacy, from life itself. We might say he fell into a hole and came back with a voice not his own."

"The hole in the earth was a hole in himself?" I whispered, grasping for the meaning. "Is that that the hole Nosei and I feel attracted to—the covered hole we share in each other, the navel?" I felt I was working on the novel again, trying to make sense of it all.

"Yes. It is the hole in you that once was your connection to a mothering ecosystem. I wasn't sure how to tell it for you, but now you will understand that it was the same for Archie. In his first session with me he described the voice as coming through his navel. You remember I transcribed that first session myself. I was so worried about how mad he would seem to others that I left the navel out of the notes. Without it, the voice was understandable as an intellectual displacement, a projection onto the site of his breakdown, the dig. A site of isolation."

"But why do we crave it, isolation? Are we in some kind of depression also?"

"Far from it. This is our cradle and you are feeling the first instincts for it."

"Then where are you, mother? Where can we be safe?"

"With the people closest to the ecosystem, Julie. In anonymity. With the restorationists, or with the indigenous people: some others are already travelling with the Bedouins in the Negev desert. You and Nosei, for instance, might find it best to find a place for yourselves on a remote Indian reservation in America, like the one in the Florida Everglades, not far from a wetlands restoration site that is related to Hula. Eventually, those reservations may become birthplaces for the new species."

"So it's still fear of human beings that makes you want to hide?"

"Oh no. There's love for the solitary; returning to the mind, yet unobstructed by the masking fears and wishes of human nature, human culture. Remember, all species have a disguise; their colors and markings, even their thoughts and the chemical communications in plants are disguised, so humans seem no more special as a species than ants. It's the buried disguises I encounter now, the spiritual ones that can see through social roles and hear the tree of Knowledge. Trees are the most successful species, even more than ants and certainly more than humans. They are everywhere, adapting to every climate. To stand before one is to contemplate the success of life both outside and inside the Garden."

"But they're cut down and turned into paper, they have no defense."

"No? Look at the Garden of Eden story again: planted at the center are the trees. They give back more than they take—taking only light, air, water, earth. Yet they produced our prehistory, the air, food and shelter that supplied the pre-human species as well as our own. Paper for Bibles, you say? Even the first clothes—fig leaves—were gifts from trees. Among the bright lights of their leaves and fruits, we were among the sheltered animals, among birds, mammals, insects, snakes, until we climbed down from them, trading some of our fruits and nuts for meat. Without trees: no elephants, no squirrels, no butterflies—and nothing, like ourselves, in between. How right the chimpanzee looks in the tree, poised there as if for takeoff, like owl or bat. Just so, Adam and Eve came down from the tree of Knowledge to taste the fruit of slaughtered meat. It was the beginning of our knowledge of death—and our taste for it."

"Don't all living things know death?" I asked. "Weren't there big sabre-tooth cats, for instance, to eat the early people, and other predators?" I felt dumb asking these questions, but I was still in a fog about it, about death, especially since the mother with whom I was speaking was living in another life.

"In place of individuals, Death itself would become our

certain predator, hunting each and every one of us down—as we became more and more aware of him. Our language growing more abstract, complicated—removed from the bright notes of the tropical tree's fruit. There it is in Genesis: 'Eat and death touches you.' For Archie and I, the voice of Wisdom is the tree of Knowledge as well as the voice of the creative ecosystem. It speaks a new language in our heads, one that wipes out death as a devourer of bodies."

I was getting very hungry, in fact, very thirsty. "I remember two trees. Shouldn't we stop for awhile and talk another time?"

"I don't know when that will be. Today is the day of the fast. You will feel better to ignore your hunger and take it all in now. It seems as if there is only one tree, and that is why many people confuse the tree of Life with the tree of Knowledge. While the tree of Life stands for the creator himself, the tree of Knowledge is in fact Wisdom, who represents the creation of life on earth through the plants and ecosystems.

"Now, when Adam and Eve left the garden it was their own decision. They intended to look for other gardens. To leave the garden, however, was to leave behind the memory of our own role as the snake—and to later repress the murder of our parental species. We killed them with our subtle language, and sometimes we ate their meat, these sweet-tasting apes—and as we did, we were separated from our natural place in the ecosystem, spreading all over the earth. You are about to be opened up to evolving again, to Wisdom's voice, and to become part of her body again, which is Eden on Earth. Other images in the Bible story should now achieve a new clarity."

"Oh yes, Nosei and I have already gone back to read Genesis. We revised but we can't see what it means, yet. How it changes the future."

"Listen: Outside of the Garden, Cain, the farmer, survived instead of Abel, the hunter and gatherer. The murder of Abel reiterated the violence in Eden, in just the way civilization developed: from hunting to farming and cities. As Cain went on to found the first city, Ir, he was marked by a sign of guilt, by something repressed. Now look: after the twentieth century has centered on urban life, the next century will be a moving out from cities again, to tend and restore the diversity of the natural world.

"All this is explained for you by Wisdom's voice, even to the story of the Burning Bush. Why did the voice of the Creator come from a bush, a plant, and why does it speak of a 'land of milk and honey?' From biblical Eden you may move again, at this millenium, into a restored, creative ecosystem. The human species confronts a completely different form of higher life, the species that evolves next.

"Only when we understood we were changing did revelation arrive. By becoming a new species we would return as the fictive dead parents—but in a new drama. The family drama had matured into a species drama. Archie could now face the psychic fact that became real because of the Scroll: that the wish to kill our parents *was real*.

"As humans, our parents were the others, the Homo genus from which Homo sapiens evolved, and whom we seem to have been capable of murdering! That is the human fear of aliens: that they will murder you. That is the basis of the anxiety which both Archie and you, Julie, knew: fear of murder, and its origin in the deep repression of the desire to evolve. But restoration of endangered ecosystems is an atonement for the repression of nature and the past. These creative ecosystems will reach other planets, too, since you will carry not just yourselves out into space but also your original ecosystems with you. Meanwhile, the new species will restore the Earth. The plants and trees will speak to us again in fruit and other delicacies."

"But how does it happen," I insisted.

"You mean, how does one let it happen. And you don't even mean that, Julie. You want me to take away the risk, the uncertainty. You will have to work through it your own way, however, for better or worse. You must have learned that from your analysis. You cannot think it or feel it. You must work through it. You have Nosei; I have Archie. And it's time for me to stop and return to my work. We must say goodbye now. Remember, the best revenge is living well."

"Revenge, mother?"

"It is something Archie used to say to me upon parting, in the beginning, when I was still trying to 'save' him from the voice. I didn't know it but it spoke to my past and my future. I think you will discover its meaning just as I did. I will wait for the book, Julie. Only you could have done it."

"You're forgetting Nosei," I interjected.

"I choose to remember you at this moment," she quickly replied. And she was gone. Dial tone.

I felt weak and lightheaded. It had been too long since I'd eaten. I became conscious of my heart beating hard and a growing panic. I began to speak to the walls: "A person can go a long time without eating." Except it was never really my body, but my mind. I knew that, but the panic felt so strong I was losing confidence in that knowledge. I walked into the efficiency to search for some food. Melba toast and milk. I ate it like my life depended on it. I wanted to leave but it was too hot outside to walk. I retreated to the desk and chair. I sat down and held the phone against my chest. I recalled I used to sleep with phones, the only way I felt safe about going to sleep. I was glad the phones worked on Yom Kippur. It was my kind of miracle. I knew what I was going to do, but it was so obvious.

[Julie]

Hoax: Protecting the Inner Ear

I was called to be the first witness to the Scroll: a philologist who could verify its authenticity. I never saw it, except for a few fragments transcribed by Archibald Shechner that I did not know how to judge. The whole business frightened me, especially after the media frenzy. I was never a person who liked the limelight, especially not in connection with a document that may have been a hoax.

Even when I had understood what happened to Shechner, I could not face a situation in which I would have been ridiculed. Anyhow, I wasn't sure who was or wasn't mad, at that point. I retreated into a shell, returning to my obscure position in philology at an Ivy League university.

One day, however, my life in the closet exploded. A trunk burst open with a wealth of transcribed sessions with Shechner that were impossible not to believe. They could not be discounted as a literary hoax this time: I was there, and I knew that neither Betti Peleg nor her daughter, Julie, was capable of such a thing. From a scholar of words I became an instrument of voices. When I left the manuscript behind to be published, I thought a voice of Wisdom from the Garden of Eden—reported and interpreted by respected scholars—would be revelation enough. I wanted to get away from the spotlight I was sure would be trained on me. I did not suspect that the media was jaded, and that the book's publisher would drop it altogether.

My love of anonymity finally paid off when I came back to the Hula backwater where the Scroll was first found. I discovered that *isolation* was the key to evolving, and that it was working in the persons of Archie and Betti. Once you change, a mutation can form to fit a newly revealed and isolated niche. Such a creative niche was the Hula restoration. I came to see it as a freeing isolation. The story of life itself—the freedom of earth and air, water and light—was contained there. While the old isolation in my college town had walled me in, fortressed me with the overheated knowledge Harriman Svitz might revel in, this hidden site allowed an unburdening of knowledge. The road opened up, all the way toward Eden.

And there I finally encountered my first Eden revelation: where the Garden is, and why we left it of our own free will. But it's one thing to understand it from words and books, and another to grasp the emotional truth. It was as if Wisdom always arranged it that a mate—myself—would return soon after the first one—Julie. As if Wisdom created me like an "Eve" for Julie's Adam. She was drawn to her mother; I was in search of an existence I had grown to believe was real, as if Shechner had been my absent father.

Here's how Wisdom arranged it: Since we had grown inured to the goals of fame and fortune, our natural inclination to hide—or to discover secrets—brought us to the very spot where evolving might still continue. This time, instead of transcribers or interpreters, we were simply listeners, our ears opened at last. Only in the arms of Julie, however, did I realize how this desire to evolve might rise to consciousness again, as our ears craved each other's navel. It was a desire to get all the way inside, past even the sense that we might trade places. Rather, I felt like we were both interpenetrated with the elements of life—earth, air, water, light—like a tree. We were not so much bounded by bodies or inside each other but inside of a living system that included the stars. The tree represents it best, creating from those elements more life.

As we ate from our own tree we let go of being merely human. It was a repressed immortality that seemed to burst out from inside, in the form of reaching out to touch the stars. I lost all sense of who I was or even how to talk. Instead, listening became everything. To hear. And in the perfect desire of that hearing, a voice did come. I can't say I can make it out the way that Archibald Shechner did.

Sometimes it is like a small scream to me, like the earth

itself is dying, like nightfall is her spilling black blood that won't be lifted again from dust. This is the fear of human origins I've learned, the snake form with arms and legs in which we were entranced by our own subtlety and created a murderous past. It unconsciously continues in the banality of destroying forests today, since we thought ourselves superior to the tree of Knowledge. We have become the parent species we ourselves killed, so is it our turn to die? This fear, then, can also wake you out of the snake's trance: instead of hiding from it, I realize the voice is liberating, drawing me toward a site of restoration, a garden of creative isolation. Instead of causing anxiety, can our parents become our saviors in their old age as they never were in our childhood? Not our "ordinary" parents, of course, but our rediscovery of Adam and Eve, parents of a new species.

How precious this isolation, leaving memory and identity behind to move so purely through time that it is exploration. Exploring a new world that had lain unconscious in us. Not intellectual but tactile, as in a huge swoop of cranes in the sky that rocks you in your boots. Here is what I learned: Since so many ecosystems are degraded—either domesticated or managed now—it is the voice in the heads of a new species that is truly wild. Wildness returns to us, so that like other wild animals and plants, we think not *about* the world but *with* it: the ecosystem is like our brain, so that we have less need of our own little swollen one.

Now that we can read fossils and DNA, prehistory tells us how each species has an origin so particular—so *historic*, in the biblical sense—in the web of natural events that after the entire universe of stars is mapped we will still not know how to locate such an origin on Earth. The brain of our species will just not be up to it. Except—and the exception is what we can know now—except if we let go of it and listen wildly. This is a step toward evolving, freeing the repressed desire to evolve. To listen wildly is also to let be. We did not evolve by our own power but rather the creative power of natural events.

The Creator set down this power, but who set the events in motion—who set them free? It was Wisdom, Archie repeats; Wisdom, Betti emphasizes, who endowed them with sexuality. Wisdom made them reflect the image of her marriage to the Creator, and so she eclipsed his desire to keep it all at one with himself. Svitz was like that. He had stopped listening, withdrawn from the world. When I encountered him the last time I saw clearly it was a confrontation with loss. He was a man who had lost his *hearing*, though his ears were fine. Without Wisdom he could not truly listen to anybody, as if he was speaking to ghosts. A ghost is a tragic, human thing, a reduction of spirit into a pale speaker without wisdom.

Svitz never could take advice—which once made me comfortable beside him, since I was reluctant to be the bearer of bad news. Archie, on the other hand, when he heard the advice of Wisdom's voice, began an epic struggle to embody that voice. I was freed of reluctance by Wisdom's voice too, as I composed Archie's sessions and notes. Wisdom wants us to explore what is most alive, what is non-human. If we can approach a natural ecosystem while aware of our desires—instead of projecting them onto other people—her advice tells us we can continue to grow. We can begin to evolve, again.

[Nosei]

The Story of Wisdom and Her Creator

They do not look so different when they begin to evolve. Their desire is different. They feel a commanding attraction that is not located in the human erogenous zones, that begins in the ears, a desire to hear Wisdom's voice, followed by desire to go where she is most present. Where?—in a wild diversity, isolated somewhere, because cities have become real estate overrun by one species. You can walk for miles in a city, you can drive around it, but in the end you will have seen only one species, with a motley of pets and ornamental trees. Driving out from the cities and their subcities into farmland, the impoverishment is overwhelming, fields sown with monospecies, pastures feeding a handful of domesticated animal species. And the rare plot left alone is choked with exotics, "weeds" which can't support a creative ecosystem. Instead of creating species, these abandoned areas resemble lawn-choked parks—albeit ghost parks.

How far does one need to drive to reach pristine ecosystems? To the preserved remnants? Or, to what is suddenly new in our time: the experimental areas. The places where ideas are tested of how to restore what is lost. These places are not on any map. They are known only to the workers themselves, because the most crucial condition is that they be isolated from human intervention. Anywhere else you find yourself outdoors, just look around. Can you imagine any new species evolving there? Of course not. Now look at any of the plants or trees—could they have evolved in that spot? Possibly, but not in a landscape that resembles our present, impoverished one.

A lost ecosystem is the human home, and that's why the new cosmology will come from ecology. That is why the work of Betti Peleg is special. It will take a long time to be understood. First, the human race has to exhaust all its playthings—genetics and such. It still thinks it can govern its own evolution, if not in the mind than with future technology. It might not be until the end of the next century that it faces up to reality—and, by that time, there should be a few more of the next species around to help. Meanwhile, the playthings of solar energy, genetics, and computers make up the trinity of future hopes for humans. What futile hope! It comes from resistance to evolving, and for some it even leads to new, irrational faiths that transcend sex and the body. But even angels have been a sign of sexual emasculation, a wish to exchange genitals for wings! What did Freud say about human dreams of flying? "Wings are a masturbatory dream."

What a paltry desire: to get free of earthbound habitat instead of evolving! Most people still don't know the difference between habitat and a creative ecosystem; even universities, from departments of the environment to departments of religion, just don't get it. Newspapers still confuse the two. Habitat for animals these days—especially Homo sapiens—is usually a degraded ecosystem that cannot evolve a diversity of life. It's sexually degraded. It can't even reproduce itself—hemmed in, encroached upon. And what humans are to a healthy ecosystem is a monospecies of wildly reproducing weed. That's why it's so important to get away from human habitats!

Archie was the first to hear this. Although he was digging in a forgotten human habitat, the voice he heard breaking through it had been kept alive by ancient humans in their creation scroll. So what happened when this civilization died? Betti asked me to fill in some history, since I am a natural scientist. And that should make the story of Wisdom and her Creator easier to understand.

Once farming and livestock spread, humans diminished the local ecosystem everywhere they went, it was lost, or buried under cleared land. Could it all have been some natural design, however? Some kind of progress? In other words, was the evolution of Homo sapiens planned by the shaping of ecosystems in which we evolved? The answer is embedded within us: the desire to evolve is still there, and that means adding to a lost diversity. We've always known that, too, because the myth in which it was encoded is the story of the Creator and his consort, Wisdom. We should have known it if we didn't.

Wisdom, hidden in the ecosystem, shaped our evolution so that the desire to evolve within drove us to exploring. Our village ecosystems, however, created in the name of human culture, made us feel we'd become like gods—just as the Genesis text feared. Like the Creator himself, we had lost the voice of Wisdom, and we built our own cultures with their great capitals, and we lived within them like bees in hives, imperial, expanding our bee empires over the globe.

Are you following me? That's why the media sees the future as space colonies, taking our own bio-engineered habitat-hives with us. How impoverished this habitat is, if we can't conceive of the infinite biodiversity that created us. For each of the millions of species we know, there are thousands more which have disappeared but whose record we carry: this library is Wisdom's realm, and the further in space we go the farther away her voice. It will take the next species to turn back toward her, toward Eden.

Already, the new creation story of Eden has been begun for us by Betti and Archie, and it restores the bride Wisdom to her Creator. How, and when, and why—even if we can't hear them, the answers may appear in our own language, as we grow to understand the ecosystem in which we evolved. As Betti told it to me, this ecosystem is an extension of our body. It leads to new language, a new kind of sex, in which our navels connect umbilically to the creative ecosystem.

Now, of three kinds of ecosystems—degraded, supportive of life, and creative—only the latter is our home, which is why we must return there to evolve. New language begins there: Remember, we started talking fifty thousand years ago and it was about wild animals and plants around us. So a new kind of speech is developing from creative ecosystem restoration. We'll need it, too, for neoteric sex. Our words are those of social animals and they won't work for the next species: they are solitary, and as they approach their intimate partner it is a first encounter that must have words of its own. It's a language of pictures as well, a mythology, a new Eden. And a new monotheism to be reckoned with.

[Aviya Nachman]

Beyond a Trunk of Transcription/ or, A New Religion

When she called the number in New Haven that Svitz had given her, Nosei's departmental office, the secretary explained that Nosei had left only last night for Israel. Why, she asked? A conference going on there? The secretary said he had given no reason, no plans. Only a phone call from the airport, explaining he needed to do emergency research in Israel. My God, Julie thought. That's just what he must have said when he left to examine the Scroll ten years ago.

Why was this happening now? Julie remembered what Svitz had called the "apocalyptic urge." From Rimbaud to Heidegger, the old prophets of modernism had said the past would be swept away and a new language born. Absurd or fanciful as it may have seemed at the time, the underlying goal was to turn the egocentric traditions inside out. How long ago that seems! Yet now it is clear that the instinct was correct, and that human language as a means of communication solely within our own species is a dead end, full of the hubris of human grandiosity. Instead, it's becoming clear that language is a tool for communion with the natural world, as it is in all species. Will another species find our ego-centered language any different than a bird's? In other words, will it mean anything? Besides, both birds and humans house a far more complex language of cells: they tell a deeper story in time and evolution than anything our conscious minds can put into words. Even a plant—and especially the long-lived trees—may be more interesting to "read" than a book produced by humans!

Plants move through time more slowly, in longer arcs, and their histories extend further back in time. Although humans are capable of Shakespeare's art, what does a page of Shakespeare tell about us anymore than a whale's song about the whale? Perhaps it shows how we long to see ourselves as from the outside, "objectively"—just as another species would see us.

For Julie, this longing was revealed through the relationship with her doctor. Each was open enough to allow it to be consummated: they became two subjects, not just the one of Julie's panic. She wouldn't have to rush to tell Nosei when they met again. She still needed his face but not in the same way. Now he stood for what she could know, really know about what someone is thinking. Now it was possible to be one species that could know itself—if we allowed that another had observed us, had known us.

So imagine a Neanderthal's description of his own history: Of what great concern would it be to us, except that it throw unexpected light on who *we* are? A bird's nest, for instance, might do the same. Now, given that we understand the longing to see outside ourselves, and that a new species may have filial feelings toward us, nevertheless they will have their own language among themselves—we will have to create our own bridge to them. So "reading" and "speaking" the ecosystem (knowing about what someone is thinking!) is the goal ahead of us, since it is our connection to all species.

Meanwhile, we have barely got started. Homo sapiens is still worthless in the natural ecosystems of the world, contributing nothing to evolutionary diversity and killing natural areas more extensively than any other species. Just compare the alligator to human rapacity. In the Florida Everglades, the alligator is a keystone species, digging huge holes that collect water during the dry season and keep alive a diversity of plants and animals. Homo sapiens, on the other hand, have come close to destroying the Everglades—a sister ecosystem to the Hula wetlands.

True, the alligator is a much older species. You could say that there is still hope that in the years ahead we will learn from the alligator. But it's hard to imagine—hard to imagine the grandiosity of Homo sapiens ever submitting to the grandeur of alligator antiquity. God described it well thousands of years ago in the Book of Job: "Could you (human beings) have created anything so wondrous as an crocodile (Leviathan)?" He asks a humbled Job in the *Book of Job.*

The key to Homo sapiens' future is to become a keystone species—that is, if we have a future. Is it possible? The hope is in communication with an alien species, with whom we might rejuvenate our role as explorers. Never mind the science fiction of space aliens; it could be a tree on the planet now, as Archie has interpreted through the early Hebraic Creation epic, the *Scroll of the History of Adam*, which still carries knowledge of having evolved. It is unfolded in the imagery of a Garden, a mothering ecosystem.

We used to be students of words, but now we have become students of voices beyond human language. How did this make sense to us? Recent history laid the groundwork: the idea that we are modern people is anchored in anxiety, after all. Suddenly in the twentieth century, seeing and hearing became one, which seemed madness to readers of modern classic books like *Finnegan's Wake* or *Tender Buttons*. But by now, a reconstruction of the voice Archie heard—which this book has undertaken—tugs at the anchor. The anxious voice of Julie and the audiographic memory of Everett sent them both into hiding, in academe—Nosei in his philology department and Julie in Professor Harriman Svitz's apartment (and the office of her doctor).

Isolated as they were, they remained full of the story of Archie and Betti's disappearance—like black holes. And sometimes, like a black hole—or Wisdom's voice from a hole in the ground—you can only tell it is there by the absence, as in the narcissistic criticism of our time: ears blocked, eyes blinkered, a scream against anything truly new. That scream may accompany this book when and if published, but then the scream can become a revelation. The voice of Wisdom may be heard even as an echo, even in the story of what happened to Archibald Shechner. It can even break through the wall that the vainest critic sets up between original story and original (natural) *history*.

Our lives, after all, are an exploration, a feeling forward, toward that tiny niche into which we may not really disappear when we die but instead be transformed. That is what happens in a natural death, because the ecosystem contains our past in its present. We don't need to invoke the doctrine of reincarnation if we just ask: When dead, are we still in time? We say no, we have been transformed into the natural material and memory of the ecosystem—we become part of her voice—until her story, her history, is told.

Meanwhile, this book is a record of what we've lost. All that is left of us. There is a voice outside of us, more than human, and it has been there before us. The rest, as Archie taught us, is the future: the joys and frustrations of interpretation. Though the book is our transformation, our story, Wisdom's true story will be told by the Creator, when he returns and listens to her voice. Then, we will find ourselves in Eden again, each male an essential part of Adam, each female an essential part of Eve. All the plants and animals will be there too, male and female, each species its own Adam and Eve.

The tree of Life was planted by the creator, and all life is descended from it, governed by the tree of knowledge, Wisdom's tree. Her tree called all trees and all species to sexuality, to exploring new bodies and new ecosystems in which to evolve. It was she, Wisdom's voice in the ecosystem, calling Homo sapiens into being, Adam and Eve. She gave us our consciousness—as we left the garden, our natural ecosystem.

Once we created a human culture, consciousness arose from knowing we were outside. Other species may be conscious in their original garden, but we are the one with memory of what went terribly wrong in our garden: the murder of the other Homo species. Our subtle language of consciousness surrounded them, disoriented them, as we infiltrated their lands. They lost the voice in their heads that balanced their lives, just as we had—except that ours was now supplanted with knowledge, a serpentine sophistication as we recreated Eden in the form of culture, everywhere.

In recent times, artists and psychologists have explored the borders of consciousness, pushing on to madness, to the unconscious. But today a new religion becomes possible—because we step beyond consciousness and view it from the outside, a new objectivity. We see that consciousness comes from the knowledge of death, individual deaths. While religions teach us to accept death the new religion teaches something newer: to *use* it. Death, after all, is what allows evolution to be creative. It is the fruit of the Tree of Knowledge, and now that we have eaten it we can utilize this knowledge—instead of burying it.

We are entering a time when the memory of Eden becomes available again as we hear the ecosystem's voice. It's a call for restoring balance, and for an opening, once again, to evolving. The garden of Eden can be restored to its original meaning, with the lost Scroll's help. An Eden revelation allows us to restore all that is missing in the account that survives in Genesis

There was no need to consult Wisdom now. She spoke to us in imagination, and we found ourselves inventing her answer, writing it down ourselves as if we were novelists and her voice the character at the center of our story.

Wisdom asks: What is the new religion? It encloses the answer to the riddle of death. Yet it is the obverse of rest: it is a union. The revelation on which it is based comes as a surprise—like all revelation—but it is also rooted in a desire whose culmination is not unexpected. It's the intensity that is earth-shaking; however, instead of transcending it, this revelation returns you to your body. There you are, isolated, bereft of clothes, your hands holding not tablets of the law but a pair of buttocks akin to your own. It is sexual, this visionary exposé, and it parallels an orgasm, the peak of experience from which comes down not a Moses, but oneself again. And not in the same body anymore, but one that is seen in the evolutionary self-knowledge of exploration. Spiralling entrances to rivers found in the ear and in the navel. It makes an original love possible again, a loving fig leaf over evolving. Culture results from this love also—from telling what happened in Eden, listening to the tree. The intimate ties of the ecosystem—the telling of them—is a record of this love, but its complexity is so much larger than the brain that the species Homo sapiens must evolve just to get back to the beginning and to set the story of sex in the garden down correctly. Here embarks the text of the new religion, for the story of sexual relations is the story of living and dying in the ecosystem. And the purpose for living is to find a door opening of itself there—a door balanced so precisely that merely the correct voice unlocks it. A voice that asks: Whose head is this in which I speak? Whose ecosystem? The answer is always two: one that is dying and one that is coming to be. A religion that holds the door open, restoring the meaning of home.

If we begin by restoring the ecosystems where we live, it won't be long before the original human ecosystem—where Homo sapiens evolved in our own garden of Eden—will be found. Only there can we become partners once again, man and woman, listening together. As we listen there, we may become partners as well with a new species.

It won't be easy. The current religion of technology will resist. Technology is about to disconnect natural selection as even a possible option for us. Thinking we are "free" because we can play with genes, our public religion of free inquiry in fact represents a dysfunctional human species that is in need of healing. There is nothing wrong with inquiry, but what is to govern this freedom? The old religions?

And here is the answer we've learned. The ear—the ear that keeps us in balance, the ear (and its spiral reflection, the navel, ear within ear) that may yet grow larger—brings a new listening that will govern our questioning. Our ears will need to hear and our eyes need to read the ecosystem, to know a creative ecosystem's desire: how the new room for growth is balanced by a letting go.

"Soon we must look deep within ourselves and decide what we wish to become," our leading biologist says. But "look within" is wrong; he should have said "listen"—and not "within" but listen without, listen to the ecosystem.

Then we'll understand the whole story of human religion, of ritual and art, of transformations of fear and panic. It begins like this: Like all animals, we turned our anxiety into a quest: the hunt. It is a gorgeous contest we can already witness in great art of the cave era. There, thirty milleniums ago, in this first of spirit worlds, we recreated the objects of the hunt in a quest to still an even deeper anxiety: murder.

While the contest of predator and prey played out on the walls, the still-conscious memory of the deaths of our closest Homo species was no grand competition. They were easy for us to kill off, and they weren't even normally eaten. Instead, we watched them suffer in ways that we recognize as our own, including their pain over the death of loved ones. This spectacle over many centuries bred in us intolerance of our own image, which is why no drawings of human figures appear in prehistory, except as symbolic stick figures. Why no images of ourselves? To see ourselves is to see our anxiety—our own death, as reflected to us in the destruction of the other Homo species.

Later, the human figure would merge with animals in representation, and subsequently, among the early monotheists, be banished again.

Ours, then, was the first anxiety shaped not by the ecosystem but by ourselves, we who had knowledge of murder hidden within us. Recreating our culture wherever we went, we lost track of our ecosystem and all our anxieties. Where did they come from, who were our predators? Restoring ecosystems now is a way to begin to understand them and how we came this way. Instead of a culture and spiritual world to serve ourselves, a new religion will serve the ecosystem. It will be like the Creator returning to his mate, Wisdom.

Even before that can happen, Julie Peleg overcame her own panic as she saw it taking up the dead space within her. It was seen from the outside, objectively, and now we have come to the point in human history where death itself can be seen from the outside. Death became known when Betti Peleg confirmed that the voice Archibald Shechner was hearing in his head had an outside source. As Shechner conquered his panic by listening to all that the voice of Wisdom said, Julie Peleg perceived that she too could preempt the anxiety of a deadness within as she listened to the tapes she transcribed. It would take a battle like Shechner had endured with her mother's help, this time with her own doctor beside her. The knowledge uncovered: Death does not exist within us but only at the balance points of the ecosystem. When we die, we inhabit such a point. Invisibly. As invisible as the bacteria, the archaea, and the eukarya—the three biological kingdoms of life—inhabit our world and live within us. All the plants and animals are but a small branch of this tree of life, a tiny portion that is visible to the naked eye. Buried beneath our sight as well: the desire to evolve, to inhabit a balance point.

[Julie Peleg & Everett Nosei]

1995

Yom Kippur. I just got off the phone with my mother. Dead but did not die. Disappeared after all.

What the new knowledge of nature teaches: how to hold another intelligence so different, so absent from your own. Yet there. You either have to embrace the complexity or kill it.

[Julie]

=====

1995: Memorandum from Seth Greene, literary agent

The last chapter of this story came by express mail, just as the first manuscript had. The address listed was the same one in Tel Aviv where Betti and Julie Peleg had lived. I tried calling the number and learned from the new tenants that they hadn't seen Julie since Yom Kippur. It was clear enough from the chapter what has happened. I will probably not hear from any of them again, although who knows? Maybe, in a year or even ten years, I'll get some further chapters in the mail.

There's a lot of questions I'd like to ask them. I guess that's the problem: so would alot of scientists and journalists. And perhaps they're not concerned with us so much, because I haven't even received instructions of what I'm supposed to do with the royalties for *The Eden Revelation*. But the real questions I have for them are scientific, I guess, or rather about what is going to happen to *us*.

A year ago, for example, there were reports from the government's Center for the Study of Evolution and the

Origin of Life. A spokesman had announced that "changes in the path of human evolution" were now being explored. "A whole cassette of genes that could enhance human intelligence" could be added to the human genome, this neurobiologist explained. "Human evolution is now in human hands," he concluded. I got the feeling that these scientific bureaucrats were so full of themselves and their labs that it was a waste of my energy to even send them a manuscript of *The Eden Revelation.* Let them hear about it once the book becomes a *cause celebre*—and then, let them recall the furor over the original Scroll.

Because what good is "enhancing human intelligence" if you don't know what it's for in the first place? One major purpose of the brain is to learn to resist threats. What the effect is likely to be is that these "enhanced" humans will be increasingly resistant to imagination. They will not want to listen to the new species because they will consider themselves too smart—or even consider themselves a new species. Do we think for a moment that they are going to listen to Wisdom describe how a tree's intelligence may be superior to ours? Are they going to learn how to listen to plants? I doubt it.

Now it's starting to make real sense to me why Archie and Betti had to become anonymous. They might really be in danger from these scientists who think human intelligence is the highest on Earth. Instead of learning to let go, to listen, they are holding on ever tighter to human mental goals. They're really like the *Celestine* people, after all. They want to put the body at the service of the mind, but they don't understand what the mind is in service to. They'd laugh if you answered: a tree, the tree of Knowledge in the garden of Eden.

So it looks like Julie and Nosei have done the right thing. When the shit hits the fan, there's going to be a war between these genetic engineers and the ecologists. Meanwhile, *The Eden Revelation* will build up confidence among many to begin the real steps toward evolving and to protect those like Archie and Betti who have already begun. But let's not mince too many words: war is war. The technophobes and reactionaries are not going to sit still and listen to any truth-telling about our past. "What was good enough for our forebears is good enough for us" is their rallying cry, and they will consider the revelation of murder at our origins a libel against the good name of humanity. They will be glad to murder us all—just as if we were hominids. We're a nuisance to them—best to just get us out of the way, so they don't have to think about us again. Not so long ago—not even a lifetime—since the Third Reich came to the same brutal conclusion about Israelites.

While the ecology haters see destiny in cultural terms—social progress as simplification—the rest of us see destiny in biological terms. It is our fate to evolve, to re-create our lives—and the choice to do so probably will mean to defend your loved ones from mass murder. But first, you've got to have some excitement to pull you in, some pleasure more than just following a new line of thought. I've said it before: there's got to be some fucking at the core. Julie and Nosei's version of Wisdom explains that the brain is a reflection of the ecosystem. "But the brain doesn't record the *unconscious* interactions of species." We know what's going on in that unconscious: seduction, submission. So when you go a level up from the brain to human culture—which is what Wisdom called "social organization"—you find it's all based on fucking. Why else get social?

Everybody goes to enormous lengths to avoid the fact. Talking about genes is popular at the moment; it allows you to say "intervene" instead of intercourse. A highly promoted science writer put it this way: "We are talking about intervening in the flow of genetic information from one generation to the next. We are talking about the relationship of human beings to their genetic heritage." Talk, talk—you see, it is all talk, instead of *not* talking: listening. Who's going to *listen*? Our writers are so conventional, but those who are the best artists among them, you worry. For them, it's been so long since they read or reviewed a truly unconventional voice that you worry if they'll know it. Except that the genetic engineers will scare them and wake them up to their own conventionality—and to the need for new kinds of listening that hurt one's ears. That's all that I can say: if it's unconventional, it's going to hurt your ears at first. In a time of conventionality, we're conditioned to virtuosity, to elegant writing or its opposite, tour de force. Genres are everything, and anything that sounds too strange doesn't fit a genre: Is it fact or fiction, novel or essay, the critics ask, as a way of washing their hands of it.

What genre is it, then, when you hear a voice in your head? Psychological drama? Case history? Science fiction?

It hurts when you can't find a place for it, and it hurts to hear it: it is not particularly artistic, not sensational or so polished as to appear artless. More than that: it *really* hurts, because it unsettles all presumptions, especially the presumption that nothing intellectual can kick us in the *tuchis* anymore.

And I'll tell you this: it's a tough sell. I couldn't find a publisher who wants to hear about such a book. They all want something that's been proven, done before. And their first question is usually, "What genre is it?" Science *and* fiction? Oh, we don't publish science fiction. No, not "science fiction," I tell them, it's a fucking scientific guide and novel *together*. Can't our feelings about the world ever come together with the real world itself?

END NOTE

Letter of Recommendation
Professor Harriman Svitz
New Haven, CT
October 14, 2020

To the future editor of *The Eden Revelation:*

Suddenly, species consciousness matters, a crucial theme in *The Eden Revelation.* Even the Corona virus is a family of viruses, of which disease "19" suggests the most recently evolved. I don't want to sound coy, however, as Corona is not part of the story. Evolution *is*, however, which makes the story unconventional: a lot of history has to be brought into play, like scenery "flats" in a theater.

"The play's the thing," said Hamlet, but in this novel the history's the thing. Human history and natural history. It's obvious to most that natural history comes first, yet in the story, human history follows close, because the earliest people started their histories with their first footsteps, telling cryptic creation myths.

Even then, the most concentrating thing to the human mind was that all people with whom we are intimate, *disappear.* Is "dying" really a better word for their disappearance? Since we don't precisely know where their human identity goes after death, perhaps it's better to say they disappear. An earlier species in our Homo line, Neanderthals, have gone extinct—yet here too we'd prefer to say they have disappeared. "Disappear" is a word that engages our full consciousness.

Archibald Shechner has disappeared—yet he very likely is still alive, somewhere. So the best his colleagues can do is search for clues to "why"—what happened? Ultimately the search proves so fruitful in itself that Archie begins to be forgotten.

More than conventional approaches to externalizing a character's interiority, all of the characters encountered here have had their minds set off-kilter when Archie, a sane, healthy archaeologist, hears a voice in his head, one he can't shake. It is both a natural voice and a mythic one, rooted in the origins of civilization.

The natural voice comes from the ancient ecosystem in which Archie has been digging; he has unwittingly disturbed it. Although the novel is set in the 1990s, it still has parallels to the Corona virus. Like it (for thinkers), the ancient "disturbed" ecosystem asks for empathy.

Empathy with a virus? Yes, it's a test of human ethical behavior. But what it really means is empathy with nature. Without microbes, some of whom involve viruses, we wouldn't exist. We also wouldn't exist without climate change, which stimulated human evolution at many junctures, including the last ice age.

In our day, twelve thousand years after that ice age, a long dormant core of an ancient ecosystem is suddenly disturbed, stimulating the archaeologist's mind in unexpected ways.

So begins the story—or rather, *attempts* to begin. We are clearly in a fiction, yet the triggering "character" will be a natural phenomenon, one that provokes a balancing act: there's a conventional drama, with characters in conflict in a historical setting, and then there's the underlying science of ecosystems and biblical scholarship.

Instead of a traditional story, then, the reader is absorbed into interlocking layers—and yet the plot unfolds in description and dialogue that resembles commercial literary fiction, although with more than one narrating voice. Nor is this a work that has emerged from experimental writing workshops. It may be unprecedented, however, in popular fiction after John Dos Passos and Virginia Woolf. Neither highbrow nor overly difficult, it can appeal to an audience comprising lovers of high concept books, recent history buffs, scientists, and psychotherapists, as well as those who are truly moved by the situation we find ourselves in today—between the evolutionary dilemmas of pandemic and climate change. There is fear, breakdown, but also dogged perseverance. There is an unusual love story. There is a background of memory loss as well as a search for recovery. There is mystery and fact.

The Eden Revelation wants an adventurous editor with a concern for climate change and evolution, as well as a taste for intellectual adventure and some breaking of boundaries. The ultimate audience for the book may extend from college students to readers of Don DeLillo and Toni Morrison. As further stimulus, appetizing notes about the novel are promised by the authors, to coincide with publication. To wit, they have provided me with one:

Communiqué about *The Eden Revelation* [sample of an entry to be uploaded monthly to the novel's "Communiqués" website]:

In a recent London review of "Eco-Visionaries: Confronting a Planet in a State of Emergency" at Royal Academy, "the gallery texts make it clear that climate breakdown is forcing the world to a crisis point. 'We are facing an ecological emergency,' the curatorial statement declares. There is talk of mass extinction, and 'in order to avoid further damage to nature, we need renewed creative thinking.'"

However, instead of creative ideas about "a sense of confrontation between humans and the earth," the exhibition "fails to address the many ways in which human lives are entangled with nonhuman creatures and ecosystems".

The word "entangled" here is a lamentable reminder of contemporary culture's unfamiliarity with natural ecosystems. Humans are creatures that were evolved within a specific ecosystem, though too often we are merely informed that we popped out of a previous species of great ape, most likely Homo erectus. But species do not simply advance from others; instead, they are cut off—tragically for most—and can survive only if they luckily find themselves in a niche of a new ecosystem. Not entangled but in sync, adaptable.

An even more benighted misunderstanding of ecosystems confuses the term with "habitat". Ecosystems are creative if they are healthy; they can open up niches for new species to evolve, which is not a requirement of habitats. How, where, and why we Homo sapiens evolved is lost to us, probably because we haven't found or properly imagined our originating ecosystem. It's in creation myths, however, that we've come closest, especially in the Bible's Garden of Eden. Yet that creation myth may only help us to think about the original ecosystem if the searcher is both scientist and poet.

The Eden Revelation required both and found the solution in a unique collaboration of two writers. And also in parallel, two of the main characters in the novel disappear—an archaeologist and his poetic analyst. To find them, the protagonists must come to grips with ancient history; specifically, how evolution works and how climate change drove our human species to evolve.

Scientists estimate that Homo erectus, an early human species pre-dating Homo sapiens, first migrated out of Africa into Asia almost two million years ago. In a recent article from the journal *Nature*: "An ancient relative of modern humans survived into relatively recent times before it was wiped out by climate change, according to a new study. Homo erectus may have been doomed on Java by climate change that turned its open woodland environment into rainforest".

While this is a vivid example of the lethal implications of climate change (there are also beneficial implications for humans, as in the change to African savannah), it answers no questions about where either Homo erectus or our own species actually evolved. It is rare to find such questions even asked, at least in the culture at large. Yet it is only within cultural art forms that *feelings* about our human origin can be addressed—feelings, for instance, that are still alive within us, in the form of anxiety and dread of extinction.

Certainly dread is evident in the widespread concern among youth today about climate change. It is a concern, however, that is disconnected from an understanding of human evolution. Science books and popular nonfiction are not going to explain that dread, for it's a deeply buried feeling that can only be artfully expressed—as was the satanically-disguised, intellectual serpent in the biblical Eden story.

That creation story, unfortunately, has become too encrusted with religious and dramatic meanings to stir our complicated feelings today about climate change and its connection to our evolutionary origins. Yet an unexpected novel just may do it, one that asks for an immersal in unforeseen ideas. Not science fiction, but a poetic unfolding of layers of understanding about what *disappearance*—entailed by extinction and evolving—can mean.

An example of a visual artwork that engages such emotional understanding, from the current "Eco-Visionaries" exhibit, "Basem Magdy's 'Our Prehistoric Fate' (2011) presents Duraclear prints of a prehistoric creature and of a text that reads 'the future belongs to us,' clamped onto Yugoslavian military lightboxes. The work effectively links anxiety about nuclear war with anxiety about climate breakdown". Although we may be jolted, we learn little about Homo sapiens history or how the unconscious mind works from this artwork. It moves us, but mainly because we think we already know its emotional message.

The Eden Revelation: An Evolutionary Novel has perhaps more to reveal about what we have never properly internalized: that for all our intelligence and creativity, we were not responsible for our evolving. Something as complex as the human brain, but much larger, had more to do with it: a natural ecosystem large and complex enough that we were lost in it until we found our niche.

The authors of this "evolutionary novel" are to be commended for rooting their work in a time and putative place older than any prior fiction in the Western Canon. By the same token, they have enlarged scientific, literary and biblical tradition. *The Eden Revelation* stands alone as a contemporary effort of Kabbalistic strength. My grizzled head is bowed.

DAVID ROSENBERG is the coauthor and editor of the NYT bestsellers *The Book of J* (with Harold Bloom) and *Congregation.* He has a Guggenheim for nonfiction, a PEN prize for *A Poet's Bible*, a Hopwood Special Award in poetry, a Canada Council grant, etc. Born in Detroit, dual nationality since 1981, Israeli-American, he and Rhonda have lived since the '90s in Miami, within proximity of the Everglades.

RHONDA ROSENBERG, born in Houston, is research associate professor at FIU. She has coauthored more than fifty peer-reviewed papers and completed many NIH grants in HIV research. With her husband, she was co-founder of *Field Bridge*, a think tank in translating ecosystem science into the cultural arts. She has also collaborated on several books about ancient biblical history and poetics.

CPSIA information can be obtained
at www.ICGtesting.com
Printed in the USA
BVHW041648280223
659407BV00011B/178

9 781959 556053